OMEGA

JASINDA WILDER

PART ONE:

Kyrie

1

AT THE END OF THE WORLD

"SO WHERE THE HELL ARE WE AGAIN?" LAYLA ASKED, standing on her tiptoes, leaning rather precariously over the bow of the Eliza, a monster luxury yacht, registered in the Bahamas, belonging to both Valentine Roth and me. "I lost track two months ago."

"Ushuaia," Harris answered, gruff and brusque, but with a trace of amusement most people wouldn't be able to detect unless they knew him well. "It's the capital city of Tierra del Fuego. Also known as The End of the World."

"And why are we here again?" Layla asked. The couple of extra inches she had gained weren't doing much to let her see the approaching city more clearly.

Really, if she wanted to get a good look she

should go up on the bridge.

I reclined in a teak deck chair, a floppy, wide-brimmed hat shielding my eyes from the sun, a glass of red wine in one hand, tugging my cardigan closed with the other. The temperature was pretty cool here at the end the world, not quite fifty degrees Fahrenheit, and it was the middle of May.

"Because it's somewhere to be," I answered for Harris. "And because it's extremely remote."

Layla turned to me with a frown. "Remote? Bitch, we're almost in fucking Antarctica. Have you seen those icebergs?"

I just shrugged and smiled. Layla was being Layla, but it was so great to finally have her with me again. "Roth mentioned that we might take a cruise down there to get a good look at them. Tomorrow, actually. I guess they have them all the time. It's like a tourist industry down here or something."

Harris snorted. "W*e would h*ire a private tour, obvious*ly*."

Layla rolled her eyes. "Obviously." She crossed the deck to sit at the foot of my chair, snatching my wine from me. "For real, though, I'm developing a serious case of cabin fever. As much as I love being here with you, eight fucking weeks is a long time for me to be stuck anywhere. I need off this damn boat. Nice as it is, and as much as I love you, babe, I need the real ground under my feet. I need to get na-ked-wasted with total strangers and pretend I'm not at the End of the World, doing dick-all with my life."

Harris let out a sigh, and we exchanged amused glances behind Layla's back. "Layla…only you would complain about being on a world tour, on a super-yacht, every need seen too, every d*esire met,*" I said.

"I'm not complaining. Much. I just…I've worked my whole life, Key. Since I was fourteen, I've worked six and seven days a week, two or three jobs at a time. Suddenly being unemployed…it doesn't sit well. I'm going crazy."

"It does take some getting used to," I admitted.

"Plus…" she leaned close to me, whispering. "I'm horny as all hell. Little Miss Middle Finger isn't cutting it anymore. Harris got me out of the States so fast I didn't have time to pack my dildo collection."

I let my head fall back against the chair *and laughed. "Jesus, Layla. Way* too much information." I glanced at Harris, who was scanning the approach-ing bay with a pair of high-powered binoculars, and lowered my voice. "What about our boy Harris over there?"

Layla didn't even look at him. "Um. No. No thanks. I'm not *that* desperate."

"Just no? That's it?"

She stood up abruptly. "I'm cold. I need a sweater." She hustled past me and retreated off the Lido deck into the superstructure of our home away from home, a steward holding the door for her as she swept past him without so much as a glance.

When she was gone, Harris glanced at me. "You know I have excellent hearing, right, Kyrie?"

I shrugged innocently. "I have no idea what you're talking about."

He narrowed his eyes, his brow furrowing. "Matchmaker is not a role that suits you." He stuffed the binoculars back into their protective case and vanished inside as well, leaving me alone.

I closed my eyes, absorbing the sunlight and wishing it was at least a *little* warmer. We'd been making our way across the Atlantic for some time now, and the temperature hadn't risen above fifty in all that time. We were well into the Southern Hemisphere and with the ever-present wind, I was always cold.

Even with my eyes closed, I could feel Roth approaching. He was as silent as ever, moving his huge form on cat-like feet, but I felt him nonetheless.

He didn't say a word, just slid an arm under my legs, another around my back, and lifted me, sitting down on my chair, and settling me on his lap.

"Where are the others?" he asked.

I shrugged. "I dunno. They went inside after I made an innocent suggestion. They both vanished on me."

"What suggestion?"

"Layla was complaining about the lack of opportunity for…certain activities."

"She's horny, you mean?"

"Exactly. I merely pointed out that Harris was a possibility, and she just…shut down. Walked away. And apparently Harris overheard me and didn't think much of the idea either."

Roth laughed. "Harris is…extremely private."

"What does that mean?"

He lifted his shoulder. "Just that he keeps his personal life private. He plays things very close to the vest."

"But he's not, like, married or anything?"

This earned me another laugh, this one sarcastic. "God no, babe. I don't think that's his style."

"What, marriage?"

"No, monogamy. Commitment. Long-term relationships with women. That kind of thing." Roth ran his huge hand through my hair, stroking my still-short hair with a special kind of tenderness. "I've always assumed he just…gets what he needs when he needs it, wherever he happens to be."

"But you don't *know*?"

"For sure? No. I mean, he's never introduced me to anyone. But when we make landfall, or when we're restocking in some city or other, he'll come back after a few hours away in a better mood. What he does and with whom, I know nothing about. Besides, it's not my business." He paused. "Anyway, as far as Layla is concerned, Harris would view her as a client, essentially, and he has very strict rules about fraternizing with clients. Rules that come from experience, I would think, but that's just a guess."

"Well, I meant it as more of a joke than a serious suggestion. But I guess I misjudged both of them—neither of them seem to have much of a sense of humor." I looked up at him. "So. What are our plans?"

There was a long pause before he replied, which I knew meant only one thing—he was assessing how much to tell me. Roth doesn't tell me everything, and I like it that way. I like letting him handle things. After recently becoming involved, unwittingly, in some seriously dangerous and scary things—almost losing my life in the process—I am only too happy to concentrate on the more mundane aspects of his business. When it comes to where we're going, and why, and when, I leave that to him. I enjoy seeing the world, spending all day, every day with him. I don't need every detail.

"We'll be heading back up to the States after a

few more days down here. I've got some things that do actually require my physical presence."

I couldn't help wondering if those things included a wedding, but I didn't ask. We were technically engaged, but we hadn't discussed actual marriage plans.

It would happen. When Roth was ready.

Yes, I admit I had my head in the clouds, and I was happy living in the protective little bubble around me. I liked pretending everything was fine, that we weren't running from anyone, that we were just idle rich people roaming the world just for the fun of it.

But I knew the reality of our situation was almost too macabre and frightening to think about. I'd only recently stopped having nightmares, after all.

"I can feel you thinking." His voice was a buzzing rumble in my ear.

I didn't even shrug. I just rested my cheek against his chest and nuzzled closer. Inhaling his scent, I said, "It's nothing."

"Liar."

"Okay. Then let me ask you…how long are we going to run, Valentine?"

"I can't take him on directly, Kyrie. I just…don't have the resources. Yet. The short answer is I don't know. Okay? And that's the truthful answer. I just don't know." He looked me in the eyes and added, "I know this isn't the life you had in mind, and I'm sorry—"

I cut him off, fingers to his lips. "You're taking care of me, and Layla. I get that. I do. And I love you for it. I just…I don't know, Valentine. I don't know what I'm trying to say."

"You want something approaching normalcy. I'm working on it, okay? I can tell you that much. All right?"

"All right."

"I'm working on creating a new normal for both of us, I think you could say. Streamlining, downsizing, looking into new business ventures that we can pursue from wherever we are." He laughed. "It may not be *normal*, but it's normal for us. That's what I'm working on."

"I'm guessing normal for us won't include a two-story Colonial in the suburbs? A Corgi, two kids, and a minivan?"

Roth laughed heartily. "A minivan? Me in a minivan? Dream on, love."

"But the Colonial and the Corgi and the kids are fine?"

"Corgis are okay. Not sure about the Colonial, though. I'm thinking I can maybe do a bit better than a two-story house, for one thing."

I noticed he was leaving something out, and I didn't push it. Now I didn't know why I even started this conversation. "Yeah, you're right. A mansion in the Hamptons is more our style, I think."

"The Hamptons? I think not, sweetheart. Too cliché, too overpopulated. Something down in the Caribbean, maybe. I've already got a property there and there are still a few islands for sale up there. They could be purchased quite easily. How does that sound?"

I laughed. "There's my Valentine. You don't do anything small, do you?"

"Never. Besides, do you know how impossible it would be to provide proper security for one of those shacks in the Hamptons? It would be very difficult. 'Logistically impossible', I think Harris would say. An island can be protected much more easily. And, besides, if we've got an entire island to ourselves, I can make you scream as loud as you want without disturbing neighbors." He said this last part *sotto voce*, in my ear, fingers skating down my ribs to then trace up and down my thigh.

"We wouldn't want to disturb neighbors, would we?"

"Keeping you quiet these last few months has been…an entertaining challenge. Let me just put it this way. I'm ready for some privacy."

"I've been quiet!" I protested.

"Ha. If my hand is over your mouth, maybe. Perhaps I should look into getting a ball-gag for you."

I twisted so I could glare up at him. "You wouldn't dare."

"I would. Absolutely I would. You'd enjoy it, too, I think. Some fuzzy handcuffs, a gag, and I could play with you for hours and Layla and Harris would never know."

"You like it when I scream, and you know it." I was getting hot and wet from this turn in the conversation.

"I do. But your screams are just for me." And then, just like that, the fly of my jeans was open and his fingers delved under the elastic of my panties and he was searching, flicking, swiping, finding my slit and spearing his middle finger into me. "You're soaked for me, Kyrie."

"Trying to make me scream, right here on the deck?"

"Uh-huh. Is it working?" He adjusted me, and now my mouth was crushed to his.

"Nope. Not yet."

He had two fingers in me now. I writhed helplessly as he scissored his fingers inside, and then whimpered in the back of my throat as he pressed a big rough thumb to my clit. Circle, circle. And then he slid his fingers out and smeared my wetness over my clit, his thumb resuming its lazy circles, and I was a mess, biting my lip, my forehead pressed against his, my chest heaving.

And then, abruptly, he stood up, depositing me on my feet. Buttoning my jeans, he gave me a twist and sent me stumbling toward the stairs leading to our quarters. "Go get naked, my love. Wait for me. I'll only be a moment."

My thighs rubbed together as I made my way to our bedroom, the buzz of my jeans brushing together sending delicious vibrations through my core. I was on the edge, mere moments from coming. Frustrated, I hurried up the stairs as fast as I could. I stripped in record time, peeling off my sweater and shirt, unfastening my bra, tossing the clothes aside, and then hopping out of my jeans. I still couldn't put all my weight on my knee for very long, but that wouldn't stop me from stretching out on the bed in my panties.

He'd said naked, but it's fun to disobey him.

True to his word, I heard him on the stairs a minute later. He already had his black T-shirt off, balling it in his fist and tossing it aside, then stepping out of his khakis as he made the top step. He crossed the room in just his underwear, tight black Polo briefs that outlined his huge cock and cupped his buttocks.

"I said naked, babe."

"You aren't," I pointed out.

He peeled his underwear off and stalked over to me, then got on the bed and crawled toward me on his hands and knees. "I am now, but you're still not naked."

"What are you going to do about it, Valentine?"

He grabbed my ankles and hauled me over to him. I let him pull me so my thighs spread around his trim waist, and then I hooked my ankles behind his back, reaching for him at the same time. But instead of taking my hands in his like I'd thought he would, he gripped both of my wrists in one hand, using the other at my hip to roll me onto my stomach. One hand still gripping my wrists in an implacable but gentle hold, he lifted me by the stomach until my knees were under me and my ass was in the air, presented to him.

He tugged my underwear down around my thighs, but left them there.

Suddenly, I couldn't breathe.

His hand smoothed over my left ass cheek, and then my right.

SMACK! His hand cracked against my buttock, stinging it, causing it to tremble, and I fought to keep from flinching or crying out. *SMACK!* The right side now.

Oh god.

Oh god.

I felt him reach past me and pull open a drawer on the bedside table. Then I watched as he produced a condom. He ripped it open, and sheathed himself with the rubber. Reaching into the drawer a second time, he found what he wanted: a bottle of lube and a thick pink vibrator. He tossed both onto the bed.

"Kyrie?"

"Yes, Roth?"

"Tell me what you want."

I swallowed hard. "You."

"Me, how?"

"Your cock."

I felt his hand smoothing over my ass, caressing the globes, and then his finger was pressing against me, back there, pressing. I gasped as he slid a finger into me. I didn't fight it, but relaxed and let it in. I swallowed a moan as he withdrew his finger and added a second. And then a third.

He'd been working me up to this for months now. Teasing me with it. Telling me how good it would feel, how hard I would come. But, so far, all he'd done was use his fingers, stretching me, getting me used to the feeling. Using the vibrator a few times.

I wanted it.

God, did I want it. So bad.

He applied some lubricant and put his fingers into me back there, then filled my pussy with his cock, and we moved together—the world stopped when I came, hard and fast, immediate, powerful, a breaking wave of orgasmic bliss.

He teased me with the tip of his cock, smearing the broad head of it against my clit, and then pushed it into my pussy again, stretching me, and I couldn't help but moan, loudly.

"Shush, baby. Keep quiet."

"Can't…help it."

"You didn't answer me, Kyrie." He plunged deep into me, seating himself into me to the hilt, filling me until I gasped at the fullness. His fingers were knuckle deep into me too, so deep. "Where do you want my cock?"

I lifted my ass, writhing against his fingers. "Here."

"Say it, babe."

"In my ass."

"Tell me what you want, love. Let me hear it."

"Fuck me in the ass," I whispered.

He groaned, this time, driving deep in my pussy and I came, hard and quiet, going tense, mouth open and trembling.

In the moment of my orgasm, he pulled out of my slit and withdrew his fingers from my ass. Then he squirted more lube onto himself and onto me, and then fit the tip of his cock to the opening of my asshole, pushing gently, gradually piercing me in fractional increments. "Like this, love? Is this what you want?"

"More." It was all I could say.

A nudge, and the round head of him was inside me, stretching me, a fiery burn. An ache. But I was coming, and that trumped the sting of pain. Roth put his fingers to my clit and circled, and I groaned as the orgasm fluttered and extended, and then his other palm cracked hard against my ass, and I cried out, the sting startling me. Another. And another. Hard enough that I cried out into the mattress, but then...then I realized he was in me deeper than ever. So deep.

"How does it feel, Kyrie?"

"Jesus, Roth. It feels good. Too good."

"Does it hurt?"

"A little," I admitted. "But don't stop."

"Can you take it, love?"

I touched myself, fingers circling my clit, bringing myself closer, closer, but then Roth stopped me, the vibrator buzzing, touching me with it. I took it from him, pressed the tip of the wildly vibrating dildo to my clit and felt stars detonate within me. Roth was utterly still, half-impaled inside me, but I felt him trembling. Needing. Waiting. I arched my back and slid the vibrator into my opening, and now I was so full, full to the point of aching. I could feel his cock rubbing against the dildo, a thin veil of skin separating them, and I was coming so hard it hurt, coming so hard I was crying with it, unable to do anything but slide the device in and out of me, letting the smaller secondary part of the dildo hit my clit just so, just there. Again. Again.

And then I felt Roth spank me, and when I cried out he filled me yet further, pushing himself deeper into my asshole with a slow glide, his hips now meeting the flesh of my buttocks.

"Can you take it, Kyrie?" His voice was guttural, frantic, on the edge of control.

"Fuck me, Valentine," I murmured, pushing back against him.

Oh god. It hurt so good. So deep. So much. So full.

And then...he withdrew. Ever so slowly. Just a fraction, but it had me gritting my teeth and shrieking into the bed, gripping the sheets in shaking fists...this wasn't an orgasm, this was raw pleasure, a thread of pain to make it potent, a fullness that couldn't be properly described, so much of him, all of my Valentine throbbing inside me.

"Jesus, Kyrie, you're so tight it almost hurts. So perfect." He pushed back in. "God...love—your asshole is so perfect. How does this feel?"

I couldn't even speak. I hung my head and bit the silk sheet between my teeth and grunted, arching my back and writhing—*more*, I was telling him, shouting it, screaming it nonverbally.

"You like it?"

"God—fuck—yes!" I managed, my voice hoarse, raspy, needing so badly to scream like a banshee but holding it back.

And then he moved again. A slow slide, and I could feel the width of his cock scraping against the taut muscle of my asshole, each stutter of flesh against flesh making me shake and gasp. Oh—fuck. Fuck. He was pushing in, slowly. So slowly. Glacial thrusts, but nonstop now, drawing out...out...and out—and then...back in...fucking me slowly. Fucking my ass with all the gentleness he possessed, but his hands, oh his hands, they gripped my hips with bruising force. As if the grip of his fingers in the crease of my hips was all that prevented him from drilling me so hard I'd break.

"Fuck, Kyrie. I can't take it, love. I need to fuck. I need to move."

"*Valentine...*" I didn't know what to say.

I wanted that. But I didn't think I could take it. Not because I was afraid he'd hurt me. No, this felt so good, so perfect, months of anal play gradually stretching me until I was prepared to take all of him like this. I was afraid if he fucked me like he so clearly needed to that the orgasm would just wreck me, would ruin me, would shatter me beyond repair.

Another slow—*ssssslllloooowwww*—withdrawal, and an even slower thrust back in, so I could feel him enter, feel myself stretched further open as the wide hilt of his huge cock filled me. And then he was leaning over me, chest pressed to my back, hands sliding under to cup my breasts, and he was gasping, heaving, growling in his chest.

"Roth—" I gasped.

"I'm right there, Kyrie. I can't—I need to go slow." He sounded…shredded…as if his control was being sorely tested, more so than it had ever been before.

Of all the sex we'd had up to this point, and there had been a lot, I'd never heard him so clearly, audibly shaken by the potency of it all. I'd held him as he cried, yes. I'd fucked him and made love to him when he was an emotional wreck after what Gina had done to him. But that was all different. This was my Valentine needing to fuck yet holding back for me, holding back from what he wanted, which was utterly unlike him. He took what he wanted, from me and from life, and never slowed down or held back.

But this was different.

"Fuck me, Roth." I reached out and grabbed a pillow, stuffed it under my stomach, drew my knees further forward, pushed back into him, driving him deeper in the process. "Just fuck me. I need it. I can take it. Just—Jesus god, just fuck me."

He straightened behind me, stilled. I felt him breathing, gathering himself. Felt his hands on my back, smoothing down my spine, caressing the globes of my ass, pulling them apart and groaning as he pushed deeper. I could only breathe and moan and grip the bedding. And then, oh god. He pulled out. Almost all the way. Squirted yet more lube on his cock, slid in, pulled out, applied more still, and now he was pushing in and out in tiny flutters, miniature thrusts, and I was driven mad. I'd forgotten about the vibrator as I concentrated on taking in all of Valentine, and now I fumbled for it, found it on the mattress under the pillow, turned it up so it was vibrating on high, touched it to my clit, screamed into the pillow, slid it out, gasping, making a shrieking, breathless sound.

Roth fucked me, a little harder now. A little faster.

I touched my clit again, and was clenched all over by a wracking wave. But still, this wasn't an orgasm. Not really. I slid the thick pink dildo—which I'd taken in the ass before, since it was smaller than Roth by a good bit—into my pussy and fucked myself with it. Slowly, at first, but then faster and faster, gasping, arching, writhing into it, letting the clitoral stimulator buzz against me. Roth couldn't hold back now, and was moving in earnest, grinding in and out of me, and it was so much, so good, so incredible I didn't want it to ever stop. I wanted to let him fuck me like this forever.

He had my hips in his hands again, tugging, and now slid one hand to the base of my spine, pressed the heel of his palm to my tailbone and gripped the crease of my hip in the other hand and I felt his hips slapping against my ass cheeks and felt his cock slam in deep and his thighs brush against the backs of mine. He was pushing and pulling, pushing and pulling with his hands, grunting, driving toward his own orgasm.

I felt him thicken inside me.

I felt him quicken.

I matched the now-relentless driving pace of his cock in my ass with the vibrator in my pussy. I was so full and being so thoroughly fucked, harder and harder now, that it was almost impossible to be able to even breathe.

"Kyrie—"

"*Fuck…*" I gasped.

"Shit, Kyrie. I'm there, love, I'm—oh, ohhhhh fuck…."

And he came, before he could even formulate the words. I felt it, felt him gush into the condom, felt him thicken yet more. I groaned and moved with him as he fucked me, moving the dildo in synch with his pace.

Everything stopped, then, as he came. My blood turned to fire, my muscles—all 640-some of them— contracted and pulsed, and my cunt squeezed and my asshole contracted and I writhed like a mad-woman, bit the sheets and screamed as an orgasm unlike anything in my life ripped through me, and Roth kept fucking, fucking, fucking, pushing me through the climax until I was quivering and moan-ing and crying. And then I came once more, and then again in an unending cycle. I barely knew what was happening as wave after wave of nuclear-pow-ered climax exploded through me, and in me.

As the aftershocks hit me like earthquakes, each one a wracking orgasm in its own right, I felt Roth pull out of me as slowly and carefully as he'd pushed in, by gradual degrees, tenderly.

When he was out of me, I collapsed to my side,

tears sliding down my cheeks. I felt him get up and heard him discard the condom, and then he was in bed with me, cradling me against his warm broad chest.

"Jesus, Kyrie. I still can't breathe right, I came so hard."

I curled into him. Gripped the back of his neck, lying completely on top of him, pressing my lips to his throat. "Valentine, I don't—I don't even have words for what that was."

"You're okay, though?"

I lifted up enough that he could see my eyes, and see that I spoke the truth. "So much more than okay. I loved it, loved everything about it, but I don't think we can do that very often. It was just…so fucking intense I don't think I could handle it every time."

"It *was* incredible. But yeah, not all the time."

We were quiet for a while, in the special place where we needed no words. We weren't sleeping, just utterly content in each other, holding on, breathing, skin to skin, heartbeat to heartbeat.

And then I felt his cock under my belly, hardening.

Still we needed no words. I reached between us and stroked him to life, slid him into my slit, fed him inch by inch into my pussy. I pressed my lips to his throat, crushed my hips to his, laying on top of him, my thighs gripping his sides. I took his face in my palms and turned it to mine and kissed him breathless, fucked him senseless, riding him until he was crazed and I was gasping and sweating, kissing him all the while, until we were writhing in utter synchronicity, right to the edge. And then, moments before we came, I went still. I pressed him onto the bed, stopping him. I held him down, my hands on his shoulders. I sat upright and looked at him.

"Look at me, Valentine," I said. He rested his hands on my thighs, and his eyes went to mine. "Don't move."

Sitting upright, his cock filling me, his beautiful blue eyes on mine, I rode Valentine slowly, rocking on him, grinding on him, bracing myself with my palms at the V of my thighs. I rolled my hips in broad, wide circles, lifting so he was almost out, sitting on him so he was fully in, stretching him away from his body, riding, riding, riding.

Sweat coated his gloriously muscled body in a sheen, and he fought to remain still.

I felt him nearing the edge, and slowed. I waited, holding him stretched away so he couldn't release. I waited some more until he tensed, until he was shaking all over with need. I touched my clit with one finger while he watched, holding us still, fluttering so he wouldn't lose the edge of near-orgasm. I fingered myself—

And then I came, falling forward, flinging my arms around his neck and writhing as he spurted his seed into me, flooding me with his wet heat, and we were groaning, mouths sloppily seeking and kissing, until there was only the orgasm still detonating in both of us, simultaneously.

When at long last the waves and shudders ceased, Roth pulled out of me. He rose and padded to the bathroom for a towel, came back and rolled me onto my back, parted my folds with gentle fingers and cleaned me with the towel, and then climbed back in bed next to me.

Another long, drowsy, lazy, sated silence ensued, both of us utterly spent.

My mind wandered and I wondered idly if we'd made port yet, but decided I didn't care.

His voice rumbled, my ear to his chest. "I was going to make it a surprise, but I've decided against that."

"Make what a surprise?" I asked.

"The reason we're going back to the States."

"Which is?"

A pause. "Well, business aside…it's for us."

"First, what's the business aspect of the trip?"

"I'm selling off a bunch of holdings and properties. Including the tower in Manhattan. I'm liquidating a bunch of assets and I've got to be there to finalize the sales."

"You're selling the tower?"

He nodded. "Yep. It's time. I want to build a place together, you and me. Somewhere that's ours." A sigh. "Plus, we're going to need a ready flow of cash for…preparations, I guess you could say."

"Be clear, Roth. Explain what you mean by 'preparations.'"

"Staying off the grid properly and effectively is a difficult thing to do. Even more so when you're as wealthy as I am. See, most of my capital is…imaginary, essentially. It's real, in the business sense and in the business world, where I have contacts at every bank, all over the world. But if you want to be off the grid, investment properties and net worth are meaningless. Cash is king, out here. And being *worth* tens of billions of dollars is no good to me unless I can convert it to cash, or make it readily available in cash. But, especially in the quantities I'm going to need, that is hard to do. As for why?" Roth paused, his hand idly caressing my side. "Honestly, Vitaly is still a very real threat to me, to us. He's out there somewhere, waiting, biding his time. He's a big venomous spider with a very elaborate web, just waiting for us to set one of his strands to vibrating. I need to find a way for us to vanish entirely, or I've got to take him out. Neither proposition is easy."

"Which approach are you leaning towards?" I asked.

"Vanishing, to be honest. Not because I want to run away from him, but because I'm smart enough, and know him well enough, to know I'm not entirely willing to start a war. And that's what it would take. Now that Gina is dead and he realizes his sanctum can be assaulted, he's going to be on high alert. And he has access to many, many times more men and weapons than I do. I'm worth more, financially, but he's a wily old fox with a network like no one else in the world. To go after him, to try and kill him…it would take a full-on war." He touched my chin, and I craned my neck to look up at him. "There's been enough bloodshed."

I nodded. "Yes, there has. I'll go where you go, and I'll support whatever you decide to do. I just…I don't want to spend my life being afraid, either."

"So, you'd go after him, then?" Roth seemed surprised.

I took a moment to think. "I've had a taste of death. The thought of going through anything like that again makes me sick. Seeing you or Layla or Harris get hurt…I'm not sure I could handle that. But at the same time, I'm not willing to run away from him for the rest of my life. I'd rather make a stand, or even go after him if that's what it takes. I'll shoot him myself, if I have to. I've done it once, I can do it again."

"Well, let's hope it doesn't come to that. I've got some ideas, which is why we're heading up to the States."

I rested my chin on his chest; stared up at his piercing blue eyes. "You said there was another reason we are heading back to the States, one that has to do with us."

He took my hand in his, my left hand, the one with the two-carat diamond engagement ring, his thumb nudging the ring side to side on my finger. "It's been six months since I proposed. I think it's time to do something about that, don't you?"

"Do something about it?" I felt breathless. "Like what?"

"Like get married."

I just stared at him, blinking, thinking, trying to process his suggestion. "Why now?"

Roth frowned, brow furrowing. "Why not now? I love you more than life itself. I want you to be mine forever. I want you to become Kyrie Roth."

"Yes, it has been six months, but Vitaly is still out there. I don't know if I could ever really relax knowing that he's still looking for us. We've got Layla here for her own safety, and we've got Harris and his team on high alert on our behalf. I want to get married, I really do, but I'll be with you no matter what. I'll change my name, if that's what you want."

He blew out a breath, frustrated, confused. "I'm not following, Kyrie. Just a bit ago on the deck you were suggesting a house in the suburbs with kids. Now you're saying you don't want to get married?"

I sat up, put my back to the headboard, and scraped my thick blond hair backward. "Roth, no, I'm not saying I don't want to. I just want to know why now. Is it what *you* want, or are you doing it because you think it's what *I* want?"

"Both, actually. Does it really matter *why*, though?"

"Yes! It really does matter. It's marriage, Roth. It's not something to take lightly."

He didn't answer right away. "I guess maybe I see it differently. Anyone can get married. It doesn't have to be a big deal. It's just a ceremony, a piece of legal documentation. Unless you make it meaningful, that's all it is."

I laughed, but it wasn't entirely mirthful. "You're not making any sense. Why do you want to get married if it doesn't mean anything? It seems like you've got your arguments confused."

He stood up, paced to the window, naked. Even in the midst of what was shaping up to be a pretty serious argument, I couldn't help appreciating his taut, muscular ass, the rippling muscles of his back, his broad shoulders, the fall of his blond hair.

"I'll admit I didn't see this coming, Kyrie. I thought you'd be all over this. A chance to see home again, maybe get your brother to walk you down to the aisle to me."

"First, where's home, now? This ship? New York? Detroit? Second, I love Cal, but I'm not sure I want to risk his safety by bringing him within a hundred miles of us and our problems. He's an innocent kid."

"Home is wherever we are, I suppose. Here on the *Eliza*, France, New York…but I see your point. As for Cal, Harris has two of his guys in Chicago, keeping tabs on him. I doubt he even knows they're there, but they'll make sure no one else is sniffing around him."

"I'm relieved to hear that."

"I told you I'd keep an eye on everyone. I know you've sort of kept your distance from him, for his own safety. And I know that's hard for you. And I just… I hate that you've had to do that because of my problems, because of my past."

"It's *our* past now, and *our* problems. Not just yours. We're in this together." I got out of bed and padded over to him, pressing myself up against his back. "I love you, Valentine. And yes, I want to marry you. However, whenever, wherever. And as long as you can promise me he'll stay safe, I'd love a chance to see Cal."

"I can't give you a traditional wedding, Kyrie. I can't give you a wedding with your parents on one side and mine on the other, or a little white church, or months and months to make arrangements and compile guest lists."

I kissed his shoulder. "I don't care. I'm not the kind of girl who's spent her whole life picturing her wedding. I mean, maybe when I was a little girl I thought about it, daydreamed or whatever, but after Dad died, I just…I didn't have time to think about that. I shut it down. It wasn't relevant anymore. And now, with you, I love you and I'm with you, no matter what. Whether we get married or not, whether we have a permanent home or not, it's you and me together. That's all that matters to me. Yeah, I want stability. I'd love a real home, something of *ours*. But I'm not sure we can have that yet, not while Vitaly is out there, plotting his revenge or whatever it is he's doing. But, if you want to plan us a wedding, I will marry you in a heartbeat. I'd be proud to be Kyrie Roth."

"I'm going to set up a meeting with Harris, to-day, to tell him about our wedding plans. We'll work out the security angles and then give you the safety parameters, so that you and Layla can get to work planning our wedding."

"How about *you* plan the wedding, and just let Layla and me pick dresses and flowers? That's all we care about anyway."

"If you mean it, that would be infinitely easier. We'd find a good defensible location, fly in whomever we want, get security arranged...but still create a beautiful event."

"I just have one request," I said.

"What's that, love?" He twisted in place, putting our bodies chest to chest. He palmed my backside possessively.

"Can we get married somewhere warm and sunny? It's interesting and all, being down here in Tierra del Fuego, but it's a little chilly."

He laughed. "Sure, darling. We can do that. Somewhere warm and sunny it is."

2

DISCUSSIONS

LIFE ONBOARD THE SHIP HAD ITS OWN PATTERNS and routines, and everyone, from the Captain down to the deckhands, was engaged in keeping this huge craft running smoothly. Layla and I also had our own routines. We spent a lot of time during the day in what Roth called "the salon", or the living room, watching movies, reading, listening to music, playing cards. But Layla was right in that without a job to do, boredom was a constant specter of life aboard a ship. Especially when, like Layla and me, you were used to working all the time or studying for classes or just living life.

Roth had arranged for Layla to finish her degree via online courses, using his encrypted satellite internet signal, but that only occupied so much time.

I audited classes here and there, studying whatever interested me, but I wasn't working toward a degree; I just didn't see the point.

As for Roth…he was always busy. He stayed in constant communication with Robert, his business guru in New York, staying abreast of the few businesses he'd not already liquidated. He always seemed to be on a call via encrypted satellite phone. And when he wasn't on the phone, he attended to what seemed to be an endless stream of emails. And when he wasn't doing that, he and Harris spent a lot of time behind closed doors.

Usually, the four of us all had dinner together and, typically, it was a pretty lively affair. It had become another one of our onboard rituals, I guess. Harris was often gone a lot during the day, taking the helicopter from the ship to whichever shore was closest, doing some mysterious business or other. He never really said, and I never asked. But he was almost always back onboard ship for dinner.

Dinner that night was anything but lively; in fact it was slightly awkward. Layla's mood hadn't improved since she'd left the deck earlier in the afternoon. She wasn't even looking at Harris nor really talking to me. Harris was his usual taciturn self, except maybe more icily silent. Roth appeared to be lost in thought, working through plans, I supposed.

Even under the best of circumstances I wasn't the best at idle chatter, and tonight I had even less to contribute in the conversation department.

So we ate in silence.

As soon as he was done eating, Harris thanked the steward, then excused himself from the table and disappeared from the dining room. Roth followed soon after, leaving Layla and me alone at the table. She continued to move her food around her plate, and I let the silence between us stand for all of perhaps three minutes, and then I had to break it.

"What's eating you, Layla?"

She shrugged. "Nothing. I'm fine."

I snorted. "Please, Layla. We've been friends for too long for you to feed me that bullshit."

She sighed, and set her fork down on her plate with a clatter. "Kyrie…I've lost track of time. Like, legit, I don't even know how long we've been on this boat. I never know where we are. I don't know how long this is going to go on, and worst of all, even really *why* I'm here. I know what you and Roth and Harris have told me, but it's hard to have my entire life put on hold just because other people say 'Oh, Layla, you're in danger!' I don't get it, especially when I don't have anything to be worried about." She glanced at me. "Don't get me wrong, I love you, Roth is cool, and even Harris is pretty okay. And this boat is absolutely unbelievable. But…I just want to go home."

"I get it, babe. I do." I moved from my seat across the table from her to go and sit beside her. "I don't even *have* a home to go back to. This *is* my home now. And as for why you're here…I don't *want* you to have to understand it. Believe me, I don't want you to know firsthand what could happen when you least expect it. You're here on this boat with us so we can keep you safe. Please, trust me on that. I've got your best interests at heart. I know it's…disruptive. But it's for the best. Believe me."

She nodded. "I hear you, Key. But hearing you say those things doesn't really help." Layla leaned back in her chair, tipping it backward, balancing on the back legs. "I know it may seem trivial to you, but when I said I was horny, it wasn't a joke. I've never gone this long being totally alone. I'm not good at it."

"At being horny?" I said, trying to make a joke.

Layla just glared at me. "No, you tool. I'm *great* at being horny. What I don't do well is celibacy. I don't need a serious boyfriend or anything, but I do need a booty call, at the very least. I have needs."

"And those needs aren't being met on the boat."

"Not even a little bit." She jabbed a finger at me. "And don't you fucking dare suggest Harris again. We are *not* having that conversation."

"Why not? What's wrong with Harris?" I'd probably regret ignoring her warning, but something about her reaction to my line of questioning niggled at my suspicions.

"Dammit, Key. Just leave it alone, would you?" She shot to her feet so fast her chair almost fell over. "It's not happening. Let it go."

"Jesus, Layla. You don't need to bite my head off." I followed her as she stalked out of the dining room and made her way topside.

"Well you keep harping on it, and it's pissing me off."

"'Methinks the lady doth protest too much,'" I quoted at her.

Layla laughed despite herself. "Really? You're going with Shakespeare?"

"If the quote fits."

To our left, Ushuaia was a crescent of urban life against the wild majesty of snow-capped mountains. Layla slumped over the railing and stared down at the waves. "You ever just have this feeling that something is a bad idea? Like, you don't have a reason, you don't have any proof or anything to really go on, you just have this gut feeling that it'd be super, super bad?"

I stared at her in silence. "Layla. Hello? I went blindfolded into the private residence of a mysterious billionaire to whom I owed several hundred thousand dollars."

"Yeah, and look how that turned out," she quipped.

"Um. In love? Happier than I ever thought possible? Fucked senseless by the most amazing man on the planet multiple times a day?"

"Whoa! Way more than I needed to know." She shook her head in disbelief. "And what about the whole business about being pursued by an underworld crime kingpin? On the run for your life? What about the part where you were almost raped, where you were shot, beaten up, kidnapped, and had to be rescued by fucking mercenaries?"

I shrugged. "I'd go through it all again if it meant getting to be with Roth."

A long, fraught silence. Finally, Layla looked at me intently, skeptically. "Really? You would?"

I nodded slowly. "I would. That's the honest truth. I mean, shit, yeah, it sucked hard. I've never been so afraid in my life. I still have nightmares sometimes. More about shooting Tobias and Gina than anything else. I wouldn't choose to have all that happen to me again, for sure. But would I run from it? Not if it meant losing Valentine. I'd go through it all again, do it all again."

"Roth means that much to you?" Layla asked.

I met her gaze. "More."

"Damn. Wish I had that." Another silence, then Layla turned away and fixed her eyes on the city in the distance. "This is the first time you've really talked about what happened to you."

She'd asked, of course, but I hadn't wanted to burden her with the details. Nor did I really relish the idea of reliving it by talking about it. I sighed. "It wasn't pretty. I'm not sure I'll ever really be able to talk about a lot of what happened."

"You never told me you shot anyone."

I couldn't respond for a long moment. "Roth was kidnapped by an ex-girlfriend. I woke up one day and he was just…gone, and there was a note. Harris and I went after him. We rescued him. The details don't really matter. It was shitty, and horrible, and awful. Not knowing where he was, or if he was alive. After we'd gotten him back I worried if he would ever be the same again…that was the worst part. She'd done some horrible shit to him. Not gonna say what, because it's just too…private, and too awful to say out loud. It was ugly, though, the aftermath of that. We thought we'd gotten away, but then Gina, the ex, she kidnapped me. Shot me in the knee and sent a picture of it to Roth. Just to hurt him. She took me to this private island in the Mediterranean and held me captive in a dungeon." I paused to gather myself, then continued. "Gina had this guy, Tobias. Huge, nasty, ugly, a vicious monster. They had me tied up, bound and gagged, and naked. Alone. I was terrified. I figured she'd torture me or kill me just to piss off Roth, but that didn't happen. They left me there for...I don't even know how long. Days, I think. Eventually Gina showed up with Tobias, and this...innocent young girl. Gina held a knife to my throat and forced me to watch while her trained ape did...unspeakable things to her. There's no way to describe what he did to that girl. I'll never—I'll never ever forget it. It was the most...vile, disgusting, evil thing I've ever seen. And that was just to fuck with my head. It was for no other reason."

"Jesus, Kyrie," Layla whispered.

"Yeah." I paused another long moment to summon my fortitude. "I puked on Gina's shoes, and that was when she cut my hair off. She did it with a pocketknife. Cut it all off, and then dry-shaved my scalp, which felt pretty fucking terrible. Anyway, hours later...Tobias came for me. He wasn't supposed to, she'd told him specifically to leave me alone. She wanted all the fun for herself, see, and Tobias had a tendency to ruin things...he couldn't get hard unless the victims were bloody, and after they were dead, *that* was when he got his rocks off."

Layla's face twisted. "He was a necrophiliac?

That's fucking nasty."

"You have no idea. So yeah. He was planning to—honestly, I don't even want to know what he was planning to do to me. I had a bullet hole in my knee, I hadn't eaten or drunk anything in who knew how long. I'd been beaten up, and I had to pee. So I let him get close, then I got a scissor-hold on his neck with my legs and I—I pissed all over him. Right in the face. And then I stole his gun and I shot him. Three times. Then I put his clothes on and waited for Gina to appear. I waited until she was right in front of me, and I shot her, too. Seven times."

"Jesus. I don't even know what else to say, Key. Just...Jesus." She turned and looked at me. Tears glistened on her cheeks. "I had no idea."

I wiped her face, pushed her curly black hair away from her wet cheeks. "Don't cry, Layla. I'm fine, now."

"You shot her seven times?"

I nodded. "I hope you never know what that's like. That kind of—*hate*. It's...like a bad trip, almost. It consumes you, takes over. And then after I shot her the first time, I just couldn't stop. It felt so good to see her hurt, to see her bleed. To watch her die. That's the part that scares me, that gives me nightmares. I didn't feel bad about it. I still don't. I mean, I have nightmares about it, because it's hard to forget when you watch someone fucking bleed to death because *you* shot them. You see it over and over in your mind, again, again, and again. But I don't regret it, and I don't feel guilty about it."

"And you'd do it again, for Roth?"

"I love him that much. If I never touch a gun, if I never see another dead body for as long as I live it'll be too soon. But for Roth? Yeah, I'd do it all over again."

"What does that kind of love feel like?" Layla's voice was so quiet I barely heard her.

"Indescribable. Loving him isn't a choice. It's not something I have control over. Being his, being with him…it's all of me. I don't know, Layla. It's—*everything*. And it's worth going through hell for."

"I'm not sure I'm brave enough for that." She followed the path of a cawing seagull as it carved through the evening air overhead. "I'm not sure I'm *capable* of that."

"You loved Eric," I pointed out.

She snorted. "Eric was convenient, and I didn't dislike him. But, ultimately, he was a loser. He was *my* loser, sure, but he was still a loser. I always knew it. He was good enough in bed that I never needed to go elsewhere, you know? I mean, I would have dumped him had that been the case. I'm no cheater, you know that. But did I love him? Hell no. Not even close. We were together for almost three years, yeah, but that was more because it was just...*easier* to stay together. Good enough that we didn't break up, but not good enough that it really meant anything. Love? I don't know what that looks like." She shrugged, traced the cold metal railing with a short, unpainted fingernail. "I never have, and I never will. I'm glad for you, but it's not for me. It's not gonna happen for me. I just...I don't know how it ever could."

"You think I expected this with Roth? You think I knew what I was doing? Shit, you think I know what I'm doing *now*? You close yourself off to it, it won't happen. But if it comes along, you jump at it and you hold on for dear life."

Layla rolled her eyes. "Yes, Mom."

"What happened with Eric, anyway?"

"I told him I was moving." She shrugged. "You called and asked me to come out onto the boat with you, so I just...told him I was moving. Didn't tell him where, or why. He just lit a joint and was like, well, I'll miss you, see ya."

"Wow. You're right, he is a loser."

"Tells you how much I meant to him." She waved a hand in dismissal. "The only thing he was gonna miss was my half of the rent and the BJs when I didn't feel like fucking."

I stared at her. "Wait, what?"

She glanced at me. "Even I'm not in the mood all the time."

"So you'd suck him off?"

She shrugged. "Sure. Why not? It only took a minute or two, and he'd shut up and leave me alone for a day or two."

"A minute or two? I thought you said he was good in bed?"

"Okay, number one, no, I said he was *good enough* in bed. Not great. He had decent stamina and didn't mind letting me use a vibrator so I could get off faster. Plus he was pretty well hung for a skinny white dude."

"But back to the blowjobs. A minute or two?"

"Well, if you do it right, yeah. When it's not about foreplay, it doesn't have to last forever. You just…work him until he shoots off. That's the point."

"I think you may need a new set of standards, babe," I mused.

She smacked my arm. "Hey, now. My standards assure me of sex when I need it. And besides, not all of us have billionaire sex gods to pleasure us until we scream." She quirked an eyebrow. "In related news, you should think about looking into gags or something, because bitch, you scream *loud*."

I flushed. "You can hear us?"

"Nope, I can hear *you*." She started moaning

loudly, mimicking an orgasmic scream, thrashing her hair all over the place, and generally doing her best Meg Ryan/*When Harry Met Sally* impression. "And that's how you sound *before* you come. I don't have the lung capacity to do an impression of you orgasming. If I didn't know better I'd say he was murdering you…over, and over, and over…and over. And over—"

"Shut up, Layla."

"—And over, and over. All night. Every night. Like Jesus-fuck, woman, don't you ever take a break? Does he have *any* refractory period at all, or can he just fuck all night long? And you wonder why I want off the damn ship. It's like living on a porn set."

"All right, Layla. I get it." I pretended to be extremely interested in my cuticles. "I'll try to be quieter."

But Layla wasn't done. "You know, I'm not a voyeur or anything, but you scream so loud for so long I can't help but be a little curious as to *what* the *hell* that man is doing to you. I mean, earlier today he had you screaming so loud Harris and I had to go down into the very bottom of the ship and turn on the music to drown you out. God knows what the crew hears. And even then, I swear you two were rocking the damn boat. In the middle of the day, no less!"

"Layla—"

"We've sailed through twenty-foot waves that didn't faze this fucking aircraft carrier of a yacht, but you two, fucking?" She pretended to be tossed side to side, lurching wildly. "Swear to god, I thought we were gonna capsize or some shit."

"SHUT THE FUCK UP, LAYLA!" I shouted.

"*You* shut the fuck up!" she shouted back at me. "How's a bitch supposed to sleep with you yowling all night long like a damn cat in heat?"

"I'm about to shove you overboard," I warned, laughing in spite of myself.

"Good. I'll swim my ass to shore and find a dick to sit on. I swear I've got cobwebs in my cooter."

"Cooter, Layla? Seriously? Who the hell even says *cooter*?" I was laughing, though, which I need-ed. "You are so vulgar, sometimes, I swear to god."

"Like you're any better!"

"I would never refer to my lady parts as a cooter! That's nasty!"

""Lady parts'? What are we, twelve?" She snort-ed and rolled her eyes. "Besides, what do you call it? Besides *lady parts*—which, I submit, is equally as embarrassing as calling it a cooter, if not more so."

"I don't call it anything, usually. I mean how of-ten are you in a situation where you use an actual word for it?"

"In everyday life, I suppose you're right. But what about during sex?" She leaned close. "You guys talk dirty?"

I flushed again. With Roth I was bold and willing to talk nasty. But with Layla? Not so much. "I'm not having this conversation with you."

"You do!" She laughed like a hyena. "You totally talk dirty, don't you! You'd only avoid this question if you had something to talk about! I bet you call it a pussy during sex, don't you?"

"Jesus, Layla. Shut up, already."

"You have to know we can all hear you when you're fucking, and you don't seem to care about that, but you can't talk to your best friend about whether you talk dirty during sex?"

"I get caught up in the moment, okay? And you and I don't usually talk about this kind of stuff, do we?"

"Well, you never did. I don't give a shit. I'll talk about anything."

"No kidding. So what was Eric's favorite position?" I asked.

"Doggy-style," she answered right away. "Problem was, he liked that position a little *too* much. We had to save that until he was ready to come, because he'd just blow right away otherwise. He just couldn't hold it. Soon as he had this big ass of mine up against him, he was just...*bam*, done."

I shook my head. "You are shameless."

"Hey, you asked. And besides, I ain't with him anymore, so it's not like you have to see him again."

"So then...what's your favorite position?"

"You answer first," Layla said.

"I don't have one. I like all the positions equally." I couldn't hold back a grin. "And yes, we talk dirty. Makes it that much hotter."

"Tried that with Eric a few times. He just...he couldn't deliver the lines without both of us cracking up. It always ended up sounding like a joke. I don't know. The guy I slept with before Eric liked to talk dirty, though. God, he was good at it, too. Too bad he talked a better game than he could actually deliver."

"That was...Tom, wasn't it?" I asked.

"Yeah. Tom. That boy was *fine* as *hell*. He did two things really, really well, and that was basically all he had going on, except for being sexy. He could talk dirty like no one's business, and I mean he could get me wet and ready just by talking. And he could eat pussy for hours. Like, legit, that was the only way he could make me come, and Jesus, I've still never come harder than when Tom had his tongue working me. But if he wasn't doing those two things, forget it. His dick was forgettable at best, which isn't really a deal-breaker if the guy knows how to use what he's got, but Tom didn't. He and I were just fuck-buddies, though. I don't think I even know his last name, come to think of it."

"Kurzweil. Tom Kurzweil," I filled in.

"How the hell do you know that?"

I shrugged. "He told me, when he introduced himself. He was like this...caricature of a person. He swaggered everywhere, and he'd shove his hand at you and squeeze yours hard as he could, and he'd be all like 'Tom, Tom Kurzweil. Pleasure to meet you, buddy.' Like, for real? Who for real says their first name twice when they introduce themselves? And Tom called *everyone* buddy."

"How do you know all this?"

"You dated Tom for six months, Layla. Is something wrong with your memory?"

She stared at me. "I wouldn't say we dated. We fucked, and that was it."

"Okay, well, whatever. You brought him over all the time, and he introduced himself to me at least three times, the same way every time. He was a douchebag and I never got what you saw in him."

"Aside from his six-pack and those fuck-me dimples?"

"He used more hair product than I did."

Layla laughed. "He was kind of a douche."

"So you just kept him around because he was good at cunnilingus?"

"Yeah, basically," she said with a shrug.

"See what I mean? You need better standards. I don't remember you ever bringing around a guy who was…I don't even know…the whole package, I guess. They were all either hot douchebags or losers who weren't exactly ugly. It's like you choose guys intentionally who you know there's no chance of falling for."

The humor was gone, now. Layla wasn't looking at me, she wasn't laughing anymore, and she wasn't shooting back at me with a snarky reply. All I got from her was a small shrug. "I told you. Falling for a guy? That's just not my style."

"And *I* told *you*, you need a new style."

"Know any other mysterious, available, billionaire sex gods?" She looked at me with a sharp, cutting expression. "And do *not* say Harris. We aren't going there."

I held up my hands in surrender. "I wasn't going to."

"You were thinking it, though."

"He's a good guy, Layla. A *great* guy. He's saved my life more than once. He taught me to shoot a gun. He's even killed for me. And knowing how well Roth pays, I guarantee you he's not hurting for money. And he's good-looking. I mean, I'm with Roth for life, but Harris…well, let's just say I don't understand your reticence."

The scuff of a shoe echoed from above us, and we both craned our necks to look up. Harris stood two decks up, his expression inscrutable, impassive, green eyes glittering. He stared down at us for a moment, then turned and vanished.

Layla smacked my arm. "That's the second time he's overheard us talking about him. Or rather, *you* trying to fix me up with him. It's not happening, so please, for my sake, for the sake of our friendship, *please* let it go." Yet, she glanced back up again, to where Harris had been standing.

I held up my hands again. "Fine. Not another word from me, I swear."

"Perfect. Thanks." And just like that, she was gone.

Was I out of line? Maybe. I don't know. My friend wasn't just horny, she was lonely. I could tell that much. She was with me, so it wasn't the loneliness of being actually by herself, alone, but rather the kind of loneliness that stems from not having someone to share her life with, someone to talk to at night in whispers across a shared pillow, someone to hold her. Despite her somewhat harsh description of her relationship with Eric, I had a feeling she missed him. She may not have loved him, but she'd spent three years with him, lived with him, spent every day in his company, every night in his bed. That meant something, no matter how much she may have claimed otherwise. The way he'd let her go had hurt badly, I could see that much as well.

I ruminated on the deck by myself for a while, and then I heard a quiet footstep, and assumed it was Layla come back to talk. I didn't turn to look, just spoke facing the water. "Listen, hookerface, I'm sorry. I shouldn't have pushed it. I promise you I won't bring up Harris again."

"I'm not who you were expecting, clearly," I heard Harris say behind me.

"Shit, Harris—" I said, turning with a jump.

He leaned against the railing beside me, a bottle of beer in his hand, an unlit cigarette pinched between the index and middle fingers of the same hand. "It's a subject you would do well to forget, Kyrie. For her sake, and mine. As she has said more than once, it's not happening. I appreciate your good intentions, but…no." His voice was how it always sounded, low but not particularly deep, cool, even, hard. Yet, because I knew him, I could hear a certain tone, a wistfulness, perhaps? A strain of regret, maybe? I wasn't sure, and with Harris, it was impossible to tell. "A man like me is not the right type for a woman like her."

"She doesn't have a type, Harris. That's the point. The guys she's dated or whatever…they're all over the place. Black, white, Italian, buff, skinny, short, tall, and everything in between."

"Why are you telling me this?" Harris asked, then tilted the bottle to his lips, swallowing a mouthful of beer.

"I don't know. I just think you and Layla—"

"We aren't compatible, Kyrie."

"If you'd asked me a year ago if I thought I'd be compatible with a man like Valentine, I would have laughed at you. And that's *before* knowing about his involvement in my father's death."

He sighed, dug in his hip pocket and produced a lighter, then lit his cigarette. "You are fixated on this, aren't you?"

"I didn't know you smoked," I said.

"There's a lot you probably don't know about me." He took a long drag, letting it out slowly. "But I don't consider myself a smoker since I don't do it often or regularly. It's a vice I allow myself once in a while."

I let the silence hang for a while then, by way of changing the subject, I asked, "So when will we be back Stateside?"

He lifted a shoulder. "Depending on the weather, I'd say a month? Give or take a week either way."

"I need some bridal magazines. Can you get some for me next time you go ashore?"

He nodded. "Sure thing." A glance. "Roth would never say it this bluntly, so it's up to me. This wedding will be extremely small and private. It's not going to be a traditional wedding. It can't be, not if we want to keep Vitaly off our scent."

I didn't mention that Roth *had* said pretty much that exactly.

"So Roth wants to keep running," I said.

Harris didn't answer right away, inhaling instead, blowing out a stream of smoke, and then he did it again. When he spoke, he chose his words carefully. "Taking on a man like Vitaly Karahalios is no small undertaking, Kyrie. He's out for blood, and he plays a long game. If it were just me, I'd go after him. If it were just Roth, I'd go after him. But it's not. Not anymore. Vitaly has made it clear he's willing to spill innocent blood, and that's not a risk either of us are willing to take. Your brother, your mother, Layla, Roth's parents, even Robert. Vitaly is aware of them all and will target them if we force his hand. He's completely capable of slaughtering all of them if we go after him and fail to take him out the first time. It's a complex situation, Kyrie, so I wouldn't necessarily call it running. I would call it prudence.

I would call it avoiding collateral damage."

I nodded. "I guess I see your point. It just…it doesn't sit well with me."

"Me neither. But let Roth and me worry about that, okay? Keeping you—all of you—safe…that's my job. So you just focus on planning this wedding."

"Thanks, Harris."

He nodded, extinguished his cigarette on the side of his now-empty beer bottle, then tossed the butt inside. "Of course, Kyrie."

He started to walk away, but I stopped him as a thought occurred to me. "Harris?"

"Yeah?"

"Layla…she's getting a little bit of cabin fever. Plus, all this is getting to her. The sudden change, life on a ship without work to do…it's bugging her. So just…keep an eye on her, please? I don't want her to do anything rash."

"She is prone to making rash decisions, isn't she?"

"Under the right circumstances, yes. When she decides she's had enough, she's capable of just about anything."

Harris nodded. "I'll have both eyes on her, all the time. Nothing will happen to Layla, you have my word."

I knew Harris's word was good, but I still had a

strange, unsettling, niggling feeling in the pit of my stomach.

3

FAREWELL, MANHATTAN

I SAT IN THE BACK OF THE CAR, A BLACK MERCEDES-Maybach Pullman limousine. It was luxurious beyond compare, soft and supple quilted tan leather, soothing classical music piped in crystal-clear surround sound via invisible speakers. There were a thousand other details that made the car worth more than half a million dollars. I sat in the rear passenger seat, staring out the window gazing up, up, up. Tinted, reflective glass rocketed skyward to a dizzying height, and I saw the face of a Manhattan highrise that had been the scene of a life-changing series of events for me. Up there, on the very topmost three floors was Roth's former home. *My* former home, really. In what seemed like a lifetime ago I'd stood behind a pair of rich mahogany French doors, my heart hammering, waiting to meet the man who essentially owned me.

I'd been blindfolded. My heart had hammered like a drum. Fear had pumped through my veins in place of blood. Yet through it all, there had been an element of excitement. Seduction, even, that began from the first moment I'd heard his voice, sensed his presence, smelled the spicy undertone of his cologne, felt the brush of his fingers on my shoulder. He'd owned me, financially, but from that first moment, he'd also owned my body, my soul, my heart.

When we first made love, he'd taken possession of my whole being.

I could never go back, now. I could never be a normal girl, dating normal guys. Even if I wanted to—which I didn't—the experience of Valentine Roth had ruined me for all other men.

And it had all started a few hundred vertical feet away from where I sat. The place where Roth was right now personally attending the sale of his building. His home, the core of his company. I wondered if he would walk the halls once more, visit the shower where we'd done…such delicious things to each other. The bedroom, where he'd finally allowed me, of all people, to see the real him, to know him, taste him, feel him.

I thought about the library up there, where

Gina Karahalios had shot me in the knee and then kidnapped me. The hallway near the foyer, where I'd first encountered Roth...where I'd seen Eliza's dead body. Eliza, Roth's housekeeper, friend, and one of the few people other than Robert, Harris, and me that he truly trusted or cared for. Eliza, the namesake of our ship.

I inhaled sharply, then blinked. I ignored Layla's curious glance at me and focused on breathing and pretending it was just another day. People passed by on the sidewalk just a few feet away, staring curiously, but the windows were mirrored, preventing anyone from seeing in.

Long, long minutes later—fifteen minutes, or maybe an hour, I'd lost track, lost in memory—Harris emerged from the rotating doors at the entrance, followed closely by Roth. God, Roth. All seventy-six-point-eight blond-haired, blue-eyed, gloriously gorgeous inches of him, clad in a trim black bespoke suit, crisp white button-down, no tie, top two buttons undone, striding confidently toward the limousine, unfastening the center button of his suit jacket as Harris opened the back door for him. I knew from his expression that my Valentine wasn't in a good mood. He had on what I thought of as his "shit-kicking" face, brows drawn, lips pressed in a thin flat line, jaw muscles flexing, eyes glittering and shifting.

Harris took the driver's seat, buckled his seat belt and checked his mirrors. "All set, sir?" He glanced in the rear-view mirror through the lowered partition between the front and rear seats.

Layla, sitting in a rear-facing jump seat, glanced from me to Roth and back, and then slid toward the passenger door. "Hang on, Harris, I'm coming up front."

She exited and took the front seat beside Harris, who shot another glance back at Roth. A nod from Roth, and Harris pulled the long, powerful vehicle out into the stream of traffic, and then closed the partition.

I waited a few minutes more in silence as Roth stared out the window, brooding. Finally I reached out and pried his hand open, threading my fingers through his. "Babe? You okay?"

He shook his head. "No. I hate selling that building. I built it from the ground up. I formed the construction company myself, handpicked the foreman and architect, and chose all the subcontractors myself. Every tile, every slab of marble and every board foot of imported wood, every door handle and cabinet pull and roll of carpeting...I chose it all myself. My handprints are in the foundation. I poured the first load of concrete. It was the first place since I left

England as an eighteen year-old boy that really felt like home, you know? It just…sucks."

"You didn't have to sell it."

He glanced at me, finally. "Yes, I did. Number one, we need the cash. Number two, could either of us have walked into that library ever again? I couldn't. I just…couldn't. I went through the bedrooms, the kitchen, and all the other rooms. But the library…I just couldn't go in. Couldn't stand to see the place where she…where Gina…." He shook his head, once, sharply, and then rested his chin in his other hand. "I couldn't. And, besides, for better or worse, I'm done with New York."

"So now what?"

"Now…Robert condenses the businesses that remain into one umbrella company." Another glance at me, this time with a small smile. "We're calling the new structure St. Claire, Incorporated. You're on the board, and you have your own majority share."

"What?" I stared at him; he never ceased to amaze me.

"You and I are the controlling shareholders, each of us owning a third of the shares, with the remaining third split between a few others."

"So…what does being a majority shareholder entail?" I asked.

He shrugged. "As much or as little as you want.

You can become involved in the day-to-day operations of the company, if you want; I can teach you anything you need to know that you don't know already. Or, you can just sit back and do nothing and collect the earnings, which will go directly into your personal bank accounts."

Ah, yes, my private bank accounts. Roth had set them up for me after Harris and I had rescued him from Gina. They were my insurance, in case anything happened to Roth, or if—god forbid—I either left or became separated from Roth. The accounts were mine, and only mine. He had no access to them. In my purse there were debit cards, checkbooks, and a slip of paper with series of codes written on it, allowing me access to…six accounts? Seven? I wasn't sure. There were a whole bunch of Swiss and offshore accounts, each in my name.

They contained, in total, something in the neighborhood of eight hundred million dollars.

Every once in a while, I would remember I had that money, and I would try to imagine what it meant. Eight hundred million dollars. It was a gobsmacking amount of money. Enough that I could live in utterly ridiculous luxury for the rest of my life and never have to work another day, never have to pay taxes—something that was handled without my needing to do a thing. I wasn't sure how he'd worked that magic, and didn't honestly care; he wasn't a criminal anymore, so it was all legal. Of that I was positive.

"I tend to forget about those bank accounts, honestly," I said.

Roth laughed. "How do you forget about nearly a billion dollars, Kyrie?"

I strived to look innocent. "Out of sight, out of mind? I don't use the money since you take care of everything for me." I shrugged as if it didn't matter, which to me it really didn't. I had total confidence in Roth's ability to provide for us financially. "So... why did you add me to the business, and why name it after me?"

He grinned, a cute, sexy tilt of his lips. "Because you're half of me, sweetheart. And everything I have is yours. All of it is meaningless, without you." He turned toward me, finally. "I've never exactly been *poor*, but I can tell you without hesitation that I would live my life in utter poverty, as long as I could do it with you."

I shook my head. "Roth, baby. You're a spoiled brat. You have no idea what poverty is like. But...I believe you."

He laughed. "I only said I'd do it, not that I'd like it."

"You would hate it."

He nodded seriously. "I'm sure I would. I have a taste for the best things in life. But I assure you, my love, if we were to somehow lose everything, every penny, every company and subsidiary and property and stock share, we wouldn't remain poor for long. I would work day and night until you were provided for as you deserve."

"I know it, Valentine. I have absolute faith in you."

He just smiled and squeezed my hand. After another few minutes of silence, the vehicle stopping and starting and weaving through traffic, I recognized that our path was leading to the airport. "So, where next?"

"A private airfield a few hours from the city."

I furrowed my brow. "Private airfield? Like your own airport?"

He shrugged. "Sort of. It's nothing but a few acres in the middle of nowhere with a hangar and a landing strip. But it's owned by a dummy corporation and was purchased through a complicated series of transactions that would be…very difficult to trace back to me. It's a secure facility, surrounded by razor wire and protected by heavily armed guards from Harris's security company."

"Wow." Roth never ceased to amaze me. "When did you do all this?"

"Oh, I've had the airfield for years. I first purchased it back when I was still running guns, but I essentially sold it to myself via a long and complicated process to erase any connection to me personally. And then I just let it sit, kept it maintained, but that was it. Then, a few months ago I had it overhauled, had the landing strip repaved, upgraded the fence, and had Harris set a guard. I had a feeling we might need a place to fly in and out of that was totally off the radar."

"And where are we going from the airfield?"

"It's a surprise."

"A wedding surprise?"

He grinned. "Maybe."

"But Layla and I haven't done any real planning."

"Once we're at our destination, you two can go crazy. As long as you follow Harris's security rules, anything goes."

"What are the rules?"

"He'll tell you when we get there."

"When will that be?"

Roth lifted an eyebrow at me. "Soon." He turned toward me and lifted the armrest up out of the way. "You aren't eager at all, are you?"

I slid away from him, putting my back to the door. "No," I gulped. "Not at all."

He was all over me, a hand cupping my hip and

tugging me down, toward him, pulling me horizontal. The movement made my knee-length skirt hike up to mid-thigh, and then Roth's hands were helping it upward, pushing it up around my hips, baring me to him.

"Why, Kyrie..." he whispered, pressing his lips to my ear. "You aren't wearing any underwear."

"You know what being in a limousine does to me."

"We have company up front." His fingers trailed up my leg, tracing from calf to knee to thigh. "You'll have to be silent."

"I can do that."

Roth just huffed a laugh in my ear. "No, you can't. You are many, many things, my love, but quiet during orgasm isn't one of them."

"I can't help it if you have a knack for making me scream," I said, and then lost the capacity to formulate sentences, because Roth's fingers were inside me, scissoring, spearing, withdrawing, smearing my juices over my clit and sliding back in.

I moaned, and Roth covered my mouth with his, not kissing but rather eating my groan, swallowing my sigh, smothering my whimper. I slid further beneath Roth, arched my back, ground my core against his fingers. Eager, hungry, ready. I rode his fingers, writhed against him, sucked his tongue into my mouth and tasted him, bit his lip. I fisted my fingers in his hair and let my knee fall aside, opening myself for him, hooking my other heel on the back of the seat.

"Are you close, Kyrie?" Roth whispered against my lips.

"Yes…fuck yes."

"Squeeze my fingers, darling. Don't make a sound." He had his index and middle fingers deep inside me, and now pressed his thumb against my clit. I clenched my teeth on the shoulder of his suit coat, groaning, writhing, stifling a scream. "You're there, aren't you? You want to come, don't you?"

"I need it, Roth," I said past gritted teeth.

"Not yet." He slowed his plunging fingers, curled them inside me to knead his fingertips against that perfect spot, the ridge high on the upper wall, circling my throbbing clit with his thumb.

I was wet, dripping wet, each motion of his hand making a thick squelching sound. He was alternating now, circling with his thumb and pressing with his fingers, and then switching so his fingertips swiped and scraped and pressed inside me while his thumb was stilled against my clit. No rhythm, no predictability. Just enough to make me need it more, driving me crazy.

I knew what he wanted.

I clamped down with my vaginal muscles, and he started fucking me with his fingers, giving me rhythm now. In and curl, thumb pressing in hard and fast circles. Harder. Faster.

I bit his earlobe and moaned as softly as I could, which…wasn't very quiet.

"Shush, Kyrie, love. Keep quiet for me."

"Can't."

"You can. Or I'll stop." He made good on his threat when I moaned again, his hand going still.

I whimpered in frustration, writhing against him, needing to come, needing to fall over the edge. "Roth, *please.*"

"Yeah? Not above begging, are you, sweetheart?"

"Hell no. I need it, Roth. Let me come. Please let me come."

"Not yet. I don't think you're desperate enough." He went to work again, starting all over, kneading, circling, and finger-fucking arrhythmically, slowly, maddeningly, until I was grinding and biting his sleeve and trying desperately not to scream from the raging need inside me, the whirling fireball of need, the hurricane of sexual desperation.

"*Please*, Valentine, please. God, I can't take anymore." I whispered this in his ear in my quietest voice, barely audible.

He thrust a third finger inside me, hooking them to rub against that spot, fucking in and out faster and faster, the only sound now my ragged breathing and the wet sucking of his fingers.

I felt the edge approaching like an on-rushing cliff, like a detonation building, building. Every muscle tensed, my spine arched off the quilted leather, my heels were pressed against the opposite door to keep me aloft, and my teeth clenched against the scream.

I squeezed his fingers as they fucked in and out, in and out, and then I was beyond all control, focusing only on not screaming. He was in control now, his three fingers and one thumb ruling my universe.

He pressed his lips to my ear, and nibbled my earlobe. "Come for me, Kyrie. Come *now*."

I had to clench my teeth so hard my molars ached as the orgasm blasted through me with nuclear force. I felt myself gush, squirting all over his hand and wrist, and he kept finger-fucking me with relentless speed, pushing my climax to the absolute zenith, pushing it until I was frantic and writhing helplessly, coming and coming and coming.

When it finally slowed, he withdrew his fingers and murmured in wordless satisfaction as I collapsed against the seat, gasping.

"Look at this, Kyrie." I forced my eyes open, and

saw him examining his hand. "You soaked me, love."

His hand was dripping, his shirtsleeve and the cuff of his coat were dampened. Even the leather beneath my ass was wet with my juices.

I felt myself blush in embarrassment. "I made a bit of a mess, hmmm?"

Roth kissed each fiery cheek. "You did indeed. My hand is going to smell like your pussy all day now."

I buried my face against his neck. "I'm sorry?"

He laughed. "I'm not."

I shifted to a sitting position beside him, and noticed a certain problem. "Your turn, I think."

His eyes cut over to me. "My turn?"

I swiveled to partially face him, curled one leg up on the seat. "I mean, I can't let you suffer, can I?"

"Certainly not." He brushed a flyaway strand of hair away from my face, an eager gleam in his eyes.

There was no protestation that I didn't have to. Obviously not. We were past that, long past. I knew what he wanted, and how he liked it. He knew I wouldn't do it if I didn't want to. He just sat there, waiting, his eyes on me.

I shot him a smile as I unbuckled his belt, careful to not let it jingle. I unfastened his trousers, unzipped him. He lifted an inch or two off the seat, and I slid his pants and boxers down to his thighs, baring his cock. It stood tall and straight, rigid, veined, pink, and huge. Begging for my mouth. Pleading for my touch.

I wrapped my fist around him, slid my fingers down the shaft and back up slowly, watching his expression go heavy-lidded. He inhaled deeply, letting his breath out in a slow gusting sigh. With my other hand, I cupped his balls, kneading them gently, sliding my middle finger down, down, finding his taint. He shifted lower, let his knees fall apart as wide as his pants would allow, brushed my hair out of my face, lip curling in pleasure as I stroked his length.

I kept it slow, teasing. Toying with him. Just touching him. A thumb across the tip, smearing the droplet, squeezing around the broad head until it popped out over the top of my fingers then plunging my hand down to the root. Again. Again. And again, and this time his hips flexed involuntarily. I squeezed harder, and he sucked in a breath.

"You like that, don't you?" I asked him in a nearly inaudible whisper. "When I squeeze your cock?"

He nodded. "Yeah, I do."

"You like it hard and tight, don't you?" I kept my eyes on his as I bent over him. "I know why, too."

"Why's that, love?" His voice was even, steady. But his eyes betrayed him, gave away his need, gave away how much he was enjoying my ministrations.

"Because it feels like my asshole, and I know how much you love to fuck me there." I said this, and then wrapped my lips around the thick head of his dick.

"Jesus, Kyrie," he mumbled, and let his head fall back against the seat.

I took him in my mouth, flattening my tongue to taste the salt of his taut flesh as he slid between my wide-stretched lips. I backed away, letting him pop out. "Don't you?"

"Don't I—what?"

I felt a wild thrill of satisfaction; I knew I was doing it right when he lost composure. I squeezed as hard as I dared, and leaned close to whisper in his ear. "Don't you love to fuck me in the ass?" I plunged my tightened fist down from tip to root, squeezing, clenching around him. "Like this? Tight and hot?"

He made a sound low in his throat. "God yes... just like that." He thrust his hips, his groan rumbling deep in his chest.

I pressed a kiss to his jaw, and then his throat, and then bent over him and licked the tip of his glans, tasting pre-come, and then stroked his cock with my hands, taking him deeper into my mouth as I lowered my fist around his girth. He groaned again and leaned forward, thrust upward, and I took the thrust willingly, letting him fuck my mouth, letting him fuck through my squeezing fist and between my lips.

But then I backed away and glanced up at him. "That's enough, now, Valentine. Let me make you feel good. Don't move."

His eyes narrowed, Roth nodded, resting his head back against the seat once more. He threaded his fingers through my hair, tucked his other hand behind his head, and let out a sigh.

I waited another moment, drawing it out. Then, keeping my eyes on his, I pulled his shaft away from his body, tilted my head to the side, and took him into my mouth. He sucked in a sharp breath, nostrils flaring, chest swelling, jaw tensing and flexing as he watched his dick slide between my lips. Back away, bend closer, take him deeper, let him almost slip out...I matched the rhythm to the pace of his breathing, faster and faster and faster, until I was bobbing almost frantically.

And then I stopped, and Roth groaned. He'd never apply force or pressure, but his grip on my hair tightened.

I let his saliva-glistening member pop free of my mouth, and then, eyes on his, moving slowly, deliberately, I licked him from root to tip, pressing my tongue so it was wide and flat against the veined flesh. As I reached the apex, I took him back into my mouth and this time wrapped my fingers around him just beneath my mouth and stroked him with both at once. I took him to the back of my throat, and then I added my other hand around the base— god, I'd never get over how huge his cock was, how perfect, that I could fit both hands and my mouth around him and still have room to move, that I had to stretch my lips and jaw around him, that my fingertips didn't quite meet when I gripped him with my fist.

I began moving slowly, then. Torturously slowly, gliding down with my mouth, stroking with both hands, pulling upward so just the soft and springy head of his cock was in my mouth, and then I began sucking. Fists moved, sliding up and down, faster and faster.

Harder and harder.

And then slower. I removed my mouth, pulled him away, looked up at him, maintaining eye contact as I stroked him hand over fist, smearing my saliva and his leaking pre-come all over his cock. He groaned again, fisting my hair even harder, so the roots tugged. He was close, then.

I jacked him with one hand, the tip of his cock at my lips, kissing, licking, sucking, a gentle careful scrape of the teeth, and then he was flexing his hips and clenching his teeth to keep from making too much noise.

"Just your mouth, love. Give me your hands."
His voice was an unexpected rumble.

I reached up and he took my hands in his, cupping my small ones in his much larger paws. I rested
my cheek against his stomach and slid lower, closer, and let his cock slide into my mouth. Sucked.
Bobbed. Paused to lick the tip and flick my tongue
against the hole at the very apex, tasting the smoky
essence. And then bobbed lower and took as much
of him as I could, setting no rhythm.

And then he was rasping in his throat and his
hips were flexing, and I knew it was time to stop
playing with him and make him come.

I tugged one of my hands free from his grip and
cupped his sac in my palm, slid my middle finger
against his taint and pressed in. His breath caught,
and I began fucking with him my mouth in earnest,
now, no finesse or technique, just my lips and tongue
on his throbbing cock, faster and faster.

I pressed harder with my finger, slid it a little
further back, earning a grunt of surprise from him.
He didn't protest, though, so I pushed yet farther,
until I was right there, tip of my middle finger
pressed against his asshole and he was fighting to
relax, wanting to tense, but not allowing himself. I
found the center of the knot of muscle and pressed,

slid the tip of my finger in, and he groaned helplessly, his muscles going limp even as his hips flexed and stayed taut.

All the while, I was going down on him, not hard or fast, but with a consistent rhythm. He wanted it faster, wanted it harder. But I didn't give that to him. My goal wasn't to make him come quickly, but intensely, and to that end drawing it out as long as possible was best.

He was close, though; I could feel it, taste it.

And I wanted it. I wanted to taste him. I wanted to feel him let loose, feel him take his pleasure in my mouth.

Until Roth, giving blowjobs was something that was just...a thing. Not a bad thing, or a good thing, just something one did as a routine part of sex. I didn't mind doing it, but I didn't enjoy it. I always knew my partner enjoyed it, obviously, because every male whether straight or gay loves few things more than getting his dick sucked. But this...with Valentine?

This wasn't about sex, really. It was about an expression of love, about showing him how much I loved him, showing him how much I wanted to make him feel good, showing him that his pleasure was paramount to me. I loved his body, every inch of it. And I especially loved his cock, all the glorious length of it. I'd never have thought it was possible, but I loved feeling him in my mouth, loved the sensation of stroking his hardness with my hands, tasting the pre-come on my tongue, feeling him tighten and grow harder under my touch. I loved feeling him go crazy, watching him lose control, knowing it was *me*, knowing I could make him feel so incredible that he couldn't hold back. I loved the way his cock would throb and thicken as he got closer to orgasm...like he was at that moment, rock-hard abs taut as a drum skin, balls tight up against his body, hips flexing involuntarily, eyes squeezed shut, breath coming in short wild gasps...

Yes, here it came, the release.

I loved this too, when he cut loose in my mouth. I felt him thrust deeper into my mouth and pressed my finger deeper, felt him tense, flex. He gave my hair two sharp tugs as a warning signal.

I slowed my pace.

He groaned, growled, sounding almost feral.

I slowed yet more, pulling back until he nearly popped out, and then plunged down, taking him to the back of my throat. He growled again, thrusting up as he prepared to come.

I hummed, moved my finger ever so slightly in and out, and gave him one more long slow stroke of my mouth, and then I tasted salt and heat, felt the initial spurt as I was backing away. Felt it on my tongue, splashing into my mouth. I swallowed, continued my slow deliberate stroke, until I was at the edge of my gag reflex.

I wrapped my free hand around the thick root of his cock and stroked him there too, hard and fast now, while moving my mouth up and down slowly, slowly. The contrast of the slow movement of my mouth versus the quick hard jacking motion of my hand drove him crazy, and he shot another thick stream of come into my mouth. I swallowed. He groaned, a low but loud rumble, and I kept the contrasting pace going, milked his orgasm for yet another spurting gush, another smaller one, and then one last dribble.

Finally done coming, he let out a sigh.

But I wasn't done. I used my hand alone now, caressing him slowly from root to tip, coaxing more semen out of him, casting a glance at him as I licked it away. Again. And only when he was finally starting to subside and go limp did I let him go, helping him tug his underwear and pants back into place.

And at that moment, as I was tucking him back into his boxer-briefs, the privacy glass whirred and lowered,.

"Hey, we were thinking of stopping for—oh *Jesus*! Seriously, you two?" Layla's voice shifted from casual query to disgust and outrage within a single breath. "You're for real blowing him right there in the back of the limo? We're right *here!*"

I glanced at Layla as I zipped, fastened, and buckled Roth. "That's why it's called privacy glass."

"Yeah, but—" she faked a dramatic shudder. "Seriously did not need to see that."

"Good thing you didn't open the window any sooner, then," I said, resuming my seat and smoothing my hair back.

Layla just stared at me for a long moment, and then her brows drew down. "Um. You've got some… right by your mouth—oh god. I'm not sure I can look at you anymore."

I wiped at my face and grinned at her. "Oh please. Like I've never walked in on you before. In fact, I think I did, and you didn't even slow down, if I remember right. You just kept on going."

Layla looked equal parts embarrassed and angry. Roth was silent, but clearly enjoying it, and Harris? I wasn't sure about him. He kept his eyes straight ahead, hands at ten and two on the wheel.

"Yeah, well—" Layla started. But then she laughed despite herself. "That was so damn awkward. We were in the shower and you had to use the bathroom. But he was right there so I couldn't just *stop*, and you were about to wet yourself."

I laughed even harder. "I pretended I didn't know what was going on, and you pretended I wasn't there. Only, there was a shower curtain between us, clear from the waist up. Thank god it wasn't glass, but I could just see the top of your head moving..."

"You wouldn't look at either of us for weeks after that."

"Yeah, well, your creeptastic whatever-of-the-month didn't have that problem. He'd look at me like 'yeah buddy, you want some, too?'"

"He did?" Layla asked.

"Um, yeah? He stared me down all the time after that. Gave me these looks, wiggled his eyebrows. Shit, he all but pulled his junk out and offered it to me."

Harris coughed, then, and Layla glanced at him, and I saw her expression shift from amusement to embarrassment, and from there to walls-up defensive anger. "What?" She turned to him. "Got something to say, *Harry*?"

He swiveled his head ever so slightly. "No, Miss Campari."

"Oh please. 'Miss Campari' my ass. You know my fucking name."

"True."

"So what?" She tilted her head, and I could tell by the set of her shoulders that she was spoiling for a fight, Layla-style. Poor Harris. Layla in pissed-off or embarrassed mode is scary. She could flay the red off a brick with nothing but a few well-turned phrases. "You don't like to hear about my sexual exploits… *Harry*? Got a problem with it?"

"Not at all."

"Well it sure as fuck seems that way. That little cough, like *excuse me*? Sounded to me like a judgmental sort of cough, know what I mean?"

"Not at all. It isn't my place to judge."

"But you are, aren't you? Bet you're wondering how many dicks I've sucked in the shower, aren't you?" She leaned close, enunciating each syllable very clearly and carefully. "A *lot*. Not just in the shower, either. In the car. In the bed. On the couch. Public bathrooms. Behind the bleachers. Everywhere. I *love* blowjobs, Harry. They're my fucking *specialty*."

Harris's shoulders lifted and lowered as he took a long breath and let it out. His fingers flexed on the steering wheel. "Very clever play on words, Miss Campari."

"My name is *Layla*."

"I'm aware."

She traced the shell of Harris's ear with her finger. "Bet you want a sample of the goods, don't you? A little test run? Right here, right now?" She leaned closer. "You want some road head, Harry?"

"My name is Harris. And no. Not while I'm driving a half-million-dollar automobile." He didn't flinch, didn't bat her hand away, and didn't look at her. "Ask me later, though, and I might have a different answer."

Not the response she was expecting, I gathered. She snorted and turned away, catching a glimpse of Roth, who was barely restraining open laughter.

"Glad you think this is funny, Roth," she snapped.

"Oh, I do. Very much so." Roth gestured at Harris, chuckling. "You've managed to fluster Harris, and that is no mean feat, I assure you. Harris is so unflappable he could be British."

Harris shook his head. "Very funny...*sir*."

This only made Roth laugh even harder. "So it's sir, now, is it? You never call me sir."

I had to defuse this, somehow. "I feel like we've gotten off-topic, here. Layla, you were going to say something about stopping somewhere?"

She tossed her thick, curly black hair. "Never mind. I ain't even hungry anymore."

Uh-oh. Layla rarely reverted back to what she referred to as "old Layla" slang. She'd grown up in a pretty rough area, and her manner of speech had shown that. She'd worked hard to eradicate it, and had taught herself to speak more properly, even if she still swore like a sailor. But when she was *really* upset she'd speak in street-slang.

"Layla, I—"

She raised the privacy glass, cutting me off.

Roth glanced at me. "That was unexpected."

"She gets prickly when she feels like she's on the defensive."

"She going to be okay?"

I shrugged. "Eventually. Layla is Layla. You can never tell with her."

"YOU KNOW I CAN HEAR YOU, RIGHT?" Layla shouted. She lowered the glass again. "I am *not* prickly, and I am *not* unpredictable. Jesus."

I had to laugh at that. "Layla, come on—"

"Just—shut up, Key. You're just gonna piss me off even more."

"Please, Kyrie," Harris cut in. "Whatever you do, don't piss her off anymore. I have to ride with her up here."

"Oh shut your fucking mouth, Mister Unflappable."

"You first, Miss Blowjobs-for-Everyone."

"Oh…shit," I murmured.

"I didn't mean—" Layla started, and then shut her mouth on her words so fast her teeth clicked. "You know what? I don't owe you dick for explanations. That's not what I meant and you know it."

"That's what it sounded like to me." Harris was speaking as calmly as ever, but there was something in his voice, a hint of ire, a note of irritation…something I'd never heard before.

"I was making a point."

"About how much you love blowjobs. Point taken."

Layla hissed. "About how my decisions are mine to make and I won't be judged for them!"

"I'm not judging. I have not uttered a single word in judgment. I haven't said one syllable that could be construed as negative towards you in any way, Miss Campari—Layla, I mean."

"It's the way you're looking at me. Or not looking at me." She sounded petulant, and less sure of herself, somehow.

"Then you're misconstruing the way I'm looking at you. And, honestly, my focus has been on the road, not you."

"What, you can't divide your attention?"

Harris let out a breath, a very frustrated breath. "Oh for fuck's sake. You're impossible."

Layla had no reaction to this. She just crossed her arms beneath her prominent breasts and stared out the window at the rural New York State scenery.

I glanced at Roth as this exchange occurred. We

traded looks, both of us surprised at our respective friends.

I'd never seen Layla interact with anyone this way. She dominated conversation simply by virtue of being louder and talking faster, by being in your face and unapologetic and rowdy and bawdy. She was beautiful, tall, strongly built, had curves for days, and a personality that naturally took up all the attention in any given room. Every guy she'd ever dated or slept with or whatever she wanted to call it, they'd all just gone along with her, because trying to buck her need to control and trying to steer her at all never worked. Not for anyone. She was the epitome of the no-fucks-given mentality, not because she genuinely didn't care about how she came across, but because she refused to be cowed or dominated or controlled by anyone.

But Harris, with his quiet, calm, unassuming mannerisms, had somehow taken her down a few pegs without even trying. He'd gotten under her skin. No one—*nothing*—ever got under Layla Campari's skin. Her skin was so thick it was like armor.

This interaction with Harris had me thinking. Combine this with the overly quick denial that anything could ever happen between her and Harris…

The lady doth protest too much, methinks.

4

THE SYSTEM

WE WERE GOING TO THE TURKS AND CAICOS islands.

Population roughly 33,000 people. Geographically, it was an archipelago of forty islands, governed by the UK as a "British Overseas Territory". Their currency was the US dollar.

It was a paradise with turquoise water, white sand beaches, tiki-hut bars on endless beaches.

I couldn't wait to get there.

After transferring from the limousine to a small twin-engine jet, Harris took a few minutes to go over his flight plans and to make final arrangements for the trip. Within a few short minutes he had us airborne, flying us several hours south to the Caribbean.

Layla spent much of the flight ignoring Roth and me, her earbuds plugged in, music blaring, reading a book on her Kindle. Then, partway through the flight, without explanation, she went forward and knocked on the door to the cockpit. Harris let her in, and the door closed, and we didn't see her again until after landing.

As the islands of the Turks and Caicos came into view, I watched with interest as we began our descent. It truly was a special kind of paradise. Under perfect blue skies, Harris made his approach to the Providenciales International Airport and we landed a few minutes later with a perfect no-bounce touchdown.

We taxied to a private hanger where an old-school white Range Rover waited, engine idling. After transferring our baggage to the Rover, Harris drove us away from the airport...in complete silence.

I wasn't sure what was bothering Layla, or whether Harris was pissed off, but you could cut the silence with a knife. Harris was hard to read when it came to facial expressions, but that was just his way—he *liked* being quiet and inscrutable. Layla was easier to read. She was my best friend, and had been for many years. I knew her inside and out, so it didn't take much for me to figure out that she was indeed still stewing. *What* exactly her problem was, I wasn't sure. It was her own filterless, sassy mouth that had embarrassed her, not me.

It was a long drive across Grand Turk Island to a marina where a yacht waited for us. During that time she didn't look at me, didn't look at Roth, didn't look at Harris. She just stared in silence out the window.

The silence between Harris and Layla especially was rather icy and pronounced, and a little awkward. Maybe I was imagining things…or maybe not. Maybe they'd argued while alone together in the cockpit. Or maybe something else had happened.

I watched Layla intently the whole way to the marina. She was leaning against the door, forehead to the glass, watching the scenery, her lovely half-black/half-Italian features schooled into neutrality. I knew that look. It was the look that said she was battling intense inner turmoil, keeping an emotional tsunami from overtaking her.

Layla was an intense person. Everything she did was done at full speed, no holds-barred, all-in. But, emotionally, she could be closed off. Anything real, anything personal, anything deep, and anything that could leave her vulnerable she avoided or kept behind those walls of hers. Even with me, she was very rarely openly emotional, using her smart mouth and colorful vocabulary to deflect anything that got too personal. And if things got too intense she closed down completely, putting out spikes, and refusing to interact until she had it under control.

I would be willing to bet money that something had happened in that cockpit.

Things didn't improve on the boat ride either. Harris piloted the big antique boat out of the marina and away from Grand Turk in silence, black Oakleys shielding his eyes. His only concession to the Caribbean climate was that he chose to wear a white short-sleeve button-down and khaki trousers, rather than the two-piece suit he usually wore.

The boat was long, low, and open-sided, with a roof to block out the sun. Benches lined the sides, and there was a screened-in sitting room/saloon at the bow, two small cabins belowdecks and the cockpit aft. As soon as we were out of the marina, Layla walked along the outer railing and stood as far forward as she could, her thick, curly hair tied back, a cheap pair of knock-off Ray-Bans on her face, looking completely miserable.

I was tempted to go forward with her and try to get her out of her shell, but something told me she wasn't ready.

I left Harris alone, too. He was busy piloting the ship, navigating around the many small islands and reefs. I knew him well enough to know he wouldn't say a word to me about whatever may or may not have happened between him and Layla.

That left Roth and me to lounge on the starboard-side bench, the wind in our hair, warm salt water leaping up in spits and sprays as we rolled over the shallow waves.

"She okay?" Roth asked, nodding at Layla, who was visible standing at the port railing, staring out at the water.

I shrugged. "I'm not sure. I think something is going on with her and Harris."

"Should you talk to her?"

I shook my head. "Not yet. Not here, anyway. I think she needs some time to work through whatever is bugging her."

"But you think it's something with Harris?"

"I'm not positive, but that's my hunch. They either had a conversation on the plane ride here, or something happened in the cockpit. I don't know. She's not usually like this. Silence from Layla is usually a sign of something being really wrong."

"It's harder to tell with Harris. You'd have to know him really well to even know anything was upsetting him."

"You think something's upsetting him, too?"

"He's always taciturn, and he tends to like his

solitude. But he's been especially closed-mouthed recently. It's hard to say. Our friends are both rather difficult to understand, I think."

I laughed, somewhat mirthlessly. "No kidding. I was best friends with Layla for two years before we ever had a serious talk about anything personal. She keeps her shit seriously private."

Roth laughed. "Harris has worked for me for… nearly ten years. I know very, very little about his personal life."

"When we were sailing across the Mediterranean to go get you, we talked a little. He said he came from a totally normal family, joined the Army at eighteen, the Rangers at twenty. Said he joined the Army out of sheer boredom. And…that's about all I learned, actually."

Roth laughed again. "He hasn't told me much more than that. I know his retirement from the Rangers was…hard for him. Came on the heels of a mission gone wrong, I believe. I don't think I really want to know what happened, if I'm being totally honest. If it was something traumatic enough to cause a man like Nicholas Harris to quit a career he loved, it had to have been extremely upsetting. I hired him mere months after he left the Rangers, and I know he availed himself of my company's rather generous medical package so he could hire a therapist."

"Harris went to a therapist?" That was difficult to picture.

Roth nodded. "Every Monday morning for four and half years. The only reason I know is because he requested that time slot off specifically, and getting him to tell me why he needed it was like pulling teeth."

"I still go see Dr. Mancuso on occasion, actually," I heard Harris say from behind us. Silent as a cat, he had appeared out of nowhere.

I wasn't sure what to say. "Harris. We were just—"

"Gossiping about me. I know, my ears were burning." A small smile brightened his features, telling me he wasn't upset. He crossed his arms over his chest. "Any combat veteran will have demons to exorcise," he said, leaning back against the railing. "I'm no exception. My father was a Vietnam veteran, and he refused to talk to anyone about his experiences or the effects they had on him. I saw firsthand how well that works, so after I left the Rangers I knew that if I didn't want to end up like Dad I'd have to see someone. So I did. Purely out of a motivation to be something close to normal, I guess."

Then, changing the subject abruptly, he added, "Even the auto-pilot needs help. I'll see you later."

And then he was gone again, just like that, back in the cockpit, pulling the throttle back as we approached a low-lying island.

The island loomed large in front of us, water fading in color from jade to turquoise as the water shallowed out nearer the shore. The beach was a thick white line rimming an explosion of green, with just a hint of glass reflecting sunlight from between branches. Still about a hundred meters from shore, Harris cut the engines, letting the antique boat coast to a stop, and then he went to the forward starboard side and loosened a crank to let the anchor rattle free. It hit the water with a huge splash. He returned to the aft of the boat, more rattling and fussing with mechanical winches or cranks or something, and then he lowered a wide white ship's boat into the water.

"All right," Harris called. "Down to the skiff. Roth, you first, please."

A rope ladder tossed over the side allowed Roth to descend. I followed him, and then Layla, and then Harris used a thick rope and a tie-off point to lower the luggage, which Roth stowed in the bow of the skiff. Harris came down last, untied the ropes connecting the skiff to the yacht, and used the end of an oar to push away from the ship. Layla and I watched as both Roth and Harris then set the long oars into the locks and began pulling, just Roth at first to bring the skiff about to face shore, and then both of them in unison.

For the first time in the twelve hours since we'd left Manhattan, Layla cracked a smile. "Never thought I'd see *the* Valentine Roth doing manual labor," she said.

Roth had unbuttoned the top three buttons of his shirt revealing a V of tanned skin at his chest. The muscles on his strong forearms flexed as he set a rowing rhythm. His blond hair was windswept, and he had an easy grin on his gorgeous face. God, so fucking hot. I don't think I'll ever get used to how insanely sexy my Valentine is, just how perfect he is.

His shirt strained across his chest as he pulled the oar in perfect synch with Harris. "Get a good look," he said to Layla, "this doesn't happen often."

And thus ended the brief exchange. The rest of the ride to the island occurred in silence.

When the hull scraped on the sand, Harris pulled in his oar, removed his socks and shoes, and rolled his pants legs up to his knees. Roth did the same, and they both leapt out of the boat, one on either side, setting it to rocking gently, and then each of them grabbed the bow with both hands and hauled the skiff further onto the sand, until the water was lapping at the aft end.

And then something bizarre happened.

Harris moved to the end of the boat where Layla was preparing to step out of the skiff. He reached for her, put his hands on her waist, lifted her easily, and set her down on the damp sand.

And she *let* him.

She even reached for him, balancing herself with her hands on his shoulders. As her toes hit the sand, Layla sank slowly down, her eyes locked on Harris, her hands trailing from his shoulders to biceps to forearms.

And then, abruptly, she turned away, tossed her hair, and stalked away, almost angrily, through the surf.

I'm unable to emphasize how utterly alien that behavior is for Layla.

She's the epitome of the independent woman— and not in the angry-feminist sort of way. She won't bitch out a guy for opening a door for her, and if he offers to pay for a date, she might let him if she likes him. But she's fiercely independent. She never asks for help. She's not the sort to hold a guy's arm or be handed down from a truck, not the type to engage in any kind of public touching. Around me, at home, when we shared an apartment, she might let me see her kiss her current boyfriend, but that was it. She's not a hugger, not a cuddler, and certainly not a trail-her-hands-down-his-arms girl. And certainly not a gaze-with-rife-and-conflicted-emotion-into-his-eyes girl.

But yet that just happened.

With *Harris*.

With Mr. Tall, Dark, and Handsome, Mr. Strong and Silent, Mr. Cool as a Cucumber in Any Situation, Mr. I Can Kill a Man Without Flinching.

I exchanged a glance with Roth as he lifted me out of the skiff.

"What the hell did I just see?" he whispered.

I could only shake my head. "Fuck if I know, babe."

The house was incredible. Roth had arranged it, so of course it was. But...*incredible* barely describes it. It was only one floor, but it sprawled out to cover over fifteen thousand square feet, carefully crafted to make the most of the views, perched on a slight rise that looked out over the Caribbean, each room facing the water on one side and the forest on the other. The kitchen was the centerpiece, taking up the entire width of the building, connected in an open floor plan to a sitting room and a dining room. All four exterior walls of the building were folding glass doors that could be pushed open from corner to corner, making it totally open to the salt-scented breeze and the soothing sound of the surf in the distance. To the left and the right, walkways made of what looked to be reclaimed driftwood meandered away, leading to freestanding bedrooms each with an *en suite* bathroom—which included cleverly hidden outdoor showers. There were six bedrooms in total, three to the left of the kitchen and three to the right, arranged in a semi-circle around the main structure and connected by the same driftwood path to the kitchen, to each other, and to another large structure opposite the kitchen.

The secondary building held a movie theater, a gym, a wine cellar, and a small library. Each room occupied an outer quadrant, with another sitting room at the center. Every exterior wall of the entire home could be slid open from corner to corner, even the movie theater, which used glass that could be electronically tinted to block out the light so one could watch a movie during the day.

In the center of the property was a swimming pool lined on one side by a tiki-hut bar and lounge chairs on the other. The courtyard also held a fire pit surrounded by semi-circular couches, and an outdoor kitchen—a grill, a pizza oven, an induction range top, and a built-in under-the-counter refrigerator.

Roth took us all on a tour, pointing out all the various features. Even Layla seemed excited by the place. We ended the tour in the kitchen, sharing a bottle of white wine. "All the bedrooms are equal, in terms of size and amenities," Roth said. "So it doesn't matter which one you pick."

"When you said you had a place in Turks and Caicos, I wasn't expecting this," I said. "Why haven't we come here before?"

Roth lifted one shoulder. "It's brand new; I had it custom built. This is the first time I've been here myself."

I tilted my head. "But you said—"

"I did have a place in the islands, but I sold that several months ago," he explained.

"Why?"

He glanced at Layla, and then Harris. "Would you excuse us?"

Harris put a hand—just three fingertips of his right hand—to Layla's lower back, and subtly but effectively guided her out of the room.

When we were alone, Roth returned his attention to me and sighed. "Lots of reasons. First and most importantly, I was on record as the owner. I bought it during a time when I hadn't heard from

Vitaly in many, many years. I'd hoped he'd forgotten about me. I assumed he had, I guess, so I figured it was safe to own property in my own name. I sold it, knowing I'd never want to go there again, because he could easily find us there. When I built this place, I purchased the land and hired the contractors through a series of false corporations, which I dissolved after the construction was complete. It's inaccessible except by water, and it's owned by a company that can't be traced back to me."

There was something he wasn't saying. "Roth." My tone of voice was all I needed.

"My previous property in these islands was a getaway. It wasn't a home, but more of a private resort, I guess you could say. When I needed time away from the chaos of Manhattan, I would retreat there."

I read between the lines. "But you weren't alone, is that what you are saying?"

He nodded. "Precisely. Not alone."

I swirled wine around the bowl of my goblet. "Explain."

"Why?" he demanded. "Surely you understand without needing a detailed explanation."

"You know every last detail of my life, every guy I dated or slept with, absolutely everything. I, on the other hand, know little or nothing about your past, romantically speaking."

He nodded, letting out a sigh of acquiescence. "True enough, I suppose. This requires more wine, however." He reached under the island in the middle of the kitchen where there was a wine refrigerator, and withdrew another bottle of chilled white wine, opened it, and refilled both of our glasses. "The first thing you need to know is that I don't have a romantic past. The only woman I would claim any sort of romantic attachment to would be Gina, and you know about her."

"But there were other women?"

He shrugged. "Of course. Many. But none of them held any real meaning." He glanced at me. "Do you remember our first conversation about the difference between sex, making love, and fucking?"

I nodded. "I remember the conversation, yes." I thought back. "You said something about how all of your previous sexual partners were—how did you put it?—carefully chosen for their willingness and discretion? There was something about a contract, too, I believe."

He nodded, taking a long pull on his wine. "Correct. I didn't have girlfriends, or fuck buddies, or anything like that. I would choose a woman, bring her to my office, explain the contract to her, have her sign an NDA regardless, and then if she was agreeable to the arrangement, she would sign the contract."

"I have so many questions, babe," I said. "Like, how did you find them? How did you choose them? And what was the contract?"

Roth hesitated. Or, rather, took a long moment to consider his response. "They were not prostitutes or escorts, which I know is what you're thinking. They were mostly employees of the corporation, or one of the subsidiaries. Never anyone that worked in the tower itself, never anyone who might accidentally come in contact with me on a day-to-day basis. I perused the employee dossier registry, if you want total honesty. They were chosen primarily for their looks. Every employee of VRI Incorporated, as part of the hiring process, was required to take a basic psychological profile test, males and females, no exceptions. I had an assistant who would comb through the list of single female employees and create a file of potential candidates, which I would look through and choose a girl based on a criteria of looks and psychological willingness to participate in the arrangement I had in mind. Not every female employed by VRI fit that bill."

I frowned. "Jesus, Roth. That's...very...I don't even know. Logical. Mechanical."

He just nodded. "Well, yes. Of course. That's the

idea, after all. It wasn't about a connection, or about romance, or seduction, even. It was about meeting a physical need. So, I would have the individual brought to my office, and I would lay the proposal out for her, which was very simple, actually."

This system just seemed so...odd. So calculated, so cold, so utterly logical. Choosing a sexual partner isn't a logical thing, it's a chemical thing. Attraction, lust, need, desire. Not psychologically profiling someone to filter out the attachment-prone. Not sorting through a roster of potential candidates and choosing the most suitable among them. Was I disgusted? Sad that he was so closed off, that this system of his was all he was capable of? Glad that he kept himself so aloof, because it meant I got to have you for myself?

A little of all of the above, I think.

I was quiet for a long moment, trying to sort through my feelings. "I don't know what to think, Valentine," I said, eventually.

"It was a long time ago. When I decided I had to have you, I stopped all that. When I brought you to my home, I hadn't touched anyone else in...months. Nearly a year. And you were the one and only woman to ever enter my home."

"So you just...used them for sex, and that was it."

"They used me just the same," he pointed out, a note of frustration in his voice. "That was part of the psychological profile. I chose women whom I thought would have a more…pragmatic approach to sex. Never anyone emotionally vulnerable or given to attachment. Casual, consensual sex was the purpose of the entire agreement, and that was made clear from the very beginning. So I feel they used me just as much as I did them. We used each other, by contractual agreement. They each had the ability to say no, to back out. One girl got cold feet once we were there. I never even touched her, never removed a single article of clothing, but the moment she saw the bed, she asked if it was too late to say no. I put her on a plane within the hour and sent her home."

"It just…I don't like it."

"Why?"

I shrugged miserably. "You're mine."

"I am now, yes."

"I don't like the thought of you just…casually fucking other women. You didn't just have a fuckpad and a little black book, Roth, you had a goddamn system. An entire *roster* of fuckable employees, and a fuck-resort you took them to.." I stepped back, walking over to the covered deck circling the building. "God. I'm…I don't know. I wish I hadn't asked."

He moved to stand behind me. "Kyrie, love. I

will never lie to you. That's why I told you. That was the truth. That was my life. Am I proud of it, now? No. It was all I was capable of, then. After Gina, I just…shut down. I wanted nothing to do with an emotional connection. I thought I loved her, but she turned on me. Controlled me, used me, tried to have me killed. Tried to own me. I wanted, after I'd gotten away from her and her father and that whole life-style—I wanted something I could control. Something easy, no strings attached, simple."

"I get that," I said. "And I don't…I guess I don't hold it against you. Like, I'm not mad. I just…I don't know. I knew going in that you'd had other sexual partners. But the reality of it, hearing your whole system…" I shrugged again. "I'm just jealous, I guess."

"They weren't *partners*, Kyrie. It was just sex. Nothing else—maybe that only makes it worse, I don't know. It doesn't lessen your right to jealousy, though. Or mine." He turned me around, and his eyes were intense, but warm, the eyes of my Valentine once more. "You think I'm not jealous of your exes? I hate all of them for getting you before I did. I hate the thought of anyone else putting their hands on you. It makes me sick to my stomach just to think about it."

I sighed and pressed my forehead to his chest. "There weren't that many of them, though."

"So? Is that supposed to make it better, some-how? You're *mine*. All mine. Whether it was one man or a hundred, I hate the idea of anyone ever having any part of you." He touched my chin and lift-ed my face. "But at the same time, I know that each of our respective experiences led us together. Your past makes you who you are, just as mine makes me who I am. And…it's hard to put this into words." He paused to think, and then continued. "In a way, I'm glad we didn't meet each other as virgins. I want all of you, forever. But…that you had experience before you met me…it meant you knew what you wanted, what you liked, it meant you knew what to do with me. And my past meant I could make you mine, it meant I knew exactly what to do with you, how to make you scream, how to make you need me."

"I never thought of it that way," I admitted, rest-ing my cheek on his broad, hard pectoral.

"Regardless of jealousy or our pasts, how we feel about any of it…there's nothing we can do about it, is there? We're here, and what happened, happened. We each have the right to our feelings, to be upset or angry or jealous. But the real question is, what are we going to do about it? Will it change our present together? Our future? Does knowing how I chose which women to engage in sex with before I met you change how you feel about me right now?" He brushed his hand down my back, smoothing and scratching over my shirt.

I shook my head against his chest. "No, it doesn't."

"Good." He was silent for a moment, and then tilted my chin up so I had to look at him. "And to be totally honest, I sold the…fuckpad…as you called it, precisely because I didn't want to be anywhere with you that I'd been with anyone else. I want us to make new memories together, in a place that's totally ours."

"That makes me feel a bit better," I said. "I do have one potentially stupid question."

"What's that, love?" He sounded resigned, and slightly amused.

"You never felt anything for any of them?"

He was quiet for a moment. "Hmmm. That's not what I thought you were going to ask."

"What were you expecting?"

He hesitated. "A number."

"I don't think I want to know the number."

"Probably not," he agreed.

I didn't even like that answer, as vague as it was.

"No, I never felt anything for any of them. I didn't let myself. I…I didn't let them get close to me, see the real me, and I didn't try to get to know them. I didn't want to."

"Did it ever backfire, the proposal? The contractual casualness of it?"

"Yes. More than once. If they got clingy, started asking too many questions, demanding things that smacked of intimacy, if they got too personal, I'd send them home. That happened…not frequently, but more than I liked. I suppose it was inevitable. This is going to make me sound like an ass, but I'm going to say it anyway: if you present women with the unobtainable, a mysterious man, however unapproachable, however cold or distant, however clearly he may make his intentions, there will always be those who try to…get him. Change him. Make him hers. Someone will always think she's different." There was truth in his words, and in his preface to the statement.

"And me?" I asked.

"You didn't try, Kyrie. You tried *not* to. You were you; you played by the rules and just tried to get through it with your own heart intact. But…you were different from the beginning. It was always different between us. I tried to convince myself otherwise, but it was in vain." He tilted my face up again. Kissed me slowly, gently. "Can we be done rehashing the past, Kyrie? Please? I don't like to think of that any more than you do. That's not why were here; we're here for the future—our future together. Let's just focus on that, all right?"

I nodded, reached up and clung to his neck. "I like that plan."

"Me too."

5

LAYLA, THE NOPE-FISH

I found Layla by the pool, lying in a lounge chair, clad in a neon-orange bikini that would have fit in a Tic-Tac box with room to spare. God, I loved her, but she dressed like a skank sometimes. She had huge round bug-eye Audrey Hepburn shades on her face and her hair pulled up in a sloppy knot.

I had a glass of sweet white wine in each hand, and I extended one to her as I took the lounge chair beside her.

She accepted it, took a sip. "If you gotta be exiled from everything you know…this is the way to do it."

"Right? Roth has amazing taste."

"This place is awesome. I could hang out here for a minute." She still wasn't looking at me.

"Layla."

"I'm enjoying the sunshine and this really tasty wine. I don't want to get into it."

"Dude."

She swiveled her head on the chair back. "Don't 'dude' me, Key. It's fine. I'm fine. Everything's fine."

"I'm a woman too, Layla. You can't fool me with the 'it's fine' bullshit."

She laughed at that. "Okay, well then…whatever. It's not fine, but I still don't want to fucking get into it. We're cool, I just need a minute to figure my shit out."

"We're not cool. I have no clue what's going on with you." I grabbed her bottle of sunscreen lotion and squirted a dollop into my palm, spreading it onto my arms. "We can't be keeping things from each other, hon. We're all either of us has, right now."

"You've got Roth," she said, pushing her sunglasses higher onto her nose.

"And so do you. We're a family, Layla."

"Fuck that. You and him are a family. You and me are a family. But he's just your fiancé to me. We're sort of friends, I guess, but I'll never be close to him. Not that I don't like him, because I do. He's great. He's supercool. But he's not my fucking *family*." She spat the last word with something approaching actual hate.

"Whoa, Layla. What the hell?"

"Don't worry about it. Just…forget it." She set her wine glass down and stood up, tugged the bottom of her bikini down and the top up, and then stalked away, storming through the kitchen and out toward the beach.

I followed her, of course. She was a good thirty feet away by the time I made it through the house and down to the beach. She strode angrily through the lapping surf, bare feet leaving fading footprints in the wet sand. I jogged after her, caught up, grabbed her arm and spun her around.

"Layla. What the *fuck* is wrong with you? What did I do?"

She jerked away. "You wouldn't understand."

"I'm your best friend! What wouldn't I understand?"

She backed away, shaking her head. "Me! Why I'm mad! Everything! Anything! Pick one, *bitch*, they're all true." The term we threw back and forth at each other in a joking, loving way for once didn't feel very joking or loving.

Tears pricked my eyes. "Layla…what…? I—I don't get it."

"No shit. You're so caught up in *you*, in fucking Roth, in whatever the hell we're even running from that you don't even know what's going on with me. We've been best friends for so long, but you sure don't understand how throwing around the idea of family would be hard for me?"

I shook my head. "I know being away from home is hard—"

She laughed bitterly. "See, that's exactly what I mean. Home? You think fucking Pontiac was home? And family? You can honestly throw that word at me?"

"I'm so lost, Layla. Talk to me."

She turned away and walked deeper into the water, till it was up to her knees. I went in as well and stood beside her.

She twisted a flyaway curl between a finger and thumb. "What do you know about my family, Kyrie? My real family, I mean. The one I was born in to."

I shrugged. "I had the impression that it wasn't… bad, just that they weren't really…I don't know— caring. Loving." I blinked, thinking hard. "I—I guess I don't know much more than that."

She sniffled, and I realized she was fighting tears. "You think it's an accident you don't know more than that? Jesus, Kyrie. I mean, I love you like hell, girl, but you are *so* clueless sometimes. Like, just…clueless. You can only see what's going on with you, most of the time."

That made me angry, and I opened my mouth

to say something in response, but then…I thought about it.

And she was right.

I knew little about her because I'd never bothered to find out. Granted, she was prickly and defensive and refused to talk about herself or her past or much of anything personal, but then…I'd never pushed. And Layla…when she knew something was going on with me, she'd turn tenacious, refusing to back down or shut up or give up until I'd spilled it all. And I always did, and she was always there for me.

"Shit. Layla, I—"

"We've been friends for over five years, Key. I know a lot about you. I accept it all, and I love you. And granted, the shit you've been through over the last two, two and a half years, ever since that douchebag Mr. Edwards propositioned you and then you got that check…it's been crazy. Totally crazy. Everything with Roth and finding out about your dad and then getting whisked away by mister sexy billionaire and living all over the world, and then Roth getting snatched and whatever else…I don't blame you for not following up on little old me."

I was crying now. "I'm a shitty friend."

She just laughed. "Yeah, but you're *my* shitty friend. And you've made up for it. You brought me here to be with you on your...your fucking aquatic skyscraper. I get that it's for my safety...intellectually, I get it. But I guess I still sort of resent being yanked out of my life, you know? But there's a lot about me you don't understand."

"So help me understand," I said. "I want to understand."

Layla just shook her head. "It's not that easy. I can't just...unburden myself. There are layers and layers of shit."

"For real, though, Layla. You can't jump all over me like you have been and not explain, not give me a chance to understand what the fuck is going on."

Layla walked out of the surf and sat down in the dry sand, letting the water lap at her legs, and I sat beside her. She stared out at the water for a long time, and then started talking, her voice low, soft, hesitant. "So, I may not have told you the whole truth about me. I let you think my childhood was just...average-shitty, I guess. Like, I think you probably have the impression I grew up with both parents, and that it was fine, just not...great."

I shrugged. "Yeah, basically. Average-shitty sounds about right."

She shook her head, the loose bun of her hair coming loose. "It wasn't average-shitty, Key. Not even close. It was...super mega awful shitty, like whoa shitty."

"How?"

"In any way it could be," she said, with a bitter laugh. "Momma never really said so right out loud in so many words, but I'm pretty sure I'm a rape-baby. She always seemed to…resent me, I guess. She didn't beat me or nothing, but she…sometimes I felt like she hated me. Like she couldn't even bear to look at me. I mean, maybe my father was just a colossal dick and I remind her of him. It could be that. God knows I'm nothing like her, that's for damn sure. My mom, she's this tiny, skinny, quiet little Italian woman. She's an immigrant, actually. Came over when she was…twelve or thirteen, I think. I'm like her in that neither of us likes to talk about ourselves. So I don't know much about her past. She came over with her folks, I think, but I never met them, so I don't know if they died or she ran away, or they moved back to Italy. I just don't know. She had no education. Spoke really poor English. She was a hard worker, though. Gotta give her that. I'm like her in that way too, I guess. She had me, didn't abort me. Maybe she couldn't afford to, I don't know. But she kept me, and I was always fed, always had clothes to wear. Hand-me-downs and shit from Value Village or whatever, Salvation Army, but I wasn't naked or hungry."

I traced an abstract pattern in the sand. "I sense a 'but' coming."

She laughed again. "You got that right. Things weren't too bad until I was…eight? Nine? It was just me and Mom, doing what we had to do, getting by. And then she met Mario. Yeah, legit, his name was Mario, and he was old school New York Italian, hair slicked back, shiny shoes and windbreakers, like something from fucking *Goodfellas*. I *hated* Mario. But he took care of Mom, and I think he loved her, in his own sort of way. They never got married, but they were together for a long time. He knocked her up, and suddenly I had this little half-brother who they both seemed to like a whole hell of a lot better than me. And again, I gotta say Mario never did anything bad to me. Never beat me or molested me or anything. But once the baby arrived it was as if I was not even there. They just focused on Vic. Like he was all that mattered. By nine years old, I was basically on my own. Got myself to school, took care of my own lunches, got myself home. Got myself dinner and breakfast usually, too, because Mom and Mario would take Vic and leave, go to breakfast, go to dinner, go away somewhere for the weekend and just leave me to fend for myself. They just didn't care. I took care of myself, no big deal." She dug her heels into the wet sand, pausing for breath. "Here comes the other 'but'. Only, it's more of an 'and then…'"

"Shit."

She nodded. "Yeah. Vic got leukemia when I was seventeen. Mom and Mario…they just checked out. When Vic got sick, it was…it happened so fast. Like, one day he was fine, the next he was in the pediatric oncology ward, bald, tubes in his nose… and then he was dead. Like, within months. He didn't stand a chance, the little shit." She sniffled. "He was a good kid. Weird and gumpy and annoying, but sweet. I liked him. He'd come in to my room while I was doing homework and just pester me for hours. 'Layla what's this, and why that, and what are you doing, and do you have a boyfriend…'" She shrugged, and I saw a tear drop from her face to the sand. "I was messed up when he died, and Mom was just…*wrecked*. It ruined her. Mario too. They just… checked out. Stopped caring. Mom started drinking, Mario was gone all the time, started coming home hammered, smelling like the strip club, they started fighting. It got nasty. That last year of high school was just raw, unmitigated hell. I was on my own for real by then. I'd been working since I was fourteen. Had my own car by the time I got my license. I was still living with them because they refused to emancipate me. I tried when I was sixteen, and they were just like 'fuck you, no.'"

"Layla, Jesus."

She shrugged. "It is what it is. So then—yeah, it's not over yet—then Mario gets drunk at the strip club one night and tries to drive home, slams his Cadillac into the back end of a semi, kills himself and injures two others. Mom was a fucking mess, of course, so I had to set up the funeral for a stepfather who barely spoke to me, a stepfather who when I asked for a ride to the doctor so I could get birth control at fourteen was like 'take the bus, you little slut', and kept drinking. That was fun. So anyway, a few weeks after the funeral, Mom took a bottle of Ambien with a bottle of One-Fifty-One. Easy way out, I guess. I found her. I got home from graduation to this godawful smell. So then—hip-hip-hooray! I got to arrange yet *another* funeral, the third in less than six months, because guess who took care of Vic's funeral when Mom and Mario were too wasted to do it themselves?" She sucked in a deep breath and held it, let it out with a shudder, shook her head as if to clear away the memories. "So, yeah. There you go. Layla's Shitty Upbringing, the abridged version."

"That was the abridged version?" I asked.

She laughed, a low chuckle rife with dark humor. "You don't raise yourself in the worst part of Highland Park as a mixed-race girl without getting into some shit, Key."

"Goddamn, Layla." I felt like I should say something understanding or supportive or compassionate, but I just…had nothing.

"You don't want to know any of that shit, though, and I don't want to talk about it. I made it, and that's all that counts. I made it out. I graduated high school, got a scholarship to Wayne State, fucking did something with my life. Sort of." She glanced at me. "None of that really has anything to do with you, though. Except that before I joined you on the big yacht I was a couple semesters away from getting my degree. I had an internship set up at a law firm. I was gonna be a paralegal. I finally had an end in sight to the whole poor college girl thing. I had a plan. And then you…you, with one fucking phone call, you fucked all that up. You brought me on your stupid boat, and now I don't know what I'm going to do. You and Roth are so in love it's disgusting, we're always in the middle of nowhere, thousands of miles from anyone who speaks English, and we're in fucking hiding so I can't even hit up a bar and find a dick to ride."

"I'm sorry, Layla. I wish I knew what else to say."

"I'm lonely, Kyrie. I'm so lonely my pussy has cobwebs. You and Roth are this perfect couple, which only makes it that much harder for me. I mean, I'd seriously just started to really get over being depressed about Eric. And then you have the gall to talk to me about family. To act like you and your rich, gorgeous, perfect boyfriend are my family. Like your fucking *butler* is my family. God. It makes me so mad, and you don't even get it. I don't *have* a family. I never have. It's always been just me. But I love you, you're my sister from another mister, and that won't ever change. I've got your back and I always will. *Always*, no matter what. *You* are the closest thing to family I got, but you were gone a long time, Key. You left me. You vanished with your rich boyfriend and left me to fend for myself. When Eric left me—"

"Hang on second, now. You said you broke up with him when I called you about coming with us."

She shrugged. "Yeah, well, I lied. He broke up with me and asked me to move out. Said he wasn't really 'feeling it' anymore." She curled the index and middle fingers of both hands to make air quotes. "He wasn't feeling it anymore. What the fuck does that even mean? Three goddamn years, and you just stop *feeling it*? He kicked me out. I came back from work one day and he'd packed all my clothes, all my shit for me."

"Are you kidding me?"

Layla shook her head, digging her heel into the

sand furiously now, making the hole bigger and bigger. "I wish. So I left. I put my shit in the back of my piece of shit '91 Silverado and left. And I didn't have anywhere to go, Kyrie. You were gone. I was just about broke, and I'm not exactly the type to call and hit you up for cash, you know?"

"Where did you go?" I asked, not wanting to know the answer.

"NOWHERE!" She shouted. "I was fucking homeless for a month and a half! I lived in my truck and took showers at the YMCA. When you called me to come with you, the ink on my brand-new lease was still wet. If you'd called literally two weeks before, a month before things would have been different…but you didn't. You just whirled back into my life like a goddamned tornado and whisked me off to Neverland or Oz or whatever the fuck. And now you want me to help you plan a wedding. And for *who*? Who's gonna be there? Your mom? Cal? When was the last time you talked to Cal? What about Roth's parents? Does he even have parents? And what the hell do I know about weddings, Kyrie? Since when am I into girly touchy-feely shit like weddings and flowers and bridesmaids dresses? Jesus. I love you, but wake the *fuck* up! I don't belong in your life. Not this life. Just let me go back to Detroit and live my shitty life. I'll find a shitty boyfriend and work a shitty job, eventually I'll probably get knocked up and have a shitty kid. I'm okay with taking my chances with this Vito or whoever he is. If he wants to roll up to the 'D' and come for me, let him. I'll kick his ass. I'm from Detroit, motherfucker, I will fuck him up. You don't even know."

I didn't know what to say. This was all coming from left field. How had I known Layla for over five years and not known any of this? She'd been homeless while I was floating around the world with Roth? I could have helped her. I could have done something. I could have—

I broke down into tears.

Layla, of course, wrapped her arms around me and pulled me against her, and we both fell back into the sand. "Oh quit your blubbering, you little sissy. I'll stay for your wedding and then I'll have Harris fly me home. I bet I can get a job and an apartment in a few weeks."

"Layla, you can't leave. You don't understand. Vitaly isn't the kind of man you just 'take your chances with.' You don't 'kick his ass.' He won't just… it won't be a drive-by or something. It'll be someone showing up at your house with a drill and some duct tape, and they'll torture you for weeks just to piss Roth off, and then they'll kill you once they've had their fun. Which will probably include a lot of rape, just because they're monsters like that."

"So, tell me: your dear sweet billionaire fiancé knows these guys…how?"

"That's a long story, and it's not mine to tell. Let's just say his background is even more colorful than yours."

"Gotcha. Well, all I know is that I can't live like this anymore. I just can't. I'm sorry. I just can't do this much longer."

"I'm not joking about what they'll do, Layla. Roth and Harris are working on a plan to fix things. Just be patient a little longer—"

"Kyrie. I'm going crazy. You want to have Roth buy me a new identity? Fine. Relocate me to Atlanta or New Mexico, or Tokyo or something. Fine. But I live to have my own life, Kyrie. I *have* to."

I sighed in defeat. I knew Layla well enough to know she wouldn't budge on this. I may not have known the details of her past, but I was realizing I did know her. I knew her moods and I knew the shape of her walls and the color and taste and texture of her soul. I *knew* her. She was my best friend, and a life that had long ago become normal for me—traveling constantly, not working a real job—just wasn't pos-sible for her. She would end up resenting me even more than she already did. And I could beg her all I wanted, refuse to let her go home, and she would do what she had to do anyway. When Layla made up her mind, no force on Earth could sway her.

"I'll talk to Harris and Roth. We'll figure something out. Get a security detail on you, or something."

She laughed uproariously at that. "Can you even hear yourself? Talking about getting me a security detail like you're the fucking president or some shit. God, you're funny. You've changed, girlfriend."

A silence lingered. Eventually, I broke it. "I have to ask one more thing. You and Harris, on the flight over—"

She cut me off, standing up abruptly. "Nope. Nopenopenope. Not going there." She sucked her cheeks in and pretended to do a doggy paddle. "Look at me, I'm a nope-fish, swimming in a sea of nopes. Nothing happened. There's nothing to talk about. I don't know about you, but I think a bottle of wine or four is in order, to celebrate being on dry land." And then she was walking away again.

God, she was difficult. I let her go. I felt like I'd taken one step forward with her, and two steps backward. I knew why she was acting pissy with me, but I still had no idea what the deal was with her and Harris—and there *was* a deal, no matter what she said—especially *because* of what she said. And I also had no idea how to keep her safe while letting her live her own life. She may have grown up in Detroit—I did have some idea what a childhood like that entailed—but she hadn't been through something like I had. Drug dealers, pimps, bullies, assholes, prostitutes, teenage pregnancy…all that was rough and difficult and hellish to grow up in, I was sure, but it wasn't the same as dealing with international black-market criminals like Vitaly Karahalios.

I was supposed to be planning a wedding. Yet, after that conversation with Layla, I didn't really feel like shopping for wedding dresses. Not without my best friend at my side.

I sat on the beach, thinking about a lot of things, as the sun slowly dipped below the horizon, a fiery red ball that seemed a lot like Layla herself.

6

THE DRESSMAKER AND
THE GUARDIAN ANGEL

I WATCHED IN FASCINATION FROM ONE OF THE REAR seats of the twin-engine floatplane as Harris walked Layla through the takeoff checklist. She had on the headphones with the mic, and she was flipping switches as Harris pointed them out, checking them against the clipboard balanced on her thigh. They were close together, shoulders brushing, Harris's right arm propped on her seat back. Once, as Layla shifted to reach a switch, Harris caught the clipboard before it fell, and his fingers brushed her thigh when he rebalanced it on her leg.

I watched her body language through the whole exchange, and she was digging it. Digging him. Letting him get physically close, letting him touch her.

Little, innocent touches, incidental contact. But for Layla, letting him that close was a big deal.

Roth sat beside me engaged on his phone call, so he was oblivious to everything going on up front. But I wasn't missing a thing—they had my rapt attention.

"Okay," Harris said to Layla. "We're up and running. We're untied, we've been through the checklist, and now we're ready to go. Hold the yoke with one hand, and gently—and I mean millimeter by millimeter—push the throttle forward."

Holy shit. Harris was letting Layla do the takeoff? Not just take the controls while we were in the air, but actually take off? Harris was a control freak, I was pretty sure, so this was a big deal.

The seaplane inched forward as the sound of the engines increased to a deafening roar. Harris talked her through guiding the plane away from the dock and out into the bay, toward the open water.

"Now gradually throttle up, bit by bit. Keep the yoke straight and level, pedals even. Great, doing great." He had his hands on the controls, too, I noticed, ready to take over. That made me feel a bit better. But, having flown a good bit with Harris by this point, I knew Layla was doing really well. "Okay, now you feel it pulling? She wants to lift, so all you're really doing is letting her do what she wants. Help her up a little, pull back. No pedal, no tilt. Just pull it back, inch it back. Nice and easy, no sudden movements. And…we're airborne! That was awesome, Layla. Very smooth."

Layla glanced back at me then, and she had a huge, shit-eating grin on her face. "Did you see that, hooker? I took us off! Me! I'm flying a plane!"

"Yeah, and you have to focus, or we won't go far," Harris said. "Hold our angle of ascent right here, nice and shallow, and when we reach two thousand feet, level us off and bring us around to a southwest heading."

After that, it was a fairly uneventful flight. Layla was at the controls the whole way, Harris explaining and lecturing the entire time, pointing out dials and explaining their purpose, quizzing her on things he'd already explained. We were on our way to St. Thomas for the day, as Roth claimed the shopping on St. Thomas was better than on Grand Turk.

When we were about one nautical mile from St. Thomas, Harris took over, calling in our arrival over the radio, and then talking Layla through the landing, explaining what he was doing, how, and why. She was rapt, soaking it all in, hooked on every word.

Nothing going on, my ass.

Roth and Harris trailed behind Layla and me as we ducked into store after store, shop after shop, trying on clothes, jewelry, hats, and trinkets. Neither of us bought anything, though. I was too irritated with Roth to be focused on shopping; he'd been sucked into his phone the whole time, physically present but mentally absent.

Finally, an hour and a half into the trip, he stuffed his phone into his pocket, looked up at our surroundings, checked his watch, and then set off at a quick pace, grabbing my hand and tugging me after him without a word.

"Roth! Where are we going?"

"We have an appointment," was all he'd say.

He pulled me into a shop, taking me to the back and up a narrow flight of ancient, rickety stairs. There was a door with white peeling paint at the top, a brass doorknob. Roth knocked three times, and then entered without waiting for a reply. I followed him in, curious.

The room beyond the door had a high ceiling, three wide-blade ceiling fans turning lazily, stirring the air, the three fans connected to each other via a long tube, one fan turning the other two. The walls had once been wallpapered in white and pink stripes, but the paper was so old and faded it was nearly invisible. The floor was faded as well, smooth and shiny in places from long wear. There were several seamstress dummies around the room, two stools, rolls and rolls of fabric stacked on the floor, leaning against the walls, and hanging on homemade wire racks that were screwed into the walls. There were clear boxes of pins on the windowsill, and at least one pair of shears that I could see, and measuring tapes everywhere.

"Ella!" Roth called out. "We're here."

A door opened somewhere, then closed, and a woman appeared. She was short and thin with black hair going silver at the temples, and a pair of glasses hung from a cord around her neck. She had a measuring tape in one hand, a mouthful of pins, and a length of fabric trailing behind her.

"Ah. Mr. Valentine. You come, good, good. So glad to see you, dear." She wrapped both arms around Roth and hugged him tightly. "I have not see you in too long. Where you go?"

"Oh, I've been busy, Ella. You know how I am." He kissed both of her cheeks, held her by the arms. "How have you been?"

Ella shrugged one shoulder. "I am well enough. Some days I am still sad, of course, but what can one do, hmm?" She turned to me. "And this must be your bride, yes? Oh…she is beautiful, Mr. Valentine. So beautiful. You say she is lovely, but you did not say *how* lovely."

I blushed. "Hi, Ella, I'm Kyrie." I extended my hand to her, but Ella pulled me into a warm, strong hug.

"Kyrie, so wonderful to meet you."

Roth took my hand once Ella released me. "Kyrie, Ella is Eliza's sister."

"You knew Eliza?" Ella asked, her sharp brown eyes going watery. "I miss her every day. Every day."

"I knew Eliza, yes. Not anywhere near long enough, but…she was amazing." I had to fight back tears.

"Every day after she finish working for Mr. Valentine, Eliza would call me. Just to say hello, to say I love you. We were very close, even though we did not live near for much of our lives. I am here, living here, working here, and she is in England for the elder Mr. Roth, and then she moved to America with the Mr. Valentine, but every summer Mr. Valentine, he give her three months off to come see me, to stay with me." Ella let out a long, quivery sigh. "And now she is gone."

Roth cleared his throat roughly. "I'll never be able to tell you how sorry I am, Ella. I'll never forgive myself for…for what happened."

Ella turned away from me, putting her palm to his cheek. "I forgive you, Mr. Valentine. I have already tell you this. I *forgive* you. And Eliza, up in heaven, she forgive you too. I know she does. She know you from when you just a boy. You are her family, Mr. Valentine. I forgive you, she forgive you, now *you* must forgive you." She smiled, patted his face, and then turned to me. "But we are not here for the chatter of a silly old woman, are we?"

She grabbed me by the shoulders, hustled me over to a stool and up onto it, and pushed my arms up and out and began taking my measurements.

I glanced at Roth. "What's going on, babe?"

"Ella is a dressmaker." He smirked at me. "You really think I'd allow you to wear something off the rack?"

I laughed. "I suppose not."

Ella spoke while measuring and jotting the numbers onto a pad she'd produced from somewhere. "I am not a famous designer, but I can make you a pretty dress to marry Mr. Valentine. I think, because this is the islands, you have something with no straps, something the wind can play with. It will be on the beach, yes?"

I shrugged. "I suppose. I'd marry him in a kitchen, if I had to."

Ella paused and glanced up at me. "A kitchen? Not so romantic, you ask me. I think he can do better than that, probably." She straightened, draped the measuring tape around her neck, and tucked the notepad into a pocket, the pencil stub behind her ear. "I have a dress all made for you, in my mind. Say…two days? Maybe less, but come here again in two days, I will have the most beautiful dress for you to marry Mr. Valentine."

We were at the door when Ella stopped Roth with a hand on his arm. "You shouldn't have done that, you know."

Roth kept a blank expression. "Done what, Ella?"

"Pay my debts. I am proud woman. I don't need no help." She looked almost angry.

Roth sighed. "It doesn't give you your sister back. It doesn't take away the grief. But…it's the only thing I could do."

Ella's face softened. "Well, thank you. I know you mean well."

"We'll see you on Friday," Roth said, and leaned in to kiss her cheek.

I watched as Layla tugged the hem of a dress down a little further, so it just barely brushed the tops of her knees. It was short, tight, low-cut, and everything

Layla loved in a dress. So sexy it was just this side of slutty, fully emphasizing her remarkable assets. At five-foot-nine, Layla was a couple inches taller than me, and she was also a good bit heavier than me, all of it in her curves. Long, thick, curly black hair done up in a sloppy bun, flawless caramel skin, exotic, exquisitely beautiful features, tits and ass that wouldn't quit…my best friend was stunning. I knew I wasn't homely by any stretch of the imagination, but when placed next to Layla I was the ugly friend.

I cleared my throat as Layla swiveled side to side, smoothing her palms over the bell curve of her hips. "Layla, babe. It's a wedding, not a night at the club. Can we go for something a little more…beach wedding and a little less 'fuck me in a limo?'"

Layla shot me a glare. "It's *cute*. And it does great things for my ass."

"Your *ass* does great things for your ass, honey. You could fill out a burlap sack."

Layla shook her head. "You're just trying to ruin my fun."

"All I'm saying is, can you try on something that's past the knee and that you can actually walk in?"

She let out a groaning sigh. "*Fine*. You pick something, then."

I went over to the rack and flipped through it

until I found something. I checked the size, and then handed it to her. "Try this one."

Layla held it up and examined it suspiciously. "Okay, but I'll hate it."

It was totally unlike Layla's usual style. Floor-length, bright yellow, cut straight across the chest, tucked in at the waist and flowing loose from the hips. Tasteful, but still sexy, especially if the skirt was as sheer as it looked. Layla ducked into the changing room, tossed the dress she'd chosen over the top of the door and tugged my choice down over her head. I heard her suck in her breath when she first saw it on herself.

"I hate you," she mumbled, pushing the door open.

"Oh…my…*god*. Layla, you look—"

"Classy, for once?"

I shook my head. "Beautiful. Bitch, you're gonna steal the spotlight."

She really did look incredible. The skirt was nearly sheer from the waistline down, giving tantalizing glimpses of her long legs, hugging tight to her waist and bust. It wasn't a low-cut bodice by any means, but with Layla's build, she didn't need it to be cut low to have banging cleavage. The bright yellow of the fabric highlighted the caramel shade of her skin, making her look that much more exotic.

I reached up and freed her hair from the elastic of the ponytail holder, feathered my fingers through the curls, spreading her hair out around her bare shoulders. "There. A couple flowers in your hair, and it'll be perfect."

"I hate it," she declared, but her voice said she was lying.

"I'm so nice for buying you a bridesmaid-of-honor dress that you can and will wear again," I said.

"Bridesmaid-of-honor?" Layla asked with a laugh.

"Yeah, you're pulling double duty."

"Do you think—" Layla started, but then cut herself off with a shake of her head.

"What? Do I think what?"

She shook her head again. "Nothing. I'm just being an idiot." It was too hard to tell with her dark skin, but I was pretty sure she was blushing. I'd have bet money her cheeks would be red as apples if she had my fair skin.

"Layla, say it before I smack it out of you."

Layla tossed her head again, swiveling to get a look at herself from the back. "Hooker, you hit me and you'll be getting married in traction."

"Layla."

She rolled her eyes and turned back to face the mirror, adjusting her breasts and then fluffing her curls so they sat on her shoulders just so. "You really are a bitch, you know that? All I was going to ask was if you thought…" She trailed off, and then mumbled the rest under her breath in a rush—"… *IfyouthoughtHarriswouldlikeit.*"

"HA!" I laugh-shouted. "I KNEW IT!"

"Don't make me regret saying anything, Kyrie. I swear to god I'll never talk to you again if you make fun of me."

"You used my actual name, which means you must be really serious."

"Serious as taxes, babe."

I stepped up behind her, hugged her hard. "Layla, I'd never make fun of you. Not for real. You look absolutely gorgeous, honey, and I think Harris is going to have trouble breathing when he gets a look at you. I want you to be happy. I don't know if Harris is the man for that particular job, but as far as I'm concerned, you have my blessing to give it a shot. He's an amazing man, he's just…hard as diamonds, cold as ice, and a complete mystery."

"When you say he's cold as ice, what does that mean, exactly?"

I'd never really told her much about my desperate mission to rescue Roth from Gina's clutches. Harris had been the one to get it done. I'd seen a side of Roth's bodyguard, pilot, driver, personal assistant—and, I suspected, best and only friend—that I suspect few ever saw in action. Being an ex-Army Ranger, he was lethal, cunning, capable, without doubt and without mercy. I'd watched him calmly walk up to a man who'd been chasing me, trying to kill me, and I'd watched Harris put two bullets in the man's skull from point-blank range. Harris had wiped the blood from his face without expression, and had driven us away.

I'd watched him kill again and again in the process of getting Roth back, and every time he'd done so coolly, confidently, and quickly, without any sign of remorse. Of course, every man he'd killed had been a ruthless criminal who had probably done more than his fair share of evil, knowing the kind of people Vitaly employed, but still. Watching someone gun people down without even flinching…it makes you wonder what goes on in his head, and then you think maybe you don't really want to know.

Did I want to communicate any of this to Layla?

I wasn't so sure. I shrugged. "I just mean that Harris is the kind of man who will do whatever it takes to get the job done. I'd be dead if not for him, and Roth would still be a prisoner on that island."

"You won't ever tell me what really happened, will you?" Layla asked.

I shook my head. "No. Some stories are best left

untold. You said you grew up rough, but…the things I saw, the things I did…" I had to choke back a lump in my throat. "It wasn't pretty. I wouldn't wish any of it on anyone. I'd do it all again to save Valentine, mind you, but…shit got ugly, Layla."

"And Harris?"

I shrugged. "Harris was my rock through it all. Kept me sane, kept me going. He never wavered, and never hesitated." I let out a breath. "I don't know much about him. I don't think anyone does. Just…if you decide to see where things go with him, just be careful, okay?"

She must have heard something in my voice, something that spoke louder than my actual words. "I don't know what's going on between us. He's not easy to get to know, you know? Getting him to say more than a single sentence at a time is like having a root canal without Novocaine. I'm intrigued, I guess you could say, 'cause he's something totally different than what I usually go for. But I'm not gonna chase him out of his shell. He's gotta come out to meet me, since I've got a shell of my own."

"He's different with you, from what I've seen. He's usually all business, buttoned up, silent, Mr. Stoneface, you know? And with you, he's…human."

"I'm done talking about this," Layla said, sweeping past me and into the changing room. "It's not going anywhere, and besides, you're getting married, and then I'm going back to Detroit. So for now, let's just focus on making you Mrs. Kyrie Roth."

I grinned. "I like the sound of that. Kyrie Roth."

"It does sound good," Layla said from the other side of the door. "I still can't quite believe you're actually getting married. I never thought either of us would, to be honest. I was all set to be old maids together with you, and then you had to go and fuck up all my plans."

"Oh, come on, Layla."

"What? Until you met Roth you didn't exactly have the most sterling taste in men, either."

"My taste in men was fine. I just didn't have time for anything serious."

"Remember Steven? That guy creeped me the fuck out."

I'd never told Layla about some of the things Roth had revealed to me, when we first met. I'd dated a man named Steven who, it turned out, had been into some very unhealthy sexual practices. Such as torture, and, Roth suspected, murder. I shivered at the thought of what Roth's vigilante stalking of me had saved me from.

"That was an exception," I said, my voice flat.

Layla emerged from the changing room, dressed once more in a tight orange tank top and khaki shorts that just barely covered her booty. She gave me a quizzical look. "What aren't you saying?"

I sighed, took the dress I'd picked out for Layla, brought it to the register, and paid for it. Harris was standing just outside the door of the store, leaning back against the wall, one heel hooked over a shin, arms crossed over his chest, eyes hidden behind sunglasses. He pushed away from the wall and fell into step behind us.

I glanced at him. "Harris knows what I'm not saying."

Harris remained expressionless. "I make it a point to not eavesdrop on private conversations," he said.

"Layla was calling into question my taste in men, before I met Roth. Specifically, she mentioned Steven."

Harris was silent for a long moment before responding. "I take it you didn't tell her."

"Tell me what?" Layla demanded.

"Harris?" I prompted.

"This is your story to tell, Ms. St. Claire," Harris said, and I knew I wouldn't get anything else out of him.

I sighed, and thought about where to start. "Okay, so I told you about Roth's involvement with my dad's business, and that whole mess. Well, after he—after Dad died, Roth started keeping an eye on me. From…afar, you could say. Not in a creepy-stalker sort of way, just more in a…making sure I was okay sort of way."

"He was watching you, you mean?" Layla said, glancing at Harris. "Meaning, he had Harry watching you?"

Harris didn't correct Layla's misuse of his name, which was pretty shocking. "Correct."

"And what does this have to do with that creepy fucker, Steven?"

"Remember what happened?" I asked.

She nodded. "He just vanished, between one day and the next."

"It turns out your creeper radar is pretty accurate," I said. "Harris didn't like the looks of Steven any more than you did, so he did some digging. Turns out Steven was into BDSM."

"Holy shit!" Layla said. "I knew it!"

"Actually, that isn't entirely accurate. I've known some people who were into real BDSM," Harris said, "and what Steven was into *wasn't* BDSM. Real BDSM—bondage, dominance, and sadomasochism—functions around three basic tenets: safe, sane, and consensual. What Steven liked was just…sick. The photos I provided in that file were just the tip of the iceberg, and the more palatable ones at that.

When he was done with a woman, she was never the
same again. Most of them were too traumatized and
too permanently damaged to be capable of pursuing
criminal charges. And he was also good at vanishing
under the radar when he was done, so it was pretty
hard to find him. And with no one pressing charges
against him, there was no one looking."

"Jesus," Layla breathed. "What the hell was he
into?"

"Torture," Harris answered. "It wasn't about
sex, or bondage, or any of that. It was about inflict-
ing pain, and getting off on it. And trust me, it was
never consensual. Maybe it started out as consensual sex, but by the time his victims realized what he
really wanted, he had them tied up and helpless. It
was fucking sick, and I've never enjoyed ridding the
world of filth so much as when I ended that sick bastard."

Layla missed a step. "You—what?"

I closed my eyes briefly. "You did kill him,
then?" I asked. "I was never sure. Roth wouldn't tell
me."

"We had a little…*conversation*…first," Harris
said, and the tone of his voice was terrifying. "He admitted his plans for you. Let's just say that you were
going to be getting special treatment. He had some
extra sick shit planned for you. I won't repeat any of

it. Gina could have learned a few things from him, let's just put it that way."

Layla was noticeably quiet. "So you tortured him and then killed him?"

"Does that turn your stomach, Miss Campari? He was a predator, and planning to rape and torture your best friend. Rape and torture, in fact, aren't quite the most accurate words for what he had in mind. He knew about you too, actually. He had photographs of you." Harris's voice was quiet, low.

"He...did?"

"When he was done with Kyrie, he was going to just flat-out abduct you and have fun. You had no one who would miss your absence, and he was planning to take advantage of that fact."

I stopped and faced Harris. "You and Roth never told me that."

"No reason to. He was taken care of. No need to worry you with something that wasn't going to happen."

"I just—" Layla halted, as if unsure what she was planning to say. "I suppose I owe you a thank you, then."

"That's not the only time Harris saved our asses without us knowing," I said. "Remember that night in college when we got hammered after finals?"

Layla laughed. "Which time?"

"Exactly. Well, this particular instance, you were so shitfaced I had to basically carry you home."

Layla nodded. "Ah, *that* time."

"Well, apparently we had some company."

"Company?" Layla frowned. "What's that mean?"

"It means if it wasn't for Harris, we'd both be dead," I said.

"How? I don't follow."

"You were colossally wasted, so you may not remember, but a few blocks away from the bar, there were these three guys on a street corner, shouting at us in Spanish. I guess they were following us. According to Harris, they were planning to break into our apartment and…well, I'm sure you can guess."

"Holy shit, really?" Layla looked from Harris to me and back. "And you stopped them?"

"I took care of the problem, yes. I found out later that those three young men were wanted in connection with several other violent sexual assaults and at least one murder. They were probably guilty of more of both, though."

"Damn. So you were our guardian angel, huh?" Layla asked.

"Something like that," Harris said.

"Harris is being modest. Not 'something like that', but *exactly* that," I said.

None of us had much to say after that, but I noticed Layla giving Harris a speculative look. Either I'd just scared her off of Harris, or intrigued her all the more.

I wasn't sure which.

7

PERIMETER BREACH; THE BONFIRE

"I have a surprise for you," Roth said, after dinner the next night.

I glanced at him. "What's that, babe?"

He checked his watch and, as if that was a cue, I heard the distant buzz of an approaching airplane. "Here they are."

"They?" I asked.

"Harris and Layla…and your surprise."

Harris and Layla had left together in the seaplane the night before, and I hadn't gotten an explanation as to why. I'd assumed, at first, that maybe it was just a quick trip, a chance for Layla to practice her newfound love of flying. But then when they hadn't returned that night or the next day, I realized it hadn't just been a quick trip. I'd asked Roth, but he'd just shrugged and changed the subject, via the effective but unfair method of cunnilingus.

And now here they came, nearly twenty-four hours later, with a "surprise" for me.

I couldn't begin to imagine what Roth had planned; he was far too adept at surprising me.

I went out to the beach, holding Roth's hand, watching the evening sun glint golden on the wings of the approaching seaplane. The wings wobbled side to side, and the aircraft lowered itself toward the water with something less than Harris's usual perfect economy of motion, making me wonder if in fact it was Layla attempting a landing.

Foot by foot, the pale blue twin-prop seaplane went lower and lower until the floats sliced through the water, sending spray up into the air to catch the setting sun like droplets of liquid gold. A bounce off the water, a wobble of the wings, and then another bounce, and then it touched water once more and this time stayed down, sending water sluicing away in arcs to either side. Then the noise of the propellers slacked off and the nose was settling forward and the airplane was gliding across the surface of the water toward us, cutting to the side at the last minute. The maneuver toward the dock was sharp and efficient, which meant it was likely Harris bringing it in the rest of the way.

"That was an ugly landing," Roth muttered.

"I think it was Layla," I said.

"Oh. I didn't know she flew."

"She doesn't. Harris is teaching her."

Roth glanced at me in shock. "Holy shit. Really?"

"Really. She took off when we all went to St. Thomas. You didn't notice?"

He made a face. "No, I didn't. I was following an auction of one of my companies. Robert was sending me the updates via email."

"I thought you seemed preoccupied."

He kissed my temple. "I have been, haven't I? I'm sorry. Dismantling an international, multi-billion-dollar corporation with dozens of subsidiaries isn't exactly a quick or easy process. I should be there, in person, handling it all. But I can't be, so…" He shrugged. "I do what I can. The process is almost done, though. The new corporation is in place, and we're down to the last few odds and ends. Hopefully by this time next week, VRI will be history, and St. Claire, Incorporated will be up and running."

"I wish you could have been there, too," I told him.

"This is good practice," he said, as we moved toward the dock, where the floatplane's props were slowing to a halt. "The new setup allows me to operate remotely one hundred percent of the time. It puts a lot on Robert's plate, but then, I've given him a rather enormous raise to compensate. And he's more than capable. He's the only person other than Harris and you that I trust implicitly."

"Does Harris have security on him?" I asked.

Roth laughed. "So much that it's driving Robert batty. Harris has more security on him than the president, I'm pretty sure."

"Yet we have just Harris?"

"Just Harris?" Roth said, eyebrows raised. "Are we talking about the same guy?"

"Yeah, but—"

"And no, it's not *just* Harris. He's got guys out there right now, protecting us. You just can't see them. And, hopefully, you never will, which is the entire point."

I glanced around, but all I could see was the forest, the house up on the hill behind us, the sea and, anchored out in the bay, the *Eliza*. "Where are they?"

Roth shrugged. "I don't know for sure. There are some outbuildings hidden in the vegetation around the house, there are some guys out there. There's a sniper on the *Eliza*. Alexei is on the grounds around here, somewhere, prowling. We have half a dozen pairs of eyes on us at all times. I assure you."

"At all times?" I asked, a little disconcerted at

the thought of eyes watching us at…certain intimate moments.

Roth just laughed again. "They are discreet, I promise. If we're…intimate, shall we say, they keep their eyes on our location, but not on us directly, and any audio input is muted. Standard protocol, I'm told."

"So Harris is…"

"The tip of the spear, you could say. The visible portion of the iceberg, with the real bulk hidden below the water. If you think Harris is frighteningly efficient, the rest of his men make him seem like a harmless kitten. He's by far the most…*personable*… security expert I've ever met."

"Harris is…personable?"

"Compared to the barely-reformed villains in his employ? Yes. I've met a lot of his men over the last few months. He chooses well. Let's just say you don't hire private security personnel based on their shining personalities."

"I'm not sure I want to know what that means."

"No, you don't."

"Are they like Vitaly's men?"

"*Hell* no. Vitaly employs murderers and thugs. His men are little more than barbarians. The men closest to him, his personal security force, *those* men are a little more human, but the rest are monsters turned loose on the world. Harris's men are competent, efficient, well-trained, and most of all…have at least a modicum of humanity. A spark of morality, I suppose you might say. They're still mercenaries who fight for the highest bidder, but none of them will tolerate the kind of evil Vitaly propagates."

"What about Alexei?" I asked. I'd met Alexei in the middle of the whole thing with Gina and Vitaly. He seemed nice enough, even if his eyes were a little hard and distant. Good-looking in a rough-hewn sort of way, he was also an accomplished musician, having played guitar and sung beautifully at the dinner at which Roth had proposed to me.

"Alexei was assigned to interact directly with us specifically because he can actually behave himself. But he's still not a man I'd like to meet in a dark alley."

By this time, the propellers were still and the door was opening, disgorging an exuberant Layla. "Did you see that? Holy shit! I landed a plane, bitches!"

Harris was next, a faint, amused smile on his face. "A plane which needs to be tied off so it doesn't float away, Miss Campari."

"Yes sir, right away sir!" Layla barked, with a sharp, dramatic salute. "And why is it whenever we get around other people you call me 'Miss Campari', but in private you'll call me by my first name? I don't get it."

Harris's face immediately wiped itself of expression. "I'll get the bags." And then he was back in the fuselage, out of sight.

Layla finished tying the rope around the dock pylon with a knot Harris had obviously shown her, and then straightened and stared after Harris. "Touchy little shit, ain't he?"

"Wait, that wasn't your first landing, was it, Layla?" came a familiar voice.

A voice I hadn't heard in far, far too long.

"Cal?" My voice cracked.

"Yes, it was my first landing, *Calvin*," Layla asked, her voice a little too formal. "Why do you ask?"

He emerged from the plane, all six foot three of him, blond hair cut short and spiked stiff, mirrored aviator shades on his face, tank top revealing muscled arms, bright pink floral print board shorts. God, my little brother had grown up.

Cal took one glance at Layla, and thought better of whatever he'd been about to say. "Just…that it was great. Great job. Glad those lessons are paying off. Awesome."

She smirked at him. "Lessons? Oh, I haven't taken any real lessons. Harris has been teaching me."

"So…you don't actually have a pilot's license?" Cal asked, looking a little green.

"Pilot's license?" Layla laughed. "Buddy, I barely got my *driver's* license."

Harris emerged with a suitcase in each hand. "Don't worry, Mr. St. Claire. I was in control at all times. Miss Campari is a natural pilot, and very careful. I wouldn't have allowed her to touch the controls of my aircraft if I didn't have confidence in her. She just likes to tease you, it would seem."

"Yeah, well, Layla's been teasing me since I was fifteen. You'd think I'd be used to it by now." He turned back to me, and his expression brightened. He rushed over to me, wrapped me up in a bear hug, lifting me clear off the dock. "Jesus, Kyrie. It's so good to see you. I've missed you. I thought maybe you'd fallen off the face of the earth for good, this time."

"I have, for all intents and purposes." I slapped his shoulder. "Now put me down, you ogre."

He set me down, but kept a grip on my shoulders. "You owe me a shitload of explanations."

I swallowed hard. "I know."

"I mean, I haven't seen you in, what, two years? You used to call me once in a while, at least, but then even that stopped. I mean, I get that you're busy and whatever, and that I'm just your little brother, but—"

"*Cal,*" I snapped. "I said I *know.*"

He eyed me, and I saw that under the smiles and the hugs, he was pissed at me. I really did owe him a lot of explanations. "Sorry. I just—I woke up this morning and Layla was in my room, rifling through my magazines. It's been a weird day, needless to say."

"Your *porn*, you mean?" Layla said, with heavy emphasis on the "porn". She raised an eyebrow at him. "I mean, for real. Who actually buys *Juggs* anymore? And where do you even *get* that shit?" A glance at me. "You know your brother has, like, hundreds of porno mags? Not just *Juggs*, but pretty much every other porno mag there is. Hundreds of them. I'm not kidding."

I shook my head. "Jesus, Layla. I did *not* need to know that about my brother."

Cal scratched his forehead with his middle finger. "It's a collection, and it's not all mine. My roommate and I have both been collecting for years."

"Wow, so you both collect nudie mags?" Layla mimed male masturbation. "Do you whack off together too?"

"JESUS, LAYLA!" Cal and I shouted, simultaneously.

She shrugged and endeavored to look innocent. "It's an honest question."

I turned to him. "For real, though. Why do you

collect porn?"

He pushed past me. "I'm not having this conversation with you, either of you. It's not happening." He paused as he passed Valentine. "Mr. Roth. Nice to meet you. I'm Cal."

"Nice to meet you, Cal. Just call me Roth." He shook Cal's hand. "Welcome. Your room is the second on the right after you pass through the kitchen. Make yourself at home; grab a beer from the fridge on your way. I know you have a lot of questions, and I promise you we'll answer as many as we can without risking your safety. In the meantime, why don't you collect your bags from Harris? He's not a butler, so he won't be carrying your bags for you."

Cal stalked back to Harris, grabbed his suitcases. "Thanks for the flight, Harris."

"It was my pleasure, Mr. St. Claire. Although, in the interest of full disclosure, most of that was Layla."

"Even the jet?"

Harris nodded. "I did the takeoff and landing, but Layla did the level flying."

"Well...damn. I never noticed." He glanced at Layla. "You didn't kill us, so nice flying, I guess."

She shoved his shoulder. "Go get a beer and decompress, jackass. You wouldn't be here if we didn't love you."

"I know. Like I said, it's just been a weird day."

Layla laughed. "Dude, you have no fucking clue what a weird day even is. Wake up on a boat in the South China Sea and go to bed in the Indian Ocean, and then we can talk."

He just shook his head and made his way up to the house. I heard a distant "holy *shit*" as he made his way through the kitchen and saw the courtyard beyond.

"You shouldn't push his buttons, Layla," I said.

She just eyed me. "Have you *met* me? That's what I do. Buttons are meant to be pushed, and it's so easy, with him. Seriously, though, Kyrie. You should have seen all the porn. It was a truly awe-inspiring collection, I will say that much."

"*Juggs*? For real?" I asked.

"*Juggs*. For real. And *Penthouse, Hustler, Playboy*…if it had naked women in it, he had every single extant copy of it."

I shook my head. "I don't know, Layla. He's a guy. Guys do weird things."

Layla turned to Harris. "Do you collect porn?"

He just stared at her from behind his sunglasses. "The only thing I've ever collected is scars, Miss Campari. And the memories that go with them."

"Well shit, Harris," Layla said, "way to just take the fun right out of the conversation. Also, that was the most badass comeback I've ever heard."

"I aim to please, Miss Campari."

She stared at him. "I swear to god, you call me that just because you know it irritates me."

"Buttons are meant to be pushed," Harris said.

"I feel like maybe you understand me on a spiritual level, Harry."

"And I feel like maybe I heard a slight flutter in one of the engines, and if you fly prop planes, you should have a basic understanding of how to fix them."

"I better not get any grease under my fingernails."

"Haven't you heard? Engine grease is the newest thing in beauty care."

"Wait? Was that a joke?" Layla laughed. "You'd better be careful, Harry, or I might start thinking you're a human after all."

"As opposed to what, exactly?"

"Um. A Terminator?"

Harris actually laughed, a smile cracking his features. And even with the black Oakleys hiding his eyes, his features were transformed by the smile. "You haven't met Thresh yet. *He's* a real-life Terminator."

And then, to my intense surprise, Harris helped Layla climb up onto the wing, showed her how to open the cowl over the engine, and pointed at various parts of the engine with a wrench, explaining while Layla watched and listened carefully, asking questions every now and then.

Layla, working on an airplane engine?

Would wonders never cease?

It was well past midnight. We had a bonfire going on the beach, lighting up a circle of sand and dimming some of the stars directly overhead. Beyond the firelight, however, the night was huge and dark, the moon new, a black circle visible only by its absence, stars scattered overhead in countless millions, a glittering, winking, twinkling, scintillating fall of silver light arcing from horizon to horizon and down to the edge of the sea.

I was drunk.

Valentine was drunk, and I was on his lap, wrapped up in his arms.

Harris was…well, not drunk, but loose. Telling stories, laughing at jokes, sunglasses gone, wearing black board shorts and a white short-sleeve button-down, unbuttoned to show a hard, lean, well-muscled torso with a scattering of dark hair. He had a beer in one hand and a long stick in the other with which he ceaselessly poked at the fire, stirring it, moving the logs around, turning them, prodding the coals.

Cal was on the sand beside Valentine and me, and he too was drunk, and god, he was hysterical. He was, honestly, the life of our little party, making us all laugh with stories of his and his friends' ridiculous antics as wild college boys cut loose on unsuspecting Chicago. It struck me how little I knew about Cal, about the twenty-one-year-old man he was now. He'd been so young when Dad was killed, and I'd been responsible for him. I took care of him, made his lunches and got him to school and made sure he did his homework, made him dinner when he got home, made sure he had clean clothes. Gave him money when I had some to spare. Dropped him off at the mall with friends, sniffed his breath for pot and alcohol when he got home. But then he graduated at seventeen and got a scholarship to Columbia College, and I'd made sure to keep tabs on him. I'd paid for the tuition his scholarship didn't cover, and we got together for Christmas and Thanksgiving, visited Mom together.

At least until everything with Valentine happened. And then I'd sort of, as Cal had insinuated, fallen off the face of the earth. Valentine had made sure both Cal and Mom were taken care of, financially, and I'd sent an email to Cal explaining that I'd started dating a guy who was "well off", as I'd put it. Just to throw him off the scent, I guess. I mean, how do you explain a man like Valentine Roth to a nineteen-year-old kid? And, since then, I'd called Cal every once in a while.

Mom? Not so much. Mom didn't talk on the phone. Didn't send or receive letters or email. I'm not sure Mom ever even noticed that I'd stopped visiting. I still felt guilty, though. But...I couldn't exactly visit her, for her own sake. If I showed up at her hospice, it would have given Vitaly a bullseye to aim for. Harris had people checking in on her, making sure no one bothered her. But that was about all I could do.

I tuned back in to the story Cal was telling that involved his roommate, a two-hundred-pound potbelly pig, and the last day of classes at Columbia last year.

"...And I swear to god, that pig was faster than a damn cheetah! You should have seen the security guard trying to catch it! Funniest thing I've ever fucking seen."

Layla was—I wasn't really sure *what* she was. She was drinking, but slowly, and I would guess that she'd nursed one drink all night. She was laughing at the stories, but there was something subdued about her. But the thing I noticed most was that she was watching Harris's every move. Hanging onto his every word. It was weird. Beyond weird. She had very little to say, occasionally offering a comment or cracking a joke, but she was mostly quiet—which was entirely unlike her. At any party, any gathering of people where alcohol was involved, Layla was usually in the thick of it, driving the energy, and typically getting, as she puts it, naked-wasted.

I tried to keep up with Cal's story, which had morphed from something about the pig prank to an adventure he and his roommate had experienced involving a misplaced bag of pot and an undercover narc. It sounded like the kind of story that was funny now, but wasn't all that funny while it was happening.

Okay, maybe I was nodding off. I tuned into every fifth word, smiling lazily against Roth's chest. Layla was sitting in the sand right beside Harris; both of them back in the shadows away from the fire. Just their faces were visible, turned toward each other. Harris was saying something I couldn't hear, and Layla was nodding and smiling. And shit, that smile? It was...I had to search for a word. Intimate. Private.

My heart melted. God, if Layla and Harris ended up together, things would be just about perfect.

But then something truly odd happened. A patch of shadows near the waterline detached itself from the shifting glint of the ocean and the gleam of starlight and the darkness of night, resolved itself into the shape of a man. Alexei. Tall and broad, hard and lean, a wicked, gnarled scar running down his face from forehead to his chin. He was dressed in shades of gray and black: BDU pants tucked into calf-high combat boots, a short-sleeve gray shirt with a black bulletproof vest, a gray ball cap on his head decorated with a black patch that had "A1S" embroidered in scarlet letters. He had a compact assault rifle hanging barrel-down across his chest, the strap clipped to his vest rather than hanging over his shoulder. He had a pistol at his side, a knife handle in a sheath on his vest, and several other accouterments on his belt I couldn't identify.

He stopped in the shadows well outside the circle of the firelight, crouched near Harris and murmured in low tones in what sounded like it may have been Russian. Harris nodded twice, muttered something back, and then stood up, setting his half-consumed beer bottle in the sand.

"Harris." It was a statement from Roth, low, a command.

"Possible perimeter breach," Harris said as he

vanished into the shadows, reaching behind his back and producing a black handgun, checking the clip, and returning it. "Probably nothing, but I'm going to check it out anyway."

"Should we stay here?" Roth asked.

"No. Alexei will escort you to your rooms." Harris glanced at Layla. "There's nothing to worry about. Just being cautious."

"I'll trust you on this, Harris," Roth said. "It goes without saying that I want you or Alexei to inform me the moment you have discovered the exact nature of the breach."

Then Roth stood up without letting go of me, an arm under my legs and the other around my shoulders, taking the lead behind Alexei, who moved in a swift, silent prowl across the sand toward the staircase leading up to the house. His weapon was held low, barrel still down, but his head was constantly swiveling from side to side, and every few steps he would pivot and walk backward, checking our rear and making sure we were all together.

We stopped at Cal's room first and Alexei entered the room alone, ensuring that it was secure. When he was satisfied, he allowed Cal to enter with instructions not to leave, informing him that a security detail would be patrolling the area.

Next we stopped at Layla's room and Alexei repeated the protocol, this time taking time to ensure that Layla had everything she needed.

Just as she was about to close the door to her room, Layla looked at me questioningly, not saying a word. I could tell she was a little unnerved.

Seeing the expression on her face, Roth said, "Layla, please don't worry. It's better to be safe than to take chances. Harris has us covered. There will be a security detail right outside your door."

Layla just nodded, not looking convinced, and we continued through the house. Alexei preceded Roth and I into our room, sweeping the bedroom and the bathroom before leaving.

My heart was pounding. "You think there's anyone out there?" I asked. "For real?"

Roth shook his head. "No. If Alexei thought there was a real danger, we would have been taken to the ship, rather than to the house. There's a Zodiac on shore at all times, ready to take us to the *Eliza* in the event of an emergency. As Harris said, they're just being cautious."

"What did Harris mean by perimeter breach?"

"There are hidden motion detectors running around the perimeter of the property, including along the water line. There are also buoys in the water out about five hundred yards, with line-of-sight lasers connecting them to the shore, so if anyone approaches from the sea, we'll be alerted. The crew on the *Eliza* has the radar active at all times as well. Plus, there's another motion-sensor perimeter immediately around the house itself. So, to answer your question, a perimeter breach could be a fishing boat that wandered into our waters. The ocean-side crew would hail them and send them on their way. Or it could be some animal in the forest that set off the motion detectors. There's nothing to worry about, sweetheart."

"I had no idea there were so many different security features in place."

Roth laughed. "You think I'd bring you ashore anywhere on the planet without making sure it was as safe as humanly possible? When we went ashore on St. Thomas, Harris's men were there an hour ahead of us, sweeping everything. They poked into every building, every rooftop, every bathroom and rental counter. They were there when we landed, sweeping ahead of us, and they followed behind us. There was a sniper in place following our every move, as well. Up on a rooftop somewhere, I guess."

"A sniper?"

Roth nodded. "Andrei, I think his name is. Alexei's cousin. There's Sasha out there somewhere too, who is Alexei's brother. I guess when Harris and company stormed the island to get you out, Andrei's brother—Alexei's cousin—was killed. So they all three signed on with Harris, for a chance to get even with the Karahalios clan. Good men to have on our side, but really, *really* scary fuckers. Men I would *not* want to have as enemies. Ex-Spetsnaz, I guess."

"Spetz-what?" I asked. I'd heard of it, but I was fuzzy enough to not be able to remember.

"Russian special forces. Like the Navy SEALs."

"I'm glad they're out there, then."

"Me too." He brushed a thumb across my cheek-bone. "You should sleep. Ella is bringing your dress tomorrow for the final fitting."

"I haven't made any plans," I said, leaning against his chest.

"I know. I have, though."

I peered up at him, smiling, surprised. "You have?"

He sounded very pleased with himself. "I have. Some very special plans. Which is why you'd better get some sleep, because tomorrow is going to be a long day. Lots to do."

"Like each other?"

He lifted an eyebrow. "If you're good."

I tried to look innocent, the whole wide-eyed blinking look. "And if I'm bad?"

"Don't tempt me, Kyrie. You're too cute to handle when you're this drunk."

"I'm not *that* drunk," I protested.

He let go of me, and I promptly stumbled. "Oh no?" He turned me around, faced me toward the bed. "I bet you can't make it to the bed without falling."

"And if I do, I get to tie you up and have my way with you. I never got you back for Vancouver, if you remember."

His eyes went hungry. "Ah, Vancouver. A delightful night. I think I still have marks on my back from your fingernails." He bit my earlobe, whispering. "If you make it to the bed without stumbling even once, I will allow you to tie me and do as you wish."

"I'm going to have you tied up for hours." I twisted to glance at him, and somehow ended up sideways, his hands holding me upright. "I'm gonna keep you on the edge of orgasm for so long you'll beg me to let you come."

"You don't have to tie me up to make me beg for you, Kyrie." He unzipped my shorts, letting them fall to the floor. He stripped off my T-shirt, unhooked my bra, and tossed both aside. "All you have to do is get naked and I'll be ready to beg."

Clad in nothing but my underwear, I forced myself upright, focused on the bed, which suddenly seemed to have propagated into more than one bed.

Stupid multiplying Tempur-Pedic. Focus. Focus.

I maybe possibly spread my arms out like a tightrope walker, much to Roth's amusement. And then I took a step. A single, very wobbly step. And then another. My arms windmilled, and the world tipped sideways, but I managed to remain upright and take another step. I *really* wanted to tie up Roth. Dear Jesus, to have him spread-eagled on the bed, hands bound, feet bound, big juicy cock bared and begging for me to play with…? I was all wet just thinking about all the various ways I could torture him. The more I focused on what I could do to Roth, the closer I made it to the bed without stumbling. But shit, when had this room gotten so big?

I could fellate him until he was ready to come, and then stop. And then I could kiss him all over, everywhere *except* his cock, until he was starting to lose his hard-on, and then I could lick him like an ice cream cone but never actually put my mouth on him. Oh god, that would drive him absolutely *nuts*. Ha. See what I did there? It'd drive him…*nuts*? I'm so funny.

And then I was at the bed, triumphant, spinning in place to gloat—which, it turned out, was my downfall. Literally. I fell over and landed sideways on the bed.

"That counts! I made it!" I shouted.

Roth was there, standing beside me, lifting me upright. "You fell, darling. It doesn't count."

"I made it to the bed first!"

He squeezed my nipple between a thumb and forefinger until I gasped. "You fell without touching the bed first. It does not count."

I pouted. "But I want to tie you up."

"Why?" He pinched the other nipple, and then bent to take it in his mouth, suckling until my nipples were both rigid and hypersensitive.

"Because I want to."

"But *why* do you want to, Kyrie? You know my history regarding being bound."

I let my head tip backward as he sank to his knees, sucking hard on one nipple and then the other, drawing my panties down as he went. I gasped when his tongue touched my clit, momentarily lost my train of thought. "I—um. Because…" I glanced down at him, at his head, blond hair longer than it had ever been, curling around his collar, caressing his temple, brushing over his forehead and in his eyes. He'd grown out a beard, too, which I really liked. It tickled, but it was soft, now. At first it was scratchy—which led to a few weeks of a no-pussy diet for Valentine, but when he insisted it was grown out enough to be soft I let him go down on me again, and Jesus, it was amazing. The tickling made it all the more intense, because it was a counterpoint to the ecstasy of his talented tongue. So now he was long-haired, bearded, rugged. And I *liked* it. I didn't usually go for the rugged look, but with Roth, anything was sexy as hell.

But looking down at him, I had a memory of him on the old boat, somewhere in the Mediterranean, handcuffed to the bed, naked, crazed, bruised, bloody, wild. And I remembered.

"Because you're *mine*," I growled. "And I won't let her have any part of you. I want to tie you up so I can take the experience away from her."

I was airborne, twisted, and I bounced down on the bed in a sitting position. He undid his khaki cargo shorts with one hand, and I helped him with his underwear while he peeled off his shirt. I groaned at the sight of his cock, waiting for me. Hard, veined, thick, balls heavy and straining with come, belly flat and grooved with chiseled abs.

He gripped my hips and pulled me closer to him; I wrapped my legs around his waist and gazed up at him as he drove into me. No warning, no gentility. Just one hard thrust and he was balls-deep in me, vivid, piercing cerulean eyes hot as blue flame.

My tits jounced as he fucked me, wordless. He was wild, suddenly. Feral. Primal.

I knew I'd said the right thing.

"You're *mine*, goddamnit," I hissed. "I'm going to tie you up and I'm going to tease you until you beg me. And then—"

"What?" he demanded, pulling out of me, grabbing me by the hips and twisting me, shoving me with delicious roughness to the bed, pushing me to lean forward, spreading my thighs apart and driving into my pussy from behind. "What are you going to do to me then, Kyrie my love?"

"When you're desperate to come, I'm going to ride you like a fucking wild stallion until you fill my tight wet pussy with your come. And I'm going to leave you tied up, get you hard again, and I'm going to ride you and ride you and ride you. I'm gonna fuck you raw, Valentine. I won't let you touch me even once. Because I'm going to prove to you all over again that you belong to me as much as I belong to you."

"You've proved it, my love." He was moving slowly now. Making love to me with aching, tender gentility. I loved the juxtaposition. Usually from behind he was crazed and primal, and slow and gentle face to face. But this time he was caressing my spine, my shoulders, brushing my blond hair out of the way, cupping my ass cheeks and gripping my hips, his cock gliding in and out of me with a slow, deliberate slide.

Oh fuck, I was close.

He was, too. I stretched out, pushed back into his thrusts. Felt him take my hips at the creases, pulled me into him, my ass crushing against him, providing a thick, bouncy cushion. God, yes. Yes. I knew I was being loud, and I buried my face in the mattress and let myself scream into the comforter as he made sweet slow love to me until I came.

And god, did I come.

But he held out. He waited until I was gasping and trembling before pulling out.

I twisted in place and lay back on the bed, wrapped my legs around him, reached between us and guided him back in. I knew his needs, his rhythms; he needed to look at me when he came, knew that's what I needed too.

I was almost hanging off the bed, just my upper spine and shoulders still supported by the mattress, the rest of my weight held up by my Valentine. He drove into me now in slow hard thrusts, his eyes on mine. I felt him thicken with each thrust as he drew closer and closer to the edge, and when I knew he was right there, I reached up, grabbed him by the neck and pulled him down to me, crushed my lips to his and kissed him with all that I had.

He lost it then. He groaned into the kiss, broke it to rest his forehead between my breasts and thrust into me wildly, all control abandoned.

"I love you," I whispered as he pushed into me again and again. I made it a chant, clutching his head and writhing against him. "IloveyouIloveyouILOV-Eyou—"

And then he was emptying himself into me with a shout against my skin, sweat slicking his hard flesh, his hot wet seed gushing into me in wave after wave, thrust after thrust. When he was finally spent, he lay on me for a long moment, gasping. I loved the weight of him against me. I caressed his scalp, his neck, his shoulders, his arms, feathered my fingers through his hair and listened to him breathing.

"I'm sober, now," I said, when he lifted up to gaze down at me.

"How do you always know exactly what I need to hear the most, Kyrie?" he whispered, thumbing a stray lock of hair away from my face.

"Because we're one person split into two bodies, Valentine. I know what you need to hear because it's what I need to make you understand, what I need to say to you."

"I love you more than I know how to express, Kyrie."

"You should marry me," I said with a grin. "That will express it pretty damn well."

"Then you'd better get some sleep," he said, his

expression going serious. "Because that's happening tomorrow."

"Tomorrow?"

He nodded, then leaned down and kissed me. "Tomorrow."

I reached up and clung to his neck, squealing in happiness. "I can't wait to be Mrs. Kyrie Roth."

"You want to take my name?" he asked, sounding pleased.

"Well…*yeah*. Of course I do. I want to be yours in every way there is."

"I know this is a strange time to ask, probably, but…what about children? When this is all sorted, when we can relax and be somewhere permanent, would you consider having children with me?"

I had to swallow hard against a thick hot knot of emotion. He wanted kids? Roth? My Valentine, my sexy, reclusive, billionaire fiancé wanted to have children with me?

"When we can be somewhere safe and permanent and there's no threat," I said, blinking against the welling tears in my eyes, "then yes, Valentine, I will have your children."

"Then I have all the more reason to settle this than ever." He scooped me up and set me at the head of the bed with a kiss. He fetched a towel and cleaned his seed away with gentle, loving strokes, and then lay beside me, wrapping me up in his arms.

"Kyrie Abigail Roth."

"That's me," I murmured sleepily, realizing I wasn't quite as sober as I'd thought.

"Tomorrow you become my wife." He sounded as if he couldn't quite believe it.

I felt the same way, but I was too near to sleep to form words. "Mmmm-hmmm," was all I could manage.

His breathing matched mine, and then we slept.

8

LIGHTNING STRIKE

FOUR SHORT, SHARP RAPS ON THE DOOR JOLTED ME awake. I glanced out the window and saw that it was probably an hour or two before dawn, the sky still black but with muted shades of gray staining the horizon where it met the rippling, glinting sea.

"Mr. Roth." It was Alexei. "Your presence is required, sir. Immediately as possible, please."

I was still blinking myself awake as Roth scrambled out of bed and jumped into his shorts, not bothering with underwear, shirt, or shoes.

"Stay here," he commanded as he glanced briefly at me.

"Fuck that. I need to know what's going on." I was out of bed too, grabbing an ankle-length stretchy cotton sundress, not bothering with any undergarments either.

"I said stay, Kyrie."

I pushed out the door past him. "I'm not a fucking dog, Valentine."

Alexei was waiting just outside the door, dressed exactly as he had been the last time I'd seen him, but now his jaw was dark with beard growth and his eyes had circles under them, although his gaze was as alert and sharp as ever. He had his finger along the outside of the trigger guard on his weapon, I noticed, rather than just casually gripping the handle. The webbing on his body armor now held three magazines of ammunition, as well as two grenade-like objects which I assumed were flash-bangs.

Something significant had happened, I realized.

Something bad.

Another man dressed and equipped identically to Alexei stood at the back door of the kitchen, rifle held in both hands, his finger as well snugged across the trigger guard, rifle butt tucked against his shoulder. I glanced out at the darkness of the forest beyond the courtyard and saw a shadow move in the darkness, starlight glinting on a gun barrel. Another figure emerged, this man wearing a pair of night vision goggles on his face, which he lifted as he approached us, leaning close to Alexei and muttering in his ear. Alexei keyed his mic and spoke into it in

Russian.

Looking from Roth to me, Alexei simply said, "Follow me."

He jerked his head toward the dense forest, and set off toward it at a quick walk. He had his rifle tucked into his shoulder, held at the ready, moving in a crouch and sweeping the barrel from side to side. The man with the goggles brought up the rear behind Roth and me.

"What the fuck is going on, Valentine? Where are Layla and Cal?" I asked.

He shook his head. "I know as much as you do, but I'm certain that Harris has Layla and Cal under protection."

There was no clear path that I could see, but nonetheless Alexei led us unerringly between the trees through near complete darkness to a long, low building. He held open a thick steel door and ushered us in. I glanced back the way we'd come and realized I'd never be able to find the house by myself; a few yards into the undergrowth and everything looked different. Wilder, less tamed. And this place was hidden well, screened by foliage. The building was surrounded by a good twenty yards of clearing—for sight lines, I figured—but until you were right at the clearing, you'd never see it.

The building was windowless, lit only by flu-

orescent tubes. One entire wall was taken up by a
bank of monitors, each screen showing a room in
the main house. Most rooms, including the beach
itself, were shown from two different angles. There
were even cameras positioned in the forest. Opposite the bank of monitors was a floor-to-ceiling case
containing an arsenal: assault rifles like those I'd already seen, as well as a huge assortment of handguns, shotguns, sniper rifles, machetes, flash-bangs
and actual grenades, body armor, night vision goggles, and even something huge and terrifying that I
thought might be a grenade launcher.

Harris was sitting at a metal table, a map spread
out in front of him, a red pen in one hand and a ruler
in the other, marking lines and Xs on the map. He
was dressed like the rest of his security force: gray
BDUs, black body armor, black "A1S" ball cap, sidearm, knife, and a rifle hanging by its strap from the
corner of his chair. He had extra magazines on his
body armor webbing, as well.

Harris didn't just have a security company; he
had a small mercenary army, each man armed to the
teeth, loaded for bear.

So what had them on high alert?

I was about to ask when the door opened, and
another member of the security team entered with
Cal behind him. Cal looked overwhelmed and be-

wildered, and not a little amazed.

"Holy shit, Key," he said. "You people don't fuck around, do you? What's going on, you have any idea? Ivan here won't tell me."

"Name is Sasha, Mr. St. Claire," Cal's escort said, his voice thick with a Russian accent.

"No, Cal, my people do not fuck around," I said, "and no, I don't know what's going on. I think we're about to find out, though."

Cal went over to the rack of weapons. "Fuck me running, dude! Is that an M-203?"

"Touch that and I'll break your fingers, kid," Harris said, not looking up. He marked one more X on his map and then swiveled on his chair. "All right, now that we're all here—"

"Wait," I protested. "We're *not* all here. Where's Layla?"

Harris's expression hardened, fury darkening his face. "That's why we're here. I'm not going to mince words, Kyrie: Vitaly took her. Snatched her right out from under my fucking nose."

"How the *fuck* is that possible, Harris?" Roth said, snarling. "I thought you had this place more secure than the Pentagon?"

"I *did*," Harris said, his voice a little too calm. "About an hour ago they set off some kind of low-tech EMP bomb that fried our circuits. At the same time, they hit my guys on the beach as a distraction. Lucas and Thresh both took heavy fire. Lucas is down but not out, and Thresh is—well, I'm pretty sure Thresh could lose a limb and still wreck shit, so I'm not worried about him. They also went after the *Eliza,* which, along with the the beach hit, was just a distraction. While that was going on four men infiltrated Layla's room and took her. Dane gave pursuit and took out two of them, but received a wound to the throat in the process. Not sure he'll make it. They had a launch waiting down by the beach, and by the time we had comms up and running and could coordinate with each other, they were gone. This was a pro hit, Roth. These weren't Vitaly's usual half-assed gorillas with AKs. It was quick, precise, and coordinated, and done by serious professionals."

I was having trouble processing what he was saying. "Hold on, Harris. You—you're saying someone *kidnapped* Layla? And someone is dying? Why did the gunfire not wake us up?"

Harris lifted his assault rifle. "Suppressors. Ops like this, you can't have machine guns going off in the middle of the night or the local government would be all over our asses."

"People were killed?"

"Vitaly's guys lost six men and one was injured. Lucas took a round to the thigh and will be out of commission for a few months. Thresh took two rounds, one to the shoulder blade and one to the bicep, two more direct hits on his body armor, but that'll leave nothing but bruises. Dane took a single round to the throat. He's alive for now, but I don't like his chances."

"What about—what about Layla?" My voice cracked as I said her name.

"Before he lost consciousness Dane was able to communicate that she was unhurt." Harris's jaw clenched, his molars grinding. "It's both good and bad that we're dealing with Vitaly directly now rather than his crazy-ass daughter. You did the world a favor when you took her out, Kyrie. Vitaly has a different approach than his daughter. He doesn't do things rashly out of passion. He won't kill her or even hurt her unless it benefits him. If he wanted her or all of us dead, he would have just hit us with an airstrike or something. If he knows where we are and chose not to wipe us off the face of the planet, he has something else in mind. So that works in our favor. He won't kill her unless he has to, because he really wants you two—" he pointed at Roth and me with a sweep of his index finger, "but we know he *will* kill her, which works against us. We don't know where he has her, or what his long game is, which also works against us."

Cal cleared his throat. "Hold on a fucking second, people. I have so many questions I don't even know where to start. Who took Layla, and why? And when you said Kyrie 'took her out', what does that mean? Who did she take out? Kyrie...*killed* someone? And—"

I left Roth's side and put my finger to Cal's lips, silencing him, although I had to reach up to do so. "Calvin, little brother. Do me a favor, okay? Shut the hell up."

"Don't tell me to shut up, Key. Layla is gone, people are dead, and now I'm hearing that *you* killed someone? How did I not know about this? You've got to tell me what the hell is going on!"

"Cal, look—"

Roth stepped forward and put himself between Cal and me. "It's a very long story, Cal, and we don't have time to fill you in. The short version is this: I've got enemies you don't want to know about—for your own good. My enemies are Kyrie's enemies now, which she found out to her detriment several months ago. She did what she had to in order to stay alive, the details of which are her story to tell, not mine. And because my enemies have become hers, they've also become yours. Which means I've had—or rather Harris has had—men watching you for nearly a year now. Every move you made, every date you went on, every night spent studying or fucking or partying, they've been there out of sight, watching and protecting. You never knew, because you didn't need to. But now that Layla has been abducted, you've been forced into a more serious situation. Going forward, you will be given information on a need-to-know basis, and you'll stay here in this bunker under guard and you'll keep your mouth shut, because it's for your own good. We'll have you returned to Chicago as soon as we deem it safe to do so, which could be a matter of days, or a matter of weeks. Months even. All of your needs will be seen to. I've been paying for your tuition and room and board for months now, and I will continue to do so for the foreseeable future, because you are important to your sister, and thus you are important to me. But, for now, what I need from you is for you to step back and shut up. Got it?"

Cal's mouth snapped shut and his eyes glittered. "Got it."

Roth turned to Harris. "Contact Ella and tell her—"

"Already done. I've got a man on her as we speak, sitting in her living room, watching the exits. I've got visuals on Robert, your parents, and Kyrie's mom as well, and I've heightened security on all of them. Shit is locked down."

Roth crossed the room to stand in front of Harris. Roth had two inches on him, and used them to good effect, staring down at him with anger in his eyes. "Swear to me right now that this couldn't have been prevented, Harris."

Harris stared back, chin lifting. "It was a calculated strike, Mr. Roth. It was fucking surgical. The whole thing with Layla took less than three minutes from first contact to when Thresh lost visual on the Zodiac. There was nothing else we could have done, sir. I've got two wounded and one dead or…as good as dead."

Roth stepped back. "What are we doing to get her back?"

"I will rip this planet open to find her," Harris said. "I swear on my immortal soul I will find her, and I will end the life of every motherfucker involved in taking her." The vicious look in Harris's eyes sent shivers down my spine.

"Get her back, Harris," I said. "Please get her back."

Harris moved to stand in front of me. "I'm so sorry, Kyrie. You have my word. I got Roth back, I got you back, and I'll get her back. I promise."

Roth took me by the arms, turning me to face him. "I hate to have to say this, love, but I think we have to postpone—"

I cut him off. "You think I'd get married when my best friend is missing? Really? I love you more than life, Roth, but I'm not getting married without Layla. She's my family. So get us aboard the *Eliza* and get us out of here."

Harris pointed at Alexei. "Alexei, you're with them, Sasha, you too. You are to maintain direct visual at all times. Guys, I'm sorry, but privacy is going out the window until this is over. Either Alexei or Sasha will be in the room with you twenty-four hours a day. We've got the ship refueled and stocked, so you won't be making landfall anytime soon."

"Are you going after Layla alone?" I asked.

"Hell no. I'm bringing Thresh with me. I'd rather have him at my side than a dozen other men. Thresh is…well, he's one of a kind. He makes the Terminator look like a pussy."

Harris turned to scan the monitors, and then keyed his mic. "*Eliza*, prepare to receive primary. Immediate departure, emergency profile Zulu-Echo-Romeo-Oscar." He turned back to us. "You guys are gone. Cal stays here. I'll send an update when I can, but don't expect word from me for a few days."

We were out the door in a matter of seconds, Alexei in front, Sasha behind. I glanced back and saw a man lying prone on the roof of the building, holding a sniper rifle.

Harris stood in the doorway, ball cap turned backward. "I'll get her back."

"You better." It was all I could say.

I didn't even say goodbye to Cal. I saw a glimpse of him over Harris's shoulder, and he looked pale, even a little green. His usual bravado was replaced with an embarrassed silence.

Layla. God, Layla.

Be safe, hooker. Stay alive. Harris is coming for you.

PART TWO:

Layla

9

KIDNAPPING IS FUN

Fuck. Fuckfuckfuck. I do *not* like being kidnapped. I don't recommend it.

I've seen some pretty gnarly shit in my life, but that scene? I'll have nightmares for the rest of my life, that's for damn sure. One second I was sleeping and having a nice little dream about Harris—although I'd deny that if pressed—and then the door was exploding and four dark shapes surrounded me. They tossed a black bag over my head, jerked my arms behind my back and wrapped zip-ties tight around my wrists, and shoved me forward.

The assholes didn't even let me put on my fucking pants. That's right, they kidnapped me wearing nothing but a thigh-length white V-neck T-shirt and my favorite red thong. No shoes, no pants, no bra.

Then they forced me into a run, one guy on each arm, pretty much carrying me across the courtyard. I couldn't see shit, because it was nighttime still and because they'd put a damn sack over my head. This was a legit third-world mafia kidnapping. I heard something behind me go *poppoppop—poppop—poppoppop*. And then there was a wet *thwack*, a grunt and the hands on my left arm fell away. Someone had been shot, I realized. Different hands grabbed my free arm and lifted me, carried me in a flat-out run.

Poppoppop—poppop; this was a different weapon, similar silent clicking, but a different tone. The good guys were getting closer. My kidnappers were firing back with everything they had. Then I heard a gurgle from behind.

"Dane! Shit!" A voice, male, low, American.

That wet gurgle, then the voice of someone calling out to the guy who'd clearly just died trying to help me...nightmare fuel right there.

I felt my feet hit the sand, and I heard the surf followed by the quiet rumble of an outboard boat motor. I was lifted clear off the ground, and a gust of wind kicked up, tossing my T-shirt up to bare my ass cheeks and a good portion of my naked titties.

This was not lost on my kidnappers: I heard them exchanging what I assumed, judging by the tone of their voices and the lecherous laughter, were disgusting guy-comments about how sexy I was. I didn't need to speak whatever barbarian language those fuckers spoke to understand what they were saying. So I did the only thing I could. I started thrashing and kicking, biting at whatever flesh was closest to me.

"LET ME GO YOU FUCKING FUCKS!" I screamed. I felt my foot connect with bone, and I kicked again, as hard as I could. I heard a grunt and a curse. "I'll kick all ya'll's fucking asses. Put me the fuck down!"

Something hard, cold, and round touched my temple. "Shut up, cunt, or you die. Be still, or you die." This was in a thick accent, Greek, or Italian, or—who the hell am I kidding? I don't know one foreign accent from another.

I went completely still and let them set me in the boat, cold, hard, wet rubber under my thighs. The gun barrel was pressed against the back of my skull, digging in hard. It hurt like hell as the boat was shoved into the water, and then the outboard motor kicked to life and I was thrown to the side as the pilot pulled the craft sharply around. We hit a wave and I was tossed airborne, only to slam back down with a slap of flesh on rubber and a curse, which only earned derisive laughter from my captors.

I had no way to brace myself for the next wave, not being able to see, or grab onto the sides of the Zodiac. So I was tossed like a rag doll as the boat hit wave after wave, and the farther we got from shore, the larger the waves got. This was a tiny boat, I sensed, and we were heading out into open water. I wondered how far they were taking me, and why, and where, and who, and how soon I could expect to raped, tortured, and killed.

Thank you, Kyrie, for the terror-inducing warnings as to what I could expect if these dick-nuts got hold of me.

Well, they've got hold of me. So now what?

The worst part about being tossed around in the stupid little boat was that with every slam of the boat bottom on the water, cool salt spray hit me, soaking my face and my T-shirt. Did I mention my shirt was white, and that I was naked underneath it? No bra, and a tiny little thong. I mean, that thong barely covered my hoochie-coo in front, and didn't cover a damn thing in back. I like to both look and feel sexy, but not for the benefit of goons like these.

Also, I had been kinda hoping to let Harris get an eyeful of what I've got going on—which didn't happen, obviously. What can I say?

So…*slam*, slide down a wave, rocket back up, airborne—*slam*…and I'm wetter and nakeder. More naked? I don't know. Grammar isn't my strong suit under the best of circumstances and certainly not when I'm under duress. I've almost got a college degree, so I can put together a coherent essay on pretty much any topic, but it takes some effort to make sure I've edited the ghetto out.

It wasn't cold out, not by a long shot. But being three-quarters naked and wetter by the second will leave you shivering regardless of the temperature. So my teeth started chattering, my skin was covered in goose bumps, and my nips could cut glass.

None of this was lost on my captors. More than one pair of fingers pinched my nipples, hard enough that I ground my teeth together to keep from whining about it. I wasn't about to let these fuckers see me hurt. Let them pinch. Let them see me in a wet white T-shirt. I had one goal from here on out, and that was to stay alive. Dignity, virtue—heh, who am I kidding? I ain't got none of that anyway—privacy… none of that mattered. Men had died. This wasn't a game. It wasn't a prank or a joke. Real bullets had been fired, and real blood had been shed. Someone named Dane had gotten shot because of me. He was probably dead trying to protect me.

I spread my feet to brace them against the sides of the boat, leaning forward as we slid down a wave, then felt myself leave the bench and slam back down.

God, my tits hurt from the constant bouncing. I'm stacked as hell, and I do mean *stacked*. I'm not saying my tits are my best asset, because I've got a pretty bangin' ass too, but dem titties? Big, juicy, and bouncy. All natural, of course. Which meant that without the support of a bra, they were flopping all over the damn place with every slam of the boat onto the water. I'd have killed for a bra, or even to have my hands free to keep 'em pinned down.

All the while, the men were talking about me. I heard two voices, one deep and gravelly, as if he had a cement mixer in his voice box. The other had a smoother voice, but his had a more worrisome tone. Calm and quiet, but even though I couldn't understand a word, I could tell he was talking about me. He leaned close every now and then and muttered in my ear. His fingers pinched my nipples, traced my kneecap and up my thigh.

I fought to keep still: he still had his gun pressed to the base of my skull.

Let him touch. Let him say whatever filthy bullshit he was saying. Honestly, the fact that it wasn't English made it easier to ignore. I still knew he was talking shit, though, because shit-talk sounds the same in any language.

And then he dug his hand between my legs, under the hem of my shirt, and jammed his finger against my opening. Which, considering how negligible the thong was, meant he got a good two knuckles deep into me, by virtue of the little patch of fabric over my pussy slipping aside to let his finger in. I kept still, didn't squeeze my legs shut like I wanted.

I mean, I could have broken his wrist if I'd wanted to—I knew some basic self-defense moves, and a good bit of groundwork I'd learned from an ex-fuck-buddy who was an MMA fighter. He'd shown me how to do leg locks and wrist-breaks and takedowns and shit like that, all courtesy of his black belt in Brazilian jiu-jitsu. Of course, he and I had practiced naked and always ended up doing the nasty on his apartment floor, but I'd learned the moves. Point is, I could have wrapped my leg around his arm, twisted in place, and snapped it like a twig. But with a gun to my head? Nope. Let him cop a feel.

But then something odd happened: cement mixer voice guy barked something sharp in whatever language they were speaking, and the hand fell away, but not without what sounded like a petulant curse from Groper McDicknuts. We slid up another wave, crested, slammed back down with a wet splash. By now my shirt was absolutely soaked, probably totally see-through, plastered to my skin.

I'm not shy, not by any means. I've got no problem with nudity under most circumstances. Feed me tequila at a party, and I'm the girl who might end up flashing the room just for kicks. It drives my more straight-laced best friend Kyrie batshit crazy, because she thinks I should have more—I don't know…decency? Prudishness? Concern for my image? Maybe so, but that's not me. I don't give a shit. Tits are tits; you've seen one pair of boobs, you've seen 'em all.

But what I don't like is having the choice taken away. If I want to flash a roomful of horny drunk dudes, I will. Because shit, if I do, I'm likely to get a good bang out of it, and that's never a loss. But having the choice to cover up taken away, *that* pisses me off. Not that I could do anything about it under those circumstances, but I was still pissed off about it.

At least anger gave me something to focus on besides fear and worry.

Scary-smooth voice whispered something else to me in his language, which I ignored. And then he spoke in English. "Maybe we stop the boat, yes? Have some fun. Yuri, he follows the orders. Me? I think boss won't know difference if we stop and have a quick fuck of you." Something sharp touched my breastbone, right at the apex of the V of my shirt.

He had a fucking knife to my skin while we were in a boat in the middle of the fucking ocean? Crazy dumbass. I fought fear, fought the urge to scream, to beg. I didn't want to be cut open. I didn't want to "have a quick fuck of me."

Cement Mixer said something, again short and sharp, a command.

The knife slid down between my breasts, dull edge to my skin, sharp edge slicing open my shirt. Down, down. The tip nicked the inside of my thigh, and I flinched as it pricked me, loosing a trickle of blood. My shirt flapped open in the wind now, leaving me bare to the air.

I kept still. Clenched my teeth, shut my eyes inside the black bag over my head. Bit down on the whimper as salt spray stung the knife-prick on my thigh.

The motor cut out, and Cement Mixer repeated his command, and this time he accompanied it with the distinctive sound of pistol slide being pulled back and released. I knew that sound. Yes, I've hooked up with drug dealers too, and gang-bangers. Even an on-duty detective, once, and he pulled the slide on his piece with the same exact motion as the drug dealers. I can see the movement: arm held out straight, piece tilted at an angle, jerk the slide, and let it go.

Smooth Voice said something, but it was placating and rebellious at the same time. I felt him move slightly, folding the knife maybe, or sheathing it? I wasn't sure. But then he cupped my boob, gripped it with a hard, cruel grip, laughing. I kept still, ground my teeth together and held my breath.

BLAM!

I was splattered with wetness, hot and sticky. Something heavy hit the rubber at my feet, and I smelled iron.

I kept still. Cement Mixer muttered to himself, grumbling it sounded like. I smelled him as he moved past me, cigarettes and salt spray and body odor. I felt the boat rock, heard him grunt with effort, and then the boat was rocked again violently, followed by a splash.

I heard velcro ripping, and then something heavy and scratchy was tugged over my sack-covered head and jerked down roughly over my torso, crushing my breasts to my chest. He didn't fasten the vest—his bulletproof body armor, I assumed, and didn't untie me to let me put my arms through. But I was covered.

"Thank you," I said.

"Shut the fuck up." He said this angrily, greatly irritated, in accented English.

"Okay, then."

The motor coughed to life we set out again, up and down, up and down, for long minutes I couldn't count. We had to have traveled more than a mile at least, judging by how much time had passed. I had no way of judging our speed, but it felt like we were traveling pretty damn fast.

And then I heard a rumble in the distance, the heavy growl of mammoth diesel engines. The tone of the outboard motor lessened and our speed slackened. The diesel clatter increased in volume until it was directly overhead, and then Cement Mixer cut off our motor and I felt us coast and halt with a bump against the large vessel.

The boat shifted as Cement Mixer—Yuri, I think he was called—as Yuri leaned over to me and snatched the bag off my head.

Jesus shits, he was fucking ugly. Thick brows, heavy forehead, high cheekbones, fleshy lips, beady eyes, pox scars dotting his face. But he'd stopped the dead guy from raping me, so I owed him one.

I glanced up, and saw the other boat. It was a fishing boat, high prow, low stern, cockpit just big enough for one or two people, boom arms and nets and lines hung off the sides. There was a rope ladder tossed over the side, and a number of figures milled around on the deck, several carrying machine guns. Or maybe they were assault rifles. I didn't know the difference, and for real, who the hell cared? Not me, that was for damn sure.

Yuri moved to sit beside me, reaching down to his waist and producing a long, wicked-looking knife. I tensed, but he moved slowly, watching me.

"I cut you free," he said in his guttural voice. "Do not move."

I leaned forward and stretched my arms out behind me, tried to open my wrists as far as the zip-ties would allow. There was a momentary tightening of pressure as he pressed in with the knife, and then the plastic parted and my wrists were free. I kept still, knowing my best plan was to cooperate and wait for an opportunity. Mostly naked on a boat in the middle of the Caribbean, hours before dawn, surrounded by men with machine guns? Not the best time to be stubborn lunatic Layla.

That time would come, but it wasn't now.

Yuri gestured with the knife, stabbing the tip at the rope ladder. "Climb up. No bullshit, or you die."

I put my arms through the openings of the vest and then slid across the bench to the rope ladder, grabbed a rung, and hauled myself up. Can I just take a moment and point out that this maneuver is not as easy as they make it seem on TV? The fishing boat was riding up and down on the waves, and so was the little black rubber boat I was on, and neither were going up or down at the same time. Plus, I was shaky with fear, and had guns pointed at me. Also,

I've never climbed a rope ladder before, and they're not easy to use either.

And I had to pee.

So yeah, it was a difficult operation, getting a good grip on the rope ladder, getting a foot on the ladder and not losing my balance. If I fell, I'd probably end up in the water under the boat, which sounded like even less fun than I was having already. But I managed it, and climbed up, up, up, swung a leg over onto the deck, and straightened to face a group of men so hardened, rough-looking, and heavily armed that I almost peed myself. Seriously, each one had a machine gun on his shoulder and most had a pistol too. Several had lit cigarettes hanging from the corners of their mouths.

They all just stared at me like I was a fish that had sprouted arms and legs and decided to forgo the net and just climb aboard for the slaughter.

One of the men snarled something I couldn't understand, and Yuri—climbing up behind me—answered with a shrug and few quiet words. The first speaker gestured at me, and Yuri waved out at the water, pointed at me. Explaining what happened with the other guy, I guessed.

The first speaker, a tall man with a black beard and a red bandana tied over his skull like an actual pirate, stalked over to me and ripped the bulletproof vest off me, and then smirked as he realized I was essentially naked underneath. My shirt was cut open from top to bottom, leaving my front bare for their leisurely perusal. Feigning calm I didn't feel, I slipped my arms out of the arm-holes and rotated the shirt, stuffed my arms back through so I was at least a little less naked in front of a bunch of hard-as-fuck criminals.

They'd all gotten a gander at my goods, so they were all probably hoping Bandana would take the remnants of my shirt away.

Bandana held the vest and stared down at me, dark eyes narrowed. "Make no trouble, and I will not let the men molest you. Cause problems, and I will not be so strict with them, you understand me?"

"What are you going to do with me?" I asked.

"Take you to the boss."

"Am I going to be killed?"

Bandana shrugged. "Probably, but not until he has made his use of you."

"Do I get clothes?"

"No. Shut up with the questions." He gestured at Yuri and then to the deck hands, barking an order in their language.

Yuri grabbed me by the arm and hauled me toward the cabin, then pointed at a ladder leading below the deck. I climbed down, and Yuri followed, jerked open a thick steel door, and shoved me through.

The room was tiny, barely wide enough to let me stretch out my arms in any direction. It was cold, dark, featureless, and stank of fish. There was nothing in it at all, not even a prison cot.

And I had to pee.

Super.

Kidnapping is fun!

10

SÃO PAULO

YOU REALLY DON'T KNOW BOREDOM UNTIL YOU'VE spent countless hours in a featureless ten-by-ten room in the dark, without so much as a fucking bed to sit on. Did I mention it stank like fish? Well, it did. It stank very, *very* badly of fish. It sure as shit wasn't me stinking like that, because I keep my snatch clean. I mean, you can't let a guy go down on you if you don't keep your shit so fresh and so clean-clean.

But I digress.

I'M FUCKING BORED.

That was my mantra for so long I lost the capacity to think of anything else. There wasn't room to pace, except for maybe a step in either direction. It was pitch black. It was cold. The boat didn't toss me around too badly, but once in while the boat would angle up, sending me sliding backward, and then it would pitch down, sending me forward… over and over and over. There was nothing to hold on to, nothing to brace myself with or against. I tried sitting in each of the four corners, but a pitch or a roll of the boat and I'd be sliding all over the place anyway.

I was hungry. Thirsty.

Tired.

And bored.

Did I mention bored?

I'm an active girl. I'm busy from six in the morning to past midnight most days—or I used to be. I'd worked two jobs and gone to school full time, plus I usually found time to swim for an hour every day between classes, and between shifts on the weekends. That was my dirty little secret, that hour of swimming every day. I scheduled my life around it, to be totally honest. I ate horribly, regularly pigging out on bacon cheeseburgers and milkshakes and pizza and boozing it up as often as I could. But, to keep myself from ballooning into a walrus, I swam. Hard. Every day for an hour, I'd do laps at the local pool, back and forth, as hard and fast as I could without stopping. I'd change my stroke every four laps: crawl, breast, back, butterfly. Fuck, those four butterfly laps were a bitch. But they kept me relatively fit. I mean,

I'd never be a size four, much less a zero, but I had a pretty firm body for a woman with my build. Genetics did not bless me with anything approaching skinny, which is fine. I'm built like a brick shithouse, and an hour of swimming every day meant great muscle tone, low BMI, and provided a hell of a cardio workout. I just wasn't skinny.

Again, I digress.

What was I thinking about?

Oh yeah, being busy. I never had down time. If I wasn't working, or at school, I was studying, drinking, or fucking.

And yes, fucking counts as a workout too, especially if you do it right.

So to go from that to sitting around on Roth's boat all day long, not doing dick? That was a hard adjustment. Fortunately, Roth made sure there was a killer gym on that Caribbean cruise liner he called a "yacht", which I took regular advantage of. No pool, but plenty of exercise equipment, including a rowing machine. I avoid any exercise that involves excessive jostling: I just bounce too much. Running in particular is a special hell for me, so I avoid that. Stair steppers, treadmills, even exercise bikes are things I stay away from. I'll lift weights, row, swim, anything with low or zero impact. No bouncing means no lower back problems from hauling the girls around.

No bullshit.

God, I was so bored I was thinking about exercise? What the fuck?

Eventually the door scraped open, blinding me with sudden light. I cowered in the corner and hissed, shielding my eyes as a silhouetted figure leaned in, set a tray on the floor, and backed out, closing the door once again.

I smelled food.

My stomach went crazy, growling like crazy as I scrambled across the floor toward the tray. I smelled garlic, meat, onions…a gyro, maybe? I did my best blind-person impression, touching everything carefully in an attempt to figure out what was in front of me. Definitely a gyro, plus a bag of chips, and a can of something cold. Really? Was this a prison, or a shopping mall food court? Not that I was complaining. I cracked open the can and sipped at it, tasting cola of some kind. Diet; blech. I normally stayed away from diet soda because the stupid aspartame gave me headaches and diet cola was generally worse for you than regular soda. But beggars can't be choosers, and I was very definitely in a beggar sort of scenario, so I drank the diet. The gyro, now…that shit was delicious. Roasted lamb cut thin, cucumber sauce, some crunchy red onions, tomatoes. I devoured that thing so fast I barely tasted it. The chips were kettle cooked, too.

A much better meal than I had been expecting as a kidnappee. I was honestly expecting to either not get anything at all, or moldy bread and smelly water. The fucking gyro basket tasted like it was from Athens Coney Island.

Turns out stuffing yourself that fast after not eating for who knows how long isn't the greatest idea. Talk about sitting heavy in my stomach. It sat like a goddamned gut-bomb.

Also, I still had to pee.

After banging on the door for what felt like an hour straight, it jerked open, revealing a very pissed off Yuri.

"What the fuck you want?" he growled.

"I have to pee."

He gestured at the floor. "So pee."

I scowled at him. "Really, Yuri? I know I'm a prisoner but come on. Let me use a toilet. We're on a fucking boat, where the hell am I going to go?"

He stared at me in silence. "Fine." He jerked his head and I followed him around the corner and along a low, narrow corridor to a tiny bathroom.

"Door open."

I shrugged, shucked my thong and lifted my shirt, staring at him as I pissed. "You want to watch, then watch. I don't give a shit. I'm warning you, though, it's gonna be a long one. Like, you might need a book."

The corner of his mouth twitched ever so slightly, and he grunted in irritation. He didn't want to like me, but he did. Hell, he couldn't help it; I'm a funny gal. But he shut the door, so I decided to take care of some other business while I had the opportunity. Gut-bombs away!

And as a bonus, I saw a blue Papermate ballpoint pen on the floor in the corner under the sink, long forgotten. The pen is mightier than the sword, right? I mean, I've seen pens used as weapons on TV a bunch of times. Better than nothing.

Where to hide it, though?

It wasn't exactly like I had any pockets, so you figure it out.

And, yes, I rinsed it off first.

You want to talk about uncomfortable? Jesus. I've now got mad respect for those crazy druggie bitches who smuggle bags of coke up their shit, that's for sure.

I walked funny on the way back to my cell, but Yuri didn't notice. Or if he did, he didn't think anything of it.

The strangest part was, the length of the pen made me think about the various guys I'd been with, and how they measured up to my new boyfriend, Mr. Papermate. A few did not measure up so well. Others…well, that's a different kind of walking funny. But then, as we all know, it's not the size of the cock that's important when it comes right down to it; it's how well he uses it. Girth can be pretty important, but foreplay trumps everything.

Mr. Papermate didn't really do it for me, but at least I now had a weapon.

Once I was returned to my cell my first instinct was to take it out, but then I got to thinking. I knew I was gonna need it at some point, but not when that would be. Probably not on the boat—that would be a waste. I'd probably need it when we got where we were going, wherever that was. Or maybe when Harris showed up I could help him effect my escape by stabbing some of these assholes in the throat with Mr. Papermate the Pussy Pen? That seemed like a more likely scenario.

So in it stayed. I really didn't like the idea of having a foreign object up there for any longer than I had to because that was just begging for an infection, but I'd take the fiery agony of a vaginal infection over being raped and killed any day of the week.

I mean, I'd really rather not have either, but no one was asking me what I wanted.

And the sensation also gave me something else to think about, and at that point in my boredom, something to think about was welcome, even if it was strange to have a ballpoint pen lodged up my cooter.

Eventually we stopped, but I had no clue as to how much time had passed. I had no way to measure that. Days? Weeks? I was fed on a regular schedule, but with no point of reference, it could have been once a day or three times a day…When you're in a black hole, shit gets relative real fucking fast. And by relative, I mean you go batshit, arm-flapping, hoot-like-an-owl crazy. Or at least, I did.

When Yuri opened the door and gestured for me to come out, I literally crawled out on my hands and knees, blinking, hissing, and generally acting like a looney toon.

"Stand up, stupid." He grabbed my arm and hauled me to my feet. "Crazy fucking American. You only been in there three days."

I stood up and brushed my knees off, unconsciously keeping them pressed together. The pen wasn't in danger of falling out, because let's be honest, I keep my shit tighter than a drum. Kegels, bitches. Flex those PCs. I'm like a goddamn body builder, but for my pubococcygeus muscle. But still, one worries, in this situation. As one would.

He led me back up to the deck of the boat, which was now swarming with activity. Men were scrambling everywhere, shirtless, sweaty, and cursing as they hauled crate after crate out of the hold and onto a platform suspended from a crane-arm, which would then swing it across from the boat to a shipping container. Each crate had 'VK' emblazoned on the side in huge black-painted letters. They all looked heavy, since each one required two men to lift it, although there was one really huge motherfucker with arms the size of my waist hauling them around one in each hand like bags of groceries. As Yuri led me across the deck, all work stopped.

Eyes were fixed on me.

Lips curled up in lecherous grins. Wrists wiped at sweaty brows.

I focused on Yuri's back, ignored the stares, and made sure I was walking as normally as possible. Under other circumstances, I'd have relished the amount of male attention I was getting. I'd probably have swayed my hips a bit, put some bounce in my step, maybe winked and flirted.

This wasn't a typical situation, and I was pretty sure I wouldn't enjoy the kind of attention those particular men had in mind.

So I kept my eyes straight forward and hustled after Yuri. Of course, the shirt that was my only article of clothing was ripped open, leaving my back bare from neck to ass and, as I've mentioned, my choice in undergarments left my buttocks bare as the day I was born. So those big sweaty gorillas all got a free show anyway.

Good thing I worked hard to keep my ass nice and round and firm, huh?

Thank god this time there was a ramp leading from the deck down to the dock. I followed Yuri off the boat. Looking around, I realized we were in a very urban port, but I had no idea where. We walked past mammoth shipping containers stacked three and four high, forming a maze that blocked out the sun as we passed between them. The ground underfoot was damp industrial concrete, a rainbow sheen here and there from leaking oil. I heard a diesel rumble somewhere to my left, shouts, the beeping of a machine of some kind backing up, and then a container high above our heads slid away.

"Where are we?" I couldn't help asking.

"Caracas," Yuri grumbled.

"Ca-who-what?"

"Caracas. Venezuela."

"What's in the containers?"

"Business for big boss." A shrug.

"Drugs, you mean?"

"Not only drugs. Guns also. Cars. People."

I stumbled. "People?"

"Prostitutes. Brides. Slaves."

"Where is it all going?" I felt dizzy, sick.

"Whole world. Miami, Hanoi, Vancouver, London…everywhere."

"You're okay with slavery?"

Yuri swiveled his head on his thick neck, and his small dark eyes fixed on me, hard as chunks of marble. "Not my job to like or not like. My job is only to get you to boss. I like, I don't like, no one cares. I tell boss I don't like, you know what he does? He shoots me dead, like I shoot stupid Nico. Easy. So, I don't like be shoot dead, I keep my words to myself, and stay alive."

"Oh." What else was there to say? Subtext was, he didn't like it, but couldn't do anything about it.

"Am I going in one of those?" I pointed at a container.

Yuri shook his head. "*Nyet*. You are more valuable than them. You go in one of those, you end up in a shithole in Naypyidaw, fucked fifty times a day for a handful of coins you don't get to keep, and you stay there until you die."

"Napyih-what?"

He actually chuckled at that. "Naypyidaw. Capital city of Myanmar. Once used to be Burma."

"Well that doesn't sound fun."

He had nothing to say to that other than a grunt. He led me along a path around and between stack after stack of containers so circuitous that I couldn't have navigated it again even if I'd been paying closer attention. Eventually we emerged at the base of the kind of crane used to build skyscrapers, the machine itself dozens of stories tall with a boom arm hundreds of feet long, a box at the top only accessible via elevator. The boom arm was in motion far above us, swiveling over our heads with a shipper container in its grasp. I ducked involuntarily as it crossed over me, even though it swung easily a hundred feet over my head. Yuri laughed.

"If it falls you die, even if you duck." He gestured at a waiting helicopter. "This is our ride. For a prisoner, you get nice ride."

It was a small helicopter, big enough for maybe four people plus the pilot. The door was open, revealing plush leather seats, each one empty. Yuri climbed in and held out his hand to help me up, but I ignored him and stepped in on my own, and then sat down and buckled in.

I was seated so I could see the cockpit, and I watched avidly as the pilot manipulated the controls with deft hands, skillfully lifting the helicopter off the ground without so much as a wobble. It looked hard as hell, honestly, a lot more to control and not as intuitive as an airplane. I'd picked that up easily enough, but then that was a lot simpler; one yoke, push in to descend, pull back to lift up, turn it left to bank left, right to bank right, foot pedals to pivot horizontally in either direction. Keeping all the buttons, switches, and dials straight was trickier, but not exactly difficult. The helicopter controls, however, looked a lot more involved, as you had to manipulate the craft on several axes: pitch and yaw, as well as bank, plus ascent and descent vertically, all combined with velocity.

Maybe after Harris rescued me, he'd teach me to fly choppers as well as fixed-wing aircraft.

That thought sobered me: I was operating on the assumption that Harris was coming for me—I didn't doubt that part. I knew he'd be looking. But how could he find me? These guys had vanished me very effectively. I'd gone from a little Zodiac speedboat to a fishing boat, and from there to a helicopter. No witnesses, no records. From the helicopter I figured they'd probably take me somewhere even further afield, maybe on a private jet to the Mediterranean, or somewhere deep in the heart of South America. Either way, how could Harris hope to find me?

I'm not a crier. Never have been, never will be. But the thought of what awaited me had me choking up with fearful tears. So far I'd been left alone, but something told me that was just because I was meant for "the boss", one Vitaly Karahalios, international crime kingpin extraordinaire. I had no doubt that whatever *he* had in mind wouldn't be at all pleasant. Rape, torture, and murder had all been suggested as possibilities for what awaited me.

I had to hold on to hope that Harris would, somehow, find me and rescue me. Preferably before anything too fucked up was done to me.

I made a new mantra: Harris *is* coming. Harris *is* coming. Harris *is* coming.

The helicopter angled inland, and after maybe twenty minutes flight time, we landed in an empty grass field beside an old twin-engine prop plane. The grassy field, I realized, was a makeshift airstrip, meaning Caracas, Venezuela still wasn't my final destination. The fixed-wing airplane's engines were spinning, and as I was hustled off the helicopter, the airplane's rudder and flaps wiggled as the pilot prepared for takeoff. I tried to distract myself from

my ever-present fear with mental images of flying, checking dials and flipping switches and going
through the checklist—all the boring shit you have
to do to get to the good stuff: soaring through the air,
free, high above it all, a bird's-eye view of the world
and all its attendant troubles. I was shoved—none
too gently, and with a lingering touch on my ass—up
the stairs and onto the plane. There were a few metal
chairs bolted to the floor up front near the door to
the cockpit, but the rest of the fuselage was empty.
It had clearly once been a passenger plane, but had
long since been retrofitted to serve as a cargo plane,
with tie-downs bolted to the walls and floors.

Yuri buckled me in, took a chair beside me, and
then called out in his language. The plane rotated in
place, and then I heard and felt the engines ramp up,
felt the ground bumping under the wheels, and then
the lurch as we left the earth, angling aggressively
upward.

And then…?

More boredom. Hours and hours of absolutely
nothing, not even anything to see, as the tiny round
windows were too far away to show me anything except the blue sky and the occasional scrap of cloud.
Hours and hours of flight, Yuri snoring beside me. I
could have unbuckled and jumped out, but I didn't
have a parachute, didn't know how to use one, and

didn't fancy my chances of surviving a fall from an airplane. And his weapon was tucked in against his body, which meant if I tried to take it, he'd wake up and I'd be in trouble. Nothing to do but wait, it seemed.

So I endured the boredom as best I could.

We landed, eventually, and Yuri woke with a start when we hit the ground. As soon as the plane was stopped, he hauled me off the airplane and into yet *another* fucking aircraft, this one another helicopter pretty much identical to the first.

I groaned out loud. "Jesus, really? More flying? This has got to be the most tedious kidnapping in the history of kidnapping."

Yuri shot me a glance. "You would like it to be more exciting, then? I can think of ways."

"Well, when you put it that way, maybe boring is good."

"In your place, boring is good."

The helicopter lifted off and we headed south over lush greenery. No one said a word. I contemplated jumping out and taking my chances in the jungle, but Yuri's gaze flicked over to me regularly, as if to assess my inclination for just such a move. He was close enough that he'd probably be able to grab me before I even got myself unbuckled.

"Where are we going?" I asked, after an hour or

so had passed.

"São Paulo," Yuri muttered. "No more questions. Nearly there."

Harris is coming. Harris is coming. Harris is coming.

A city came into view, vast and sprawling, the jungle giving way very suddenly to an urban landscape ensconced a few miles inland from the sea. God, the urban sprawl. It was dizzying. The helicopter zipped in low, only a few hundred yards above the tallest buildings, making a beeline across the city. I heard the pilot speaking—Brazilian? Portuguese? I was pretty sure they spoke Portuguese in Brazil, and São Paulo was in Brazil. Right? God, I was so ignorant of world geography. Anyway, I heard him speaking, and then the aircraft slowed as we approached a specific building, our destination. A hotel, by the looks of it, a big, fancy one, the kind that had helicopter landing pads on the roof.

The landing was gentle as a feather wafting on a breeze, the touchdown barely registering. The rotors didn't stop or slow as Yuri unbuckled himself, threw open the door, and leapt out past me. I had myself unbuckled but he refused to let me get down on my own, grabbing me by the waist and lifting me down. The wash from the helicopter forced me to bend almost double, making a tangled nest of my already gnarled hair. Yuri grabbed my wrist and dragged me across the roof at nearly a run, through a door and into an elevator, inserting a key and twisting it.

We descended briefly, and then the doors opened.

"Ah. Miss Campari." The voice was accented, deep as a canyon, smooth as silk. Quiet, like a predator. "Welcome."

I saw the man who owned the voice. Only a few inches taller than me, but broad and powerfully built, he had thick wavy black hair, piercing dark eyes, weathered olive skin, and a square, granite jaw. He exuded threat and power. He wore tailored black slacks, and a dove-gray polo shirt left untucked. Barefoot. Clean-shaven.

Something in his eyes as he assessed me made me shiver. This man was…terrifying.

I wanted to hide behind Yuri, but he was already backing into the elevator, twisting the key, and then the doors were sliding between us, leaving me alone. I stood alone, facing Vitaly Karahalios. All but naked, and completely terrified.

He stalked over to me, flicked a loose curling tendril of hair with a fingertip, circling around me like a cat toying with a mouse. His fingertip traced down my spine where the shirt gaped open. I shivered and fought the urge to shy away. Another brief touch, this time to my shoulder. Nudging the shirt off my shoulder; the cotton slipped down to my bicep on one side, and then he nudged at the shirt on the other side, and it fell even more.

He circled back in front of me, hooked his finger in the collar and tugged. I let him remove the shirt, standing before him in nothing but my thong. I kept my back straight, my knees locked, my chin high.

Defiant.

Don't show fear—I knew his kind all too well.

"They brought you here like this?" he asked. "I will have to scold them. You are a guest."

"I don't feel like a guest," I ventured.

"Perhaps not. Nonetheless, you should have been treated better. How was your trip here?"

I stared at him. "They threw me in a tiny room on a ship that had no windows and stank of fish. The airplane and helicopters were okay, though."

"Not in a proper room?" he demanded, seeming genuinely puzzled.

I shook my head. "It was worse than a prison cell."

"Idiots." He withdrew a cell phone from his trouser pocket, touched a speed dial number, and put the phone to his ear. He spoke briefly in a foreign language, his voice sharp but quiet. After replacing the phone in his pocket, he bent and retrieved my shirt, handing it to me. "I will arrange proper clothing for you in a moment, after we've had time to acquaint ourselves. But first, I must have a word with Yuri."

As if on cue, Yuri emerged from the elevator. If I was any judge of his facial expressions, he was shitting bricks. He glanced at me as if in question, and I just shrugged.

"Yuri," Vitaly said, his voice barely above a whisper. "This is not what I was expecting. I am not pleased with you, I'm afraid."

"I brought her here, boss," Yuri mumbled. "Not hurt. No one messed with her. Nico, he tried, and I shot him. He was gonna stop the boat and—you know. But I stopped him."

"Where are her clothes?"

"This is what she was wearing when we take her. Swear."

Vitaly was quiet a moment. "And why is her shirt cut open?"

"Nico. I told you, boss, he—he was gonna rape her."

"And why did you not give her your shirt? Or find her something else to wear?" He stepped closer to Yuri, staring at him. "And why was she put in a *cell*? She should have had the captain's quarters. I *told* you, Yuri. She was not to be mistreated."

"I'm sorry, boss, I didn't think—"

"No," Vitaly murmured. "No, you did not think."

Perhaps I only thought I saw the movement. It was so fast, so neatly and easily done. *Snick*, a blade shot out of a handle that had appeared in Vitaly's palm, and then with a sudden flash of his wrist, the blade was snugged between Yuri's ribs on his left side, angled upward. Vitaly stepped back after a moment, withdrawing the blade. Yuri stood for a moment, blinking, confused, and then he toppled to the floor, slightly sideways and backward at the same time. Blood darkened his shirt, trickled slowly to the floor and began pooling, dark red on the white marble floor.

"Maria!" Vitaly said, his voice raised just a bit.

A woman appeared. "*Senhor*?"

"Get Gutierrez in here, tell him he has a mess to clean up."

"*Imediatamente.*" The woman vanished without so much as a glance at me or the dead body.

Vitaly knelt, wiped the blade clean on Yuri's shirt, and then stood. He turned to face me. "My apologies for the unpleasantness. Sometimes these men I hire, they do not do as they should. Now, where were we?" He eyed me, as I held the shirt up to my chest. "Ah, yes. Follow me, please."

He pivoted sharply on his heel, and led me to a short hallway that ended at a set of wide French doors. He pushed them open, revealing an extravagant bedroom overlooking São Paulo. He ignored the bed—thank god—and gestured at the door leading to the bathroom.

"A shower, I think, might be welcome?"

"That would be great," I said. "Thank you."

He nodded as I entered the bathroom, and then followed me. I waited a moment, and then two. Vitaly did not grin, or smile, or make a lecherous comment, but when he leaned a hip against the counter edge and folded his arms over his chest, I realized he had no intention of leaving.

I let out a long breath, then steeled myself. Nothing mattered but staying alive. *Harris is coming. Harris is coming. Harris IS coming.* I just had to stay alive until he found me.

I dropped the shirt, hooked my thumbs in the sides of my thong and wiggled out of it, all too aware of Vitaly watching every move. Turning on the spray, I adjusted the temperature, made sure there was shampoo and such in the shower, got a washcloth, and then stepped under the steaming spray of hot water.

I took my time, trying to pretend Vitaly wasn't there. I even washed myself down below, trying to act normal, like I didn't have a pen stuck up where the sun don't shine. His eyes followed my every move, every jiggle and bounce and sway.

When I was done, I shut off the water, wiped my face, and found Vitaly extending a towel to me, held open. I moved to take it from him, but he withdrew it, made a negative sound in his throat, and then held it out to me again.

Shit.

I stood still, dripping on the marble floor.

His hands never came in direct contact with my skin as he gently and carefully wiped me dry with the towel, dabbing and scrubbing all over from my shoulders to feet, breast to calves, but nonetheless I felt…not violated, exactly, but aware of the consequences of disobedience, and disgusted with what I knew I would have to endure. I held my breath and tried not to flinch, tried not to fight him. It took every ounce of self-control I possessed, but I got through the entire process without protest, verbal or physical. My skin crawled, my stomach rebelled.

I wanted to get back in the shower and scrub myself all over again.

His eyes roamed my body, and once he even pressed his nose to my flesh at my hip and inhaled deeply, and then gazed up at me.

He dried my breasts, lingeringly. Slowly. Lifting

and caressing with the towel.

Oh god. Oh god.

I endured it silently. I kept my eyes open, expressionless, staring straight ahead.

He dried my ass last, once again doing it slowly, leisurely, and once again I had to focus on breathing and keeping still.

He neglected to thoroughly dry one small part of me, much to my good fortune.

When he was finally finished, he lifted a thick white robe off the hook on the back of the door, settled it over my shoulders, waited for me to slide my arms into the sleeves, and then tied it around me. Loosely, so my breasts weren't quite covered. Of course.

Vitaly stepped away, back into the bedroom. "You have an iron will, Miss Campari. You did not react at all."

"I'm either going to get out of this alive, or I'm not. That's all that really matters."

He stood in the center of the room, hands in his hip pockets. "You determine what happens, Miss Campari. I do not really have any issue with you, personally. I think you know with whom my anger lies."

"Roth."

Vitaly frowned. "Not really, no. It is your friend,

Kyrie St. Claire. She killed my daughter. It is she who must suffer."

I shivered at that. "So what do you want from me?"

"Little enough. You are bait, nothing more, nothing less. She will come for you. She will send someone. That barbarian, Nicholas Harris, first, perhaps. Others, maybe. Eventually, she herself will stand in front of me. That is when the suffering will begin."

I swallowed hard. "She was only acting in self-defense."

He shrugged. "This I know. But it does not matter. She killed my daughter. I cannot excuse this, no matter the reason." He eyed me. "Until then, all I require from you is...cooperation. You are a diversion, no more."

A diversion.

Shit.

I *really* didn't like the sound of that.

11

ROAD TRIP

As the days passed, I played a game with myself.

Vitaly was always present, always a gentleman to me. He never swore, never smoked, and never raised his voice. In fact, he never raised his voice at all, to anyone. He was always totally even-keeled, calm, smooth as a glassy lake. His household help seemed to respect him, but did not seem to fear him. The men, though—the foot soldiers or base level thugs or whatever you wanted to call them, now *they* were scared shitless of Vitaly. And with good reason. He killed them regularly, for the slightest infraction. A misstatement, a failed job, an ill-advised glance at me…and that switchblade would find their ribs. They never saw it coming. It was like a serpent striking, sudden, vicious, and final. He never missed, never hesitated. Right to the heart, and they just dropped dead.

And it was always a man named Gutierrez who cleaned up the body. Gutierrez was short, thin, balding, and always wore mirrored aviators, black cargo shorts, black crew-neck T-shirt, sports sandals. It was a uniform, it seemed. He was never armed that I could see. And he was scarily efficient at disposing of bodies. It was like a scene out of *Scandal*: he'd appear with a huge blue tarp, roll the body onto it, wrap the body in the tarp and seal it with duct tape, heave the wrapped corpse onto an appliance dolly, and wheel it away. Moments after that, Maria appeared with an armful of towels and disinfectant, and the blood stains were gone. The whole process took less than ten minutes.

So, the game I played with myself was pretty simple, and rather morbid: I woke up each day and asked myself what I would be willing to do to stay alive. What horror would I willingly endure, if it meant my heart kept beating? What barbarity would I perpetrate if it meant another day closer to Harris rescuing me?

I chanted my mantra like it was a "Hail Mary", over and over and over: *Harris is coming, Harris is coming, Harris is coming.*

Thus far, four days into my captivity, I'd been

very well treated, if scantily clad. Vitaly provided me with a new pair of underwear, a tiny red thong. No shirt, no bikini top, nothing. Apparently his claim that I would be properly attired was a lie. I lived in that thong, and forced myself to act as if I was fully dressed. I endured the eyes of his lackeys as they came and went with reports, the eyes of the maids and the chef as he brought meals, the bodyguards always lurking just around a corner. And Vitaly's eyes, always his eyes.

A touch, now and then. A palm across my ass, a brief caress of my boob. A hand on my hip, an inhalation of my hair.

I was forced to shower with Vitaly as my audience once a day, in the morning, after breakfast.

Vitaly was a creature of habit, I discovered. He woke at six a.m., rolled out of bed and exercised for thirty minutes. Squats, lunges, two kinds of push-ups, crunches, obliques, planks, five reps of twenty each. On the third day, he made me do it with him. Asshole. At six thirty he had breakfast, plain yogurt with fresh-cut strawberries, four eggs scrambled with cheese, four slices of toast lightly buttered, three cups of coffee, and a handful of vitamin supplements. Then he showered, shaved, dressed, and watched me shower. By eight he was ready to go, and usually left the penthouse via helicopter with two bodyguards in tow, and an older, weather-beaten man with salt-and-pepper hair at his side. The older man's name was Cut. At least, that's what Vitaly called him.

Cut never so much as looked at me, but I felt his attention somehow, anyway. I didn't like his attention. It made my skin crawl, made my gut churn.

And yes, the entire time I had my old buddy Mr. Papermate the Pussy Pen in place, ready when I needed him. Fucking uncomfortable. Definitely not meant to have something hard up there at all, much less for so long. It was starting to hurt like a bitch, and I was never able to forget about it. I was, for sure, gonna end up with a bitch of an infection.

Super fucking fun.

But I had no doubt in my mind that I'd end up needing Mr. Papermate at some point in this little adventure. Especially with Cut around.

Cut scared me worse than Vitaly. Cut was an unknown quantity, whereas with Vitaly, at least I knew for a fact that he could and would kill without compunction. I knew he liked to look at me, liked to watch me shower, like to grope a bit. He made me sleep on the floor at the foot of his bed like a goddamn dog, which really pissed me off, but I dealt with it without complaint because I liked being alive, and it didn't mean anything in the long run.

No blanket, no pillow. Just the carpet, my naked ass hanging out, my arm under my head. Vitaly was toying with me, testing me, pushing me to my limits. Trying to elicit a reaction.

Unfortunately for him, he was absolutely correct in his assessment of me: I had an iron will. If I decided to do something, no force on earth could sway me. Usually I just did what I wanted, whatever seemed fun or easy. But if I got something in my mind, there was no stopping me until I did it. That was how I managed to work two full-time jobs plus fifteen credit hours at Wayne State University. It was how I survived the shit I did, growing up. I survived the ghetto as an outsider, not black, not white, not Hispanic, but as a girl alone on the streets and in the schools, which were often as dangerous as the streets, if not more so. In school, they could trap you in the locker room or the bathroom. On the streets there was usually somewhere to run. I'd survived that—not necessarily unscathed, but I'd survived it. I didn't talk about that shit with anyone, though. Not anyone, not even Kyrie.

But I survived. I'd push through fucking anything, no matter what. I'd made it this far, made it out of the ghetto on my own, I'd paid my way through school, damn near got myself a bachelor's degree, and a good set of skills. And I would be damned if some motherfucking Greek kingpin would end me. He wanted to watch me shower like a fucking nasty-ass creeper? Let him watch. He wanted to make me sleep on the floor like Fido? I'd sleep on the floor.

He wanted to rape me?

Wouldn't be the first time.

Wanted to beat me into a bloody pulp?

Wouldn't be the first time.

I hadn't been tortured, but I'd survive that too.

And besides, Harris was coming.

So each morning as Vitaly's expressionless black eyes watched me shower, I'd envision a hellish new scenario, and figure out my best options.

Turns out, one of them came true.

Vitaly was gone, leaving me alone in the penthouse. The elevator was locked, no call button, only a keyhole. All points of exit or entrance were either guarded or locked. I had a TV—in the local language, of course—and magazines, again all in the local language, and most of those were nudie mags anyway. Not my thing.

BOREDOM SUCKS.

I flipped through all the magazines, tried to figure out words and phrases, I watched TV I didn't understand. I did a lot of pacing, and a lot of staring out the window. A lot of watching people come and go far below me, wondering if one of them was Harris.

And then it happened.

The elevator opened, revealing Cut. He was bloody from head to toe, splattered, painted crimson. Unhurt, though, it seemed, which meant the blood was someone else's. He swaggered toward me, leaving bloody footprints on the marble, dripping gore from his fingertips. He even had blood on his face, his neck, on his ears.

A grin curved across his features, splitting his scarlet-bathed face with white teeth. "Everyone is gone."

I glanced at the doorway Maria usually came through. "Oh. Okay." I backed away.

He stuck a hand in his pocket, casually, and stalked closer. "Just you and me."

"Where is Vitaly?"

"He was called to Brasilia. He won't return for many days."

I swallowed hard. "Oh. Um. Okay."

My skin crawled as Cut stepped close enough that I could smell the blood and the death on him. He touched the center of my chest, leaving a red streak on my skin as he dragged his fingertip down between my breasts. "Now you're mine."

"I...I don't think that's a good idea, Cut." I forced myself to stay calm, to breathe. "He'll come back, and he'll know if you do anything to me."

"He won't know."

I lifted my chin. "I'll make sure he does." I faced him square, nose to nose. Put all my attitude into my eyes. All my contempt. "You want a piece of me, it won't come easy. Which means he'll know. And that won't go well for you. He killed Yuri just for not treating me well enough on the way here. What do you think he'll do if you hurt me?"

Cut just leered. "I am his oldest friend. You think he would kill me like he does those piece of shit pissants?" He spat onto the marble. "He won't. I want a piece of you, I'll take it. And bitch, you make it hard, you will regret it. I promise you this."

I backed away. "Fuck you."

I never saw his fist move. Just *BAM!* I was on the floor, my cheek throbbing. And then he was leaning over me, rancid breath on my face. "Wrong answer." An open-palm slap to my cheek, and then again on the other side. Again and again, until I was dizzy from pain.

I swallowed the pain, clenched my teeth, and kept breathing. When Cut finally stood up, my lip was split and my face pounded with fiery pain.

I stared up at him, unblinking. "You hit like a pussy."

"You want more?" Cut sneered.

He smacked my tit, and Jesus, *that* hurt. Again, again, again. I gritted my teeth and endured it, eyes stinging and leaking, but I didn't so much as whimper. And then he pinched. And by "pinched" I mean clamped down and twisted so hard I thought he was trying to rip my damn nipple off. A shriek escaped, but I bit down on it.

I had blood smeared on me from his hands and clothes, and I was writhing in agony when he finally let go. A moment to breathe, and then I scrambled away, realizing this was all just foreplay to him.

"You going to cooperate now, bitch? Or you want me to start really hurting you?"

I should just cooperate. Pretend it was a drunk fuck. He was bit old for my taste, and it wouldn't be pleasant, but if I cooperated, he'd be done in a few minutes and I'd still be alive.

I thought about it. Shit yeah, I did.

For about four seconds.

"Fuck. You." I spat the words, and then spat on the floor near his feet.

CRACK! His fist split my lip open and loosened a tooth. Knocked me to the floor. Hurt, but I'd been jumped and had the shit kicked out me more than once, even badly enough to need hospitalization on one occasion, so this wasn't exactly new territory for me. Of course, he was a big guy who'd been pummeling people for longer than I'd been alive, so he could hit significantly harder than the teenaged dickweed gangbangers who'd jumped me when I was in high school.

He hit me twice more, and I felt the pain building enough to feel like maybe it was time to stop taunting him.

But then I heard rustling, and peeked through swollen eyes to see him unzipping his pants.

Fuck that. Fuck him. Not without a fight, douchebag.

Under the guise of rolling around and moaning in pain—which I didn't exactly have to fake, mind you—I twisted onto my side, away from him, and withdrew Mr. Papermate the Pussy Pen, slipped it out of myself as swiftly and surreptitiously as I could.

Jesus, it stank.

I curled into a ball, hiding it from him. Pried the cap off the point, blinked hard to clear my vision, held it in my fist, point down—yeah, it was a little... slippery. Eew. Just...eew. This would serve his ass right, though.

I waited. Curled up in a ball, fighting the urge to

whimper in pain. I wasn't gonna cry. Fuck no. Bitches like him wouldn't make me cry. Nothing could.
No one could.

His foot crashed into my back, sending me rolling across the floor. I nearly dropped the pen, but
managed to hang onto it. I groaned, curled into a
ball again, and waited.

This time, he grabbed my arm and rolled me to
my back, straddling my prone body with a leg on
either side of me. Still standing, he bent over me.

Dumbass.

I silently thanked Brad the MMA fighter and
our six months of hot monkey sex-slash-Brazilian
jiu-jitsu practice.

I almost laughed at the irony: I was about to use
Brazilian jiu-jitsu, and I was in Brazil. Heh-heh-heh.

Let's break some shit.

I stuck the pen in my teeth—yuck—and
grabbed his palm with both hands, then twisted until it wouldn't twist anymore, hooking my leg around
his arm so the back of my knee braced the cap of his
elbow. Grinning up into his surprised face, I then
pulled back with both hands while rocking my body
in the opposite direction. *SNAP*. His elbow now bent
in two directions.

The entire move took less than three seconds.

He screamed, I screamed, it was glorious.

Cut fell to the floor, writhing and grabbing at his ruined arm. I rolled over him, hooked my leg around his throat and got him into a good strong leg-lock; look at the little bitch turn blue.

I wasn't done.

Rape me? Fucker, I don't think so.

I took the pen in my fist, spat into his face. Steeled myself, jaw clenched, squeamishness locked down tight. He saw it coming. I made sure he did. I held the pen up high, palm of one hand cupping the back of my pen-wielding fist, slammed it down as hard as I could into his eye socket, putting all my weight, all my strength into the move. It pierced his eye like...well, like an ink pen through Jell-O. I hit resistance, and the pen stuck. He was thrashing, gurgling, twitching. I smelled shit. I put my palm to the end of the pen where it protruded from his skull, slammed my fist down onto the back of my hand like a hammer, driving the pen deeper into his brain.

He went still.

I puked until I had nothing left but bile.

I released my leg-hold on him, kicked his inert bulk off me. I stood up shakily, staring down at him, and retched again.

The elevator stood open, key still in the hole. That was my chance out of here. I made quick work of Cut's blood-soaked shirt, unbuttoning it, peeling it off his torso, and then slipped it on, shuddering at the warm wet stickiness of it. God, so fucking gross. But I was covered. I untied his boots, pried them off, stuffed my feet into them, tied them as tight as they'd go, and then patted him down for a weapon. I found a black folding knife in his pocket, the blade clean while the handle was tacky and bloody. Clearly, this was the weapon used to create all the blood covering him, and now me.

No matter, I was covered, shod, and armed.

Time to go.

I ran at a stumble, lurching into the elevator, his huge boots flopping and clopping like clown shoes. I looked ridiculous, but that was no concern. I mean, it was, because the thought crossed my mind while in the middle of a life-and-death scenario that I looked utterly ridiculous, wearing a man's blood-soaked white shirt, the edge hanging to mid-thigh, and a pair of men's huge, smelly work boots, ten sizes too big. But I wasn't naked, and wasn't running barefoot through São Paulo, so there was that in my favor.

Also, I'd just killed a man.

There would be time to process that later, hopefully. Now, I had to get out of here.

I twisted the key to the P, for parking lot, I assumed. I hoped. The door slid closed and the lift lurched into motion, descending rapidly. A couple gentle bumps, and the elevator halted, the door slid open, and I was through, knife blade open, cutting edge up. A guy I'd hooked up with once had taught me that; hold the knife with the blade pointed up. He was a pretty rough character, obviously, but he'd explained that if you gotta cut someone real quick, cut up, start low and jab up. You can exert more force by jerking upward, do more damage.

Thanks, Lil D. Looks like that'll come in handy.

The parking garage wasn't empty. There were a bunch of valets standing around smoking pot, chattering, laughing. They went quiet as they caught sight of me, and one of them came over to me, a lit joint between his teeth, holding his hands palms out, chattering at me in Portuguese.

"I don't speak that shit, bro. *Habla usted Inglés?*" That was Spanish, not Portuguese, but it was all I had.

"No English." He gestured at the knife, saying something else.

"You can have the knife over my dead body, asshole." He understood my tone of voice, at least, and backed up, holding his hands up. I lunged at him, grabbed his shirt front. "I need a car."

"*O quê?*" He seemed surprised by my sudden aggression, but not particularly worried.

"A *car*. Un auto? Das Auto? Shit, that's German. Um…" I mimed driving, making a zoom-zoom sound.

The other valets laughed like fucking hyenas, but the guy whose neck I had my knife pressed against wasn't laughing. He was sweating and waving at his buddies, chattering in Portuguese. *Give her the damn keys, you idiots*, I imagined. One of them dug in his pocket and produced a key attached to a ring with a tag shaped like a soccer ball. He tossed me the ring and gestured at a beaten-up old jalopy, something small and once-green, now more rust than paint. Probably a stick-shift. Good thing I'd learned that skill too. How? You guessed it—a fuck-buddy. See? Being a slut comes in handy, as long as you learn valuable skills along the way.

I hopped into the driver's seat, thanking my lucky stars that it was on the left, which meant they drove on the right here, which would make my get-away that much easier. I turned the ignition, and the engine caught with a cough and a sputter, and then set to idling. I was about to put it into reverse and pop the clutch, but one of the valets banged on the hood, shouting something at me. I just stared at him in the rear-view mirror, shrugging broadly.

He smacked the trunk again, miming opening it. I fumbled, found the latch, and opened the trunk.

Maybe it was his car and he wanted to get something out of it? I didn't think there would be immediate pursuit, not until someone found Cut. The valet, the one who'd tossed me the key, closed the trunk again, pocketing a baggie and what looked like a wad of cash and a pipe. Yep, his car. He also had a pair of shorts, a T-shirt, and a pair of flip-flops in his hand.

He tossed them through the open window onto my lap. "Big Boss, up there? Asshole."

I nodded. "Yeah. He's an asshole, that's one word for him."

He pointed at me. "You steal my car. I no see you."

I grinned at him. "See who?"

He laughed and backed away, and I shoved the shifter into first, popped the clutch, and hit the gas. The ancient little car bolted forward and the valets all scattered out of the way, laughing at me. I squealed the tires as I slammed the gears into second and took off, up, up, toward the light and out into the city. I nearly got in a wreck immediately upon exiting the parking garage. Super great. A big truck full of fruit swerved out of the way, earning me shouts and what I assumed were rude gestures. I just flipped them off and peeled out, zipping past them and through an intersection. Of course, the light was red, so I caused two T-bones and one head-on collision as I darted through the intersection, flooring it once I was past. This piece of shit could move, it turned out. I mean, it was no BMW, but it had a little get up and go. Enough that I could cut around slower-moving cars and rush through intersections.

But then a thought occurred to me: I was an American woman, without a passport, without a Brazilian driver's license, and I was wearing nothing but a bloody shirt, with a bloody knife still clutched in my shifter-hand. Maybe I shouldn't draw too much attention to myself. So I braked to fade in with the traffic, forcing myself to keep calm and look like I knew what I was doing.

I didn't.

I hadn't thought past getting out of the hotel.

So now I was in a strange city, alone, half-naked, with no money, no ID, no means of communicating with anyone. I mean, I knew Kyrie's cell phone number by heart, but I didn't have a phone, and I didn't know how to dial out of the country.

I turned at random, weaving around the city with no particular destination in mind, trying to come up with a plan. I needed money, and I needed to get hold of Kyrie so she could tell Harris how to find me.

Step one, change out of the bloody shirt.

I pulled into an alley and drove halfway down,

put the jalopy in neutral and set the e-brake, left the motor running. I shucked the bloody shirt and tossed it out the window and into a nearby Dumpster. I slipped the boots off and threw those away too. I changed into the valet's shirt, shorts, and flip-flops. Thank god he was a short, skinny little shit; the clothes were actually a little small. The blue shorts ended up hugging my thighs and ass, and the maroon shirt barely covered my tits, and when I did get it over them, it was tighter than a damn sports bra. The sandals were a little big, which worked out. My hair was a mess, so I searched around on the floorboards on the passenger side—this guy obviously lived in his car, as it was an unholy disaster area of random crap. I found a rubber band eventually and used it to tie my hair back—it'd be a bitch to untangle later, but it kept my hair out of my eyes for now.

There was even a scratched-up pair of dollar-store style sunglasses in the back. And—score!—some tightly-rolled dollar bills in the glove box. Pesos? What did Brazil use for currency? I unrolled one and examined it; they were *reals*, apparently. Pink, with a picture of a sculpture on the front, the numeral 5 in the top right and bottom left corners. I counted them—I had a hundred *real*. *Reals*? The correct plural didn't matter. Thank you Pedro—I would nickname my valet benefactor Pedro, I decided—for being a money squirrel.

Attired more like a normal human being rather than a horror movie victim, I felt like maybe I had a chance, now. A slim one, but it was something.

It's amazing how a set of non-bloody clothes can improve a girl's mood, huh?

I backed out of the alley carefully, watching oncoming traffic for a clear spot. I pulled out, and headed away. I drove at a sedate, unhurried pace, sweating buckets, cutting a direct line one way, then turning left and driving for several more miles, and then turning right and going even further, just trying to get away from the scene of the crime. I checked my mirrors regularly, watching for signs that I was being followed but, so far, nothing.

I found a gas station with a small market, put one of my precious five-*real* bills'-worth of gas into the tank, and went in to the little shop. I got a bottle of water, what I hoped was a protein bar, and a map of the area. At the counter, I saw prepaid cell phones and minute cards. Of course, the instructions were in Portuguese, but I'm a smart girl, I hoped I'd be able to figure it out. I grabbed a phone and a card and passed it to the cashier. He rang me up, passed it all back to me.

And then, squinting, he spoke. "American?" He was an older guy, a little salt in his hair, wrinkles and weather on his skin.

You'd think with my hair and skin color that I'd be able to pass for a local, but apparently not. I just nodded. "Yeah. American."

He chewed on something in his mouth, and then ripped open the phone, took the minutes packages and withdrew the SIM card, glanced at the instructions, and then spent a few minutes pressing buttons and listening. Eventually, he closed the phone—an old clamshell-style phone, the cheapest one he had, as it was all I could afford—and handed it to me.

He circled a set of instructions on the minute plan packaging and shoved it at me. "Dial home. Ring America. Easy."

He must have assumed I was a student or tourist, lost, and trying to call home. True enough, and thank god there were still nice people in the world.

I was closer to tears at his kindness than I could remember being in a long, long time. "Thank you! Thank you so much! *Gracias!*"

He laughed at me, waving a hand. "Nah. *Não é nada.*"

I got in the car with my purchases, and as I checked my mirrors, I happened to get a good look at my face. Well shit, no wonder the old guy took pity on me: I looked like I'd gone three or four rounds with Manny Pacquiao, with predictable results. My left eye was quickly going purple, my lips were split and puffy, I had a cut on my right cheekbone, and I'd bled from the nose at some point, although it had stopped on its own, but had left a sticky trail of dried blood on my upper lip.

I got back out of the car and went in to the market, making a beeline for the bathroom. There wasn't much I could do but wipe at the blood and rinse my face with cold water, but it was better than nothing.

"Bad boyfriend," the clerk said, as I passed him.

"What?"

He gestured at me. "Boyfriend no good."

I nodded, and felt an absurd compulsion to laugh. "Yeah, but you should see what he looks like."

"You kick ass?" His face lit up with a grin.

"Yeah buddy, I kicked his ass good."

He nodded, his expression fierce. "Hit girl no good. Hit pretty girl? *Very* no good." I laughed at that. Apparently hitting any girl was bad, but hitting a beautiful one was especially bad. Good thing I'm pretty, then, right? The old man gestured. "You go Guarujá. Drive to *o mar*. Very pretty, much relax."

"I will. Thanks. *Gracias.*"

He laughed again, pointed at me. "No *gracias.* No *Espanhol.* You say '*obrigado.*'"

"*Obrigado,*" I repeated

"*Sim, sim. Obrigado.*" He waved at me again,

and I left.

I got back into my "borrowed" car, the interior of which felt like it was at least a hundred and fifty degrees, even with all the windows down. Brazil was fucking *hot*, dude. I sat in the driver's seat, the engine running, the radio playing some kind of local club music, examining my map. *Rodovia dos Imigrantes* seemed like my best shot for driving to this Guarujá—which I wasn't even going to pretend I knew how to pronounce. Now I just had to figure out where I was currently and how to get to the *Rodovia*-whatever-whatever. But first, it seemed, I had to go through both São Vincente and Santos, across a bridge, and through Guarujá. But then if I wanted to go the ocean, why not just stop in Santos? The old guy had specified Guarujá, though, so I'd go there.

I found the most direct route according to the map, dug a pen out of the glove box, and outlined the path I'd need to take, memorizing the numbers of the roads—the 160 to the 101 to the 248. So not through Santos at all, now that I checked the route again; I would be skirting north of there, staying to the mainland as opposed to going through the island of São Vincente. Whatever. I just had to get out of São Paulo. Find somewhere to lay low, get hold of Kyrie, and wait for Harris. Hopefully without any more super-fun run-ins with Vitaly's army of assholes.

So, I took my map *back* inside the market and showed it to the clerk. He spent a few moments staring at it, finger tracing one road or another until he located our current location—which, it turned out, was only a few miles away from the highway I needed. He grabbed a pen from the counter and drew a path for me on the map so I'd know how to get to the interstate, or the highway, or whatever the road was called. The big road out of São Paulo. *Rodovia dos*-something-about-immigrants.

Let me try this once more, this time with feeling.

I actually left the gas station, followed the helpful clerk's directions to the *Rodovia dos Imigrantes*, and hit the highway. Except for a bunch of cars whose makes and models I didn't recognize, and all the signage being in Portuguese, the trip was a lot like any road trip across anywhere in the US. Green grass on either side along with some scrub brush, palm trees in a hot breeze, semis and buses and passenger cars zipping back and forth.

I had two major concerns: running out of gas, and running out of food and water. I had one lonely little five-*real* bill left, unless my buddy Pedro had more cash stashed somewhere in his ride. I felt bad about stealing the dude's car *and* all his bank, but a girl has to do what a girl has to do, right? I was alone in a foreign country, didn't speak the language, and I'd just killed the right-hand man of a crime syndicate's top boss.

Not going there. Not thinking about putting a ballpoint pen through Cut's eye. Not thinking about the way he twitched and gurgled, or the fact that he shit himself. Shit. Shitshitshit.

I had to swing off the road and onto the shoulder so I could lean out the open window and retch.

Keep it together, Layla, I told myself. I couldn't afford to fall apart. Not now.

Iron will. Iron will.

I steadied my breathing, pushed away the images of Cut's violent death at my hands. Pushed away any and all emotions. Feel nothing. There was nothing in this moment, nothing but doing whatever was necessary to get myself out of this.

While I was stopped, I followed the instructions for calling out of the country and dialed Kyrie's number from memory, pulled the car out onto the freeway and tucked the phone between my shoulder and my ear, since I didn't think the archaic cell phone had speakerphone technology.

The line rang once, twice, three times...four, five, six. "Come on, bitch," I muttered, "pick up the damn phone."

I heard a click, and then a smooth male voice. "Who is this?"

I choked, blinked back blurry stinging salt out of my eyes. The relief I felt was immeasurable. NOPENOPENOPE. I'm not crying. For sure I'm not crying. "I—Harris? It's—It's Layla."

A pause. "Layla?" Another pause. "Sit-rep? Um, I mean, what is your situation?"

"I know what a fucking sit-rep is, Harris—I watch TV. I'm fine. I got away."

"Where are you?"

"Brazil. Heading out of São Paulo toward— well, I don't know how to pronounce it. A city on the coast, south of São Paulo. Starts with a 'G' and has an 'A' with a slant over it at the end. *Gwar-yooh-jah* or some shit."

"Guarujá." He said it *gwar-ooh-zha*. "Good plan. I can be there in—less than twelve hours. Are you hurt?"

I hesitated. "I'm fine. I can last twelve hours."

"Layla." He said my name…softly. Strangely inflected, like with emotion and shit. It made my heart squirm and my stomach flop. "What did they do to you?"

"Nothing, really. Nothing to worry about. I got away. I'm alive, not permanently damaged, and I'm in transit."

"How'd you manage that?"

"I stole a dude's car. He had some money in it, so I bought a prepaid cell phone. A nice gas station guy hooked it up for me. I don't know if I'll have enough gas to get all the way there, but I've got my route mapped out. I can walk if needed."

"I'm impressed." It sounded like he wanted to say a lot more, but kept it to himself.

"I grew up in Detroit, Harris. This shit is cake."

"Think you're being pursued?"

"No. Not yet, at least. When they find—well, when Vitaly finds out what I had to do to get away, I'm sure he'll send guys after me with a vengeance. But for now, I'm not being followed. Vitaly's in Brasilia for a few days, Cut said, so it might be hours at least before Vitaly is even aware that I'm gone. Depends on if his maid at the hotel knows how to get hold of him or his guys. We'll see."

A rife pause from Harris. "Layla…? You met Vitaly?"

"I met a lot of people. But yes, I met Vitaly hisownself. He's a scary motherfucker, Harris." I tried to keep my voice even and calm but couldn't quite stop a quaver.

"What did you have to do to get away?" This, said softly, in that same concerned tone.

"Nothing I'm willing to talk about on the phone.

I gotta keep my shit together. Maybe after you've rescued me I'll let myself think about it. But for right
now, don't worry about me. I'm fine."

"Get to Guarujá, Layla. Find somewhere to hide
out. Don't talk to anyone. Don't stop for anything.
I'll be there as soon as I possibly can, okay? You're
going to be fine. I'm on my way."

I wanted to say so many things. "Harris?"

"Yes, Layla?" God, that tone in his voice. No
one had ever spoken to me like that, as if I mattered
more than anything.

"I'm fine. This is like a road trip. Just…in Brazil."
I was trying to convince myself more than anything.

"You're just fine. Everything is fine. We're on va-
cation together."

"I'm gonna go lie on the beach and put on my
bikini and get some sun. Drink a few dozen mai tais."

This earned me a chuckle. "Mai tais are more
Hawaii, babe. You're in Brazil. Have a piña colada."

He called me 'babe.' I tried not to love that, and
totally failed. "How about straight tequila?"

"Does tequila make your clothes fall off?"

"I hate country music, Harris."

He laughed. "Yet you got the reference. Must
not hate it *too* much. And I bet tequila does make
your clothes fall off."

"Yeah, it kind of does. But then…so does whiskey, and rum, and wine." I hesitated. "I can't afford that many minutes, so I should go. Save them for emergencies."

He laughed, and then sang a few bars of the Joe Nichols song, his voice surprisingly smooth and melodic. "Keep your eyes open," he finally said. "Don't trust anyone. And…do whatever you have to."

"Just get here," I said, and then ended the call before he could hear the knot in my throat.

I didn't cry. I was just sweating…from my tear ducts. I had a little sniffle. A summer cold.

No big deal.

Harris is coming. Harris is coming. Harris is coming.

12

LOST AND FOUND

I MADE IT TO THE OCEAN. THE 248 ENDED IN THE middle of the city, which got me turned around and required a lot of circling and hunting before I found the shore, but I made it. I was puttering along a road whose name I couldn't pronounce—something-something-*da Fonesca*, the ocean on my right, cars crawling slowly bumper to bumper and parallel parked and honking, tourists and locals moving in packs on the sidewalks, and the engine coughed, sputtered, and gave out.

Right in the middle of the road, the engine just up and died. I turned the ignition, the engine sputtered a few more times, wheezed, turned over, and then, surprisingly, caught just long enough for me to hang a left onto *Avenida Puglisi* and drift into a handicap parking spot before the motor coughed like an asthmatic smoker and died again. I rested my head on the steering wheel, sweat dripping off my nose and sliding down my spine, smeared on my face and my shoulders and…everywhere.

Brazil is fucking hot.

I'd long since drunk the last of my water and the protein bar was also long gone. I had five *real*, and a pocketknife.

But Harris was coming.

Time to hide.

I spent a few minutes ransacking Pedro's car, digging under the seats and in the glove box and in all the crevices, but only came up with a single crumpled one-*real* bill. I popped the trunk and checked in there, but he'd taken anything of value out of it, leaving only some garbage, an empty plastic bag, a tire iron and donut spare, an empty red gas can, and some empty baggies that had once held pot.

I found a scrap of paper and wrote "*obrigado*" on it, set it on the driver's seat with the keys under the seat, and then set out on foot.

I trudged out from the relative cool and shade provided by the buildings of the downtown area and down to the beach, removing my flip-flops and stuffing them in my back pockets. The dry sand was hotter than Satan's asshole, but I trotted through it to the surf, letting the water slosh over my bare feet. There wasn't a cloud in the sky overhead, only a stiff, steady, hot breeze from off the water.

I just walked. North, I was pretty sure, but it didn't really matter. The beach was actually fairly deserted, only a few couples and individuals here and there. I tried to seem at ease, as if I was just a lone tourist taking a walk on the beach.

I made it as far north as the beach would go until it ended at a cluster of high-rise condo buildings butting up right to the edge of the sea, hiding what looked like an outcropping of rock covered by a scrim of jungle. I kept walking, following the narrow streets uphill and around the ridge jutting out of the hillside and back down to the beach.

Know what I did then?

I walked.

And walked.

And walked.

Theoretically, I could probably just keep walking up the coast of Brazil until there was no more beach. In reality, I was fucking tired of walking. But what else could I do? I didn't have money for a hotel, or food. I couldn't just sit down on the beach and wait for the next ten hours. I didn't want to stop, didn't dare stop moving. If I stopped moving, I'd start thinking. If I started thinking, I'd have a nervous goddamn breakdown because I'd killed a man two hours ago. And once I started dwelling on that happy little fact, I might never stop bawling like a baby.

So I walked.

I followed the beach and tried to just enjoy the sunlight and the heat and the ocean and the beauty of Brazil, and tried not to think. I just walked. Eventually, after maybe three miles, the beach ended at another rising mountain of jungle, this one much larger and more permanent, as in not the kind of outcropping you could walk around. So I picked a road and started following it, passing a lovely café right on the water, the kind of place where I'd have loved to be able sit at a table and watch people come and go, eat, drink, argue, kiss. But I didn't dare stop. So I followed the road, up, up, up. It just kept going up, half-finished high-rises on my left, the jungle on my right stopping just at the road's edge. Not a nice area, necessarily, not for tourists. But I kept going. Unwisely, perhaps, but I was committed to just walking, walking, walking.

The jungle gave way to a mammoth hotel, and I realized I was topping the rise. Sort of.

Okay, no, not really. There was still a lot of hill left to climb.

A *lot* of hill.

Jesus.

I started climbing and was sweating balls, out of breath, and exhausted beyond all comprehension, but I'd started up this hill and by god I'd make it to the top. Just because I'm fucking stubborn that way.

Up. Up. Up.

It eventually crested with the sea far below and off in the distance, blue and hazy, nothing but an outcropping of tree-covered rock ahead and a handful of dilapidated, white-washed buildings off to my right. The road turned into ancient, cracked octagonal cobblestones, angling to my right toward the cliff's edge. A hand-painted sign announced a telephone number, and beneath the number were some Portuguese words, and one word in English that I recognized: "camping"—a campground, then. Rundown, out of the way, and shitty.

Perfect.

A trio of chickens meandered past me, clucking to each other, seeking shade under a lone palm tree, hustling a little faster as I passed them. At the road's edge was a white-washed cinderblock building topped by a slab of corrugated tin, nothing but some cheap chicken-wire fencing at the very cliff's edge. A couple of yellow signs announced something or other in Portuguese, which obviously I didn't read. But I did know enough back-of-the-house restaurant

Spanish to recognize that "*fritata*" and "*coco verde*" probably meant food of some kind. That, plus the rickety plastic table and chairs and the bright pink umbrella, meant this was very likely a restaurant of some kind.

Way out here, five *real* might just get me something to drink and somewhere to sit and not have to walk for a few hours.

In I went. It was dark, the ceilings low, and it smelled wonderfully of frying food. It was hot, but cooler than outside, a window AC unit puffing away noisily somewhere, and a wide-bladed fan overhead lazily stirred the air.

So… "restaurant" may have been stretching things a bit.

But it was a public establishment, and it was deserted, so I could probably kill time here without attracting any attention.

There was a table near the door, and I sat down with my back to the wall so I could watch the interior as well as the door and the street beyond. I heard voices in the back chattering in Portuguese, but I was in no hurry. I was just glad to be off my feet and out of the sun. Eventually a tiny, hunched old woman emerged from somewhere, saw me, and started exclaiming excitedly, hustling over to me, placing a twenty-year old laminated menu in front of me. It had maybe six items on it, none of which I recognized, but at least the numbers next to the items told me I could probably make the last of my stolen money stretch enough to get me a meal and something to drink.

I spoke over the old woman's excited rambling. "American. I speak *Inglés.*"

"Oh...no, no. No *Inglés.*" And then she was off again, chattering way too fast for me to catch anything even if I did speak the tiniest amount of Portuguese, which I didn't. Except "thank you", which was *obrigado*.

Um.

"*Agua?*" That was Spanish again, but it was all I had to go with.

She understood, bustling away and returning with a tall translucent red plastic cup, the kind you used to get at Pizza Hut. It was full of ice water, and I took it and guzzled it down greedily, offering my best version of "*obrigado,*" which made her grin and chatter something else at me.

I fished the crumpled five-*real* bill out of my pocket and set it on the table, gestured at the menu with a shrug, and then patted my belly. Which hopefully translated to "Pick something for me, lady, because this is all the money I have and I don't read Portuguese."

Apparently she understood, because she took the money, stuffed it into her apron pocket, and vanished. She returned with a fresh glass of ice water and then vanished once more. This time she was gone for about twenty minutes, which were gloriously silent, except for the occasional crackle of ice against the red plastic. When she returned, it was with a plate loaded down with a shitload of food.

It looked like little balls of something deep fried, a large *empanada* sort of thing, but bigger and flatter and crispier-looking, and then a huge glop of rice and beans topped by what looked like a fried flour substance mixed with bacon and peppers of some sort. It smelled like heaven. But way too much food for a measly five *real*. I stuffed my hands in my pockets and turned them out to show that I had no more money, and then shrugged broadly.

The woman just waved at me, and a dismissive grandmotherly wave is the same all over the world, it seemed. "*Comer! Comer!*" she said, gesturing at the plate.

I'd seen the gesture before, but in Italian—"*Mangia! Mangia!*", or "Eat! Eat!".

I thanked her again, picked up the fork and tried one of the deep fried balls. Ho-leeee shit. Best. Thing. Ever. It had some kind of creamy melted cheese and shredded chicken inside it, and it was divine.

The woman pointed at the deep fried balls when I stabbed another one. "Coxinhas." *Co-sheen-yas*.

Delicious.

The empanada-thing was next. I forked it open and discovered that it contained more melted, gooey cheese, ground beef, sautéed white onions, and jalapeños. She called it a *pastéis*. I didn't care what she called it, as long as I could keep eating it. The rice and beans and flour concoction was just as amazing as everything else, so by the time I finished I was sated, stuffed, and happy.

I wished I had more money to give her, but I didn't, so I had to settle for effusive thanks, which the woman just waved away. I took my cup of ice water—my third one—and moved out to the table on the patio, sitting in the shade of the umbrella, and stared out at the sea.

Gradually, my belly full and my anxiety lessened, I decided to rest my head on my arms for a moment.

A scream woke me.

Not mine, but someone else's. A woman's. Terrified. Panicked.

I bolted upright, reaching into my back pocket for the knife. The patio was empty, but there was a big black SUV sitting with its engine idling and all four doors open. Definitely the kind of big black SUV a kingpin would send his thugs out in to look for a certain American girl.

I realized as well that my spot at the table with my head down and hidden behind the tilted umbrella meant that they *might* not have seen me. But they'd followed me here, somehow. I heard shouting, a gunshot, and a scream, the sound of a bullet piercing the tin roof.

What to do?

Duh. Only one thing *to* do: steal the truck. I hated letting the nice old lady get hurt over me, but hopefully the thugs wouldn't actually kill her if she didn't really know anything about me. I was essentially defenseless, anyway, so what could I do to help? Don't bring a knife to a gunfight and all, right?

Cursing under my breath, I watched the door for a split second, and then bolted, vaulting the low fence separating the patio from the parking lot, slid on dirt, ran around the SUV slamming the doors closed on my way to the driver's seat. I jumped in, hauled the door shut, and threw it into reverse, gunning it and jerking the wheel around. The powerful vehicle skidded backward and spun in a circle on the gravel, scattering hens and pebbles all over the place. I almost crashed into a nearby hut but I recovered and jerked the gear shift into drive, shoved the gas pedal to the floor.

I heard gunshots, and the back window shattered and the round buried itself in the passenger seat headrest. More rounds hit into the body, the rear quarter panel. Then I was around the corner and out their field of vision.

I hauled ass down the hill at a reckless speed, hit the beach and turned into the city.

How the hell had they found me?

My phone rang. Because of the traffic I was forced to go slow, so I answered it, watching my mirrors for signs of pursuit.

"Harris?"

"Yeah, it's me. I'm in São Paulo right now, headed down your way." I heard road noise in the background. "Where are you?"

"Still in Guarujá, although I've just run into trouble." I glanced in the rear-view mirror just then and saw a black SUV identical to the one I was driving cut into oncoming traffic, pass three cars, and pull up behind me.

"Trouble?"

"Yeah. I had this nice little spot out of the way

at this tiny little café. And they just…showed up. I don't know how they found me. I walked there, and didn't stop to talk to anyone. I didn't think anyone even fucking saw me." *BLAM*! A round slammed into the radio. "Shit. They're shooting at me."

"Do you have a gun?"

"No, but I have a knife. Hold on one second." I tossed the phone onto the passenger seat and jerked the wheel to the right and stood on the brakes.

This earned me a rear-ending which jolted me forward and gave me a nasty case of whiplash, but my pursuers shot past me, which was my goal. I gunned the engine and pulled up next to them, gritted my teeth, and hauled the wheel left, bashing into them. My window shattered and the door crumpled against my leg, but the other SUV didn't fare as well. I'd forced it into an oncoming cargo truck, which plowed into the black SUV, demolishing its front end. I floored the gas pedal and pulled away, cut left onto a one-way street, and then made a couple more turns at random.

"Layla!" I heard his voice distantly, tinny, and remembered the phone.

"Harris, hey, I'm here. Sorry about that."

"Are you okay?" He sounded panicked. Well, maybe not panicked exactly, but concerned at the very least.

"Yeah, I'm okay. I sideswiped them into oncoming traffic. I think I lost them."

"Don't assume. There are always more."

"Thanks for the reassurance," I said, deadpan. "I'm pretty sure I just caused a lot of injury and death."

"You want me to lie to you?" he asked.

"No," I admitted. "Keep telling me the truth."

"The truth is you're going to be fine. Keep doing whatever it takes to avoid letting them get their hands on you. Don't worry about the collateral damage; just pretend you're in a Jerry Bruckheimer movie, all right? Get back to the 160, the road you took south out of São Paulo. Head north, and call me when you're on it. We'll figure out a place to meet."

"Got it."

"All right. See you soon."

"Promise?" I hated how vulnerable I managed to sound in those two little stupid syllables.

"I promise, Layla."

Click. I hung up on him, to save him the difficulty of saying goodbye. And because if I didn't hang up right then, my thin façade of strength would come crumbling down. I'm a tough bitch, but everyone's got a breaking point, and I was nearing mine.

I managed to find the road north, totally by accident. I was checking my rear-view mirror regularly, watching for any more black SUVs, but so far I'd seen nothing. They'd managed to find me when I'd been absolutely positive I'd gotten away clean. Had they planted a tracker in me, like some kind of Tom Cruise spy movie? I mean, how else could you explain them just showing up like that? Only sheer luck and a big pink umbrella had prevented them from seeing me.

When I was out of the city proper I called Harris back, told him I was on the 160 heading north, and hung up before he could say anything.

With two broken windows, the ride was noisy and windy. My leg ached from where the door had crumpled, and I was pretty sure I didn't want to look down there to assess the damage. My neck was sore and stiff too, from the whiplash. Also, the climb up the hill had exhausted me.

But at least I wasn't hungry, right?

Always look on the bright side of life.

If you're humming the Monty Python song, then I love you forever.

Thirty minutes of driving lulled me into complacence; my phone rang, startling me enough that I shrieked and jerked the wheel, nearly sideswiping the car next to me.

"Hello?"

"It's me," Harris said. "We should be getting

close to each other. Have you reached the point where the north and southbound lanes merge, yet?"

Leaving Guarujá, the north- and southbound traffic lanes were often far apart, taking totally different routes through the mountainous terrain, only joining a good thirty miles or so north and west.

"No," I said, "not yet."

"Okay, good. When the lanes start merging, I want you to pull over and hide in the woods in the median. Get as far north as you can, so you're at the very edge of the woods, looking north. I'll find you. You see anyone else but me coming for you…well, do what have to."

"Okay. Got it."

"Any questions?" he asked, his voice firm and brusque and calm.

"Just one."

"What is it?"

"Does knowing you've killed someone ever get easier?"

He didn't answer right away. "Yes and no. Like anything else, the more you do it, the easier it becomes. But that comes with a price." Another pause. "We'll talk more when we're together."

"It was ugly, Harris." Why the hell was I saying any of this? I didn't want to think about it. I'd been trying not to.

"Death *is* ugly, Layla. No two ways about it."

"I'll see you soon."

"Yes, you will." He was the one to hang up, this time.

I tossed the phone on the passenger seat and focused on driving, focused on watching the terrain and watching for pursuit. After another ten minutes, I saw the southbound traffic lane in the distance, off to my left, just a strip of gray in the green of the forest, sunlight glinting occasionally on windshields. When the lanes were a hundred yards or so apart, a thin screen of trees appeared in the ever-decreasing space between lanes. I moved into the left-hand lane and slowed down, earning horn honks and angry shouts as the faster-moving traffic swerved around me.

Another three minutes, and the median narrowed yet further and the trees thinned to a point. There wasn't a shoulder, so I had to pull off the highway and directly onto the grass, thudding and bouncing as I braked to a halt. I shut the engine off, left the keys in the ignition, palmed my phone in one hand and my knife in the other, glancing in both directions. I was earning a lot of looks, but no one was stopping, yet.

I took off running for the trees.

As I made the tree line, I heard a car door close

somewhere behind me.

Shit. Of course.

It was a big black SUV, parked directly behind mine. Five men were moving toward me, and each one was blatantly carrying a machine gun. They strode toward me calmly, unhurried, making directly for my position.

Now what the actual fuck? I'd been watching behind me every step of the way, and I would have sworn on a stack of bibles that I hadn't been followed. Yet here they were, coming right for me.

"Fuck. Fuck. FUCK!" I shouted it the last time, and one of the men laughed.

It wasn't a pleasant sound.

I ducked behind a tree, unfolded my knife, and dialed Harris.

He answered before it had rung twice. "Layla?"

"Yeah, it's me. I'm where you told me to go, in the trees on the median. They're right behind me, Harris, they're coming for me. Five of them, and they have big fuck-off machine guns. How did they find me, Harris? What do I do?"

"I'm almost there. Run south, okay? Stay just inside the trees, but run south, closer to the southbound lanes. You'll know what to do when the time comes."

"What the fuck does that mean?" I sounded

shrill, but I had reason, I'd say.

"Trust me, babe. Run south. Watch for me."

Click.

Super.

I twisted and glanced around the trunk of the tree. They were approaching the trees, now. Shit-shitshit. I took off running south, bouncing off tree trunks and ducking branches.

Crack! Crackcrackcrackcrack! Bark exploded to my left, spraying my face with splinters. I ducked and cut right, then left, not daring to look behind me. The machine gun cracked again, and then another one, off to my left. They weren't playing around, obviously. No more orders to bring me back alive, clearly.

Kill the bitch, I was sure they'd been told.

I poured on speed, running as fast as I could, as hard as I could, arms in front of my face to knock aside branches. I felt something cut my right arm, followed a split second later by a snapping sound, and then the report of the machine gun. An angry buzz sounded on my left. I wasn't sure quite why, but the *snap* scared me more than the buzz.

To my right, off in the distance, an engine roared; I glanced that way and saw a green SUV with a white roof bouncing at full speed across the grass. It's strange the details you notice in high-adrenaline situations: I couldn't have told you what kind of car the SUV I'd stolen was, nor the model of the jalopy I'd stolen in São Paulo. But somehow, in a split-second glance from over a hundred yards away, I knew the vehicle Harris was driving was a Land Rover Defender, the older kind you see used for African safaris in documentaries narrated by the late, great Richard Attenborough.

I left the cover of the trees, machine guns still barking behind me and to my left. I ran out in the open now, risking glances every couple seconds at Harris. He didn't slow down, and as he approached behind me, I saw that his window was open and he was driving with one hand, a small black pistol in the other. I heard the bark of his pistol, saw the muzzle flash—silver dents appeared in the rear driver's side door, two, three, four, evidence that they were shooting back. Harris jerked the huge SUV to cut behind me and braked to a sudden halt, the rear end of the truck sliding and ripping up chunks of grass and spraying mud. He leaned over and threw open the door, and I leaped into the opening, landing hard on the bench. Harris didn't wait for me to get the door closed, just gunned the engine, slewing around in an arc, his right hand jerking the manual gear shifter down into second as his feet moved like lightning, popping the clutch and flooring the gas. The door swung open, bounced at the apex of its hinge-range, and then swayed toward me as the truck darted forward, hitting a hillock in the grass and going airborne. I got a handhold on the seatback and leaned out, hooked the door handle with three fingers, and jerked the door closed with a slam.

Somehow, Harris was driving with one hand, firing his pistol out the window with the other, and still finding time to shove the shifter through third and into fourth as we picked up speed, still jouncing violently across the grass heading south.

"I'm going to swing us around," Harris said, without looking at me. "I want you to get down under the window as we pass them." He accompanied his words with actions, downshifting to second and slamming on the brakes, hauling the wheel around so the truck juddered around in an arc, swaying and tipping precariously.

All five of the bad guys were lined up abreast, guns lifted to shoulders, pointing at us.

"Layla, get *down*!" Harris snapped.

Gunfire erupted from all five of them, and I heard several metallic *thunks* as rounds hit the body of the Range Rover.

"Fuck you," I growled. "Give me that."

I snatched the pistol from him, held it in both hands and pointed the barrel at one of the bad guys.

I squeezed the trigger, expecting the roar and the kick but still shocked by it. We passed by them so fast I wasn't sure if I'd hit anything, but it was the thought that counted.

"You know how to shoot?" Harris seemed surprised.

"I used to hook up with a guy who was a manager at a firing range. He showed me how."

"Well it was a good shot," he said. "I think you winged one of 'em." He grabbed the gun back as we bounced along parallel to the northbound traffic.

Holding the wheel and the pistol in the same hand, he shifted up into fourth and we went briefly airborne as we merged onto the blacktop, causing a pile-up when a little blue sedan had to brake and swerve to avoid us. I heard the crash behind us, but didn't spare it a look.

"Just like a Jerry Bruckheimer movie," I said, hearing further metal-on-metal impacts.

"You should have ducked. I fucking told you to duck, goddamn it." Oooooh shit. Harris was pissed.

"Yeah, well...I never do what I'm told. Get used to it, buddy."

"You want to live? You'd better learn to listen."

"Are you really going to argue with me about this right now?" I asked, glaring at him. "You haven't even said hello."

He stared at me, incredulous. "Hello, Miss Campari. How are you? Having a nice day? Would you care for some tea?"

I flipped him the bird. "Don't be a dick, *Nicholas*."

"I swear to fuck I'll throw you out of this car," he snarled. "Do *not* call me Nicholas. Not even my mother calls me that."

"I'm having trouble reconciling the idea of you sitting in a tasteful Midwestern bungalow, drinking sun tea with your sweet little mother."

This earned me a chuckle. "Everyone has a mother, Layla. Even me. But no, they don't live in a *bungalow* in the Midwest, they live in a condo in Florida. And my mother is not sweet, nor particularly little." A pause, and then he grinned at me. "Although, she does drink sun tea, funny enough."

"What does she call you, then?"

He didn't respond right away. "Not Nicholas," he said, eventually. He gestured behind us. "See if they're back there. Look back several car lengths."

I twisted on the bench seat, peering into the dense traffic behind us. "Shit. Yeah, they're back there. Quite a ways back, like maybe half a mile or so, but they're there."

"Vitaly's men don't give up. They'll keep coming until we kill them or they catch us."

"No shit. They don't dare go back to Vitaly without results to show him," I said.

Harris glanced at me, his gaze sharp, and his voice soft. "No?"

I shook my head as I returned to my seat and buckled up. "No. They don't dare. He doesn't accept failure or excuses. You do what he tells you to do, or you die trying. If you show up and you haven't carried out his orders to the letter, he'll kill you. And you'll never even see it coming."

"How does he kill them?"

I blinked hard. "Knife to the ribs." I tapped two fingers over my heart. "He's got this switchblade, keeps it in his pocket. He'll just be talking, calm as anything. One second he's smiling, hands in his pockets, casual, the picture of understanding and congeniality. The next? That blade is between their ribs, and they're dead. He does it so fast, so easily. Doesn't even blink. I saw him do it at least six times in the four days I was his prisoner. He must pay those guys really well if they're willing to risk death any time they're in the room with him."

"Recruit from the poor and desperate, pay them well, and they'll put up with just about anything," Harris remarked. A few minutes of silence, and then he glanced at me again. "Layla, when you were with Vitaly—"

I shook my head, cut him off. "Not now, Harris. I can't go there right now." I focused on breathing slowly and evenly, staring straight ahead, refusing to blink, refusing to unclench my teeth. "Get me somewhere relatively safe first, and maybe I'll tell you what happened."

Harris nodded. "I can do that." He checked his rear-view mirror. "So I just gotta figure out how to lose these guys."

"Do what you'd do if you were alone. Don't worry about me."

"I just rescued you, Layla. I'm not about to put you in harm's way again."

"Meaning you'd stop and shoot it out with them, if it were just you, right?"

He bobbled his head side to side. "I'd ambush them."

"So let's ambush them."

"No offense, Layla, but I'm a highly trained combat veteran, and you're—"

"I stabbed a guy in the eyeball with a pen I'd kept hidden in my cunt for over a week. I shoved it so far into his fucking brain that he died instantly. And that was after I broke his arm like a twig. I did this because he was in the process of raping me. I put on his blood-soaked clothes, his smelly boots—I had to wear his clothes because Vitaly had kept me naked the entire time—and I stole a car, stopped for supplies, drove to fucking Guarujá, walked several miles in the blazing heat, most of that distance either in the sand or uphill, without having any food or water. And then I stole a car right out from underneath the very men who were hunting me." I was getting a little worked up at this point. "And then— and *then!*—then I was nearly shot several times just now by those *assholes* back there. So I think at this point, Nicholas, there isn't much that's going to faze me. Figure out how you want to ambush these fuckers, and I'll help you kill every single goddamn one of those pussies."

Harris's jaw worked up and down, as if he was trying to respond but didn't actually have any words. "Jesus, Layla."

"If you were hoping for a damsel in distress, you've got the wrong bitch. I may be in distress, but I'm sure as shit not a fucking helpless damsel."

A long, tense moment passed, in which Harris tried to figure out what to say. "You called me Nicholas again."

"Yes I did, and you can either deal with it or shove me out of the car. I don't care. I'll figure this shit out, one way or another, with you or without you."

"You're fucking impossible," he grumbled.

I laughed. "You're just now figuring that out?"

He shook his head. "No, you're just reaching an all-time-high impossibility factor."

"Buddy, you ain't seen nothin' yet."

"That's a scary thought," Harris said.

"I'm from Detroit. Don't fuck with me." I crossed my arms over my chest and kept an eye on the passenger-side mirror, watching as the black SUV closed the distance. "They're getting closer. If you've got a plan, I'd start putting it into play if I were you."

A body of water rippled pale blue in the distance; traffic was getting thicker and thicker by the moment.

Harris gestured at the water. "Once we're past this causeway, we'll be hitting Batistini. I'll make my move there."

"What's in Batistini?" I asked.

"There isn't shit in Batistini, it's just the first suburb of São Paulo we'll get to. It's hard to ambush someone in the car on the freeway."

"I guess that's true. But I've never ambushed anyone, so I wouldn't know."

We were on the causeway that stretched out over the lake, and a sign over the road announced the exits for Batistini. It struck me as funny that despite the fact that I was in a totally different country and that I didn't speak, read, or write the language in the slightest, the highway signs were totally under-standable anyway. I mean, I didn't understand the words, but based on the layout of the sign, *saída* was probably equivalent to "exit", and *diadema* was close enough to "diadem" that it probably represented the ring of highways around the city of São Paulo.

Harris took the exit for Batistini, and sure enough, the SUV behind us followed, staying at least four or five car-lengths behind us. Obviously they had no intention of pushing the confrontation on the highway either. Too much risk of things going wrong in our favor, I guess. When we hit the resi-dential area—which was a graffiti-tagged, run-down area—Harris gunned the engine and pulled away from our pursuers, twisted around a tight right turn, gunned it again so the tires spat gravel, pushing me back in my seat, the engine roaring. I heard tires squealing behind us, still several car-lengths back. I revised my estimate of the area as being poor, sim-ply judging based on the number of well-kept cars parked on the street.

Another long straightaway, a left turn, and then we were on a narrow gravel road running parallel to the highway, the scrub-covered hillside leading up to the highway on our left, a cinderblock wall hiding a junk yard on the right, full of rusting semi trail-ers, ancient buses, and random bits of metal. Harris pulled into a driveway, the highway on our left, a ramshackle warehouse or factory on the right. There was a short, low awning under which Harris parked the Land Rover. The outside of the warehouse on our right had been roofed over to create a porch, and on this makeshift porch was a cluster of middle-aged men, all of them hard-bitten and hard-eyed, weathered faces lined with wrinkles, sweat dotting their foreheads, brown glass bottles of beer in their hands, cigarettes hanging out of their mouths. As Harris and I exited the Land Rover—which was older by a decade than I was, at least—the men on the porch stared at us, unblinking, mute. They were giving us the kind of stares a blond white girl would get if she were strolling down Cass Corridor at midnight. The kind of stares that say, "You are in the *wrong* neighborhood, and you'd best keep going if you know what's good for you."

Harris circled around to the back of the Defender, opened the trunk, and hauled out a huge black duffel bag. He hung the bag on his shoulder, and it gave a heavy, ominous *clank* as he did so. One of the men on the porch said something in Portuguese, and if I was any judge of tone of voice, it wasn't polite. Harris reached behind his back and leveled the pistol at the man who'd spoken, stepping closer to the porch in that quick, careful, lithe movement men trained in combat all seem to use, keeping his torso swiveled to the side, presenting as small a target as possible. Harris spoke in fluent Portuguese, his voice low and smooth and even, but still somehow fairly snarling with threat. He gestured with the pistol, and the entire cluster of men stood up, gripping their beer and cigarettes, and vanished into the warehouse.

"Do I want to know what you told them?" I asked.

"No," was all he said, and grabbed me by the hand and hauled me across the road, where a break in the wall had been hastily boarded over with lengths of two-by-fours and scraps of corrugated iron.

I climbed over the jury-rigged fence and then waited for Harris, who pulled me out of sight and used one hand to press me flat against the intact portion of the cinderblock wall.

He set the heavy bag down at his feet and wiped his brow with his palm, then wiped his palm on his khakis. "Please listen to me very carefully now, Layla, all right? If we're going to have any chance of getting out of this alive, you have *got* to do as I say."

I blinked sweat out of my eye and nodded at him. "Tell me what to do, Nicholas."

He narrowed his eyes at me. "First, stop calling

me that."

"How about Nick?"

He shook his head, irritated. "This isn't the time for this shit, Layla. Sure, Nick works. Now, are you done mouthing off?"

"I wasn't mouthing off, actually, but if you want to see what that sounds like, I can—"

"Jesus, Layla. Shut the fuck up and listen, would you?" he snarled. I shut my mouth with an audible click of my teeth, and gestured for him to continue. "Thank you. There's five of them, and two of us. You're not trained in the use of assault rifles, I'm assuming—correct me if I'm wrong, as you have a knack for surprising me. Point is, that's what they're carrying. What that means for us is this is gonna get gnarly. Bullets will be flying hot and heavy. I'm gonna put you in a position, and you're going to stay there, come hell or high water, until I tell you otherwise. You got it?"

I nodded. "Got it."

"I mean it. You *stay...there.* I don't care what you see or think you see, you stay fucking *put.* And keep your head down." An engine roared somewhere, and tires squealed. Harris cocked his head, listening. "They're close. We don't have much time."

He unzipped the duffel bag, and sure as shit, it was full of guns. "Well fuck me running, Harris, where the hell'd you get your hands on all that?"

"You forget I work for an ex-arms dealer," he responded, digging a pair of black 9mm semiautomatics out of the bag and handing them to me.

"I didn't actually know that," I said. "Roth was an arms dealer? No shit."

He glanced at me, digging four spare clips out of the bag and handing them to me as well. "Well, now you know." He gestured at the guns in my hand. "You can reload those, right?"

I showed him I could by ejecting the clip, checking it, and sliding it back in place, tapping it home with the hell of my palm—gently, contrary to popular silver-screen mythology. "Where do you want me?"

He pulled a short, compact assault rifle out of the bag, unfolded the stock, stuffed extra magazines in his back pockets, and slung the weapon by the strap on his shoulder and let it hang, then grabbed another handgun, this one a monster silver thing straight out of *Dirty Harry*. Zipping the bag, he secured it on his back and then led me at a trot through the knee-high grass toward the row of rusting trailers. There were a good half a dozen metal drums lying scattered in the grass, the kind of thing you'd see hobos warming their hands over in movies. Harris rolled one to lay between two closely parked trailers, grabbed a second and righted it, hauled it over, and then tipped a third to lay against both of the others, creating a makeshift barricade. The wall behind me was fully intact and all of ten feet high, so I didn't think anyone would be coming up from behind. I tucked the spare pistol into my waistband at my back—which is not as comfortable as TV would have you imagine—and the clips in my pockets.

Lying down prone, I glanced up at Harris. "Well? Don't just stand there, doofus. Go find your own spot."

He shook his head at me, a smirk quirking the corner of his mouth. When he was gone I closed my eyes and let myself feel the fear. I was fucking terrified, to put it frankly. None of this was normal, even for me. I'd been through some shit in my life, but lying in wait, preparing to ambush men who were trying to kill me? It was new. And not fun.

I do not recommend it.

But I've learned something important in going through all the crazy-ass bullshit life has thrown at me: if something heavy is about to go down, give yourself a moment to feel the emotions. Let them go, let them out, let them boil. And then shut it down—*hard*—and do what you gotta do.

A few moments of sweating balls in the blazing Brazilian heat, and then I heard tires on gravel and an engine lowering down to idle, doors opening and closing, men talking. Slides being pulled, footsteps crunching. Words were exchanged, voices were raised. A gun went off, making me jump, and then more shouts. Silence.

I couldn't see Harris anywhere.

I was on my belly, a pistol in my hands, pointing it through the gap in the stacked barrels at the opening in the wall where the bad guys had to come through. I checked the weapon in my hands, made sure the safety was off—it was a Glock, apparently, since it didn't have a safety. That was a little factoid I'd learned from Oliver, the guy who'd run the firing range: Glocks didn't have safeties.

I pulled the slide, doing so as quietly as I could, and then set it in the grass at my right hand, took the spare from my waistband, checked it, racked the slide on that one, and arranged my extra clips where I could grab them easily.

My hands shook.

My pulse thundered in my ears.

I was *not* ready for this. Killing a guy in self-defense was one thing. But lying in wait to kill people in cold blood…that was another prospect.

I couldn't do it.

Shit.

Shit.

What was I thinking?

A hand appeared in the fence break, holding onto the grip of some kind of compact machine gun. Harris would probably have a proper name for it, but I didn't give a shit what it was called. A kill-Layla device. That was all that mattered. The body followed, a short, stocky man with sweaty hair and a stained T-shirt.

My finger twitched on the trigger, but I waited; I'd start shooting only after Harris had. I didn't want to spoil the ambush by shooting too early.

Heh. I didn't want to shoot too early; I wondered idly if Harris had that problem. Probably not.

Jesus, Layla. Now is not the time to be thinking about Harris's sexual prowess.

Yes it was. It was always a good time to think about Harris's sexual prowess. He probably had a lot of prowess.

A second man followed the first, and then a third, and a fourth. And a fifth. They were each armed with a machine gun. They all looked extremely unpleasant.

The first man was about ten steps into the field as the fifth and final man was stepping over the makeshift area of fence. And that was when Harris cut loose. It happened so fast I barely registered it: there was a loud chattering crash, and the fifth man collapsed, falling into and effectively blocking the open section of fence. This happened in an eye-blink.

Another loud detonation—*CRACKCRACK-CRACK*—and the first man in line fell.

The other three scattered in three different directions, and I realized this was my cue. I adjusted my two-handed grip on the pistol, aimed at the torso of the left-most attacker, held my breath…squeezed the trigger.

BANG! The gun jumped in my hands, and my target twisted, stumbled, a red circle spreading on his stomach. Shit. I'd have to shoot him again. I aimed more carefully this time, drawing bead on his face. Deep breath, hold it…*BANG!*…let it out. He dropped, gurgling. I'd missed his head, the round going through his throat.

My stomach lurched, my eyes watered.

No time for that, bitch, I told myself.

I had no clue where Harris was hiding. I hadn't seen a muzzle flash, and the sound had bounced off the walls, effectively disguising its location of origin. Clearly the remaining two thugs weren't sure either, because they had both dropped to the ground in the waist-high grass and were firing their weapons at random, spraying bullets in every direction.

One pinged loudly off the barrel in front of me,

startling me so badly I screamed. Which, in hindsight, was a dumb idea. One of the bad guys stood up and moved toward me in a crouch, an evil grin on his face.

CRACKCRACK! He fell, toppling like a bag of bricks, his head exploding in a red mist. Oh fuck, that was nasty. His entire face was gone, just…gone.

Bile filled my mouth, and this time I couldn't choke it back.

I heard shouting in Portuguese. I spat the nastiness out of my mouth and then looked up to see Harris approaching the last man left alive. Harris gestured with his gun, and the man dropped his weapon, held up his hands.

"Stay there, Layla," Harris said, not looking in my direction.

I stayed put.

The man spoke, and Harris responded, his voice terse and harsh. The man said something else, and this time Harris responded with a shout, and the man backed up, both hands high in a gesture that clearly meant "no, no, don't shoot!"

Harris shot.

CRACK! One bullet right between the eyes. Harris lowered his weapon and moved from body to body, nudging them with his boot. One, the man I'd shot, moaned.

CRACK! The moaning stopped.

"You can come out now," Harris said.

He was rifling through the pockets of each of the dead men, taking clips, currency, and weapons. He stuffed everything he took into his black bag, which he then zipped and slung on his shoulder.

I was making my way through the grass, knees weak, stomach lurching, heart hammering. I tried not to look down at the red-stained grass, but I couldn't help it.

I stopped next to Harris and stared down at the man I'd shot. I'd hit him in the stomach and the throat, and Harris had finished him with a bullet in the forehead.

There was blood everywhere. The grass was crimson and wet, and the stink was nauseating.

"Okay?" Harris asked, glancing at me.

I shook my head negative. "I'm fine."

Harris barked a laugh. "Well that was clear as mud. I'll ask again, Layla. You good?"

I closed my eyes and focused on breathing shallowly and evenly. "Just get me out of here. Please?"

He reached out and took my hand. "You're fine. You did great. We're gone, okay?" I felt him squeeze my hand. "Look at me, Layla. Eyes on mine." I forced my eyes open; his gaze was calm and cool, his eyes green as freshly mown grass. "You did great."

"I shot him. Twice."

"He was going to kill you."

I shook my head. "No, he wasn't. He was going to bring me back to Vitaly. *He's* the one who wants to kill me, now. I think Cut was important to him. So now I'm on his shit list and so is Kyrie. He doesn't want us dead, he wants us alive so he can torture us and *then* kill us."

"Don't think about that," Harris said, hiking his bag higher on his shoulder and taking my other hand. "I'm with you, now. I'll get you out of here. I promise. No one else will ever lay a hand on you, or Kyrie. You have my word."

I felt weak, shaky, and vulnerable, and I hated it. I hated myself for feeling weak. I hated myself for showing that weakness to Harris. And I hated Harris for seeing it and acting like it was no big deal. It *was* a big deal. I'm not weak. I've never been weak. I don't show weakness. I don't need anyone.

But I needed Harris in that moment, and he knew it.

And he was being totally awesome about it, and that pissed me off. I could have handled it if he'd been all cold and businesslike, but he wasn't. He was looking at me with this...softness...in his eyes that I wasn't sure any human being had ever seen before. It was odd and disconcerting and disorienting and bizarre, especially because Harris had just killed five men in less than a minute.

It hit me, then, how fast all that had happened. Less than a minute. Five men dead in sixty seconds. Well, if you want to get picky about it, the first four had gone down first, and the last one about a minute later. So the whole business, from the moment the first man stepped through until the last bullet pierced skull bone, had lasted, at most, two minutes.

"Is it always like that?" I asked.

"Is what always like what?"

I gestured around us. "Combat. Does it always happen so fast?"

He nodded. "Yeah. You're sitting there waiting, and time stretches out like fucking taffy, so slow you can feel each bead of sweat, hear each one of your heartbeats. And then once the first bullet flies..." he shrugged, "everything happens in a split second. Blink and you miss it. Bam, people are dead and you're pissing yourself and you don't know whether to cry or laugh or puke or all three."

"I puked after I shot that guy," I admitted.

"No shame in that," Harris said. "I damn near pissed my pants first time I went into combat. If you're not scared shitless before, during, or after combat, you're a sociopath."

"Even after you've done it a thousand times?" I

asked.

He nodded. "I'm scared every time. I know what to expect and how to deal with it, but I'm still scared. No matter how good you are, how careful you are, something can always go wrong. A stray bullet doesn't give a shit." He pulled me into a walk, letting me go briefly to shove the dead man out of the way, and then he helped me over the corrugated iron fence. I refused to look down as I stepped over the corpse.

Harris led me back to the Defender, opened the trunk and set the bag in, keeping only the handguns. I had no memory of doing so, but apparently I'd grabbed my own guns and clips. Harris took them from me, stuffed them in the bag, and then led me to the front passenger seat, opened the door, and helped me in. I was in a daze, running on autopilot, content to let Harris take care of things. Adrenaline was still slamming through me, pulsing in my blood. I didn't know what to do with myself, whether I wanted to vibrate like I'd OD'd on Five Hour Energy or just fall asleep.

I also felt strangely…turned on.

I mean, it wasn't hard to turn me on under most circumstances, but this was overwhelming. Waves of need blasted through me, desire throbbing between my legs, making my nipples hard and my breasts ache.

I wasn't wearing a bra, which meant I had some serious headlights going on.

The dazed feeling, I was realizing, was my circuits being overloaded. I was feeling too many things at once for my psyche to be able to deal with them all.

I wanted, like Harris had said, to puke again from the knowledge that I'd shot a man, and I wanted to cry, and to laugh. I also wanted to touch myself. To pinch my nipples and stuff my hands down my pants and finger my clit.

I wanted to strip naked and shove three fingers inside myself.

And then, the biggest need of all, I glanced over at Harris as he turned on the ignition and backed out of the alleyway. And Jesus shit fuck—I wanted him.

It made no sense, but there it was.

He'd come after me, he'd taken charge, and he'd killed for me.

Risked death for me.

From the point of view of an alpha, Type A, totally independent sort of woman, a man who could take charge was kind of sexy to me. This translated to me being attracted most strongly to men in power, to men who wore uniforms. Of course, those men were usually assholes, but I typically didn't care because I was just using them for their dicks.

But I'd never in my life felt such a strong need. Not like this. I *NEEDED*.

I ached.

I was hyper-aware of every move I made, how my thighs rubbed together—yes, my thighs rubbed together; no gap there, just flesh and muscle. I was hyper-aware too of Harris, of every move he made, of his hands on the steering wheel and the gear shifter, of how big his hands were, how strong and callused. How they'd feel on my skin, scratchy and hard and powerful. I was aware of his face, the strong jaw and the high cheekbones, the jade of his eyes, the stubble on his cheek, the dark fuzz of his hair cropped close on the sides, and long enough to sweep backward on top. He wasn't gorgeous, not in the sense that Roth was just insanely, inhumanly beautiful. Too beautiful for my taste. Harris was rugged, hard, and weathered. He was handsome, but again, in that rough and rugged sense. A steamy novel might describe his features as "craggy". Cheesy and cliché, but true. He looked so rough and hard that he might have been chipped out of granite, carved out from somewhere deep in the crust of the earth. He was lean, sharp as a razor, not overly muscled but quick and lithe.

If Harris had an animal spirit, he'd be a puma.

I almost laughed out loud at myself at the comparison. But it struck me as true. He was a predator. Cunning, able to move in utter silence, radiating threat and lethality, oozing poised grace and coiled ferocity.

I wanted him.

I didn't want to want him, but I wanted him.

God, did I want him.

It was just the adrenaline, right?

Adrenaline made you feel horny. I'd read that somewhere, or maybe I'd seen it in a movie.

Keep it together.

Don't jump him.

My hands were twitchy and itchy. I wanted to paw his shirt off and run my hands over his abs, feel his ass cool and hard and taut in my hands, I wanted to clutch his cock and feel him throb between my fingers. I wanted to taste him and touch him and lick him and suck him and fuck him.

I stole a glance, and caught him just as he was looking away, returning his attention to the road. He'd been staring at my tits.

I looked down, and totally understood. I mean, they were pretty fucking prominent, especially with arousal making my nipples so hard they hurt, so hard they could cut diamonds.

I crossed my arms over my chest, but that didn't

help. My own arms rubbing over my sensitive nipples had me squirming, aching. My core pulsed, and I crossed one leg over another, but that made it a thousand times worse.

I couldn't breathe for how badly I needed sex…

For how badly I needed Harris.

I looked left again, and this time my gaze caught his. He cut his eyes to the road briefly, just long enough to navigate a turn, and then he was looking at me again. I held his gaze, lifted my chin. Defiant. Daring.

It was an act; I couldn't fucking breathe, couldn't take another second of insatiable need. Pure, unadulterated thirst for Nicholas Harris.

His eyes flitted over my face, slid slowly and deliberately down to my tits, and then back up. I stared into his eyes when they returned to mine. Glanced down, and saw his bulge. Ho-*ly* shit, he had a bulge. Massive, huge bulge.

I swallowed hard and laced my fingers together on my lap to keep from ripping open his pants and deep-throating him as he drove.

"Don't look at me like that, Layla," he growled.

His eyes returned to the road and he gripped the steering wheel with both hands and shifted in the driver's seat.

"Then don't you look at me like that either." I

turned away and tried to focus on the scenery outside the window.

"I'm not looking at you like anything," he said.

"And neither am I." My words were given a lie by the way I tried to steal a look at him, and caught him doing the same.

Silence.

"It's just the adrenaline," I said.

"Right." His hands were twisting the faded leather of the steering wheel as if trying to choke it into submission.

"It'll pass on its own. It doesn't mean anything." I tried chewing on my lip, biting down hard enough to cause pain.

Nope. That didn't help either.

I crossed and uncrossed my legs so many times it probably looked like I was doing the pee-pee dance. Only, it was the pretend-you-don't-need-sex dance.

And Harris was doing one of his own. I stole a glance and caught him trying to surreptitiously adjust himself, plucking at the zipper of his khakis to relieve the pressure of his erection.

Shit. Shitshitshit. *Do not think about his erection*, I told myself.

Do not think about his massive, throbbing erection. Don't think about stroking him, petting his thick, veiny cock. Don't think about licking the pre-come from his tip, or wrapping my lips around the bulbous head.

Fuck.

Not good. So very intensely not good.

Now that was all I could think about.

We drove in complete silence for several min-utes. Neither of us daring to look at each other, nei-ther of us daring to cross the invisible line drawn between us.

He seemed to know exactly where we were go-ing, and it wasn't back to the epicenter of São Paulo. If I had my directions right, we were heading east. I didn't care, though. Or rather, I didn't have the men-tal capacity to care.

All I could think about was NEED.

The sexual tension in the car was at DEFCON 10. High alert. We'd gone past storm watch directly into tornado warning. I couldn't sit still, and neither could he. We stole glances, each pretending nothing was wrong.

And then a spark flew.

He took his hand off the wheel and set it on the bench at his side, and I did the exact same thing at the same time. Which meant my hand went under his. My head snapped around and my gaze fixed on our hands, his on mine, and then I looked up at him,

at his eyes, and saw that his gaze was daring, chal-
lenging.

You move your hand first, his eyes said.

I didn't. I never back down from a challenge.
That's rule number one with Layla: never dare me or
challenge me, because I have zero common sense. I
will not back down.

I rotated my wrist, turning my hand palm-up
under his. He narrowed his eyes, looking from me to
our hands to the road and back. And then his fingers
splayed apart, snaked between mine.

What the hell was this, junior high?

Clearly, because my heart was thudding against
my ribcage like a fucking tribal drum at the innocent, ridiculous, childish contact of his hand on
mine, his fingers in mine.

We were holding fucking hands.

HOLDING HANDS.

I'd never held hands. I'd skipped the silly cute
innocent stage of my sexuality, going straight from
thinking boys were stupid to making out in jani-
tor's closets within the space of a single grade—fifth
grade, if you want specifics. I'd sucked my first cock
in sixth grade, and was pretty well experienced in
the basic missionary position by the end of seventh.
By ninth grade, I was on the prowl.

Holding hands wasn't exactly on the itinerary,

needless to say.

"Where are we going?" I asked.

"Mogi das Cruzes," he said. "It's an offshoot of São Paulo. Thresh has a safe-house prepped for us." He let go of my hand and pulled a cell phone from his pocket, dialed a number, and put the phone to his ear. "Thresh. We're ten minutes out. No, just secure the perimeter and then head for Rio as we discussed. Affirmative." He hung up, and shoved the phone back in his pocket, doing that uniquely male thing where he lifted his entire body off the seat to wedge the phone into the pocket.

And then he reached out, took my hand in his once more, and threaded our fingers together. His eyes cut to mine to gauge my reaction; I'd felt strangely disappointed when he'd let go of my hand, and giddy when he took it back. None of this had crossed my face, though, hopefully.

Or maybe it did, because the corner of his mouth quirked up in a small, pleased smile.

Somehow, over the next ten minutes, my position on the bench seat shifted. I'm not sure how, or why, but I kept sliding further and further left, closer and closer to Harris. And then he let go of my hand, but only to rest his palm on my knee. This made it hard to breathe, and impossible to swallow.

When his fingers found the tender skin of my

thigh just beneath the hem of the skin-tight shorts, I had to focus on forcing each breath in, and each breath out.

I lost track of my left hand, and found it on his thigh.

What the hell was going on?

We were in a residential area, quiet, sunny, hilly, São Paulo proper in the distance, the buildings more well-kept, the cars a little newer. Kind of like Clawson or Livonia in Metro Detroit, not super wealthy but not run-down either, where people were getting by and weren't exactly poor, but weren't really close to even upper-middle class.

Harris drove with his left hand, not taking his right off my leg. His eyes were in constant motion now, though. I could feel his attention, and it was laser-focused on our surroundings, checking the mirrors and the rooftops and each doorway we passed. He slowed, made a left turn, and then stopped outside a small house with white siding and terra cotta roof tiles, a gray fence separating the driveway and front door from the street and sidewalk. A momentary pause, and then a truly massive human being emerged from the house, ducking under the lintel and straightening to a full height that had to be close to seven feet tall. The man was nearly as broad as he was tall, which was a terrifying distortion of physical proportion. Despite his gargantuan size, the man moved with the same predatory grace that Harris possessed. Quick motions unlocked the gate and slid it aside, letting Harris pull the Range Rover into the driveway.

My door was pulled open and I climbed out, straightened, and turned to face the giant. And he was, truly, a giant.

"Jesus Christ on a cracker," I said, "you're the biggest person I've ever seen."

"I get that a lot," he said. His voice was…I'm not sure I have a word for how deep it was. Metaphor also seems to fail, but I'll do my best: it sounded sort of like mountains crashing together, the sound emerging from the depths of the Marianas Trench.

"Layla, this is Thresh," Harris said, pulling his bag of guns out of the back of the Defender. "Thresh is Rambo's worst nightmare."

"Well. That's a fun thought." I held out my hand. "Nice to meet you, Thresh."

Thresh took my hand in his and shook it once. His grip was surprisingly gentle, as if he had to consciously focus on the act of not crushing my hand like a pretzel stick. "Glad to see you in one piece," he rumbled.

He turned away then and took the bag from Harris, brought it inside the house, once again ducking his head and turning slightly sideways to fit through the doorway. Let me reframe this for you. The doorway was average height and width, but Thresh was of a size that he had to not only duck to fit vertically, but had to twist sideways to get his shoulders through the door. The bag, meanwhile, which Harris had carried with visible effort, Thresh dealt with by threading two fingers through the straps. He was carrying it like it was a grocery bag full of bread. I watched his acres of tan muscle and shaggy blond hair vanish into the interior of the house, and then I turned to Harris.

"Where the hell did you find Goliath, there?" I asked.

"I was in the Rangers with him."

"Is his name really Thresh?"

Harris shrugged. "Would *you* ask him his real name? I know very little about him besides his qualifications, which are pretty self-evident. I mean, sheer size aside, he's a stone-cold killer. He's deceptively fast and silent, which should be impossible for a man of his size. I've seen him use at least four different kinds of martial arts. He's a dead shot with a rifle, proficient with explosives, fluent in four languages, good with computers, and is, obviously, the strongest person I've ever met."

"And he's unquestionably on our side?"

"I trust Thresh with my life."

"You trust him with your life, but you don't know his real name?"

"His name is Thresh. That's all I need to know. His personal life is his business, not mine."

Thresh returned at that moment, a khaki rucksack on his back. "Perimeter's clear. Sensors are in place. I'll have us a ride out of South America by the time you reach Rio." He handed Harris a set of keys. "This place is good for seventy hours, no more. See you in Rio."

Harris unlocked the gate, let Thresh through, and locked it behind him. I glanced at Harris as he pocketed the keys, and when I turned back less than two seconds later, Thresh was gone, as if he'd never been there in the first place.

"Where the hell'd he go?"

Harris just shrugged. "Who knows? Man's a ghost."

"How can a seven-foot-tall giant just fucking vanish into thin air?"

This earned me a grin. "See why he's the only one I brought with me to come get you? Now get your ass in the house. We need to keep a low profile."

I preceded Harris into the house, heard him close the door behind us and turn several locks. The interior was dark and cool, and I noticed the shadow of bars across the windows and the front door. There was a couch under the front bay window, thick tan curtains pulled across the glass. The couch was out of the seventies, lime green fake leather. Everything, in fact, was seventies, I realized as I moved through the tiny house, from the window treatments to the appliances to the wallpaper.

There was a minuscule galley kitchen, a single bathroom not much larger than an RV bathroom, and one bedroom.

I heard Harris prowling around much as I was, peering out of windows, testing locks and windows. When he was satisfied, he pulled his phone out of his pocket, swiped it to unlock the touch screen, tapped an icon, then tapped and swiped at the screen a few times.

"What are you doing?" I asked.

He moved to stand beside me, showing me the screen. "Just making sure I'm connected to all the cameras and sensors Thresh installed. See?"

He cycled through several screens, one of the front of the house as seen from the roof across the street, one of each side looking out, and two from the back, one looking out and one looking at the house from some tall structure behind the house. There were also blank screens with "armed" and "clear" written in green letters, which I assumed were motion sensors.

The next thing Harris did was pull weapons out of the bag and hide them in various places around the house: in a box in a cupboard, duct-taped to the wall behind the fridge and behind the toilet, between the mattress and box spring in the bedroom, between the cushions of the couch, a huge assault rifle stood on its stock in the broom closet. He set another handgun on the nightstand beside the bed with two spare clips beside it.

I watched him the whole time. Meeting Thresh had momentarily distracted me from my hyper-sexual awareness of Harris, but now that we were alone again, it came rushing back at me like a runaway freight train. I was aware of the way his sweat-darkened BDU shirt was sticking to his spine; of the way each movement he made seemed to have a specific purpose, no wasted motions, no wasted energy. I was aware of the bulge in the front of his pants, lessened at the moment. I was aware of his corded forearms and chiseled biceps.

I was aware of his gaze as it slid away from his phone and to my eyes.

I was aware of the way he slid the phone back in his pocket and prowled over to me, bulge in his pants getting larger as he approached. I was aware of his eyes on my chest as I breathed, intensity and anticipation and arousal making me short of breath, which meant my breasts swelled with each breath.

"Where'd you get these clothes?" he asked.

"I stole a car from the valet in Vitaly's hotel. He gave them to me."

"They don't fit you."

I shook my head. "No, not really."

A moment of silence then, as if that was all he could think to say.

I watched his chest expand with a deep breath, which he held for a moment and then released slowly. His hands curled into fists at his sides, and his eyes fixed on mine, conflicted, heated green.

And then, with a growl of irritated acquiescence, he moved so he was pressed up against me, erection hard against my belly, face tipped down, mouth centimeters from mine.

"Tell me no," he murmured.

I should have.

I couldn't.

"Layla." It was a demand, a repetition of his injunction to say no.

"Nick?"

At my use of his name, he seemed to swell and his fingers gathered the skin-tight cotton of my T-shirt into his fists. "Last chance, Layla. Tell me to stop."

Fuck that. I wanted this. I wasn't thinking beyond the moment, because that's how I worked. I wasn't thinking about anything except need, except want, except the ache between my thighs, except the way my nipples pulsed and my core was going damp and hot. I couldn't have told him no even if I'd been able to summon words. Which, incidentally, I wasn't.

He growled again, and this time it was a groan of need. Harris's jaw clenched and I felt his fists tense in my shirt at the center of my spine. He pulled, and I heard cotton rip. His arms went rigid, and the frayed crew-neck collar parted.

Holy fucking shit; he was literally ripping the clothes off me?

The maroon fabric hit the floor, and I was bare from the waist up. My nipples tightened, and I lifted my chin, stepped back, hands at my sides.

Harris's gaze roved over me, and I was rewarded by a groan scraping past his clenched teeth as he took in my body. "Jesus, Layla."

"What?" I asked, even though I was pretty sure I knew exactly what he meant.

"You," he said. "You're the sexiest thing I've ever fucking seen."

Somehow, coming from him, that meant more than any compliment I'd ever gotten, and that scared

the fuck out of me. I shoved that little box of emotion way, way down, closed the lid, locked it off, and
buried it. Nope nope nope. Not going there. Not
with him, not with anyone.

"Tit for tat," I said, running my hands over my
breasts. "My shirt…for yours." I crossed the space
between us and gripped the edges of his shirt.

I ripped it off him with a rough jerk, and Harris
took the garment from me, let it fall to the floor, and
now we were both naked from the waist up. I ran my
hands over his chest, rubbed my palms on his nipples and through the dark, curly hair on his chest.

"You've got a hairy chest, Nick."

"Sure do." The question was there in his gaze,
unspoken.

I ran my palms in circles on his chest, placed
a kiss to the indent on his shoulder where it wasn't
quite shoulder, wasn't quite chest. Another, over his
breastbone. "I like it. Real men have hairy chests."

He scraped his hands up my belly and cupped
my breasts in his big, rough hands. "Glad you think
so." There was a smile in his words, but I was too
busy tracing the grooves of his abdomen, the con-
cavity of his sides, the smooth plateau of his broad
back to actually see it.

A breath, another kiss to his chest, right above
his nipple, and then he was kneeling in front of me,

yanking open the button of the shorts and jerking them down past my hips. I stepped out of them, and looked down at Harris, meeting his gaze. He had a double-handful of my ass, and his lips were pressed to my left hipbone. Just beneath my navel. Then over to my right hipbone and to my thigh, high up, just underneath the thin strap of my tiny red thong, then over, a breath away from where the silk cupped my pussy.

He glanced up as he hooked his fingers into the side of the thong, preparing to rip it off.

I grabbed his hand. "Don't. It's the only pair I've got."

"I brought you clean clothes from the *Eliza*. They're in my bag," he said, and then ripped the thong apart anyway.

Jesus. You read about a sexy brute of a man ripping a girl's underwear off, but the reality is a little different. It kind of hurts a little, where the strap on the opposite side digs into your hip with the pressure of the pull, until it gives. And then there's the fact that it kind of creates a bit of camel toe. But then the string parts and you're bare, naked, completely bare. And that was what he did, just ripped it off, tore my underwear right off. It snatched my breath away.

Yeah, it is exactly that sexy.

And then his mouth was over my core, his tongue spearing into me, and I had to grab his shoulders for balance. "Holy shit, Nick."

I went from turned on to orgasm in the space of a heartbeat. One swipe of his tongue against my clit and I was ready to come apart, aching, throbbing, a spear of raw intensity cutting through me.

"Come now, Layla," he said.

He reached up and twisted my nipple sharply, and then slid three fingers of his other hand into my pussy. No buildup, no adding them one at a time, just a quick rough thrust and I was shredding into a million pieces. He sucked my clit between his teeth and flattened it against the roof of his mouth, twisted my nipple, withdrew his fingers and fucked them back up into me.

"Fuck, Jesus, Nick. *Fuck*." I tried to push him away. "I need a shower, I stink."

"Don't fucking care," he murmured. "Now...I told you to *come*, Layla," he growled.

"I am—oh...holy *fuck*—I'm coming, Nick." I felt everything clench, felt my muscles contract, felt the heat blasting through me, a wordless moan escaping my lips. I squeezed hard with my PC muscles, clamping down as hard as I could on his fingers, trapping them inside me. He groaned at the pressure on his fingers, glancing up at me with an appreciative glint in his eyes.

Abruptly, he was standing up in front of me and he was kissing me, pussy on his breath and his tongue demanding mine, commanding and insistent. His fingers dug into my hair, trying to undo the rubber band keeping it in place.

"It's an actual rubber band," I murmured, breathless from his kiss. "Gonna be a bitch to get out."

He reached into a pocket and I heard a *snick* of a pocketknife as he pulled my head toward him. "Hold still," he ordered.

I sank to my knees instead, and got to work on his pants. I felt him playing with the bun on the top of my head, looking for the best spot. I unbuttoned the fly, and tugged his pants down, and they fell to the floor at his feet with a *thud*. He was utterly focused, though, I had to give him credit for that. Even as I pulled his black briefs down and bared his cock, he was focused on my hair, cutting away the rubber band piece by piece until he could shake my hair free.

Only when my hair was loose around my shoulders did he fold the knife and glance down at me. "Still got my shoes on," he said.

"True." I leaned closer to him, teasing him, mouth close enough to his cock that he could feel my breath as I unlaced his boots one at a time and helped him tug his feet out of them.

He toed his socks off, kicked the pile of clothes away, tossed the pocketknife onto the pile.

And then he waited.

I took a moment to admire his penis; it was a lovely organ, long and thick with a very slight inward curve to it as it stood flat against his belly. That curve, I couldn't wait to have it inside me, pushing against me just right, hitting that spot as he thrust into me....

I wrapped both hands around it and stroked him, and then leaned over him, wrapped my lips around the head.

I got one good suck in, and then he was lifting me to my feet. "Later, Layla."

He twisted me in place and guided me to the bathroom, turned on the shower stream, adjusted the temperature so it was somewhere between cool and warm. Normally, I like scalding hot showers, but for once I was simply too damn hot and sweaty to be able to tolerate a hot shower.

Here's a thing: shower sex isn't actually sexy. It's hard to have good shower sex without anyone getting hurt, and someone is always left out of the water stream so they get cold, and there aren't really any good positions that don't involve feats of acrobatics or powerlifting—especially when you consider that I'm not exactly dainty.

Harris seemed to recognize all of this. He pushed me so my back was against the wall, the water beating against my front. He had a bar of soap in his hand, and proceeded to scrub me with it, all over. He started with my face, telling me in a gruff whisper to close my eyes, then washed my face and rinsed it carefully. He moved to my neck and shoulders, tugging me forward to wash my back while kissing me between my breasts. Then he roamed over my breasts with the soap bar, and god, that was sexy, intimate, tender…too much to handle. I closed my eyes and let him wash me. Thighs, core, ass, all over, kissing me clean everywhere. I was breathless by the time he was done, and tried to take the soap from him, but he just knocked my hands away and pulled me under the water to wash my hair. He had bottles of complimentary hotel shampoo and conditioner, and used them both on my thick, curly black hair, working them in one after another, massaging my scalp.

I was finally clean, head to toe.

I reversed positions with Nick, and did the same for him, washing him from head to toe, but I made sure to avoid his erogenous zones at first. Meaning, I washed his hair first, and then ran the soap over

his lean, hard, toned body, only touching his cock
at the end. By this time his erection had subsided
to a drooping semi, but I made short work of this
sad fact. I lathered soap onto my hands and then
worked it onto his cock and balls, massaging gently,
just washing him at first, and then as I rinsed him
clean began stroking him to full erection.

God, the man had a lovely cock. Seriously. I've
seen and handled a lot of cock, and his was—objec-
tively speaking—the best I'd ever gotten my hands
on. I mean, it wasn't about sheer size. I'd seen bigger. But there *is* actually such a thing as *too* big, in
my opinion at least. It's more about overall shape,
for me. Size factors in, clearly, and Nick had size
in spades. He wasn't hung like a horse in any liter-
al sense, which was perfect for me. I could tell as
I explored his dick with my hands that he'd fill me
enough that I'd feel pleasurably stretched. Big, thick,
long, but just perfectly shaped, mostly straight but
with a very slight curve, and that curve...I shivered
with anticipation—when he was inside me he'd hit
me just right, and I was looking forward to it.

Like, a LOT.

I may have gotten a little carried away, stroking
him in the shower. The water had gone cold, but I
didn't care. It felt good, the cool water on my skin.
I had both fists around his cock and was stroking

him, not trying to get him off, just...playing with his length, pausing now and then to cup and massage his heavy balls, rolling them in my palms. No mouth, this time, I just touched. Learned. Explored.

And he let me. He watched, head leaned back against the tile, hands on my shoulders, thumbs circling on my skin in idle affection. And that idle touch, it was enough to make me almost panic, because it was unconscious, the kind of touch that means so much, more than any sexual touching. It was like the way he had of brushing his thumb across my lips. Tender. Affectionate. Meaningful.

When I had him breathing hard and had his hips fluttering with the smooth, slow strokes of my fingers around him, Nick lifted me to my feet, shut off the water, and indicated with a push that he wanted me out of the shower. He made quick work of drying us both, and then hauled me into the bedroom. Hot humid air immediately coated my skin. Nick's eyes roamed down my body, and his lip curled up in a hungry smile.

"Now we're both clean. No more excuses."

"Excuses?" I asked.

He didn't bother answering. He just pushed me up against the bed. Before he bent me forward, however, he pressed himself up against me, erection nestling between the heavy globes of my ass, pulled me backward so my head rested on his shoulder, and kissed me, traced my lips with his thumb. He bent at the knees, his hand cupping my throat, holding me against him, and his cock nudged against my entrance.

"Oh god. Nick…"

"You want it, don't you?"

I nodded. "Jesus, yes."

"Say it, Layla."

"I want your cock inside me, Nick. I want you to fuck me."

He kissed me once more, and then his cock filled me with one hard thrust, and a scream ripped out of me.

Oh holy fuck.

This was going to be incredible.

13

FUCKED

ONE SHORT, HARD THRUST, AND HIS COCK WAS fully seated inside me, filling me, stretching me. Still standing up, his hand gently gripping my throat to keep me in place—as if I was trying to escape—I was rendered helpless. Totally helpless. I couldn't move, couldn't breathe, couldn't think. The only thing that existed in my whole universe was Harris, big and hard and hot behind me, his dick inside me, his hand on my throat, the other strumming my nipple like a guitar string.

He didn't move. Time stood still, and the only sound was my ragged gasps and his steady breathing. His lips touched my temple, and I trembled.

What the fuck was he doing?

To kiss a body is sexual, to press lips to chest or

hip or cock or pussy or ~~belly, that's sex. To make out,~~ that's sex.

To kiss one's face, one's cheek, one's forehead, a temple, a jaw…that is intimate and personal.

I didn't do intimate.

I didn't do personal.

To quote a certain fictional phenomenon, "I fuck. Hard." I didn't connect with those particular characters on any level, except for the intimacy factor. Even with Eric, my one real serious boyfriend, the only man I ever lived with, the only guy I ever let see even a hint of my true inner self, even with him I didn't really do intimacy. Sex was sex. Eric and I fucked. We boned. Don't get me wrong, I liked Eric. A lot. I dated him for a long time, and lived with him. But I didn't do intimacy with him. There was no pillow talk. There was no kissy-face hold me afterward and tell me your deepest thoughts and share your most tender emotions.

He never kissed my temple.

Harris kissed my temple, one brief, slow, and utterly confusing touch of his lips to the side of my skull, and I was lost.

Not like, falling in love lost, or drowning in his touch lost, but the *what the fuck is happening and where am I and what's going on* kind of lost.

And then, wildest of all, my body betrayed my

heart. My hand reached up and back, and my palm cupped the nape of his neck and my head twisted to the side and my mouth sought skin and my heart was crashing and thundering and cracking and twisting and my mind was rebelling, but my body was in control. My body had hijacked the rest of me.

My lips sought skin, and found it. Found his jaw. His cheekbone. I clutched the back of his head and trembled like a dry leaf in a long wind.

And still he wasn't moving. Seemingly content to just hold the pose, both of us standing up facing the bed, his shaft buried deep inside my slit, my body boneless and without strength, leaning with total trust against Harris's chest.

A breath left me in a broken sigh, and I sank down, letting my weight fall just a bit, pushing him deeper. I couldn't take the motionlessness, couldn't take the shredding intimacy of his breath on my cheek, his wordless possession of me. I couldn't handle the memory of that kiss to my temple. I needed...*more*.

"Nick..." I murmured.

"I know," he said, and pushed me forward.

Willingly, gladly, I bent over the bed, spread my feet shoulder-width apart, braced myself with arms straight, elbows locked, hands on the mattress. I waited. Breathless with anticipation, with bated breath, with every other cliché you can think of, I waited.

And Harris, he kept me waiting. Didn't give me what I wanted, didn't do what I expected. Instead of thrusting hard, pushing into me, he leaned over me and pressed his lips to my spine, right at the center of my back, ran his palms up my sides. I shook so hard I had to clench my teeth. What the actual fuck was he doing?

Another caress, downward this time, from armpits down my sides to cup my hips, then his palms circled my ass cheeks. He pulled back, withdrawing. I bit my lip, waiting for the rough slam…

He pushed in gently, slowly, and I sagged, at once defeated and exhilarated. So good. So fucking good. The feel of him, moving in me. The sweet wet slide of his cock pushing into me, I groaned with delight.

He leaned over me as his hips pressed flush against my ass. His lips touched the shell of my ear. "Rough…or slow?"

"Rough," I answered immediately.

He bit my earlobe. Hard.

I shrieked in surprise and twisted my head to look at him in shock, and he just grinned as he straightened behind me, running his palm down my spine to grab a handful of butt cheek. "Rough?"

I nodded. "Rough."

"How rough you want it, Layla?"

"Fuck me hard, Nick."

He pulled back so the tip of his cock rested just barely inside me, caressed the left globe of my ass with his left hand, gripping the crease of my right hip with his right hand.

There was no warning. He slammed into me so hard the breath left me involuntarily and his hand smacked my ass with a painful resounding *crack*.

I screamed.

I'm not a screamer. I'm a moaner, a gasper, a porn star whimperer. When I come, I usually clench my teeth and groan through them. I do *not* scream.

Nick made me scream.

He paused a moment, impaled fully inside me. Then he smoothed his palm over the stinging flesh of my bottom, and then withdrew, slowly. So slowly. Then he spanked my ass and fucked into me again, *hard*. I felt his cock spear through me, slam deep, felt his balls slap against my taint, and my ass cheek jiggled and stung from the smack of his palm. This time, there was no pause, no hesitation. Just the slow, almost tender withdrawal, and then immediately upon reaching the apex of his pull-out, Harris spanked me and thrust again. My left ass cheek was on fire, by now. My pussy was throbbing, and I was fighting for breath, for equilibrium.

He switched it, then. Right hand spanking right ass cheek, left hand gripping my left hip bone.

Smack.

Smack.

Smack.

Each slap of his hand was accompanied by a jarringly hard thrust.

Four spanks per side, four thrusts. Then he switched, back and forth, back and forth. No rhythm, no pattern. Always the slow pull-out, an infinitesimal pause, and then the slam into me.

I lost track of time, never counted the thrusts or spanks. All I knew was that I was throbbing and aching, that my ass was burning and stinging and that with each spank it hurt more but that with each spank the thrusts incited the fire inside my core to burn hotter, made each brutally powerful thrust of his cock into me that much more intense.

I lost the ability to bite down on my screams.

He spanked and thrust, and I screamed as he rammed home.

I don't know how, but he knew when I was close. Maybe it was that as I neared climax, I started pushing back as he fucked me. Or maybe it was that whimpers and groans filled the spaces between screams. I don't know how, but he knew.

And right as I reached the edge, he pulled completely out of me, leaving me empty and ready to beg.

He grabbed my left hip in his right hand and flipped me over, putting me off balance, tossing me over as easily as if I was some skinny size-nothing floozy. Just tossed me over like I was nothing. I sagged back against the bed, fighting for balance, struggling to get my feet under me.

Harris was there, grasping the backs of my knees and lifting me, his hips fitting into the V of my thighs, cock nudging my entrance. I wasn't balanced, had no control. He had me totally helpless, my upper torso resting on the bed, my lower half in his grip.

"Do I need a condom?"

I shook my head. "No, I'm protected, and I'm clean."

"Do you trust me?"

Fuck, what a question. Did I trust him? I mean, my life was in his hands. He'd risked death for me, killed for me, and that was just within the last couple hours. But did I trust him to fuck me bare, no protection against disease? Did he trust me to actually be on birth control, that I wouldn't come up pregnant, and that I really was clean?

So much trust.

So foolish.

Stupid, even.

I'm impulsive. Rash. I do whatever I want, when I want. I don't always think about the consequences of my decisions. If I fuck up, and I handle it. The one exception to this is sex. I was on birth control by the time I was fourteen, and I never, ever, *ever* had unprotected sex. Not with anyone. Not ever. Not even when I was wasted. If he didn't have a bag, he didn't bag me. That was the one unalterable, inflexible rule I never broke, no matter what. Not even with Eric, in the nearly three years we were together, we didn't have bare sex even once.

So why, oh why did I lift my hips in silent agreement, then, with Harris?

Simple. Same answer as why I was so affected by an innocent kiss to my temple:

I have no fucking clue.

I lifted my hips, pushing against him, angling and lifting so his cock slipped into me.

Harris didn't push in, though. "Say it, Layla. Out loud." His eyes were fiery jade, unblinking, unwavering, intense, pinning me.

"I trust you, Nick." Jesus, I sounded *breathy*. Seductive. Vulnerable.

Clearly, some other spirit had possessed me, because this wasn't me. This wasn't Layla.

I didn't breathe out a whimper like that, no fucking way. When Harris finally thrusted into me, I whimpered. I know I said I wasn't a screamer, that I made pretty typical almost fake-sounding porn star sounds during sex. In fact, I've been accused of faking just because of how I sound. But I never faked, it was just how I sounded.

This, though? When Harris slowly and deliberately thrust into me, the way I made this...I don't even know the right word...moan, whimper, sigh—a sound that was all three of those in one, a moan-whimper-sigh. It wasn't me. I *never* sounded like that. No matter how good it felt.

But that was the problem, wasn't it? Nothing had ever felt like this before. Not the way Harris drove into me, not the way he filled me. Not the way he held me completely in his thrall, helpless.

I pulled back from the edge of climax.

It only took him four slow thrusts to get me there again. He watched me, watched my face, my expressions. I felt his attention, laser-focused, hyper-aware. I hooked my legs around his waist and he slid his palms to my ass, keeping me aloft with a firm grip of each hand on the globes of my ass. His fingers were at the crease of my buttocks, daring in, separating the cheeks. Literally, he had my entire ass cheeks gripped, one in each hand, and he was holding the entire weight of my lower body aloft with that grip.

I felt the pressure of his fingers against my asshole, nudging but not pushing in.

He'd want in there, at some point.

I'd let him. Shit, I'd probably beg him for it, if this was how it was going to feel with him.

Once he was sure of his hold on me, once he was sure I was close, he settled closer, leaning deeper into the V of my thighs, pushing his cock as far in as it would go.

And then he started fucking.

Oh. Oh Jesus. Oh shit.

This was real-deal fucking. He left me no breath, left me no quarter, had no mercy. I'd asked for it rough, he gave it to me *rough*. Hard. He didn't ask if I was ready, didn't ease into it. Just…a single growling murmur of appreciation for my body, and he started fucking, ramming me hard over and over and over, so my whole body was jarred with each thrust.

"Play with your tits, Layla. Pinch your nipples."

I obeyed, cupping my big, bouncing breasts in my hands and thumbing my nipples erect, and then pinched them.

"Hard, Layla. Make yourself scream."

I caught my left nipple between my thumb and forefinger and pinched it so hard I shrieked; a bolt of lightning blasted through me, striking my core as I twisted the nipple and pinched it again. Pinched both.

"Come for me, Layla." The command was quiet, but spoken with razor sharpness, rife with intensity.

I shattered, twisting and pinching my nipples as the orgasm ripped through me.

"Finger your clit. Right now, while you're coming."

I kept one hand at my breast, twisting and pinching, and my right hand delved down in obedience to Harris's quiet order. I put my middle and ring fingers to my hardened clit and rubbed myself in circles, so aroused I needed no buildup, already coming so all I had to do was swipe at my hypersensitive clit hard and fast.

"FUCK!" The word was a plea, yanked out of me as the orgasm spiraled through me and out of control, making my entire body gyrate. "Oh god, Nick, Nick, NICK!"

I glanced at him through slitted eyelids, and saw a small, pleased smile on his lips as he drove into me over and over. And I realized he still hadn't come.

"Your turn, Nick," I said.

The smile spread, turned feral. "My turn, is it?"

"I need to feel you come, too."

He set me down, unwrapped my legs from

around his waist. Made sure I had my balance, and then climbed onto the bed. Rested his head on the pillow, and just stared at me. Waiting.

"Ride me," he ordered.

I took a moment to just drink in his body. So fucking sexy. Lean, corded with iron-hard muscle. Lupine, primal. Dark, curly, masculine hair dusting his chest and stomach, trimmed close around his junk. God, his cock. Glistening wet with my essence, hard and thick, the very slight curve that felt so perfect inside me, hitting me right where it felt the best.

His eyes followed my movements as I twisted in place and climbed on the bed. My heavy breasts swayed as I crawled over him, and I fucking *loved* the way his eyes just devoured my body, the way his gaze seemed to speak a thousand, million words decrying my beauty, all in silence, a poem in glances, a song in gaze. He didn't need to say a single word, and I knew I was gorgeous, to him.

But then he did speak, as I straddled his hips with my thighs. "Layla, you are...so fucking beautiful."

"Thanks, Nick."

He reached up, his knuckles brushing my cheek. And then he gathered a handful of my curly, tightly-kinked, ink-black hair, and pulled my face down. It was a rough jerk, tugging my face down to his, but

the expression on his face somehow made the gesture seem…tender. I wasn't sure how he managed
that but it was effective. My heart was leaping in my
chest, thumping painfully hard. Trying to escape,
trying to get away from what I perceived in him.

"No, Layla," he said, and nipped my lip with his
teeth. "I don't think you get it. You are absolutely
perfect."

I had nothing to say to that. I couldn't speak,
even if I had possessed the words. I was choked up,
throat tight. This was raw terror pounding through
me.

Perfect?

God no.

I knew I was good looking, but more because of
my body than because of my face. When you've got
dimensions like mine, you don't need to have a beautiful face. Most guys told me I was hot. Sexy. That I
had a bangin' body. That my tits were the best thing
they'd ever seen. That I had a ghetto booty so fine
they could fuck it for hours. More cushion for the
pushin'; legs for days. I'd taken those compliments to
heart, and I stayed in shape to keep it that way.

But no guy had ever told me how beautiful I
was, not without qualifying it in relation to my body
in some way.

And you know what? That kind of hurt, down

deep. Knowing my beauty was only because of my body? It was the kind of hurt you don't know how to express, even to yourself.

But in that moment, when Nick told me I was beautiful, that I was "absolutely perfect"? That framed it for me in a way I could finally understand.

I waited for the qualification.

It never came.

And my defenses were on high alert.

Danger, Will Robinson.

I slid up his body, dragging the tips of my breasts across his chest, brushing his face with them, swaying them over his lips, across his eyes. "Yeah? You like these, don't you?"

He lifted up and captured a nipple in his mouth. "Yes, I do."

I ground my ass on his stomach. "This feels good on you, doesn't it?"

He cupped my ass in his hand, kneading the muscle. "So good." But then, my hair still gripped in his fist, he tightened his hold so he had my hair by the roots, and firmly but carefully brought my face to his. "You have the sexiest body I've ever seen, Layla."

"Thanks—" I started, but he didn't let me finish.

He cut me off with a kiss. "I wasn't done. Don't interrupt me." I frowned at the command, but waited for him to continue. He gave my ass a gentle spank—well, it wasn't really gentle, it was still a loud *smack*, but in comparison to how hard he had spanked me earlier, it was relatively gentle—sending the round globes to quivering, and then smoothed his palm up my back, brushed my jaw with his thumb. "But that wasn't what I was talking about."

"No?" I was trying for casual.

"No. I said you were absolutely perfect." He bit my lower lip again, his palm splayed against my face. "And I meant it. *All* of you."

It was either cry or avoid the subject, so which do you think I chose?

I reached down between our bodies and wrapped my fingers around his cock, fitted him to my entrance, propping my body up with one hand on the mattress beside his face, hovering over him, tits swaying over his chest. A momentary pause, our eyes connecting, heat and intensity crackling and sparking between us. And then I sat down on him, hard, impaling myself on him.

"*Fuck*, Layla," he ground out, "that feels—you feel incredible."

I squeezed his cock as hard as I could. "You like that?"

He thrust up into me, our hips grinding together. "Fuck yes. Do it again."

I lifted up, swirled my hips so the broad head of his dick smeared in circles between my damp labia, and then plunged down on him, squeezing at tight as I could. "Like that?"

His hands coasted up my ribs to knead my boobs, cupping and stroking. "Just like that. Keep doing that. Ride me until we both come."

So I did.

I clamped down as I lifted up once more, relaxing at the apex, circling my hips again to move his shaft around and around, keeping him guessing as to when I would…slam down hard, our bodies meeting with a loud *slap* of my ass onto his thighs, squeezing with my pussy muscles on the down-thrust.

Seated on him, panting, everything inside me pulsing madly, I knew I had to draw it out. When I came again, it would be hard, and it would break something in me. I was scared of it. It was inevitable, but I still tried to push it away. I had to.

Self-preservation.

There was something real between Harris and me, and it scared the living shit out of me.

So I played with him. Drew it out. Used every trick I knew to string him along.

With his cock impaled inside me, I rolled my hips in broad circles, grinding down on him. And then I lifted up, paused, and sank down, and then ground hard on him again. Repeated this until I was shuddering and on the edge myself.

Harris was sweating, breathing hard, and clearly feeling what I was doing, but he hadn't said a word, hadn't made a sound. He'd kept his grip on my hair, and his other hand was resting on the bend of my hip where it became thigh, cupping, holding. Letting me do what I wanted.

I lifted up, planted my palms on his chest, and feathered slow, shallow thrusts around him, sliding just the top couple of inches in and out of me. Over and over and over, I teased us both with shallow movements, never letting more than half of his cock in me at any one point, sliding up, circling, sliding down his shaft again, pulling back to stretch his dick away from his body and moving in circles again.

And all the while, Harris let me.

Jaw clenched, panting, sweat gleaming on his face and body.

Finally, he growled. "*Enough*, Layla."

He thrust up, jerked my head down, and captured my mouth with his. I was on top, but he was in control. He kissed me. *Ho-ly fuck*, did he kiss me. All tongue, lips crushed to lips, demanding that I kiss him back, commanding my mouth. His body moved, his palm on my ass, pulling at me, his hips thrusting up.

I moaned into the kiss and had to glide on him, had to move. The kiss burned me, stole my breath from my lungs and the will from my soul. It was a kiss that dominated, a kiss that possessed. Took.

He fucked.

And I could do nothing but ride him, do nothing but take it. I was helpless on top of him, my face kept crushed against his by the rough and firm grip of his fist in my hair, paralyzed by the kiss.

It wasn't *just* fucking, though. The movements of his body, the rough and wild and vigorous thrusting—that was *fucking*. It was raw and primal and unrestrained. Everything that had gone before that, the spanking and the thrusts from behind, everything I'd done to him up until that moment, it was all just…a precursor.

Foreplay.

This was…something else. Not fucking. Nothing so impersonal or casual as that. This was Nick taking possession of my soul. This was Harris taking command of my body. This was…my walls being demolished. My defenses eradicated.

I think I came at some point, but I was so blown apart by the implications of how much I was *feeling* emotionally that it didn't really register.

I like sex. Duh. I mean, I *really* like sex. A lot. A

whole fucking lot. It's, like, my favorite thing, along with getting naked-wasted on cheap red wine and bingeing on Netflix.

But I'd never had sex like this. It was…new. Strange. Intense. Emotional. Fraught with meaning. It…*meant* something.

And I didn't know how to deal.

I couldn't deal.

But Nick wasn't letting go, wasn't letting me off the hook. He gave me enough slack in the grip on my hair that we could pause the kiss to take a breath, but that was almost worse. Without the kiss, I had to meet his gaze. And fuck, his eyes…the passion in them. The need. The way he looked so deeply into my eyes, the way his glance flicked down to where our bodies joined. It was all too much.

I kissed him, this time.

Smashed my mouth to his so hard our teeth clacked and my lip split. Harris pulled back, licked my lip where it throbbed and kissed it. And then, slowly, gently, masterfully, he claimed my mouth. Once again taking the initiative and control away from me.

God, he fucking *owned* me. He knew exactly in each moment and in each situation exactly how to snatch control away from me and make me utterly dependent on him.

My choice was to either cede control to him entirely, or get off and walk away.

I thought about it, I really did.

If we came together—and we would, I was positive—something was going to change.

But I couldn't walk way. *Couldn't*. I tried. Jesus, did I try. But I couldn't make myself do it.

I was too ensnared by the mastery of his kiss, too paralyzed by the throb of upwelling ecstasy, too pierced by the intensity in his eyes and the rising urgency in his thrusts.

And can I just say, holy hell, the man had extreme stamina.

He let me pull my head back, but didn't let go of my hair. His fingers were fisted in my curls at the nape of my neck, and he let me rise up enough to plant my fists in the pillow by his face. Our faces were inches apart, but we weren't kissing, now. He was thrusting slowly, long, deep glides in and out with smooth, perfect strokes. I drew my knees up under me and started pushing back into his thrusts, our eyes fixed on each other and unwavering. Not looking away.

I wanted to.

I hated the intensity, hated the vulnerability I felt in myself. He *saw* me.

I couldn't look away.

I knew the exact moment he lost the battle for control over his own body; he snarled like a wolf and began fucking in earnest, wild manic upward plunges, and his grip on my hair tightened to the point of pain, but I liked that, because it grounded me. Distracted me a little from the open passion in his eyes, from the raw furious frantic need in his gaze. From the blazing connection streaming between us. I could only push down onto him, could only ride him and take his fucking.

God, it felt perfect.

The most heavenly ecstasy ever, Harris fucking me while his eyes promised so many, many things. Tender things.

"Layla," he murmured.

I couldn't speak. Could only whimper breathlessly.

"Squeeze. Hard."

So I squeezed as hard as I could, went still and focused on squeezing.

"Oh…fuck. Layla. I'm coming." He jerked me down so our mouths touched, but didn't kiss me, his eyes on mine. "Look at me. Don't you dare look away."

"I won't…I'm looking at you," I gasped.

I felt him start to come, and my eyes watered.

He cupped my face, thumb brushing over my

lips. "Come now, Layla."

I came. Holy fucking hell, I came. So hard.

"Say my name, Layla. Say my fucking name while you come apart on top of me."

"*Nick*," I breathed. "Nicholas. I'm coming, Nick."

I felt him unleash. He bit my lip, kept my face pressed to his and kissed me dizzy, and his hand slid down my body and spanked my ass once, hard, and then, finally, he came. Jet after jet of hot seed poured out of him and into me, and I couldn't do anything but feel it and squeeze him and marvel at what I'd never felt in my life before, the hot wet gush of a man coming bare inside me, filling me, surging up into me and stuttering in his thrusts as he came, came, came, his kiss fumbling as he lost all control, his hand on my ass, gripping, kneading, pulling me harder against him.

I ground onto him, clenched him with my inner muscles, and whimpered as I came with him, not coming again, but coming *still*, a continuation of a long shattering climax.

"Fuck," he breathed, settling back.

"Holy shit." I collapsed onto him.

Instead of rolling me off him, he took my weight on his body and wrapped his arms around me, kept me from escaping.

Almost as if he understood the panic shooting

through me.

A single tear escaped my eye, because I knew what had just happened had utterly and completely ruined me.

I'm so fucked.

14

DRAW IT OUT

I woke alone, slowly and disoriented. Sore. Deliciously sore, in all the best ways.

I heard heavy breathing, even and steady from somewhere in the room. Twisting and stretching, I rolled to the edge of the bed toward the sound and saw Harris, stark naked on the floor, doing pushups.

Which might just be the hottest thing I've ever seen. His bare ass was taut and flexed, hard as granite, and the broad plane of his back was a ridged field of pulsing muscles as he lowered himself to the floor with exquisite slowness. His biceps bulged, gleaming with sweat, and he pushed himself up again just as slowly. He breathed out each time he lowered his body, and breathed in when he pushed up. Again and again, never rushing, never wavering. A hundred times, he did this. I know, because I watched each one, counting with him, fascinated and hypnotized by the sight.

Jesus.

And then he rolled to his back, touched his fingertips to the back of his head, and did the kind of crunches where he jerked his knee toward his face while lunging his torso forward, touching his right elbow to his left knee and vice versa. I know he saw me, but he didn't pause, just crunched, crunched, crunched. Another hundred.

Hooooo, Lordy.

Then he stood, his feet slightly more than shoulder-width apart, and squatted, extending his arms as he did so, then stood up. Like the pushups and the crunches, he made each motion slow and deliberate and with total control.

I might have had to stifle a chuckle at that. I mean, how could I not? He was buck naked, so his junk was flopping all over the place, and it was kind of funny.

But then he finished his hundredth squat and his eyes cut to mine, he turned and stood in front of me, and I stopped laughing. Post workout, naked, sweaty, muscles swollen...Nick Harris was a fucking beast and I wanted him.

I stared at him, meeting his eyes, and then let

my gaze slowly rake down his magnificent body to his cock. It was waking up. Stiffening, hanging down but starting to curl to the side as arousal sent blood coursing through it.

Fuck, I wanted him.

I *needed* him. I'd never needed anyone before, and it had me quaking with fear. I hated being afraid. It made me angry.

So I did the only thing I could think of: I slid off the bed and sank to my knees in front of him, staring up at him. He stood still, arms at his sides, breathing heavily. Maybe if I sucked his cock, I'd avoid the intensity, the vulnerability, the need.

I began slowly, intending to make a production of this. Make it good. Make it last. Make it the hottest goddamn blowjob he'd ever gotten, or ever will get. I carved my palms up his legs, starting at his calves and grazing them up the backs of his legs to his ass, cupping it, kneading it, digging my fingers into the impressively iron-hard muscle. I turned my eyes down to his cock, which was at half-mast, now. I held onto his butt and nuzzled his belly above his burgeoning erection, feeling it bumping up against my chin. Slid my lips around to kiss beside the root, and then touched my mouth to his tautening sack. He smelled of sweat, but it was clean, fresh sweat, and I didn't mind it. It was a manly smell, masculine, arousing. I took his sack in mouth and felt his dick hardening against my cheek. A glance showed me his hands clenching into fists and releasing, and I flicked my eyes up to his. Snared by the fire in his green eyes, I couldn't look away, wondering what he was thinking. He had his poker face on, only his eyes giving away the fact that he was feeling anything at all. I knew he felt it, though. What, I wasn't sure, but something, and powerfully.

I let the length of his penis slide against my cheek as I drew my face away from his body, and then finally the tip of his nearly-erect shaft was bobbing at my lips, hardening and straightening. I gave it a lick, a quick flick of my tongue against the head, and Harris sucked in his breath sharply.

I kept my gaze on his, opened my mouth, and took him between my lips, gazing up at him all the while, cupping his ass with both hands. He let out a breath, and his brows furrowed. I backed away, let him bob free of my mouth, and ran my tongue up and down his length, licking him over and over again, broad fat swipes of my tongue against his salty, soft flesh.

I wrapped my lips around the head now, and suckled, starting slowly and gently and increasing intensity until I heard him groan and felt his hips flutter, and then I spat him out. He sagged slightly, exhaling a rough breath.

"Jesus, Layla." He reached down and tried to lift me, but I grabbed his hands and shoved them into the tangled mass of my hair.

He buried his fingers in my hair and held on, but didn't make any move to urge me to go down on him again. He seemed content to let me do this my way, for now.

Fine by me.

I was totally avoiding things, because I knew if we fucked again, there would be talking, and shit would get real, and I wasn't ready for that. Sucking his dick nicely circumvented the whole business, pleasantly for him. And as for me? Well, let's just say his cock was not only impressive to look at, but enjoyable for my mouth as well. Maybe I'm in the minority here, but I actually kind of liked giving blowjobs. I liked the power, yes, the feeling of knowing I was able to elicit strong reactions. Control a man via giving pleasure. But I also just *liked* it, liked feeling cock in my hand, liked to stroke the skin, and the musky taste, the feel of him in my mouth, the way he'd tense and explode. It was also a good test of the man, because the good ones would return the favor, maybe not right then, but at some point. And I also really enjoyed receiving cunnilingus. If he didn't return the favor, there usually wouldn't be seconds for him. Call me a bitch, but it was a pretty handy rule of thumb. Not solely because of the oral itself, though, but more because if he wasn't willing to return the favor, he likely wouldn't be focused on making sure I got mine during sex in general. Which didn't work for me. I expected to get mine. That's the whole point, right?

But this, with Harris, this was several things at once. It was a delaying tactic, an avoidance tactic. It was also because I just genuinely wanted to go down on him, wanted to exert some kind of control over him, put him under my spell as payback for the way he had utterly dominated me during sex.

So, I went down on him.

I brought my hands around front, sank back on my heels, and curled my fingers around his shaft. He exhaled sharply, and his fingers tightened in my hair. I hadn't even done anything yet, but he was already grinding his jaws and gripping my curls for dear life.

Oh buddy. Just you wait.

I started stroking him; one hand loosely curled around his thickness and pumped up and down, my skin barely making contact with his. My other hand wasn't idle, though; I had his balls in my palm and was massaging them as gently as I could. I stroked him slowly, gentle caresses of his length, up and down, up and down. When my hand reached the top of his shaft, I cupped my palm over his head and gripped it, twisted, then slid my fingers around the plump pink mushroom head and stroked short pumps around the tip, faster and faster until his hips fluttered and his breath left him in a gust.

And then I stopped.

He made a low sound of warning in his chest, a sound of disapproval. Good. That meant he was starting to really feel things, now.

I scooted backward, pushed him a step away, and then gripped his cock in both hands and began a slow two-handed pumping, pulling him away from his body and leaning forward to take him into my mouth. Just the very tip, at first, the way you might put your lips on the very tip of a tall scoop of ice cream. Double-fist strokes, over and over. He was grunting, a low, almost inaudible sound, but a good sign. I started bobbing, replacing some of the strokes of my hands with my mouth, going lower and lower, my lips passing the groove of circumcision but no further, bobbing up and down, sucking as the springy flesh entered my mouth. He started thrusting, and his grip on my hair tightened. He really had a thing for my hair, it seemed; he now had both hands gripping the mass of it tightly near the scalp. He wasn't applying any pressure, though, just holding. His hips flexed, pushing his cock farther into my mouth. I took it, accepted more of his thickness between my lips, let my tongue slide against his flesh, stroked with one hand only now, bobbing down into his thrusts, cupping his balls and kneading them gently.

His breath was ragged, rasping grunts, and I knew he was close.

So I slowed down. Stroked his length as slowly as I could, lowered my mouth around him, opening my throat and leaning forward to let him in further, taking him deep. He liked that. I did it again, stretching his cock away from his body until it was nearly horizontal, holding it by the base with both hands. I glanced up at him through my eyelashes and deep-throated him.

"Fuck." The first word he'd uttered so far.

I hummed a questioning sound—*mmmhmmm?*

His jaw flexed and he pulled at me, very gently, but a slight pressure as I moved toward him, his cock passing between my lips, over my tongue, the tip nudging my throat. Harris was breathing hard again, his abs tensed.

He was holding back.

That wasn't gonna work. He was planning to let me take him to the very edge, I realized, and then he'd retake control and try to finish inside my pussy. Try to make it intimate. Face to face, probably. Some

way that he could make sure I was there with him,
some way he could reassert my vulnerability.

Hell no.

So I sped up, started bobbing back and forth,
taking him deep into my throat each time, until I
had a good rhythm going. I felt him shudder, heard
him grunt and sigh, muttering curses under his
breath as he neared the edge.

Closer, now.

He throbbed in my mouth, and I tasted pre-
come on my tongue. Full strokes, from the tip of
his erection against my lips to his belly against my
nose, long wet strokes of my mouth around his
shaft. I moved my hands to his ass and gripped him,
pulled against him, encouraging him to move. He let
himself thrust, then, and I kept pulling, harder and
harder, getting him to thrust, to fuck my mouth.

And then he tried to slow down, tried to stop,
jerking on my hair, but I ignored him and bobbed
harder.

"Shit, Layla. You need to stop."

"Mmm-mmm."

"Fuck, I'm close." He liked the vibrations, so I
hummed as I deep-throated him, and it wasn't just
for him. I felt him throbbing and thrusting and knew
he was close, and I was humming in appreciation for
his body, for the taste of his cock in my mouth.

But then he did something totally unexpected.

He jerked free, roughly, and stumbled backward. "I said *stop*."

I fell back against the bed. "Why?" I was genuinely confused. Most guys never questioned it when they were that close to finishing.

"I'm not ready to come in your mouth."

"Where do you want to come, then?" I asked, coyly.

He was tensed all over, fists flexing as he held himself back, growling though his teeth as he willed himself away from the edge of coming.

"Inside you."

I smiled up at him, a devious, mischievous grin. I reached out and grabbed his cock, and before he could protest or stop me, I had him in my mouth again, gave him one good deep-throat, then glanced up at him. "This *is* inside me, Nick."

I wanted it.

I wanted him to give in to me.

This was about winning, about getting my way.

It was also about retaining some distance, some objectivity, some semblance of my former self, maintaining the Layla who didn't feel intense emotional turmoil during soul-shattering sex, the Layla who was shut down and casual. The Layla who didn't fall asleep in a man's arms, content and sated and utterly vulnerable.

Like I'd just done, for the first time ever, last night.

I needed to feel like I was in control, like I was doing what *I* wanted.

"Jesus, Layla." He grunted this as I resumed my rhythm, going deep, swallowing as he entered my throat to massage his shaft with my throat muscles and my tongue.

I cupped his balls and pressed hard against his taint, gripped his ass with clawed fingers, moaning as I took him, going down hard and fast now, unrelenting and frenzied.

"*Fuck*," he growled.

"Mmmmm."

"I'm coming, oh fuck, I'm about to come."

"Mmm-hmmmm."

He buried his fingers in my hair and pulled me closer, thrusting into my mouth. I held myself still and let him fuck my throat, swallowing with each thrust, feeling him reach the edge, knowing he wasn't going to stop, now.

"Shit…Layla, oh god…"

I felt him spurt, felt it start in his balls cupped in my palm, felt it as a tense of his taint and a throb of his thrusting cock. The first load splashed right down my throat, and I swallowed it, and then backed away to suction my lips around the head, letting go of his rock-hard ass to glide my fingers around his shaft at the base. I stroked him and bobbed around the tip, sucking hard. He cursed again and thrust forward, and now his body locked, thrust forward as the orgasm ripped through him. I milked it for all it was worth, tasting come on my tongue, feeling it spurt. I swallowed it all and kept sucking, kept pumping as he came again, and again, massaging his taint the whole time.

Finally, he was done. I let him pop free of my mouth but stroked his softening length a few more times until another drop of come seeped out, which I licked away.

"Jesus, Layla."

"You say that a lot," I pointed out, standing up to relieve my protesting knees.

"You have a way of forcing it out of me."

I just smiled and swayed my hips as I went into the bathroom and shut the door. As soon as I was alone, I collapsed onto the toilet and let myself hyperventilate.

What the hell had I done?

I'd had sex with Harris.

Fucking Harris had been a *great* idea; that wasn't the problem. He'd rocked my world just as hard as I knew he would. The trouble was, he'd rocked it a little *too* hard.

He'd rocked it so hard something had been shaken loose in my heart.

I wanted more, not just more sex and, more hard fucking. Duh, yeah, I wanted that, too. But problematically, I needed more of *him*. More of Nick, the man who kissed my temple, the man who gently clutched my throat as he held himself still within me, just feeling me. More of the man who thought I was perfect.

I didn't *want* to want more of that. More of that was dangerous. More of that meant everything changing. Everything already *had* changed, and if I gave in to wanting Nick, wanting to be with him all the time like some addiction, it'd all change again, and I'd lose myself.

I shook myself. "Get a grip, Layla," I told myself out loud.

I peed, and then turned on the shower. When the water was as hot as it was going to get, I got in and soaked my hair, letting the water sluice down my body. I let myself lose focus, let myself not think, not feel, not worry. I just let the hot water beat down on my back and scalp and tried to let the water wash away my troubles.

I didn't hear the door open. Didn't notice the shower curtain slide aside. I didn't notice anything until I felt hands on my hips and lips on my inner thigh.

I jumped a mile, shrieking. "Holy shit, Harris!" I pushed his head away. "What the fuck are you doing?"

He was kneeling in the tub in front of me, staring up at me. "You didn't think you could get away that easily, did you?"

"Yeah, kind of."

He just grinned. "Good try."

"I'm taking a shower."

"No, you're not." He grabbed my ankle, lifted my leg, and draped the back of my knee over his shoulder.

"I'm not?"

He shook his head. "Nope."

"Then what am I—oh." His tongue was sliding up the inside of my thigh, slowly, inching closer to my core. "Ho—oh…*oh*—holy shit."

"You're going to want to hold onto something, babe." He pressed his lips to my pussy and sucked my clit into his mouth, and then backed away. "This might take a while."

It took a while.

It didn't have to, but he drew it out.

He got me back. Oh Jesus, did he get me back.

His tongue circled my clit until I was gasping for

breath and gyrating against his face, and then he'd stop and slide fingers inside me and fuck me with his fingers, reach in, curl his fingers and find that spot high inside and rub it, and his tongue would slide slowly against my clit until I was grinding against his face again, and then he'd stop and just flick tiny quick little bursts of his tongue tip against my clit, teasing, teasing.

I held onto the wall, pressing my palm flat against the wet subway tile for balance, standing on one foot, my back against the wall, the shower streaming down against my neck and over my breasts.

He drew it out over and over, getting me to the edge again and again, then pulling me back only to drive me there once more.

When I was frantic and desperate, riding the edge but unable to fall over because he just wouldn't give it to me, wouldn't give me the rhythm or consistency I needed, I started to growl, grabbing his head with both hands and grinding against his mouth, pushing against him.

And then…he pulled away.

"What the fuck, Harris?" I growled. "I was—I'm right there."

He shut off the water, then stepped out of the tub, shoved the curtain aside, and reached in. Lifted me as effortlessly as picking up a suitcase. Carried me dripping wet out of the bathroom and set me on the bed.

"Nick, I'm soaking wet—"

"Don't care."

"Are there new sheets?"

He leaned over me, eyes intense. "Nope. But again, don't care. We're leaving soon, anyway."

"For Rio?"

"Eventually."

"What—what—why did you stop?"

He was levered over me, face inches from mine, and I realized he was hard again, ready again. "Because I know what you're doing."

"What am I doing?"

"You can't get away from this, Layla."

"Away from what?"

He pushed into me, entering me slowly, his eyes on mine, thrusting in to the hilt. "Don't play coy with me, Layla Campari. I know you. And I know you're fucking terrified."

"I am not." This was breathy, because I totally *was* terrified, and I hated it, and also because he felt so goddamned perfect inside me, felt so goddamned perfect above me.

"It's okay to be scared," he said, and moved slowly, gliding in a smooth rhythm. "I won't hurt you. I won't disappear. I won't let you down."

"Fuck." My throat was hot, tight. "Goddamn it, Nick."

"You are the only person who has ever called me that, you know." He bent to capture my nipple in his mouth, and then my lips. "You can't escape it. You can't stop it. And deep down, you don't want to."

"Shut up and fuck me, Harris." I bucked against him, angry now.

He just laughed and kept moving slowly, gently. He pressed down on me with his weight, pinning me, and caressed my face in that way he had, thumb grazing my lips. "Oh, I will. I'll fuck you every way there is, twice. I'll fuck you until you can't see straight. I'll fuck you sideways, upside down, in your ass, I'll fuck your mouth and I'll fuck your tits, and I'll fuck your sweet pussy until it's raw."

I gasped, blinking, as he pushed deeper, lifting my legs onto his shoulders and driving deeper yet. "Oh—oh—holy fucking shit. Nick…Jesus." He was so deep now it hurt perfectly, so deep, filling me completely, stretching me and opening me.

"But you know what else, Layla?"

I took the bait. I had no choice. "What, Nick?"

"I won't *just* fuck you."

"No?"

"Oh no. I'm going to show you what it means

to be possessed by me. To be treasured. To be the object of devotion, and passion." He moved, slowly, deeply, rhythmically. Gently. Tenderly. "I'm going to show what it means to be *mine*. And you'll never want anything else again."

Little did he know, I already didn't want anything else. So ruined. I was so ruined.

Then the bastard messed me up even more. Right when I knew he was on the edge, and I was there too, he pulled out.

"I'm going to kill you," I snapped.

He didn't answer. He rolled us so I was on top, let me find my balance, and then slid his body down until his face was underneath me. Not one to look a gift horse in the mouth—whatever the fuck *that* bullshit phrase even means—I sat on his face. His tongue speared into me, and I gasped. Then his tongue flicked my clit, and I moaned. And then he sucked my clit into his mouth, shoved three fingers into my slit, reached up and twisted my nipple...and I screamed.

I rode his face like he was a goddamned penny pony at the grocery store, and he took it and ate me out until I was screaming nonstop and frantic and grinding my clit on his mouth like I'd die if he stopped. I just might have, you never know.

But the bastard wasn't done. He just *had* to up

the ante, because he was a bastard. The best kind of bastard, but still a bastard.

What did he do, you ask?

He put one in the stink. Not the pinky of the left hand he was three-fingers deep inside my pussy with, either. No, he reached around my hip with his right hand and pressed his middle finger against my asshole. Already cresting the edge of orgasm, this was nearly too much. But just because I'm a glutton for punishment, I held myself back. I wanted that finger in me, first. I forced myself to relax and open for him as he massaged the rosebud of muscle.

I grabbed his hand, pulled it up to my face, and spat on his fingers.

No shame in my game, bitches.

I heard as well as felt the bass rumble of his laughter.

He smeared my saliva against my rear entrance until I was nice and coated, and then pressed his finger in, gently, slowly, carefully. One knuckle, pulsing rhythmically in and out, tongue slowly working my clit, keeping me at the edge but not pushing me over. I rocked my hips, and got another knuckle's worth for my effort. I couldn't stop the moans from escaping then, and didn't try. He increased the pace of his mouth over my core, tongue flicking in quickening circles, fingers sliding in and out of my hot, wet slit, long thick middle finger now fully inserted, his palm flat against my flesh. Couldn't be a comfortable position, his wrist curled around like that. I let myself go, then.

I felt it start in my belly and in my chest, my muscles tightening, my heartbeat going wild, my thighs trembling from the effort of holding myself aloft over him. I cursed and started convulsing, grinding on his face arrhythmically, wildly, rocking against his fingers, the one and the three, which he used to great effect, thrusting them in and out of me in a steady rhythm.

The scream when I came probably woke up people in China.

He still wasn't done with me.

Still coming, I had no choice but to grab onto his shoulder for balance as he slid out from beneath me, rose to sit on his shins, and lifted me up. My thighs were done, toast, jelly; I had to cling to his neck, shaking all over, quaking with tremors of the orgasm that still had me in its grip.

Harris wasted no time, no motion or energy. He palmed my ass cheeks and lifted me up, and I, savvy to his intentions, reached between us and guided him home.

Fuck. Did I really just think that? Home? There was no home. I had no home.

But this felt like it. Holding onto Harris's strong neck and broad shoulders, wrapping my legs around his waist and letting myself sink down around him to sit on his thighs...that felt like home.

Clutching Harris for all I was worth, still ripped by waves of climax, feeling him deep inside me, one of his corded forearms beneath my buttocks, the other gathering my hair into a ponytail and gripping it at the base of my skull and roughly jerking my head back so I *had* to look at him...

I was *HOME*.

Goddamn it.

He just held me like that. Seated on him, my head tilted back so I was staring down at him past my nose, my hands clawed into talons gripping his shoulders. So deep. So thick inside me. Throbbing, hot. My cunt pulsed around him, oozed essence. He didn't move, just stared at me.

"You feel us?" He thrust once, hard.

"Yes," I breathed, and tried to close my eyes.

"Fucking *look* at me, Layla." He gave my hair a jerk. "Tell me what you feel. Out loud, right now." Another thrust, this one slow but forceful, lifting me up with the power of his thighs.

"I feel us. I feel you." I ground my hips on him, needing more, even though he couldn't go deeper and I'd already come so hard I was still out of breath, but there were the facts: I needed *more*, and I hated myself for it. Hated my weakness for the drug that was Nick.

"Copout."

"It's not a copout, that's what I feel."

He pulled on my hair until I bent backward, so my tits thrust into his face. He latched onto my breast, licking first the wide dark brown circle of my areola and then flicking his tongue over my nipple. A thrust, once again hard and slow, lifting me up. He was doling out the thrusts like they were in short supply, and it was working, making me want them all the more for how few I was getting.

"No shit you feel us, Layla. I'm inside you. I can't go any deeper." He bit my neck, my throat, kissed my chin, keeping a firm grip on my hair so I couldn't move to even kiss him back. "I know you feel us. Tell me what's inside you."

"You are."

He laughed. "True. But you know what I mean. Don't be a pussy, Layla."

"Tell me what *you* feel, then, Mr. I'm In Touch With My Feelings." He may not have heard the capital letters on that, but they were there.

"I've fucked a lot of women in my life—"

"Wow. Great to know while you're inside me," I snapped.

He continued as if I hadn't spoken. "None of them have ever made me feel even a fraction of what you do, Layla. You've ruined me for other women. You've ruined me for sex with anyone else, ever again. And you know how we talked about being scared every time I went into combat? Well, I'm not ashamed to admit the way you're making me feel emotionally has me all kinds of fucked up in the head. I'm scared of you. You scare the shit out of me."

"How many women have you fucked, Harris?"

"You're jealous?"

"No. God, no." I totally was. I didn't want to be, but the theme of this whole mess with Harris was me at war with myself.

"You are."

"No, I'm not. It's just a dick move to brag about how many women you've fucked while you're in the middle of fucking a woman."

"I wasn't bragging. Just stating a fact."

"Why are we having this conversation?" I asked. "Why now?"

"Because you're trying to avoid me. You thought you could avoid me by going down on me." Just to make sure things stayed...relevant, he pushed up into me, pulling a gasp from me. "You can't avoid this. It's real. It's happening. It's *been* happening."

"I'm not avoiding anything."

"You're a shitty liar, Layla."

I was, though. The man knew me. I was a bad liar, and I was lying.

"Goddamn it, Nick. What the hell do you want from me?"

"I want you to admit this is more than just outrageously incredible sex. It's more than just a good hard fucking." He pulled my hair again so I was leaning backward, spine arched, and he leaned backward as well, reaching between our bodies to caress my clit. He fucked me, then, moving hard and fast, pounding into me over and over, driving up with all of his considerable power so our bodies crashed together with a *slapslapslapslap* of flesh on flesh.

My tits bounced roughly on my chest, my ass hit his thighs and shook like gelatine.

God, I loved it.

"You like that, don't you, Layla?"

"Fuck yes," I admitted, breathless.

"You like it when I fuck you so hard you can't see straight."

"Don't stop, Harris. Please, don't stop."

He stopped.

He let go of my hair and tipped me backward so I hit the mattress, and then he was over me, above me, still inside me, his hand on the back of my knee stretching my leg up toward my chest, splitting me open, pushing deeper and deeper. He pinned my knee in place with his arm, and his free hand brushed my hair out of my face.

And he moved, slowly, gently, with a rhythm so smooth there was no way for me to know where the thrust in stopped and the pull out began.

"How about this?" he asked. "Do you like this?"

I whimpered in answer. Lifted my hips to meet his. "Yes," was all I could say.

"Is this fucking?"

I shook my head. "No."

He let go of my leg, and I wrapped my heels around his back. He braced himself with his hands beside my face, and just moved, plain vanilla missionary. It had never felt so good.

Or so intimate.

"What about this?"

"Shut up, Nick."

"What am I doing to you, right now? What is this, Layla?"

"Goddamn it." I knew what he was doing, and I didn't dare say it.

He lifted a palm and did his thing, cupping my cheek, brushing a thumb over my lips. Bent, kissed my chest, between my breasts. The slope of one breast. Licked a nipple, crossed to the other side and kissed the slope of that one, the wide dark areola and the thick, nearly black nipple.

"What am I doing, Layla?" he demanded.

I clawed my fingers down his back in equal parts ecstasy and anger. Bit his shoulder until I knew it had to hurt like a motherfucker, but he didn't even flinch, just let me bite him.

"What is this thing happening between us, Layla?" He kissed my cheekbone. My forehead. My temple. Always moving, slowly, smoothly, rhythmically, beautifully, and perfectly. "Say it, babe. I want to hear it."

I shook my head.

"No?" he said.

I shook my head again, refusing to betray myself by speaking. If I did, my voice would break. I'd be forced to admit...shit, a lot of things I didn't want to admit.

The motherfucker pulled out and got off the bed, breathing hard, eyes blazing, green orbs fiery and angry, chest heaving, sweat sheening his skin.

I threw a tantrum, kicking my feet and flailing my hands, screaming in anger. "*Goddamn* it, Nicholas! Don't do this to me!"

"Why not?"

"Why can't it just be sex?"

He was so hard it had to be painful, his erection flat against his belly, leaking from the tip, my essence smeared and glistening on the beautiful shaft of his goddamned perfect penis. I wanted it. I wanted it back in me. I wanted to feel him finish, feel him let go, wanted his breath on my skin, his weight on my body. I wanted his seed dripping out of me and sliding down my thighs. I wanted his arms around me. I wanted to wake up with him and share the intimacy of not having sex, of just talking, sharing, touching, having coffee and being together. I'd never wanted that before. I hadn't thought I ever would.

I was fucking terrified of how badly I wanted all that.

And Nicholas motherfucking Harris, the man I wanted and needed more than I'd ever wanted or needed anything in my entire stupid life—he wanted to know why I was so scared.

"Why can't it be more?" he pushed. "What the hell are you so scared of?"

"EVERYTHING!" I shouted. "I'm scared of how much I need you, how suddenly it happened. I don't believe in insta-love. I don't even believe in love at all! I don't believe in anything except my own ability to take care of myself. I don't need anyone. I've never needed anyone. I don't *want* to need anyone. But I—I fucking need you, and I hate it. I *hate* it. And I hate you for making me need you. For being so fucking amazing that I don't just need you, I *want* you. I *crave* you. And I hate that too."

"Why? Why is it so bad to need someone?" He wasn't sitting down, and his massive erection wasn't fading.

"Because."

"What are you, three? Give me a real answer."

"Or what?"

"Or nothing. Or I'll take you back to Detroit and post a guard you'll never see on you. You'll never see me again. You can have your lonely, workaholic, pathetic life, if that's what you want. I'm not going to force this out of you."

"But you are." Even in the midst of having my feelings ripped out and put on display, I couldn't take my eyes off his cock. Harris's penis was just right, thick enough to stretch me, long enough to fill me. Almost as if...

Fuck it. I knew I had to finish the thought:

Almost as if it had been custom-made specifically for me, to fit me like a puzzle, to complete me, to pleasure me and me alone.

I choked on my own emotions.

Finally, I sat up, put my feet on the floor and folded my hands on my lap, wringing them together, squeezing until my knuckles protested. Kept my eyes off his, on the floor.

What did I want? Him? This?

Or my life back in Detroit?

"Say something, Layla."

I tried. I couldn't. It was all too much, too hard too fast and all at once. I just shook my head.

"Fine." He managed to say the word with both a sigh and a snap. "Have it your way."

I watched him through lowered eyelids; he snatched his pants off the floor, sat on the edge of the bed and shoved both feet into the legs at the same time. He buttoned them over his erection, which was finally starting to subside. Made quick work of his shirt, buttoning it up with lightning speed. Socks, boots. Dug something out of the black bag, a strap of some kind. A holster, which he buckled onto his torso, shoving a pistol into it at shoulder level.

And just like that, within thirty seconds, he was no longer Nick, my lover—he was Harris, the security expert. The killer. Hard, cold, calculating.

He strode across the room and unlocked the door, pulling his phone out of his pocket.

"Where are you going?" Suddenly I was afraid of being left here alone.

"Gotta call Thresh, see if the ride out of here is ready."

"Will you be back?" Goddammit, I sounded needy, weak.

He glanced at me. "You think I'd leave you

here?"

I shrugged. "I don't know. Why wouldn't you?"

He went into the bathroom and I heard him wash his hands. He returned, staring at me. When I said nothing, he shook his head. "You're an idiot. For such an intelligent woman, you're a fucking moron."

That hurt. Fuck, it hurt.

He watched me for a second, but I couldn't look at him.

Then, with a sigh, he walked out the door.

Truly alone, everything hit me.

Like hitting the ground from ten thousand feet without a parachute, the wall of emotions and memories all hit me, and I just...broke.

Shattered.

Crumbled.

I ugly cried. For the first time in my life, I ugly cried.

I didn't ugly cry when Eric and I broke up. I didn't ugly cry when Momma died, or when Mario died, or when Vic died. I didn't cry when I got raped in my senior year of high school. Or when I had to get an abortion because I'd gotten pregnant because of it. I didn't cry when I was homeless, or when Kyrie just fucking left me to go be with Valentine God-damned Roth. I didn't cry for fucking anything. Not even when I killed that asshole Cut with my bare hands.

    But when Harris walked out that door?

    I bawled like a baby.

    Why?

    Because I knew I'd really fucked up this time.

15

SAY IT

You know why I don't cry? Because it's exhausting. It just sucks the energy right out of you, leaves you a snot-encrusted, puffy-eyed, blubbering, lip-quivering mess.

But no matter how hard I tried, I just couldn't stop. It started with knowing I'd probably just messed up the one good thing that had ever happened to me, but then all the shit I'd just been through piled on. Getting kidnapped. Getting kidnapped in a thong and a T-shirt. Being locked in a tiny, cold, fish-stanky cell on a boat. Being forced to resort to hiding a Bic pen up my poon. Flaunting topless for Vitaly, never knowing when he'd decide to just rape me, or torture me, or kill me; not knowing was the worst part. Cut trying to rape me, and having to kill him. Jesus, that in particular sent me spiraling into a paroxysm of sobs, the awful visceral memory of the way it felt to smash that pen through his eyeball, the way it just…*gave* with a nasty squish. Having to slam it deeper so he'd just fucking die, and stop twitching and thrashing. Running. Being fucking *hot*, and hungry, and alone. The hike up that motherdick of a hill. The chase through São Paulo in the stolen car, culminating in Harris finding me, and then the ambush…killing *another* human being.

And then…Harris. Stealing my heart, blatant and brazen. Just snatching it out of my chest and claiming it like he had every right to it.

He *made love* to me.

The bastard.

These thoughts caused me to sob even harder. I just couldn't seem to stop.

I had no clue what time it was. I had no idea how long I'd slept last night before waking up and sucking some epic cock. How long had that taken? I still tasted his come in my mouth. My pussy still ached. I could almost feel his finger in my ass. I felt him around me, behind me, above me, inside me.

I smelled him: sweat, sex, faint deodorant. Leather. Gunpowder, or whatever they used in bullets, now. Cordite? Who the hell cared? It was a sexy as hell smell.

With a start, I realized he *was* behind me, spooning me. I was still naked, and as previously stated, a snotty, lip-quivering, blubbering, rat's-nest hair, sex- and sweat-stinky mess. He had a hand on my hip, nose in my hair, chest against my back.

"I'm no good with words."

"No, Nick, I—"

"Shut up and listen a second, Layla," he interrupted. "Just let me speak. I'm no good with words, with expressing myself. Hell, I'm no good with people. I'm good at one thing: assessing and eliminating threats. It's all I know. I've never been in a relationship. Nothing has ever lasted longer than a weekend. I'm not the commitment type, you might say. I'm gone too much, and my job is too dangerous. And I just…no one has ever captured my interest, much less held it. I've never *wanted* to make anything last for more than a few days of feeling good. And now, I feel like I'm just too damn old to change my ways."

"How old are you?" I asked.

"I'm forty-two." He flattened his palm over my belly, low, fingers splayed, pressing me back against him. "I'm not done. Just listen. My point is, I fucked it up with you, a bit ago. I have no right to demand anything from you, to act like I did. And then I fucked up even more because I heard you crying and I stayed outside. I can face down men with guns and not flinch. I've been shot and I've been tortured and I've been stabbed and beaten and left for dead. I've had malaria, typhus, dysentery, and dengue fever and survived it all. But I didn't know how to deal with a woman I'd made cry."

"I'm glad, honestly. I wouldn't have wanted you to see me like that. It was ugly."

"No part of you is ugly, Layla. Not one thing. You're the most beautiful woman I've ever known, inside and out." He spoke just above a whisper, his voice a heady, buzzing murmur in my ear. "You don't owe me shit."

"I do, though."

"How do you figure?"

"You were right. I'm scared shitless of what I'm feeling for you. Like, where the fuck did it come from? Why is it so strong, so fast? What does it mean? I don't know how to do it. How to be—that kind of girl. How to let you in. How to be…I don't know. Like I said, that kind of girl. Because I'm *not*, Nick. I never have been. You said you've been with a lot of women, and I for real wasn't judging you for that, because I've been with a lot of men."

"Still don't get why you think you owe me anything, though."

I sighed. "Because…god, I don't even know. Because you were right. Because you had the courage to own up to how you feel, and I didn't."

"That's stupid. It makes no sense."

"Well gee, Nick, don't mince words or anything. Tell me how you really feel."

He laughed. "I'll never bullshit you. I can promise you that much."

He was still fully clothed, the holster pressing against my back, the butt of the gun cold on my bare skin, his zipper scraping my butt. He rolled to his back and unhooked the holster, setting it on the floor beside the bed, and then turned back to resume spooning me, and this time his hand slid just beneath my boobs, just barely brushing the undersides.

"I can tell you one thing, though," he said.

"What's that?"

"It wasn't quick, for me. My attraction to you, I mean. You forget, I followed Kyrie around for years. Just under seven years, to be exact. I was there when she met you, watching from a distance through a telephoto lens. I was there watching everything that happened between the two of you. I have a drawer full of memory cards with thousands of pictures of you, and her. You two together. At the bar, at school eating lunch together. Moving into your first apartment together. Every boyfriend you brought home to that apartment with Kyrie, I've got him in a picture, and I've got a file in a cloud account full of dossiers on all of them, criminal records and transcripts and medical records and financial information. Of *your* ex-boyfriends. If you hooked up with a guy more than once, I've got a file on that, too."

"That's a lot of files. I'm trying not to be creeped out, to be honest." The idea made me a little sick, actually. "Why? Why are you telling me this?"

"Full disclosure, I guess. And because I..." he stumbled over his words for the first time since I'd known him. "I fell for you a long fucking time ago, Layla. Those guys in that ambush back there; those weren't the first men I've killed on your behalf. When I wasn't trailing Kyrie, keeping an eye on her, making sure nothing happened to her, I was following you. Protecting you. I couldn't help it. I never got paid for it, because I never put it on the books for Roth to pay me for. I wouldn't have. It was personal. I had to make sure you were safe. I know about that guy in high school. I found him, by the way, and I made sure he paid in fucking blood for what he did to you."

"Holy hell, Nick." I felt tears trickle out of my eyes. My heart clenched.

"I wanted you. But I didn't dare approach you. How could I explain any of it? There was just no way. Finally, when you joined Kyrie and Roth on the *Eli-*

za, it all came to a head. You were there, lying on the deck all day long in those goddamned tiny-ass bikinis, teasing me. Torturing me. You know how many nights I jerked off, thinking about you? Picturing you in that yellow bikini, the one that's just basically strategically placed strings. Picturing you tugging the top down and—*fuck*. Every damn night for months. I couldn't think about anyone else. I went ashore more than once and tried to get it out of my system with someone else, but I couldn't follow through. I haven't been with anyone since you came aboard."

Something clicked into place. "Did you jerk off thinking about me, Nicholas?" I asked.

"Yes. I did. A lot."

"A lot?" Should I have been grossed out? Because I wasn't. It...turned me on, actually. "How much is a lot?"

He hesitated for a moment. "Every night. Every morning. Why do you think I was such a grumpy asshole all the time?"

"I thought you just didn't like me," I said.

"I felt guilty as hell about it. But I couldn't stop. I felt dirty and sick and fucked up, coming into my hand while thinking about you. And then I'd have to see you and talk to you, and that's all I could think about, what I'd done while thinking about you, just a couple hours before. And then you'd prance around in a slinky bikini and your tits would be bouncing and your ass would be swaying and I swear to fucking god I'd pop a semi just looking at you." He rolled to his back and scrubbed at his face with both hands. "Doesn't help that I'm damn near twenty years older than you. Makes me feel even dirtier."

"You're forty-two, you said?" I rolled to my other side, so I was facing him. He nodded. "I'm twenty-seven, so that makes you fifteen years older than me. Not twenty. And it doesn't make a difference, anyway."

"Fifteen years, Layla. I was a sophomore in high school the year you were born. I was a decorated combat veteran by the time you graduated from high school. It does make a difference."

I put my hand on his chest. "Your age is honestly the least of my concerns, Nick. For real. I don't care."

"You will. At some point, you will."

"Why? What makes you so sure?" He didn't answer. I sat up, faced him sitting cross-legged. "I can answer your question now, Nick. I could have when you asked it before, but I just…was too scared. I *do* need you, Nick. I need you. I want you. I've fought it for…a long time. I don't *want* to need you, even now. I still don't want to need you, but I fucking do. Not just to get me out of here, to keep me alive and out of Vitaly's hands. I need you…inside me."

He finally glanced at me, lips quirking. "R*eeee*-ally?" He drew the word out and infused it with lecherous sarcasm.

"That's not what I meant, but yes, that way too."

"What changed? Between then and now?"

"The fact that I felt scared and empty when you walked out. The fact that even with everything I've been through in my life, the thought of losing you made me cry when nothing else ever has."

His eyes fixed on mine, green and roiling. "Layla, god. I didn't mean to make you cry."

"Yes you did."

"I let you cry. Alone. For nearly a fucking hour."

"I needed it," I said. "For you, for all that back there, Cut and Vitaly and everything. For…so many things. I needed to cry alone. I needed to wake up, I guess. To see things for how they are."

I scrubbed my hand over my face, letting out a sigh.

"Fucked up. I'm fucked up. You're fucked up. This whole situation is fucked up." I let out a breath. "But I know now that I don't want to go back to Detroit. I don't want to go back to living alone, working three jobs and going to school. After what I've been through, sitting through lectures and taking tests seems…stupid."

"What do you want, then?"

I shrugged. "I don't know. I'll have to figure that out when we're back on the *Eliza*, I guess."

"Thresh has our flight out of here covered. So we can head out whenever we're ready." He rolled off the bed, stood up, and then bent to retrieve his shoulder holster.

"Wait," I said. "We're not done."

He shot me a quizzical look. "We're not?"

"Nope." I scooted to the edge of the bed, set my feet on the floor. Gazed up at him. Let him see the heat in my eyes, the need, and the desire. "You left before we were done."

I took the holster from him and set it carefully on the floor. Reached up and unbuttoned his shirt from the bottom up, and when the last button was freed, I ran my palms up and down his chest, leaned in and kissed his stomach, roamed my palms over his shoulders, brushing the shirt off. He let out a breath that was equal parts relief and pleasure as I unbuttoned his pants, shoved them down over his hips.

His dick swung free, unfurling and swaying and hardening to full erection as I gazed at it. I curled both hands around his shaft and stroked him slowly. And, of course, because it was right there at the perfect level, I had to taste him. Between my lips, tongue sliding over the tip, tasting flesh and a hint of my own essence on his skin.

But then he pulled himself free and pushed me backward. "I don't think so." Nick lowered himself over me, climbing onto the bed, and his mouth descended to mine, his tongue slid over my lips and two fingers brushed over my clit. "Jesus, Layla. You're wet already."

"You do that to me. You have this effect on me, and I don't get it. I mean, I'm always ready, but... there's something about you that just makes my pussy drip, all the time." As if to emphasize my point, his fingers speared into my opening with a wet squelch. "See what I mean?"

He pulled his fingers out of me and lifted them to his mouth, licked my juices away. "I love the way you taste. Sweet as fucking sugar."

"Liar. I taste like pussy."

He laughed. "True. But a very delicious pussy." He moved down my body. "In fact, I think I need a better taste."

I was torn. I wanted him inside me, wanted—*needed*—to feel that connection to him. But I also really, *really* liked the way he ate me out. "Nick..."

"Yeah, baby?" He spread me apart with his thumbs. Flicked his tongue over my clit.

"I need you."

"You'll have me."

"I need you *now*." He ignored me, licking at my pussy like he was eating ice cream off a cone. Lapping, lapping, lapping. I moaned, and buried my fingers in his hair.

"I don't think you're ready. I think you need to come at least once, first." He punctuated his words by sucking my clit into his mouth and sucking on it and flicking it with his tongue tip until I was writhing and gasping and grinding my core against his face.

"Fuck yes, Nick. Eat me, baby. Jesus, that feels so good."

He pushed two fingers into me, and then added a third, and then pulled them back and thrust them back in, over and over, until I was grinding against his face and riding his fingers and moaning nonstop, riding the waves until I crested the climax, and I screamed when I came, gripped his head in trembling fingers and kept him tugged against me, writhing and rolling my hips into his madly fluttering tongue.

And then he was inside me.

All at once, hips between my thighs, huge thick hard smooth cock filling me and stretching me and leaving me breathless with the perfection of it all, my spine arching up off the bed, my hips crushed to his. "Oh Jesus oh shit oh fuck." I let my knees fall apart and drew my heels up to my ass cheeks, grabbed two handfuls of his taut backside and jerked at him. "Fuck me, Nick. I need it."

"No."

My eyes flew open and met his. "No?" I sounded a little shrill, a little panicked. "Why not?"

"Because I'm going to do *so* much more than that."

"Oh." One syllable breathed from my lips, pure relief.

He lowered his forehead to mine and stared into my eyes from millimeters away, his breath on my lips, and pulled back so he could thrust into me. His lips met mine, and I eagerly deepened the kiss, demanded his tongue, held onto his flexing ass with one hand and cupped the back of his head with the other. Kissed him and kissed him and kissed him until we were both breathless.

I felt my heart expanding as he moved inside me, felt my pulse thundering as another orgasm rose up within me. This time, I welcomed the feeling, welcomed the emotion. I felt it, and let it burgeon.

I moved with him, planted my feet in the bed and lifted my hips to meet his.

I can say, without equivocation, that I've never

enjoyed missionary sex as much as in that moment. Physically, it felt like nothing had ever felt before. Emotionally, I was a mess, but a beautiful, delirious mess.

"Layla." His voice was low, intense.

"I'm here, Nick. I'm with you."

"Do you feel this?" He placed my hand over his heart; it pounded as hard as mine.

I put my hand over his and let all the vulnerability I felt shine out through my eyes. I pulled down the walls and defenses and just...*felt*. "Yes, Nick. I feel it."

He pulled his knees beneath himself, pulled my heels over his shoulders and pushed so deep into me my eyes watered.

Okay, fucking fine. I'll admit it: I was crying, because it felt so good. "Oh god, yes. More, Nick. *More*."

He thrust, slowly and rhythmically, unhurried. I reveled in each slide, closed my eyes and focused on the stretch, on the way his cock felt sliding in and out of me.

"Watch us, Layla."

I opened my eyes and watched where our bodies were joined, watched his cock pull back, coated in my essence, and then slide back in. And god, that was sexy. Watching us, watching him, his abs flexing, his hands wrapped around as much of my thighs as he could grip in one hand—which wasn't much—watching his face show his emotions.

"I masturbated thinking about you," I said, apropos of nothing. "I would lie in my bed and picture you just like this, and I would touch myself."

"How? Show me, baby."

I slid my fingers over my slit, used my fingers to spread my lips apart and circled my ring and middle fingers over my clit, gasping at the intense ramping up of sensation. "Like this, Nick. Hard and fast."

He matched my rhythm. "What would you think about?"

"This. Us. Together. I'd picture us fucking. I'd picture you eating me out like you just did, and I'd—" I broke off with a grunt as I came, suddenly, arching forward and clamping down around him. I heard him growl and felt his rhythm slow, felt him tense as he focused on holding back.

"What, Layla? What did you fantasize about? Tell me."

I didn't tell him, I showed him what I wanted, instead. I pushed at his chest, and he pulled out, rolled off. I rose up onto my hand and knees, stared at him over my shoulder, my hair falling in a black curtain of curls. Sweat beaded on my spine, and my skin pebbled as he moved to his knees behind me.

"Like this?" he asked.

I moaned. "Like this." I bowed my spine in, pushing my ass toward him. "This is how I want it. I want to feel you come inside me like this."

He palmed my ass with both hands, caressing each globe slowly, tenderly. "God, I love your ass."

I took him at face value. The way he was staring at me, touching me left no room for doubt. He loved my ass. My tits.

I did wonder, though, if he loved the rest of me, too. I suspected he did. I suspected I returned the feeling. I didn't know what love was like, how it was supposed to feel, either giving or receiving, so I wasn't sure.

But he loved my ass.

I was totally okay with that. It was a big ass, and not all guys appreciated that.

My train of thought was derailed when he pulled my ass cheeks apart. "I want you here, Layla."

I groaned. "You can have me there. But not now. For now I just…I need to feel you in my pussy."

He reached between my legs and feathered a gentle touch over my clit, found my entrance, guided his cock by feel into me. I reached down and nudged him into better position, and he slid deep.

We both groaned in unison.

I pushed back to get him deeper. "Don't hold

back anymore, Nick. Just…take me."

Oh fuck, did he take me. It wasn't hard and fast. It was hard and slow. And I *loved* it. I moaned and groaned and let myself scream as he thrust into me over and over, holding my hips and pulling me back into his crushing thrusts. He didn't relent, and this time I felt him let go, felt him release control and just…take me. No pleasing me, no manipulating admissions out of me. Just taking pleasure, fucking to release.

I touched myself as he fucked me. Rested my head on my forearm and reached between my thighs to finger my clit until I was aching and trembling.

"Layla…"

"That's right, baby," I said, voice rasping and gasping. "Say my name when you come. Shout my name."

"Layla, I'm almost there."

I was close too, but I abandoned the effort and braced myself with both hands and rolled my hips to grind my ass against him, writhing into his frantic fucking. "Give it to me, Nick! Fuck yeah, just like this, fuck me hard, baby."

He fucked me hard, and it hurt so good I didn't need to touch myself, just needed to let him hit inside me and feel lightning burst inside me with each pound of his cock into my pussy.

"Layla…" His voice was ragged and his thrusts faltered. He pushed deep, thrust until my ass cheeks were flush against his hips and he couldn't get any deeper, and still he thrust, harder, growling. "Oh *fuck*, Layla, I'm coming…I'm—Oh—Jesus, *Layla*…"

He came as he said my name, filled me with his come, a river of hot wet seed flooding me. I touched my clit once, and that's all it took to join him in release, thunder detonating inside me, making me shake and go limp and breathless.

Moments later, I was wrapped up in his arms, head resting over his beating heart, listening to his pulse slow from a frantic thunder.

I love you. I felt it bubbling up in my throat, and I shook with the need to say it, the desire to say it.

To hear it said to me.

Kyrie St. Claire was the only human being to ever utter the words "I love you" to me.

I desperately wanted to hear Nicholas Harris say it first, and I couldn't get the words past my lips.

"Layla?" His voice was a sleepy murmur.

"Yeah, Nick?"

"I'm not going to say it. I know you feel it. I know you see it." He sighed. "I will say it, because it's real and it's true. But not like this. I don't want you to think it's got anything to do with how hard I just came. I mean, it does, but that's not why."

He sounded almost awkward, and Harris was *never* awkward. It was cute.

"Nicholas?"

"Yeah?"

"Don't say it if it's not forever. I can handle just about anything. But don't say that if you don't mean it, and if it's not…for forever."

"Layla, I wouldn't—"

"I don't want to talk about it right now. I want to enjoy the afterglow."

He tightened his grip on me, his arms coiling tighter. He may not have said he loved me in so many words, but he'd made it clear he did.

It was enough for right now. More than enough. Maybe even all I could handle, at that point.

Baby steps to falling in love.

"I do, though," Nick murmured.

"Me too."

16

AIN'T OUT OF THE WOODS YET

I woke up when I hit the floor beside the bed with a painful *thud*. "What the fu—*mmmph*—" I was cut off by Harris's hand over my mouth.

"Shut the fuck up. Someone's outside." His voice was a harsh whisper in my ear, barely audible.

I went still, disoriented and sleepy still but recognizing the urgency in his voice. He was crouching over me, naked, pistol in his hand, aiming at the entrance to the bedroom. Tense moments passed, and I heard nothing, saw nothing. Light streamed in bright through the drawn shades. I smelled the thick musk of sex, and looked down to see Harris's dick mere inches from my face, dangling, heavy.

"Mmm. Penis," I whispered, and took him into my mouth, tasting us, feeling him twitch.

"Jesus, Layla! Not now." He glanced down at me and gave me an angry look. The effect of the glare was ruined somewhat by the fact that he was now hard as a rock.

And then I heard it. A creak of hinges, footsteps scuffing on threadbare carpet.

"Awesome," Harris whispered. "Now I'm gonna have to kill this guy with a hard-on. Thanks, babe."

"No problem," I responded, "I'll just wait here."

"Good plan." He moved toward the foot of the bed, holding the pistol in both hands, slinking with predatory grace and silence.

The gear bag was on the floor, and he reached into it, tugged the opening aside, found what he was looking for: a silencer, which he quickly and quietly screwed onto the barrel of his pistol. More waiting. Sounds from the living room, a voice murmuring in a foreign language and another voice responding. Two of them, then.

Harris glanced back at me, put a finger over his lips. I rolled my eyes at him to indicate *no shit, what do you think I'm going to do, start shouting?* Fuck me, he was sexy. Rugged, lean, hard—ha, that was a double entendre, now, thanks to my mouth—muscles of his back shifting in the shadows with each motion. He should have looked stupid, prowling closer to the doorway, buck naked with a gun in his hands. But somehow, he didn't. He looked primal, fierce, and deadly.

My man was deadly, and dead sexy.

My man?

Yes, my man. I decided to own it. He was my man. I was his woman. Oddly, unexpectedly, I kind of liked the feeling of being someone's woman.

I almost missed it. One second I was ruminating on the novelty of being a man's woman, lying on the floor between the bed and the wall—and then Harris was in motion, pistol rising, bucking and flashing and barking quietly, once, twice…three times, four. Still loud, but not the deafening report of an un-silenced pistol. Harris was around the door now, moving in that sort-of crouch all soldiers, policemen, and other combat-trained people all use— Harris just did it in the buff. Still sexy.

He returned after a moment, yanked the sheet off the bed and vanished back into the living room to cover the bodies, his phone to his ear, updating Thresh.

He ended the call as he entered the bedroom, ejecting the clip of his pistol and replacing it. "Okay, we're clear for now. We gotta move. Hit the shower, if you want. But be quick. I want to be gone in twenty minutes."

"But you still have a hard-on, Nick. Want me to

help you out with that?" I took a step toward him.

"It'll go away. We don't have time."

"Does it make me sick that I get horny after situations like this are over?" I asked.

"No. Adrenaline does that to you. It's a documented fact." He hefted the bag of weapons onto the bed, found a box of bullets, and was thumbing rounds into the clip. "I told you, babe. We don't have time. I'll be fine. You can make it up to me later. We have to move."

"I can make it quick. I promise." I sank to my knees anyway.

"Layla—" He lifted me to my feet, brushed his thumb over my lips, and then kissed me. "You suck at listening."

"I'm a bad girl, what can I say? And, obviously, listening isn't all I suck at." I licked my lips.

He laughed. "You're impossible. And amazing." He turned me around and shoved me toward the bathroom, giving my ass a hard, loud spank. "Go. Shower. Before I decide I'm hungry. And we really don't have time for that."

"You sure?" I ran my finger up my seam.

He growled. "Jesus, Layla." He ran a hand through his hair. "Those two were just the first. They shouldn't have found this place, but somehow they did. Which means there will be more out there somewhere. What I need from you right now is to do what I'm telling you, so I can keep us both alive long enough to get you alone on a beach somewhere far from any of this."

"And once we're alone on the beach?"

His eyes narrowed, green gone fiery. "When I've got you alone…baby, I'll fuck you until you can't walk straight. I'll make you come so many times you'll beg me to let you rest."

"That will never happen. I'm pretty sure I don't have an orgasm threshold of any kind whatsoever."

He swayed toward me. "Layla? I swear to god I will spank your ass red and raw if you don't get in the fucking shower right *goddamned* now."

"That's not a threat to me, Harris, that's a temptation."

He grabbed my hair and pulled me down for a kiss. "And I will, someday, I promise. Now…for the last fucking time. Go shower."

His eyes were serious, and I realized if this was going to work between us, I really would have to know when to obey him—no bullshit about it, this was about knowing when Harris needed me to just listen and do what I was told.

I'm terrible at doing what I'm told, but if I could listen to anyone on the planet, it was Harris.

I got my ass in the shower, and was out in three

minutes. I didn't have any of the products I needed to really do my hair properly—which was extensive, as I had pretty difficult-to-manage hair—so I settled for six small braids, which I then braided together into a single thick column. By that time, Harris had laid my clothes out on the bed: a pair of stretchy capri pants, a baby blue thong and matching bra, and a striped V-neck T-shirt. The pants had LOVE PINK written across the butt, which I suspect wasn't an accident on Harris's part.

"You picked the clothes?" I asked, hooking my bra in front and then rotating it around my body to stuff my tits into it.

He watched as I did this, halted in the act of repacking the weapons into the bag. "Yeah. Why?"

I tugged the thong on. "You picked a matching set of lingerie. And this is lingerie, by the way, not exactly practical underwear."

He shrugged, and went back to repacking the assault rifles into the bag. "How the hell do I know the difference? Panties are panties, a bra is a bra. And besides, that color is sexy as fucking sin on you."

It kind of was. Baby blue looked killer against my dark skin. "And the pants with the writing across the butt?"

Another shrug. "They looked like they'd be comfortable. I didn't pick them for the writing."

I slid them on, and then donned the shirt. "Sure. But the writing is a bonus, right? Makes my butt look even bigger, all those letters stretched across all this real estate." I palmed my ass and gave it a smack.

He smirked. "A lot of seriously juicy real estate. It *is* a nice bonus." He gestured at the shoes, a pair of plain, worn black and white Chucks. "Practical shoes, though."

He was already dressed, clean black BDU pants tucked into his calf-high lace-up combat boots, a black T-shirt, and the same hat I'd seen his guys wearing that night on the beach, A1S in scarlet letters on a patch sewn onto a black military-style ball cap.

"What's A-One-S?" I asked, tying my shoes.

"My company. After I got Kyrie back and I sent her and Roth out on the *Eliza*, I realized I'd need a lot of backup if I was going to keep them safe. So I started Alpha One Security. Technically, I'm a private security contractor hired by Roth, rather than working exclusively for him. The effect is the same, though, because right now I only work for him."

"Alpha One Security?" I chuckled. "That's... both clever and entirely unoriginal at the same time. A-One Security, basically, right?"

He zipped the bag and shoved two pistols into holsters on an elaborate system strapped to his torso. I counted two small pistols on his shoulders, another bigger one at his right hip, four knives, and six extra clips of varying sizes. He was loaded for bear.

"Yeah," he said. "That was the idea. I was in a hurry to get it off the ground. I wasn't real concerned with what the company was called, I just needed the LLC up and running ASAP so I could hire my guys. Originality was the least of my concerns."

"Makes sense." I stood up. "I'm ready. Now what?"

There was an assault rifle on the bed, and a pistol with a spare clip. He gestured at the smaller weapon. "Take that. Don't use it unless I tell you to. We get in the Rover and drive to Rio as fast as we can. We should be there already, but we got…sidetracked." A grin, eyes sweeping over my body and back up to my eyes. "I can't say I regret the delay, but we're gonna have to haul ass to make it up."

He preceded me outside, rifle at his shoulder, barrel sweeping side to side, covering me as I got into the ancient SUV. He tossed the heavy bag of gear into the back seat where we could both get at it, apparently now more concerned with access to it rather than hiding it. He was in the driver's seat within seconds and was backing up, the gate already opened.

We were twenty minutes away when I realized

I'd stepped over the three dead bodies without even glancing at them, not so much as a flinch or twist of the stomach. I was getting used to it, it seemed.

I wasn't sure if I was okay with that or not.

The drive to Rio de Janeiro was utterly uneventful. Could have been just another road trip with my boy-friend, except for the fact that we were in Brazil, and that my boyfriend was loaded down with enough guns to take on an army.

And that I had an actual, factual *boyfriend.*

Other than that, it was just any old road trip.

I was about to say something to that effect, but I never got the chance. The windshield exploded in a shower of glass, the front tire popped, and a hail of bullets riddled the body of the SUV. I ducked, covering my face, and Harris twisted the vehicle to the right. He gunned the engine, rounding a corner, the tail end sliding with a squeal of tires, the body swaying. I heard the chatter of machine guns, heard bullets *thunk* into the body. Harris cursed under his breath and hauled the vehicle around another corner. I watched him out of the corner of my eye, ducked down beneath the window, staying out of sight. He was completely focused, driving with one hand, jerking the shifter back with the other, glancing in the mirror. We were in the middle of downtown Rio, on a road that ran parallel to the beach. The sea was on our right, the city on our left, not a cloud in the sky. Another tire-squealing turn, and we were darting between the maze of buildings, flat tire flopping and the rim grinding.

I dared a peek behind us, and saw a small black sedan following behind us, and as I watched a dark head popped up from the sunroof, leveling a huge machine gun at us. "Shit!" I ducked back down, just in time.

The back window shattered and rounds thudded into the seats behind us.

"Shoot back, Layla. The driver, the shooter, the engine, doesn't matter. Just return fire."

I swallowed hard and grabbed my pistol off the seat between us, twisted in place and took aim over the top of the seatback. I aimed at the windshield, held my breath, and squeezed the trigger. The windshield spiderwebbed but didn't shatter, so I fired twice more, and finally it broke with a spray of white glass shards. I saw a face, then, dark skin and a goatee. I ducked again as bullets hit the seat, passed through, and smashed into the dashboard. I popped up, fired twice, and ducked back down.

Harris glanced at me, a smile on his face.

"What?" I demanded. "What the hell is there to smile about?"

He jerked us around a corner, jammed on the brakes, and then floored the gas and spun the wheel to swerve around a slow-moving truck. Another glance at me. "You. You're sexy, shooting my gun. Ducking down behind the bench like it's going to stop a bullet. You're just hot as fuck. A woman with a gun in her hands is kind of a turn-on for me, I guess."

All I caught was the part about the bench not stopping a bullet. "So I shouldn't duck, is what you're saying?"

He shook his head. "Do you intentionally ignore the best parts of what I say to you?"

"Me not getting shot is pretty important, I'd think!"

"True, true. But ducking behind that bench isn't going to do anything. Their shots have already gone through." He reached to the side and fingered a ragged hole in the aged leather.

I sat up, realizing he was right. I took aim at the driver and fired, and this time I hit him. He grabbed his arm, and I saw red spray on the window beside him, and his car swerved. That was all it took. He lost control just long enough to slam into the back of a service van, the front accordioning and crunching under the rear bumper. I heard shouts and screams, and then we were around the corner and out of sight.

"I hit him! I got him!" I shouldn't have been elated, but I was. "I'm a badass!"

Harris laughed. "You sure are, baby. Good shot."

"Am I bad person for not even feeling bad?"

He shrugged. "I'm not really the best person to ask, I don't think. My perspective is kind of skewed."

"I guess you're right." I glanced at him. "So when you say a woman with a gun in her hands is a turn-on, do you mean that literally, or…?"

Harris shot me a look as I posed for him, holding the weapon in both hands out in front of me, arms straight, hair blowing in the wind. "Baby, if we weren't running for our lives, I'd stop and show you how literally I mean it."

"So do you have any fantasies regarding me and guns?"

He shifted on the seat. "Um." A glance in the mirrors. "Yeah, actually. But I'm going to save that one for when we're out of this."

"Come on, Nick! Just tell me what it is."

He blew out a breath. "Let's just say it involves you wearing nothing but a bandolier of shells, with my M4 in your hands."

"I can see how that would be sexy. It'd have to be

a big bandolier, though." I smirked at him.

He pulled out his phone. "The point, Layla, is that the bandolier *isn't* big enough to cover everything." He handed it to me. "Call Thresh. He's in the contacts under his name, obviously. Tell him we're coming in hot."

I found the contact entry, touched it, and held the phone to my ear. It rang twice. "What'cha got, boss?"

"It's Layla, actually. I'm with Harris and he says to tell you we're coming in hot. Whatever that means."

"How hot?"

"I don't know what that means. I mean, I know *I'm* pretty hot, both literally and metaphorically—"

"It means you've got pursuit," he interrupted, sounding both irritated and amused at my rambling. "Bad guys after you. In danger."

"Oh. Yeah. There was one car behind us, but I shot the driver and they're dead now. Or probably dead. I don't see anyone else right now, but they have a tendency to show up when you least expect it."

"*You* shot the driver?"

"Yep!" I sounded proud of myself, because I was.

"From a moving vehicle?"

"Well, it wasn't a headshot or anything. I just

winged him, as Harris would say. He crashed."

"Nice. Okay, well, tell Harris that I'm on the runway, engines idling, ready to go. I'll be in the cargo hold, ready to cover your approach. Got it?"

"I'll tell him." *Click*. I glanced at the phone, and then handed it to Nick. "What is it with you men and not even saying 'bye' before you hang up? It's rude!"

He shrugged. "I don't know. It's a guy thing, I guess. Or maybe it's a military thing. We don't waste time with pleasantries. No point and no time."

"Anyway, Thresh says to tell you he's on the runway, engines idling, and that he'll be in the cargo hold ready to cover our approach."

"Perfect." He gestured at my pistol. "Reload."

Turns out I didn't need to reload, because there was no one else behind us and we arrived at the airfield a couple minutes later. We got out of the SUV and ran up the ramp to the cargo hold of a massive, twin-engine aircraft. The scene actually reminded me of that scene from the cartoon movie *Rio*, where the awkward American girl and the gumpy Brazilian bird guy are in the Carnival float, chasing the birds onto an airstrip. Except, there were no birds on the airplane, just all seven feet of Thresh—and holy Moses, St. Peter, Jesus, and Mary herownself...Thresh was shirtless, wearing nothing but a pair of cut-off cargo shorts, the ends frayed and ragged. He was the most heavily muscled man I'd ever seen, easily rivaling both Arnold Schwarzenegger and Dwayne Johnson—and I'd say Thresh probably had the advantage. I stumbled as I passed him, gawking openly. I mean, that kind of build didn't do it for me, sexually speaking, but it was still a hell of an impressive sight.

He winked at me. "Take a picture, sweetheart. It'll last longer." He had a massive machine gun in his hands, the kind of gun you usually see mounted on the sides of helicopters in Vietnam war movies.

"Don't call my woman 'sweetheart,' you big asshole," Harris snapped. "I'll kick your ass."

Thresh glanced from me to Harris. "Your woman?"

"You fucking heard me."

"All right then." He eyed me again, assessing rather than leering. "So, when you say 'your woman', what does that mean, exactly, boss?"

Harris was in the cockpit, flipping switches, settling a headset on his head. He turned around and glanced through the open door. "It means shut the fuck up and mind your own goddamned business, that's what it fucking means."

Thresh's eyebrows rose. "Whoa, dude. Uptight much?"

"Uptight?" Harris rose out of the seat, pulling at

the headset. "I'll show you—"

"Harris! Sit down, shut up, and fly the fucking airplane. We don't have time to measure dicks."

Thresh's eyes, already wide, widened further when Harris did as I said. The noise of the engines ramped up, and we bolted forward. Something sparked off the ramp and ricocheted around the cargo hold with angry *ping-zzzzinggg-buzzzzz*, and Thresh's hand—which was so big a fully-grown Pomeranian could have sat in his palm—shoved me to one side. He dropped to his knees, flipped a bipod out, and dropped to his belly. Our plane was howling down the runway, picking up speed, but Thresh didn't seem concerned by this as he took aim and opened fire at the black SUV roaring up behind us. I grabbed hold of the nearest object, which was a chain fastened to the floor and to the wall, clinging to it as I felt the ground fall away. The banging of the machine gun was the most deafening sound I'd ever heard, and it rocked Thresh's entire body back with each report. He fired in bursts of three shots, and on the fourth burst, the hood of the SUV crumpled, the front bumper buried itself into the tarmac, and the entire vehicle flipped forward. Contrary to Jerry Bruckheimer movies, it didn't explode in a fiery ball, instead just flopping forward onto its roof and rocking a few times before coming to rest.

We were angled upward now, so the tail end was facing the ground at a steep angle. My stomach lurched into my throat. Thresh, meanwhile, calmly folded the bipod, shouldered the huge gun, and grabbed a chain near mine. He loomed over me, glanced down at me, and winked. The man was just *enormous*. It boggled the mind, honestly.

He slammed his palm over a button, and the ramp folded up, darkening the interior and removing my view of the ground.

I let my head thunk against the wall of the plane, and I blew out a breath of relief.

"Well, that was nerve-wracking," I said.

Thresh just chuckled. "All in a day's work, sweet—I mean, Miss Campari."

"Layla."

"I'm sticking with 'Miss Campari,'" he said. "Harris can be a vicious son of a bitch."

I wasn't sure what he meant by that, so I just shrugged. "Okay. Well…I'm going up to the cockpit."

Harris may have been a vicious son of a bitch, but I still felt Thresh's eyes on my ass as I walked forward to the cockpit. I turned and glanced at him, an eyebrow lifted. He just shrugged, making a face that said *who, me? I don't know what you're talking about.*

I laughed as I took a seat in the copilot's chair.

"What?" Harris asked.

"Just Thresh. He's funny. I like him."

Harris gave me an odd look. "Thresh is funny? Since when?"

I waved it off. "So. We're finally going home?"

"Well, to the *Eliza* eventually, but our route there will be a bit…circuitous. We're stopping in Miami first, and then to the Bahamas, and then eventually we'll take a chopper from St. Thomas to the ship. Gotta make sure we really lost them."

"Think we have?" I asked.

He didn't answer right away. "I don't know, honestly. I told you I'd never bullshit you, so I won't. You killed his best friend. I don't think we'll ever really lose Vitaly's guys until Vitaly is dead. "

"Best friend?" I swallowed hard at that.

"Reports are Cut was the only person Vitaly trusted, his best friend since childhood."

"So I just made things worse, didn't I?"

Harris glanced at me. "You did what you had to do. That's all you need to worry about."

I didn't like the sound of that.

And the fact that Harris stayed quiet as we flew out over the ocean, his brow pinched, worry on his features…didn't do much to reassure me.

Nor did the roiling uneasiness in my stomach.

We weren't out of the woods yet.

17

"I LOVE YOU," FINALLY

AFTER BRAZIL, FLORIDA SEEMED RELATIVELY temperate. As soon as we landed—once again on a too-short landing strip in the middle of nowhere, Harris effortlessly bringing the big aircraft down with a single gentle bump and bark of the tires— Thresh, now clothed in a tight T-shirt and canvas boat shoes, jumped onto a waiting Harley and roared off without even waving at me.

There was a Hummer waiting for us, but it wasn't the civilian version, the watered down derivative. No, this was the military Hummer, huge, wide, tan, with a sloping rear roof and a brutally spartan interior.

Harris turned the engine over, and it made a rattling bass diesel growl. I buckled myself in and laughed as a thought occurred to me.

"What?" Harris asked.

"Just, you. I wish I knew how you do it."

"Do what?"

"Magically procure guns and airplanes and military Hummers—"

"It's not a fucking *Hummer*," he snapped, "it's a Humvee. A Hummer is one of two things: a piece of shit civilian vehicle that shares literally no DNA with what I'm driving right now, or it's a blowjob. *This* is a Humvee. It should never, ever, be called a Hummer."

I widened my eyes. "Yes *sir*," I said, with a mock salute.

He had the good sense to laugh at himself. "Sorry. I'm a soldier, and we tend to get picky about that kind of thing. A chopper is a motorcycle, not a helicopter. Pistols have clips, assault rifles have magazines. And AK-47s, M-16s, those kinds of things... those are assault rifles, not machine guns. What Thresh had on the cargo plane, *that* was a machine gun."

"Noted."

"Now." He glanced at me. "What was it you were laughing about, now that we've got basic terminology out of the way?"

"It's just...none of what's happened to me has been like I thought it would be. In the movies, shooting guns is easy. You shoot someone, and it's no big deal. You shoot a car in the engine and it explodes. Running for your life is exciting. But none of that, except for you, is true. You're just like a movie character. Like, you show up with a bag full of machine guns—sorry, *assault rifles*. You go on not one, not two, but *three* real-life car chases with people shooting at us and everything. And we *get away*. And then you've got a real life Terminator who shoots big ass machine guns like it's a goddamned toy. And there's an actual plane just…waiting for us. And when we land…there's a military-grade Humvee waiting for us. Like, who can do that? Seriously. Who do you call that can just get a fucking airplane? Where do you get assault rifles? This shit doesn't just…appear in real life. But for you, somehow, it does. It's like magic."

By now we were on a two-lane highway that led through absolutely nowhere, the horizon flat as a ruler in every direction.

Harris just shrugged. "It's not magic, it's connections. I know a lot of people. A lot…of unsavory people. Just so you're totally aware, having a bag full of assault rifles is, obviously, highly illegal, regardless of what country you're in. But that's why it's called the 'black market', right?"

I snorted. "I really do know better, I swear,

but…I've always pictured the black market as being, like, a secret warehouse somewhere, like an actual secret marketplace. Like you have a secret knock and shit, and there are tables full of guns and there's someone that runs a business called Goons 'R' Us. I mean, I do get that it's all online and whatever, but that's the mental image I have."

Harris laughed out loud. "Goons 'R' Us. God, Layla, you're fucking hysterical. I'll have to tell Thresh about that. We can make it a side business. Maybe we can invent our own gun and call it the 'thugbuster.'"

"'You're mocking me, aren't you?'" I asked.

"No, I'm not, I swear. It's just funny." I didn't really expect him to catch the *Toy Story* quote, but hey, I had to try. The situation just called for it. He shot me a glance. "And babe, life isn't like the movies. I spent a small fortune just on the guns. Being a badass is expensive as hell, which is something no one ever tells you. In reality, shooting a gun and hitting what you're aiming at is hard, and killing a man is harder. Car chases are fucking terrifying, and having people trying to kill you is worse. Cars rarely explode. Getting shot fucking hurts; I do *not* recommend it. Any of it."

"I wish I'd known all that *before* I got kidnapped."

"You're handling this better than you have any

right to, by the way," he said, reaching over and taking my hand. "I think anyone else would have gone crazy by now."

"Here's the thing, though. You don't really go crazy, do you? I mean, unless you legit have a psychotic break or a nervous breakdown, you don't really go crazy. You just deal with it. It sucks, and you hate it, and you wish you weren't going through it, but you deal, and all you can really do is keep going. And I suppose, as crazy as all this has been, it's not really *that* crazy, not if I consider everything else I've been through. But killing Cut? *That* was different. Really fucking different. I can't forget it. I'm trying. I'm trying so hard…but I just keep—I just keep seeing it. *Feeling* it. I can deal with shooting the guy during the car chase. That one I can justify as being like in the movies. I can pretend it didn't happen. I can forget it. But stabbing Cut in the eye with a pen? I can't forget that."

And just like that, I was fighting hyperventilation. Zero to sixty in nothing flat. Suddenly I was sobbing—just immediate, bam, Layla goes full on baby.

Harris pulled over on the side of the road, exited the Humvee, jerked open my door, and hauled me out. He held me against his chest. Let me cry. Didn't say a word for a long time. Just held me.

When it seemed like my hissy fit had subsided, he tilted my head back. "It'll fade. I can't say it'll ever go away. I'm not gonna bullshit you or blow smoke up your ass. You're a tough as nails chick, so I'm not gonna treat you like you're fragile. You kill someone with your hands like that? It sticks with you. You feel it. You have this...I don't know...haptic memory of it. It doesn't ever go away. You just learn to live with it. You justify it as self-defense, something you had to do, it was you or him. You're talking about it, which is a big step. Some guys, after their first kill, they won't talk about it. They clam up, suppress it. And that's no good. You've got to let it out, talk about it. Or it'll fester. And when emotional trauma turns gangrenous...that shit gets ugly."

"I didn't want to kill him. But when I did? Nick, it felt *good*. That's the part that makes me sick. I don't regret it. Not one fucking bit. I don't feel guilty. He was an evil fuck and he deserved to die the ugly death I gave him. I feel bad that I don't feel bad. And I hate the...what was that term you just used? Haptic memory? That's it exactly. I can feel right now exactly how it felt. And that's a memory I'll never, ever be able to forget. I'll have it till the day I die."

"Which will be a very long time from now, okay?" His palm was warm, rough, and flat against my cheek.

I nodded. "I know." I let out a breath and looked up at him. "Nick? I don't think I've said this yet, but…thank you."

He frowned. "For what?"

"Coming to get me? Rescuing me? Killing for me? Risking death for me?"

"Oh. That. It's very literally in the job description. I would have gone to get you even if it wasn't, though. They say love makes you do crazy things, and I always thought that was stupid bullshit. But now? Now I get it."

Love.

The word hung in the air between us. He knew I'd caught it, and I knew he knew. We just stared at each other for a long moment, each willing the other to say it first.

Eventually, I couldn't take the pressure any more. "Come on. Take me to Miami and buy me some new clothes and a fancy American dinner."

"It would be my pleasure," he said, and helped me back up into the monster Humvee.

And that's exactly what he did. He took me to Saks and bought me a whole new outfit from the skin out. Jade green lingerie the exact shade of his eyes when he was horny, lace-trimmed demi bra and boy-shorts. A white skirt that hit mid-thigh, knee-high socks and Mary-Janes, a lacy, racy, sleeveless, backless, cleavage-popping blouse in sapphire blue. Even a brand new Kate Spade clutch. Like a good boyfriend, he followed me through the store and just told me everything looked amazing, told me to pick whatever I wanted and not worry about price tags. So I did what he told me. I might have tested him on the purse, though. I mean, it wasn't Gucci or anything, but a four-hundred-dollar purse is crazy expensive to a girl who's used to working three jobs just to afford rent, food, bills, and booze. Nick didn't even blink. Just handed over a stack of hundos and told the girl to keep the change, walking away with my bag and ignoring the girl's protest that she wasn't allowed to take tips.

He accompanied me to the mall's restroom and waited while I changed. "Damn, Layla." His eyes on my body, his hands reached for me and smoothed over my hips. "You look incredible."

I smiled. "Thank you, Nicholas."

He growled. "Nicholas. Fucking Nicholas. I haven't been called that since Mrs. LaPrade, my second grade Sunday School teacher."

"I'm special, so it's fine."

"You are special," he agreed, pulling me against his body for a kiss. "Very special. After dinner, I'll show you how special you are."

"You know, this is kind of a first for me."

He pulled me into a walk. "What is?"

I tugged at the hem of the skirt. "All this. Letting you buy me this stuff. I'm not, like, a femi-nazi or anything. I appreciate chivalry and all that, but I've always drawn the line at letting men buy me things. Buy me dinner, sure. Pay for the movie, okay. That's taking care of your date, and it's fine. But I've never let a man buy me gifts. That smacks of having a sugar daddy, and I've always refused to allow that. Makes me feel like I'm being paid for sex, but in stuff rather than money."

"So what's different?" Harris asked.

I shrugged. "I don't know. Everything. Me, I guess."

A pause as he helped me into the Humvee and navigated out of the parking lot. "Look. I'm not anywhere remotely close to being as wealthy as Roth, but I'm doing just fine. I'll never want for anything. And as long as you're mine, neither will you. I don't give a shit how you want to work things. You want to keep your shit separate from mine, that's cool. You let me; I'll take care of you. I just want you any way I can get you. That's all I care about."

"There's a certain assumption in what you just said that I'm not sure we've really covered yet."

He eyed me across the space between us— which, being a Humvee, was significant. "Damn right there's an assumption. Unless you want to tell me otherwise right now…Layla, you and me? We're it. You're mine."

"Nick—"

"And I realize how caveman that sounds. You're your own woman. You do what you want. I respect the fuck out of you. But you're mine. It goes both ways, though."

"Say it, Nick."

He let silence hang for a moment. A smile curved his mouth. "You think I won't?"

"I think it's harder for you to say you're mine than to tell me I'm yours."

"I'll show—"

I cut in over him. "No shit you'll show me. I know it's true. You're mine, now, Nicholas Harris. Don't think I don't know it. I'll let you be dominant and alpha and all that, because it's hot as fuck and I like it. But make no mistake, buddy: I take what I want, and I do not sit and obey for fucking anyone. And I do *not* share. You're mine. And I want to hear that from you."

Harris's nostrils flared and his eyes narrowed.

He cut a glance at me, and then hauled the mammoth vehicle across four lanes of traffic, jumping the median and plowing over a three-foot tall bush like it was nothing, barreling through traffic without concern for anyone or anything. Down a side street, around a corner, and into an alley, parking the Humvee at an angle in front of a Dumpster.

He left the engine idling, jumped out of the driver's seat, leaving the door open. Stalked with harsh, angry steps around the hood.

"Oh shit," I breathed to myself. "I done pissed him *off.*"

My door was flung open, and his hands grabbed my biceps. I was lifted out of the car like I was a doll, set on the concrete, shoved flat up against the brick beside the back door of the closest building. I trembled, not quite sure, suddenly, of what he was capable of when he was in this mood. I knew he wouldn't hurt me, but short of that? He was capable of just about anything.

Incidentally, the shove he gave me wasn't entirely gentle. It was rough, impatient. I slammed back up against the brick, and the breath left me. Although, that had more to do with the look in Harris's eyes than the force of his push. He grabbed both of my wrists and pinned them over my head—his own hand bore the rough bite of the concrete rather than my fingers.

"Say that again." His voice was low. This was Scary Nick.

"Which part?"

"Say it again, Layla. You know what I mean." His hips pinned me to the wall, and his free hand gripped my face, held me in place for a kiss.

I stared up into his eyes, my gaze daring, fiery, rebellious. "You. Are. Mine." I breathed each word. "I do *not* share." I thrust my hips against his, feeling his erection pressing against my core. "Say it, Nick. Tell me you're mine."

"I've got you pinned against the wall. You couldn't get free if you wanted to. And you're making demands?" He laughed, catching my lower lips between his teeth. "You've got some serious balls, baby."

I ground myself against him. Pulled my mouth away, stared at him for a beat, and then darted in and bit his lip as he had mine. Bit down *hard*, and thrust rhythmically against him. "Say it, Nick. I need to hear it. I can be alpha too, you know." I let his lip go, feeling a bolt of equal parts thrill and guilt when I saw that I'd drawn blood. "I'm yours. I admit it freely. You own me. You own my pussy. You own my ass, my tits, my soul. You own my fucking heart, goddamn you. But only if I own you too."

He let out a snarling breath, reached down under my skirt, tugged the edge of my new underwear aside, and slid two fingers into me. I writhed against him, shamelessly seeking my own pleasure on his touch.

"Nasty girl," he murmured.

"Nick, baby, you have no idea how nasty I can be. How fucking sexually voracious I am." I rode his fingers with abandon, not caring that we were in an alley, in public, mere yards from a major Miami thoroughfare. "Quit changing the subject. Tell me what I want to hear."

I was impaled on his fingers, rising up on tiptoe, and I was riding the cusp of orgasm. I would have done anything he asked in that moment, just to get him to let me fall over the edge. Yet there I was, making demands of him, as if he was the helpless one.

His mouth claimed mine, briefly but furiously. Our tongues slashed and tangled and he bit my lip, once, sharply, and I tasted blood. Payback. When he bit my lip, he curled his fingers inside me and smashed his thumb against my clit, and I came. A blast of pain, and an explosion of bliss.

"Fucking *say it*, Nicholas," I gasped into his neck. "Fucking say it, goddamn you!"

He unzipped himself, and I felt his cock at my entrance. No pause, no warning, no fingers guiding him in. He just slammed up into me with unerring accuracy, filling me totally all at once, stretching me to stinging ecstasy.

"Oh fuck. Oh Jesus." I couldn't reach for him, since he still had my wrists pinned over my head. He was buried in me, lifting me up on to my tiptoes as I struggled to breathe through the orgasm still ripping through me.

He palmed my cheek, tilted my face. Slanted his lips over mine with possessive mastery. He owned my mouth and plundered my pussy with his cock. Pounded, rammed. Jarred my breath out of me. Fucked me senseless. I knew I couldn't look away, and I didn't try. I met his gaze without wavering, taking everything he was giving me and rocking my hips in a silent beg for more.

He gave me more.

Fuck, so much more.

The door beside us opened and a young man with a full hipster beard emerged, wearing a green apron, khaki pants, and a black polo. He had a clear plastic garbage bag in one hand, and a cigarette and lighter in the other. As soon as he was outside, he stuck the cigarette in his mouth, lit it, and then lifted the lid of the Dumpster and tossed the bag in. Took a drag. Two. Three.

Nick never slowed his plundering, plowing,

driving pace.

And then I moaned loudly, a breathy, erotic sound that echoed throughout the alley, and the hipster barista spun in place. "Holy fucking Jesus! What the—? Hey, you can't do that here…" he trailed off, staring, as Nick lifted my chin with his fingers and forced my mouth up to his. "God, that's hot."

Harris let go of my jaw, reached behind his back, drew his pistol, and leveled it at the hipster. "Fuck off."

"Yes sir. Fucking off." He dropped the cigarette and vanished inside, and we were alone once again.

Nick's attention returned to me as he replaced the gun. "Where was I?" He thrust up into me, hard, and I moaned again. "Oh yeah. Right there."

I hooked one foot around the back of his knee and surged against him. "Goddamn it, Nick."

He wrapped his hand around the back of my neck, buried his face in my shoulder, sucked on the skin where my neck and shoulder met, bit and sucked until I was sure I'd have a hell of a hickey; I'd wear his mark on my skin with pride.

All the while, his hips were driving his cock up into me, over and over and over, harder and harder.

I felt myself climbing toward climax again, and felt him nearing the edge as well, felt it in the way his pace became frantic and his grip on the back of my neck tightened. I felt it the way his pace faltered then, and his breathing went ragged.

I clenched around him with my pussy and held on, and felt him groan against my skin. "Say it, Nick," I breathed. I struggled against his grip on my wrist, but he refused to let go. "Say it. Fucking say it. Say you're mine."

I wasn't sure why this was suddenly so important, but it was. It was everything. I needed to hear it. *Had* to hear it.

I came, hard. I saw stars and heat blasted through me and I sobbed, buried my nose in his hair and rode the wave of orgasm, rode his cock, chanting my demand—*say it, say it, say it, say it.*

And then he thrust in, once, *hard*. Again, groaning. I felt him come, felt his cock throb inside me and felt the hot rush. "Yours…" he growled, "I'm yours, fuck—I'm yours, Layla."

He let go of my hands then, and they flew to him, burying my fingers in his hair, clutching him to me, riding his last surges and then tilting his face to mine and eating his breath and feeling him whisper it into my mouth:

"*Yours…yours…yours…*" over and over again, like the refrain of the song sung by our joined bodies.

It should have been degrading, being fucked up

against a wall in an alley; my skirt rucked up around my hips, his pants unzipped. It should have felt base and coarse and rude. But in that moment, his face in my hands, his breath on my tongue, hearing him tell me he belonged to me...it was deeply intimate, and beautiful.

The words just...dripped out of me. Were torn from me.

In a perfect world, it would have been said in a romantic moment, during a candlelight dinner, or in the afterglow of slow, tender lovemaking.

The world isn't perfect, and I said it to him as he shot his come into me, after fucking me hard and raw in an alley behind Starbucks, each of us claiming the other.

"I love you—" I choked as the three words I'd never said to a man fell from my lips. "I—god, Nick...Nicholas Fucking Harris. I fucking love you. Goddamn it, I love you."

He was still hard inside me, throbbing as the last of his seed dripped hot out of him. He thrust again, and I gasped. And then he cupped my face in both hands, thumbs brushing over my lips as if to smear the words I'd just said over my mouth. He kissed me.

This kiss was...like no other. Slow but forceful, deep, yet tender. Endless, breathless. He said it then, silently, with the kiss, before he broke away and spoke.

"I love you, Layla." He said it simply, easily.

I fell against him, cut deep, torn open. He let me down, pulled out, and fixed both my skirt and his pants with one hand, and then pulled me into his arms.

He said it.

My mother never told me she loved me.

Mario sure as fuck never did.

None of the boys or men I'd slept with ever said it. One guy started to say it to me, but it was just to get me to try anal, so I shut him up before he could say it and let him do it anyway. He didn't mean it, and I knew it, and he knew it, and I didn't want to hear it.

Kyrie said it to me, but that wasn't the same because neither of us were bi-curious.

Nick said it.

He kissed my cheekbone, the shell of my ear. I felt his lips move. "I love you. I love you." He buried his fingers in the mass of my curls and tugged my face around to kiss me again, this time with delicacy and tenderness. "I love you. And I'm yours."

"God, Nick." I kissed him back, again and again, until we were lost in the kiss and out of breath.

He pulled away. "Come on. Let's go have dinner."

He took me to a fancy steakhouse and I visited the bathroom to clean up, and then we had a long dinner during which neither of us drank much. Unusual for me, not so much for Harris, I didn't think.

He picked a hotel somewhat at random, a nice one but not the best—intentionally, he said, to avoid being found easily. Not the cheapest, but not the most expensive. Middle of the road.

He led me to our room, unlocked the door, picked me up, wrapped my legs around his waist, and was inside me before the door closed behind us.

And then he told me he loved me exactly eighty-three times in a row, as he fucked us both to orgasm against the door. And then another four times as he carried me to the bed and stripped me naked, and told me he loved me seventy-seven times as he kissed every inch of my body, top to bottom, front and back. And then when he was hard again, I rode him reverse cowgirl and I told him I loved him so many times I lost count at ninety-two.

I think we both had a lot of not loving people or being loved to make up for.

We had nearly no sleep that night. But by the time the sun was peeking through the blinds, I was reasonably sure Nicholas Harris loved me. Judging by the something like five hundred times he'd told me throughout the night.

Not that I was counting or anything.

Nor was I counting the number of orgasms he gave me.

(Nine.)

Or his.

(Four times inside me, plus a fifth in the wee hours of the morning, on my tits, right before we passed out.)

We woke up mid-afternoon, ordered room service, showered, went down on each other, ate breakfast, had sex twice more, showered again, and finally got dressed to leave the hotel.

We were at the front desk checking out when I got the feeling.

I leaned close to Nick. "Can we stay for a little longer?" I leaned my head against his shoulder. "Please?"

He glanced at me as he dug an envelope full of cash out of the backpack he'd bought in with us. "Haven't had enough, huh? Jesus, Layla. We've had sex six times in the last eighteen hours. I've given you at least ten orgasms. Plus, Thresh is waiting at the docks."

The hotel employee counting out the cash Harris had handed her was trying valiantly not to listen, but was failing. Miserably. She was blushing scarlet and eyeing us surreptitiously, and lost count three times. "*Ten*?" She squeaked. "I don't think I've ever come that many times in my entire life." She clapped her hand over her mouth, mortified. "Oh god, I'm so sorry!"

Harris just grinned at her. "Then sweetheart, you're not having the right kind of sex." He took his change and winked at her.

"It's not that," I said. "Or, not entirely. I told you, I don't have an orgasm threshold. I could come until I passed out from exhaustion and still be ready for another one."

"Then what is it?" He led me by the hand across the lobby and handed the valet his car claim ticket.

I shrugged, finding it hard to put into words. "I don't know. Just…a bad feeling. Like, dread. I don't know. I just feel like we should stay here. Like something bad is going to happen. It sounds stupid, but…I don't know. I've just got a bad feeling."

The valet arrived with our monstrosity-mobile, Nick handed him a hundred-dollar bill, and then checked the trunk, the back seats, the front end, knelt and glanced at the undercarriage, even popped the hood to examine the engine.

"The truck is clean, babe. I'm not saying we're home free, because Vitaly's not dead. But we're okay for now. All right?" He dropped the hood with a loud slam and brushed his hands on the front of his jeans.

Time distorted then.

I felt my blood thicken and slow, and my heart stop. My eyes lifted as if in slow motion.

Vitaly was walking toward me. Arm extended. Huge silver pistol in his hand, eyes dark and cold and deadly.

Stupidly, my last thought as Vitaly pulled the trigger was: *Well...fuck.*

18

THROUGH-AND-THROUGH

I heard the *BLAM!* as if through a cloud of cotton: dense, distant, muffled, thunderous.

I braced for an impact that never came.

BLAMBLAM!—BLAMBLAM!

Harris fell in slow motion to the ground at my feet. Bleeding.

People were screaming, but I barely noticed.

Vitaly was stumbling backward, pistol hanging down, blood welling in four spots on his chest, clustered in a tight group dead center, right over his sternum.

Harris, one large scarlet flower blooming wet over his heart. On his knees, one hand flat on the ground, head held up, right hand leveling his pistol at Vitaly. Harris's whole body shook, but his gun hand was steady as a rock. *BLAM!* Vitaly's left shoulder jerked backward, spouting red.

Vitaly turned in a clumsy circle, pistol dangling at his thigh, and ran in a lurch. No one stopped him, and he vanished around a corner.

Sirens howled.

Harris twisted, his elbow giving out, and he fell. He landed awkwardly, on his face and his side. He was bleeding front and back.

"NICK!" I heard myself scream, and felt myself fall to my knees beside him.

It was all happening in slow motion, and as if it was happening to someone else. I felt nothing, just vacant, numb, disbelieving. Outwardly, however, I was hysterical. Shrieking. Screaming. Sobbing.

"Lay—Layla." Harris gasped. "Shut...shut the fuck up."

I took his head onto my lap and stroked his face. "Nick. You're going to be okay. You're going to be okay."

"I—I know." He handed me his phone. "Call... Thresh."

Things happened to me, around me: an ambulance arrived and I was pried away from Nick—it took four men to get me away. I was piled into the ambulance, and two men in the blue paramilitary medic uniforms were operating on Nick, doing something to his back and then his front, trying to stop the bleeding.

I felt the phone in my hand, stared at it blankly. What was I supposed to do with this? Nick was unconscious.

Oh yeah, call Thresh.

I found his name under "favorites" and called him. It rang twice.

"Thresh," came his chasmic voice.

"Thresh…It's Nick. They shot Nick. He—Vitaly. He shot Nick."

A pause. "Who the hell is Nick?"

I felt something hot and violent erupt inside me. "HARRIS! NICHOLAS HARRIS! Your fucking boss! Nicholas goddamned Harris, you fucking ape!"

"His name is Nick?" Thresh seemed truly baffled. "Huh."

"THRESH!"

He sounded utterly unmoved. "Is he okay?"

"No, he's not fucking okay!" I screamed. "He's dying! He took—it was—Vitaly was trying to kill me, and Nick—Harris, he—"

"That's what he does. It's who he is." I heard a motorcycle engine roar to life. "Have you gotten him medical attention?"

"Yes, I'm in an ambulance right now."

"Where are you? Are you in Miami?"

"Yes, we're—" I turned to one of the medics. "Where are we going? Which hospital?"

"Jackson Memorial," came the terse answer.

"We're going to—" I started to relay.

"I heard. I'm ten minutes away. I'll meet you there." The sound of the chopper engine being feathered. "Layla, did Harris get him?"

"Yes. He shot him five times. Four in the chest, one in the shoulder."

"Did he drop? Did you *see* Vitaly die?"

"No—he…he got away. He was shot five times, though. Could he—? He couldn't survive that, could he?"

"Never count a man dead unless you watch him die with your own eyes." Thresh could have been discussing his breakfast cereal preference. "Look, I'm gonna let you go. I'll see you in ten minutes. And Layla? Harris is the toughest motherfucker I've ever met. One puny little bullet won't stop him for long. Okay? He'll be fine. He's survived worse."

"It went straight through. He's bleeding from the chest and the back."

"That's better, actually. It means the bullet isn't stuck inside him and didn't fragment. That's when shit gets nasty. A through-and-through is good news. Unless it stops his heart on the spot, fucking nothing will kill that man. I'm not worried at all."

"You're not the one watching him bleed."

"I have, though. I carried him over my shoulder fifty miles through the fucking rainforest, with a bullet lodged in his gut. He was screaming bloody murder the whole way because the stomach acid was eating at the wound. I got fucking malaria carrying his bleeding carcass to a doctor. I know how it feels. And I know he'll be fine. All right. Goodbye, Layla. I'll see you in a few minutes." *Click*.

I don't know what happened next. It was all a jumble of images: the medics tending to Harris, doing whatever it was they had to do to keep him alive, Harris being pulled out of the ambulance, the *clatter-clack* of the stretcher's wheels locking open and into place. A hallway. A doctor—who looked all of twelve—in a lab coat with a stethoscope around his neck and those weird bent medical scissors attached to his nametag lanyard. *ER*-style urgent medical shouting, something about BP and a single GSW and I didn't know what else. Doors closing in my face, hospital security trying to keep me out of the operating room, four or six pairs of hands holding me back as I screamed bloody murder.

Finally, huge paws, a giant's hands. Lifting me bodily, easily. Cradling me in burly arms like a baby, carrying me away. "Easy now, girl. They gotta fix him. I'm here. I won't let anything happen. To you, or to him. He's going to be okay. I promise." Thresh's voice in my ear was the rumble of diesel engine heard from far away, a grumbling trembling bass thunder.

I went limp and let him set me on a chair in the emergency room waiting area, hard plastic under my ass. I fell asleep against Thresh's mountainous shoulder.

After an endless time—two or three hours at least—the same young doctor approached, looking tired and a lot older than my first estimation. He had to be sixteen, at least. He took a seat beside me. "Miss Campari?"

"That's me." I sat up, rubbing my eyes with the heels of my palms.

"Mr. Harris is going to be okay. He's got a long road ahead of him, a lot of healing to do. He won't be going anywhere for a long time, and he may never operate at the same capacity as he used to, but he'll live. Of course, judging based on the sheer number of scars on his body, not to mention his rather astounding medical record, he's an insanely tough human being. So I would guess he'll probably make a liar out of me. I'm hoping he will."

"Can I see him?"

Thresh spoke up. "There's only one correct answer here, Doc." His voice carried a hard note of warning.

The doctor hesitated a moment, regarding Thresh coolly. "He's resting at the moment. But if you promise to not disturb him, I don't see why you couldn't be in the room with him." He stood. "This way, please."

We followed the doctor through a maze of hallways, the antiseptic smell acrid in my nostrils, steady beeping coming from the rooms we passed; a male nurse in pale blue scrubs ran past us, dodging nimbly around us. The doctor stopped at a room, pulled open the sliding glass door, and tugged aside the curtain, revealing Harris in a bed, clad in a loose hospital gown.

I collapsed into the chair at his side, fighting tears at the sight of him: he had an oxygen cannula in his nose, an IV taped to his arm, a thin white blanket across his lower half. His right cheek had a bandage on it where he'd scraped it when he hit the pavement.

"He doesn't belong here. This is all wrong." I wasn't sure what I meant even as I said it.

"No, he doesn't," Thresh answered. "But when he took the bullet to the stomach, they said he would need something like six months to heal. He was on his feet and running three miles within six weeks. Shouldn't have been possible, but Harris is...I swear he's not even human. The things I've seen him just shrug off like nothing would crush lesser men."

"He's saved my life so many times already. He has to be okay."

Thresh was quiet for a moment, waiting for the doctor to leave us alone. When he was gone, Thresh circled to the other side of the bed and stood staring down at Harris. "When we were in the Rangers, we had a mission go belly-up. Just totally FUBAR. All our intel was wrong. We got ambushed, our unit was taking heavy casualties. He and I were pinned down, and I took three rounds. I was bleeding out, helpless. He returned fire and managed to slow the bleeding at the same time. And then he stood over my body and fought off the tangos, fucking twenty of them. Depleted mags, switched to his sidearm. And then he stood there over my body for the next sixty hours waiting for S-and-R to find us. Fuck of it all was the mission was off the books. Volunteer only. Never happened. He should have gotten a Medal of Honor for that shit, but no one will ever know about it. The guys who never went home, only their wives and parents even remember their names."

"What was the mission?"

"Terrorists were holed up in an orphanage. Had a whole bunch of kids held hostage." Thresh went silent for a moment. "We went in HALO insertion.

Hit the ground weapons-free, immediately started taking fire. We lost three-quarters of the unit on that SNAFU, but we took down every single fucking one of those piece-of-shit motherfuckers. I personally double-tapped each one, just to make sure they were really dead. We thought we were home free, but the ambush hit us at the EZ. That's when I took the hits. The helo ate a rocket, leaving us stranded and surrounded. Which is when it got real fucking hairy. Harris is the only reason I'm here. And I will stand outside this room until we can move him somewhere off the grid."

I had no idea what most of that even meant. Weapons-free, SNAFU, double-tapped, EZ…military mumbo-jumbo. What it meant, at the bottom of it all, was that Harris was a hero. I knew that, though. And I knew I felt better knowing Thresh was loyal to the death, and would be standing outside.

"You know how to get hold of Roth?" I asked.

Thresh grunted a wordless assent. "Already did. He and Kyrie are *en route*. Alexei and Sasha are with them. With Vitaly wounded, we should be fine for a while. But I'm not taking any chances."

"I want that man dead," I snarled.

"All of us do. He's caused enough trouble. All of us are loyal to Harris, so hurting him was a big mistake. They woke the beast. Once we get you, Harris, and Kyrie and Roth somewhere safe, the shit's gonna get real fucking ugly for Vitaly."

"I'll help you. Shit, I'll pull the trigger myself."

Thresh eyed me with respect. "I believe you." He glanced down at Harris, and then headed toward the door. "I got calls to make. I'll be right outside. No one gets in without talking to me first, and showing me their orders. You rest. Your only job for right now is to be there for him. Got it?"

I could only nod.

When Thresh was gone, I took Harris's hand in both of mine, leaned back in my chair, and watched him sleep. Watched the heart monitor, the oxygen machine huffing and pumping, his chest rising and falling, mouth slack, stubble darkening his jaw.

Eventually, a nurse showed up and moved us to a recovery room. I resumed my station at his side, his hand in mine, fighting sleep and tears.

Eventually, exhaustion won out.

19

WORTH IT

I JERKED AWAKE, HEARING THRESH'S DEEP VOICE just inside the door. He had his cell phone on speaker and looked at me as he spoke. "Sasha. Talk to me."

"I hear chatter on police radio. A man was found with many gunshot wounds, not yet dead. No identification, not able to communicate. He is at the university hospital."

"Take care of it."

"How?"

"I don't fucking care. However you want. Just take care of it. *Da,* comrade?"

"You are stupid gorilla," Sasha growled. "I am from Georgia, not Russia. "

"You sound Russian," Thresh pointed out.

"I speak Georgian, Russian, Armenian, Arabic,

and English. I serve in the Russian Army for ten years, so I speak Russian most frequently."

"You speak five languages?" Thresh sounded grudgingly respectful. "I'll have to pick up another language so we're even."

"Americans are lazy. You expect everyone to learn your language, but most of you do not even speak it properly. Is embarrassing."

"Can't argue with you there. Get going. Give our friend Hell's welcome."

"I will get kill bonus?" This was so low I barely heard it.

"You get this done, Roth will give you a bonus so fucking huge your kids' kids will have more money than they'll know what to do with."

"I would do it for free. But I still want the bonus."

"No shit. You'll get it. And Sasha? I need photographic proof of completion. There's no room for error with this one."

"I do not fail."

"I know, buddy. That's why I'm sending you." He tapped the screen to end the call, shot me another glance, and then went back outside to stand guard.

I glanced at Harris, and saw that he was awake, sort of. Looking at me. He squeezed my hand, once, weakly, and then fell back asleep. I wondered if he'd heard any of that.

When I woke next, Harris was sitting up, awake, and spooning the last of a pudding cup into his mouth. Roth was sitting in the chair on the other side of the bed, Kyrie standing behind him, her hand on his shoulder.

"Layla! You're awake!" Kyrie rushed around the bed and I barely had time to stand up before she slammed into me, arms going around my neck. "I was so worried, hooker. I never thought I'd see you again."

"Sorry to disappoint you, slutty-buns." I peeled her off of me, and then kissed her cheek. "I was worried you wouldn't see me again, too. For a minute. And then Nick found me and everything was fine."

"Nick? Who's Nick?" Kyrie asked.

Thresh, standing just inside the door again, laughed. "That's what I said!"

I rolled my eyes, and gestured at Harris. "He's Nick. To me, at least."

Kyrie eyed me with suspicion. "Nick? Since when do you call Harris Nick?"

Harris was suspiciously silent, studiously scraping every last drop of chocolate pudding out of the cup. I poked his leg. "You want to tell them...*babe*?"

He shook his head. "Nope. It's all you."

Kyrie and Roth exchanged perplexed glances.

"Tell us what?" Roth asked. "What's going on, Harris?"

Harris shrugged. "Nothing."

I glared at him. "Nothing? Fucking *really*?"

He glared back. "I don't owe anybody any explanations as to who I fall in love with."

Kyrie shrieked so loud we all flinched. "I knew it! I FUCKING KNEW IT!" She collided with me again, squeezing me so hard my breath left me and I saw stars. "Tell me everything! How long has this been going on?"

"Calm your ass down, bitch." I untangled myself from her arms. "Strangle me, and I won't be able to tell you dick."

"Sorry. Sorry. I'm just excited. I knew you and Harris had a little somethin'-somethin' going on. This is awesome!"

I took Harris's hand and twined our fingers together, and wonder of wonders, he let me. Right there, in front of both Kyrie and Roth and Thresh. "It was kind of a surprise for both of us."

"I had to all but club you over the head to get you to admit you even liked me," Harris said.

I shrugged. "I may be easy, but I'm not an easy person to like."

He growled at me. "You're not easy."

"Not any more. At least, not for anyone but you."

Roth wiped his face with both hands. "I feel like I've fallen through the rabbit hole into Wonderland."

At that moment, we heard the door open and Thresh speaking in low tones to someone on the other side. "I hear what you're saying, Doc. We'll let him rest. But this is important."

"He shouldn't even have *one* visitor," a female voice said, sounding frustrated, "let alone *four*. And just because you're a fucking giant doesn't mean you can tell me what to do in my ward."

"Actually, it kind of does. You don't have enough security guards in this entire building to handle me. Which means when I say it'll be fine, it'll be fine. Our meeting will be over in a few minutes and we'll all leave him to rest. All right?"

"Shit." This was mumbled, exasperated and defeated. "Fine. But you all need face masks and you have to sanitize your hands. His immune system is weak right now. The last thing he needs is to catch something from one of you."

"Chuck Norris doesn't get a cold, the cold gets Chuck Norris."

"What?" She sounded utterly puzzled.

"Nothing. It's a joke. Never mind. We'll wash our fucking hands, okay?"

"Face masks too. Or I'll shoot your giant ass with an elephant tranquilizer and drag you out of here myself."

"I've been shot with an elephant tranquilizer, actually. It just got me high. Kind of fun actually. You wanna try that, you'll need two or three." I heard the grin in his voice. "And babe, you want to drag me out of here, you won't need a tranquilizer. It'll be more fun if I'm conscious anyway."

"Jesus. You're a piece of work, you know that?"

"Been told that, yes."

"I'm going to lunch. When I come back in thirty minutes, I want this room clear. Or we really will see how many security guards it takes to subdue your freakishly oversized carcass."

"Honey—"

"You say one damn word about bondage, and I'll stab you with my shears."

Thresh just chuckled. "We'll be gone in fifteen minutes. You have my word."

"You'd better be." And then she and Thresh left the room.

The door opened once more, admitting Thresh with Sasha behind him. Thresh had a handful of paper masks, which he handed to everyone, and then made us all use the hand sanitizing foam from the dispenser just inside the door. Thresh took up position in front of the door, and Sasha moved into the interior of the room, standing at the front of the bed near Harris.

"This meeting is regarding a certain Greek friend we all have in common," Thresh said. "After Harris's latest...encounter...there was some doubt as to his situation or whereabouts. I tasked Sasha here with finding him."

Harris adjusted the cannula in his nose, sucking in deep breaths slowly. "And?"

Sasha pulled an iPad Mini out of the cargo pocket of his pants. "I found him, and took some selfies. Here. You see." He opened the iPad, tapped on the Photos icon, and handed the device to Harris. I leaned close so I could see the pic as well. Sure enough, it was a selfie of Sasha and Vitaly.

Vitaly was in a hospital bed, wired for sound, it looked like: IVs, oxygen, food tube, a bunch of other stuff. Vitaly was unconscious, and Sasha was grinning as if they were long-lost friends reunited.

"Swipe left," Sasha instructed.

Harris swiped left. Sasha had a syringe inserted into part of the IV tube, the photo taken with his thumb on the plunger, another shit-eating grin on his face. The next showed him with the plunger depressed. The next photo showed the monitor, with the heart rate flat-lined.

"I make a distraction in another room first, so when he dies, they don't notice so quickly," Sasha said. "I put another dose into his tube, just to be sure. I also unplugged the life support. He would not have made it anyway, I do not think, but now… our friend is dancing with the demons."

Roth took the iPad from Harris, swiping through the pics several times, clearly struggling with some deep emotion. "He's really gone?" He glanced at Sasha.

"I am sure of this," Sasha answered. "I put a mirror to his nose. Felt his heart. Long minutes I waited. He is dead. I am one hundred percent positive."

Roth sighed, leaning back in the chair. "It's over. It's really over." He wiped his face again with both hands. "He took me in, when I was a clueless twenty year-old kid with more money and ambition than common sense or business skill. He taught me everything I know about being a smart businessman. More than I ever learned from my own father. He didn't even hold it against me when I left, even though I killed one of his men. He got it. He let me go. It wasn't until his crazy bitch of a daughter found me that any of this even happened. I never had a grudge against him. Not until he threatened all of you. I should be glad he's dead. And I am, mostly. But part of me…"

I kept my own opinion to myself. I felt nothing but relief that Vitaly was truly dead and I wouldn't waste a single second mourning him.

"Name your price, Sasha. Sky's the limit." Roth handed the iPad back and stood up.

Sasha didn't answer immediately. "One million," he said, finally.

"Two million," Roth said. "You'll have it by noon."

Sasha opened his mouth as if to argue, but then thought better of it. "Thank you, sir."

"All right. You and Thresh can go. Post a guard on the ward, just to be sure."

"I will cover it myself," Sasha said.

Thresh made a negative sound in his throat. "I got it. Me and the doc have a thing. A repertoire."

Harris snorted. "You mean *rapport*, lunkhead."

"Yeah. That. A thing. She's feisty, and she's not afraid to get in my face. I like it."

Thresh and Sasha left, and it was just Harris, Kyrie, Roth, and me.

Harris rubbed his jaw and fiddled with the cannula again. "So. You two lovebirds can have your wedding now. No one else will get in the way."

"Harris, you don't think we'd have it without

you, do you?" Kyrie asked. "You're like family."

"She's right, Harris," Roth said. "I've known you for eight years. We can wait until you're better."

"I'll be on oxygen for a while. Won't be bouncing back from this one too fast, I'm afraid." He gave Roth a hard look. "Take a video for me."

"Harris, come on—" Kyrie started.

"Miss St. Claire." Harris's voice was cold. "I'm not asking. Get married. You've waited long enough. Take some pictures and send 'em along. That'll be enough. We'll have a toast to your happiness when I can get out of here."

"He's right," I said. "You two shouldn't have to wait. You deserve your happiness together."

Harris shot me serious side-eye. "You think I'm letting you sit around at my bedside when your best friend is getting married? Think again, sweetheart. You're going with them."

"The fuck I am!" I said, almost shouting. "I'm not leaving you."

"Kyrie, Roth…can you give us a second?" Harris didn't take his eyes off me.

"Sure." Roth stood up and followed Kyrie out of the room.

Alone, Harris pulled me closer to him, wrapped a hand around the base of my spine so I was flush against the bed. "Layla. I want you to listen to me, okay?"

"Fuck that, you idiot. I'm not going anywhere."

He just smiled at me. "Babe. You *are*. You're go-ing with them. You're her maid of honor. Her best friend. You can come right back, but this is how I want it. I hate weddings anyway. I look stupid in suits and can't stand sitting down for that long."

"Bullshit. You're a pilot. You're used to sitting for hours."

"Layla. This isn't up for debate. You're going."

"You told Kyrie you were primarily a pilot with the Rangers. But then Thresh told me how you stood over him when that orphanage mission went bad."

He blinked at me. "Change of topic. Okay. Um…well, number one, he shouldn't be talking about that mission. It's so classified only four people on the planet even know it ever happened. It would have started an international conflict if it had been public knowledge. Number two, what Thresh didn't tell you was that I was only part of that mission as a pilot. I wasn't with the insertion team. I was the extraction pilot."

"He told me the helicopter was hit by a rocket."

"It was. Took out the engine, went into a flat spin two hundred feet up. I rode it down and jumped clear just before it hit. Rolled my ankle and dislocat-ed my shoulder and had the hair burnt off my fucking arms. He was already down by then, and most of the team was dead. The bad guys were swarming like fucking ants, and I owed Thresh my life, so I did the only thing I could. I picked up his rifle and held them off. Wasn't much choice. It was that or let them capture us."

"You jumped out of a crashing helicopter?"

"Not as badass as it sounds. More a matter of timing and knowing how to fall."

"Harris."

He grinned. "Okay, fine. It *was* pretty badass."

"I'm staying."

His expression darkened. "Layla. Please. The only thing I hate more than being bedridden is the idea of holding up Kyrie and Roth's wedding. They've been through a ton of shit. I refuse to let them wait three or four months just for me. It's not going to be a big deal anyway. Just them and you and Cal and the reverend on the beach on Roth's private island. I won't be missing anything, I swear. You do the wedding, party with your best friend, and then come back here to me."

"Nick, I don't want to leave you. What if something else happens?"

"Vitaly is dead. His daughter is dead. Cut is dead. There's no one else to carry out the grudge. It's over. You're safe. They're safe. You don't need to be afraid, okay?" He cupped my cheek. "You can Skype me when you get there. We can…what would you call sexting, but with Skpe?"

"Skype-sex?" I suggested.

He shook his head. "Not catchy enough. I'll think of something. Point is, you're going. I'm just going to be sleeping for the next few days anyway."

I sighed. "I don't like it. I'm still adjusting to the idea that this thing between us is real. And now I've got to leave you when you're wounded?"

"Thresh will be here and Sasha will be with you. Alexei and Andrei are with Kyrie and Roth. Nothing else will happen. And as for you and me…Layla, babe. It's real. *We're* real. I really love you. Which is why I'm making you go."

I rested my cheek against his. "Say it again."

"I love you, Layla."

I sighed. "That will never get old."

He tipped my face to his, and kissed me. The cannula was cold and hard against my upper lip, but I didn't care. I'd take his kisses however I could get them.

"Fine." I breathed the word against his mouth. "I'll go. But I'm coming back as soon as the reception is over. And I'm sucking you off before I leave."

Nick just smiled and feathered his fingers through my hair, then swept his thumb across my lips. "Why wait?"

I giggled; only Nick could make me giggle. It was embarrassing. "Why wait, indeed?" I slid my hand under the blanket, under the gown, found him hardening under my touch. "Watch the door."

"I'm gonna watch you, that's what I'm gonna watch."

So I pulled the curtain closed. Tugged the sheets and blankets back, shoved the gown up, and went to town. Slowly, lovingly, pulling him back away from his body and tilting my face to the side so he could watch as he entered my mouth.

His heart rate went crazy and his breathing became labored, and he came with a quiet grunt. I sucked him dry and limp, and replaced the covers over him just in time for the nurse to rush in.

"Your heart rate just increased," she said, coming over to lay two fingers against his wrist. "Are you okay? Did something happen?"

He glanced at me. I still had a mouthful of his come, which I surreptitiously swallowed, and then wiped my mouth with my sleeve.

"No," he said. "Just...I had a dream. I'm fine."

The nurse shifted her gaze from me to him and back. "None of that, you two. If you want him to heal, you need to let him rest. Causing his heart rate to skyrocket and his lungs to have to work harder isn't doing him any favors."

"She's got a wedding to go to anyway," Nick said. "She's about to leave. We were just saying goodbye."

"Okay, well, say goodbye less…vigorously." She let out an exasperated sigh.

Alone once more, Nick grinned at me and pulled me in for a kiss. "You taste like me."

"I was still swallowing when she came in." I kissed him, tangled my tongue against his.

We kissed for a long moment, and then he pushed me away. "Go. Before I tie you to the IV pole and have my way with your ass."

"Is that a promise or a threat?" I stood up, turned away, and waggled my ass at him.

He groaned. "Don't tempt me, woman."

"Can't help it if I'm a born temptress," I said. I turned back, ran my fingers through his hair. "You can have your way with my ass when you're out of the hospital. Promise."

"I'll hold you to that." He reached around and patted me on the bottom, then turned me around and pushed me away. "I love you. Go. Have fun."

I wasn't capable of saying goodbye to him. So I rushed back to kiss him once more, amazed that this was me, in love with a man who loved me back.

I even looked out the window to see if I could spot any flying pigs.

I left, pretended to close the door, and then peeked through. As soon as I was gone, Nick flopped back onto the bed, pressed the button to lower the head of the bed so he was lying down. His hand was pressed to his chest as if to physically keep his chest rising and falling. He looked weak, suddenly, and exhausted.

But he had a smile on his face.

Everything it took to get me here, to this place with Nicholas Harris?

Worth it. All of it.

EPILOGUE

"DO YOU, KYRIE ABIGAIL ST. CLAIRE, TAKE THIS man, Valentine Roth, to be your husband, for better or for worse, in sickness and in health, till death do you part?"

"I do."

"And do you, Valentine Albert Roth, take this woman, Kyrie St. Claire, to be your wife, for better or for worse, in sickness and in health, till death do you part?"

"I do." Roth had a tear in his eye when he said those two words, which was almost as surprising to me as learning his totally, ridiculously pedestrian middle name.

Albert. Heh. I'd have to tease him for both the crying and the middle name.

Sure, I was crying, watching my best friend get

married, but I was a girl, and I was allowed.

I started when a hand touched my thigh. I glanced to my left, and my tears gushed freely.

Harris, looking shell-shocked at the sight of me in my kickass dress.

He was in a wheelchair, an oxygen canister strapped to the back of the chair, tubes wrapping under his arm and connected to a cannula in his nose. He was in a tux, a red rose in his lapel. He hadn't shaved, so he had the beginnings of a beard. Yum.

"Nick?" I lunged for him, wrapping my arm around his neck. "You're here!"

"Barely made it for the I-do's." He pulled me down so I was forced to land on his lap, and then glanced up at Roth and Kyrie. "Congratulations, you two. Sorry to crash like this."

Kyrie wrapped her arms around both of us. "Don't apologize, Harris. I'm just glad you're here. We're done anyway, so now we can start the fun part."

"Actually," the minister interjected, "I haven't officially made the pronouncement yet. So…"

"Oh!" Kyrie straightened, and rushed back to stand facing Roth, taking both of his hands in hers and schooling her features to something resembling seriousness.

Roth cracked a grin, shaking his head minutely.

"In the sight of God and all these witnesses, I now pronounce you man and wife. You may—*ahem*." He stopped, a smirk on his face. Roth already had Kyrie bent backward over his arm and was kissing the ever-loving shit out of her. Like, full on tongue-sex. "Well. It seems you've got that part down."

When they straightened and broke the kiss, finally, the minister took their joined hands in both of his and lifted them high. "I now present to you Mr. and Mrs. Valentine Roth."

There was a platform laid over the sand that formed the aisle Kyrie had walked down and the area in front where the actual ceremony had taken place, and now Kyrie and Roth walked hand in hand back down the aisle and up to the thatch-roofed area where the "reception" would take place. Cal had served as Valentine's only groomsman, I was Kyrie's bridesmaid, and we both followed behind.

The reception itself was a tiny affair. Just a single bartender, a catered dinner brought out by a single server. No guests, no nonsense. The cake was appropriately sized, a simple black and white two-tier confection. The beach was less than twenty yards away, and Valentine's estate just up the hill.

Alexei, Sasha, Andrei, and Thresh were in attendance as the security detail. They wore matching tuxedos, but each of them was also carrying an assault rifle as they patrolled the perimeter. It was equal parts sexy and comical and scary, seeing men in fancy tuxedos with roses in their lapels and bowties at their throats, looking fancy and gorgeous... and carrying big ass machine guns.

The security was slight overkill, since Thresh had done some hunting and discovered that with Vitaly's demise, his assets had been seized and redistributed, and the underground crime world was too busy trying to fill the power vacuum left by his sudden death to worry about a non-factor like Valentine.

In other words, the danger was past.

But hell, sexy men in sharp tuxedos with scary guns? Really brings a wedding together, if you ask me.

"How'd you get here?" I asked Nick.

"I didn't leave them much choice. I took out my IV and cannula and walked out of the room still in my hospital gown. I told them I was going, and they could either help me or get out of my way. Also, I bribed them with a huge donation to the hospital. Roth's money, of course. They got me this stupid contraption," he smacked the wheelchair and tugged at the oxygen tube, "and I booked a flight. Checked in with the hospital here to refill the canister, got a taxi, and here I am."

"I can't believe you're here." I wrapped my arms around his neck and inhaled his scent. "It's only been three days, but I feel like I've been away from you for a fucking year. It's been hell. Never leave me again, okay?"

"I'll do my best."

I palmed his cheeks. "Wrong answer, buddy. You go somewhere, I go with you."

"What if it's a dangerous rescue mission?"

"You've seen me handle a gun. You've taught me to fly a plane. I think I can handle anything you can handle."

"Alpha One Security *does* have an opening for an informational assessment asset."

"A what?"

"Someone to sort through reams of intel and pick out the useful stuff."

I nodded. "Oh. That I can do."

"I know. I may have just invented the position just for you. You could also be my personal assistant."

"Does either position include sexual benefits? I've got a thing for the boss, you know."

"It certainly does. All the cock you can handle."

"I can handle a *lot* of cock." I touched my lips to his ear. "Remember the promise I made back in the hospital?"

"How could I forget?" He bit my earlobe.

"Think you're up for it yet?"

"You want it right now?"

"Maybe we have some drinks with Kyrie and Roth first?"

He faked a disappointed growl. "Fine. I'll wait. But I plan to be in your ass by midnight."

Kyrie appeared at that moment, just in time to hear Harris. Her eyes widened. "Holy hell. Sorry. Wrong place to come in to the convo, I guess." She took my hand. "Can I borrow Layla for a second, Harris?"

"Just have her back to me by midnight," he said, winking at me.

She pulled me across the sand to the water's edge, where the waves lapped at my bare feet and the edges of Kyrie's incredible, custom-made dress. It was a strapless lace corset bodice, with a lace panel under her breasts, smooth, flawless satin hugging her incredible figure to pool at her feet. Beautiful, flattering, yet informal enough for a tiny beach wedding. "I just wanted to talk to you real quick," she said. "I have something to tell you."

I waited, but she didn't immediately continue speaking. "Well? Out with it, hooker!"

"Roth and I, now that Vitaly is gone, we're staying here. At this estate, I mean. More or less permanently. And I just wanted you to know that you're welcome—"

I cut in. "Kyrie. Baby. Honey. Darling. You couldn't *pay* me enough to live with you and Roth another day. Listening to you two fuck like bunnies all the damn time? I've had enough." I bumped her with my shoulder. "Besides, I'm with Nick, now. I'm going to work for him at his security company, and will probably end up living with him."

She eyed me. "Really?"

I nodded. "I really love him."

"I'm happy for you," she said, hugging me. "So happy I won't even say 'I told you so.'"

"You just did."

A shrug and an innocent smirk. "Well, I did tell you so." She took my hand. "Anyway, that's not really the reason I wanted to talk to you."

"What else?"

She laid a palm on her stomach, looking nervous, suddenly. "I…Roth and I—um. I'm…pregnant."

I stopped walking abruptly. "You what?"

She shrugged. "While you were gone, I lapsed on my pills."

"Does Roth know?" I asked.

She stared at me. "Does he know? He's already building a nursery. He's painted it pink. He's absolutely convinced it's a girl. I've tried telling him we won't know for sure for another ten weeks at least, but he's…just positive it's a girl." She had a dreamy grin on her face. "We'd been talking about it a little anyway, so it's just…a little sooner than we were thinking, that's all."

"You're having a baby." I blinked hard, trying to wrap my head around a mini version of Kyrie and Roth. "Damn, girl."

"That's all you have to say?"

"I'm the godmother, right? And the honorary aunt?"

She blinked away a tear. "Of course."

"Congratulations has always seemed like a weird thing to say when someone is pregnant. Like, all you did was have sex. Biology did the rest." I wrapped my arm around her and kissed her cheek. "I'm happy for you, Kyrie. That's so cool."

"What about you and Harris?"

I shuddered. "Honey, I'm still working on letting him love me without me freaking out. Ain't no babies or wedding bells happening any time soon. You'll be the first—well, the second—to know when there is. I promise."

We walked up the beach for a while, Alexei trailing behind us at a distance. When we returned, Nick was talking to Roth, and both of them had tumblers of scotch. Nick slapped Roth on the back, which led me to suspect Roth had just broken the baby news to him.

We partied late into the night. Kyrie didn't drink, of course, so I drank enough for both of us. Harris even let loose a little. Responsibly, I insisted, since he was still wounded.

All the while, though, I was ruminating on Kyrie's question.

And Harris and I?

Marriage? Kids?

I never thought it would happen to me. I never thought I'd even want it. I always assumed I'd be arranging fuck-buddies when I was in a nursing home, visiting my various geriatric booty calls. Apparently, fate or something had a different life in mind for me.

Somehow, sitting on Harris's lap, sharing a glass of scotch with him, the idea of saying "I do" didn't seem so scary or impossible. I wasn't convinced I'd be that great a mother, since the only example I had was pretty shitty. But if anyone could make an honest woman out of me, it was Nicholas Harris.

And I was willing to try.

He pulled my ear to his lips as Roth carried Kyrie up to their room. "Just so you know, I'm gonna knock you up someday."

"Someday far from now?"

"Not yet, no. You're not ready for that. But you will be."

"I'm not so sure, Nick."

He pulled back so he could meet my eyes. "I am sure. You'll be a great mother, some day."

"Can we worry about teaching me how to be a great girlfriend, first?"

He laughed. "Sure. I'm in no hurry. We've got time."

I tugged his wrist to me, pulling his suit coat sleeve back to bare his watch. "It's 2:02, Nick."

He grinned lazily at me. "Is it, now?"

I let out a breath. "Sure is. That's a good two hours past midnight."

"I have a promise to keep, don't I?" He grinned at me, a smile full of promise.

THE END

AUTHOR NOTE

Okay, so by now you're probably familiar with the outrageousness that is the ALPHA series playlists. And this one…? It's the most outrageous of all. It's full of some seriously incredible music spanning genres from indie folk to instrumental metal to classical. All the good stuff, in other words. I hope I turn you on to a new favorite band, or to an amazing song that helps you through a rough time. Or just a good tune you can blast with the windows down and do some serious steering wheel drumming. Music is my life-blood, and the pulsing heart of every book I write.

Support art. Buy music—or pay for upgraded streaming services—share good finds.

As always, thank you to the artists listed below for creating sonic inspiration.

PLAYLIST

"Mute Departure" by Cult of Luna

"Hungry Face" by Mogwai

"The Omega Suite pt.ii" by Maroon

TEN— album by Break of Reality

A String Tribute to Skillet—album by Cello-fourte

Evolution—album by Primitivity

"Blood" by Algiers

Symphony of Shadows—album by Cello Fury

COVERS—album by Break of Reality

Every Red Heart Shines Toward the Red Sun—album by Red Sparowes

Transcend—album by Philip Wesley

"Storm" by Godspeed You Black Emperor

"Partita No. 2 in D Minor BWV 1004: V. Chaconne" by Hillary Hahn

"He Films the Clouds Pt. 2" by Maybeshewill

"Making Love on the Mountain" by The Woodlands

"Work Song" by Hozier

"Mojo Pin" by Jeff Buckley

"Revelry" by The Careful Ones

"Too Repressed" (Explicit) by Sometymes Why

"Hush" Theme from *Turn* by Joy Williams and Matt Berninger

"Vessel" by Dry the River

"The Hanging Tree" by Angus & Julia Stone

"C'est Moi" by Rupa & the April Fishes

"Wade in the Water" (Live at Spotify House) by Jamie N Commons

"Far From Any Road" by The Handsome Family

"Danger and Dread" by Brown Bird

"Snake Song" by Isobel Campbell & Mark Lanegan

"After Midnight" by Dorothy

"Red Right Hand" by Nick Cave & The Bad Seeds

One Cello x 16: Natoma—album by Zoe Keating

"Japanese Sky Transcript" by Maybeshewill

Battle Cry—album by Two Steps From Hell

Phenomena—album by Audiomachine

Epicon—album by Globus

Evolution—album by Fringe Element

Arktika—album by Pelican

Sol Eye Sea I—album by Irepress

"Gun In My Hand" by Dorothy

"The Railroad" by Goodnight, Texas

"Lie To Me" by Johnny Lang

"Suite for Cello Solo No. 6 in D, BWV 1012: 1. Prélude" by Johann Sebastian Bach, played by Mischa Maisky

"Once Upon a December" (from *Anastasia)* by Emile Pandolfi

"So Far" by Haushka

"Atlantico" by Roberto Cacciapaglia

"Woman (Oh Mama)" by Joy Williams

"Goldrush" by Paper Airplanes

"Dark Side of the Heart" by Maggie Bjorklund

"Lost Boys" by Paper Bird

"Nothing But the Water (I)" by Grace Potter & The Nocturnes

"Bad Things" by Jace Everett

"Boy Got It Bad" by Kali Baxley

"How's It Gonna End" by Tom Waits

"Stolen Roses" by Karen Elson

JASINDA WILDER

Visit me at my website: **www.jasindawilder.com**
Email me: **jasindawilder@gmail.com**

If you enjoyed this book, you can help others enjoy it as well by recommending it to friends and family, or by mentioning it in reading and discussion groups and online forums. You can also review it on the site from which you purchased it. But, whether you recommend it to anyone else or not, thank you *so much* for taking the time to read my book! Your support means the world to me!

My other titles:

The Preacher's Son:
Unbound
Unleashed
Unbroken

Biker Billionaire:
Wild Ride

Big Girls Do It:
Better (#1), Wetter (#2), Wilder (#3), On Top (#4)
Married (#5)
On Christmas (#5.5)
Pregnant (#6)
Boxed Set

Rock Stars Do It:
Harder
Dirty
Forever
Boxed Set

From the world of *Big Girls* and *Rock Stars*:
Big Love Abroad

Delilah's Diary:
A Sexy Journey
La Vita Sexy
A Sexy Surrender

The Falling Series:
Falling Into You
Falling Into Us
Falling Under
Falling Away

The Ever Trilogy:
Forever & Always
After Forever
Saving Forever

The world of *Alpha*:
Alpha
Beta

The world of Stripped:
Stripped
Trashed

The world of *Wounded*:
Wounded
Captured

The Houri Legends:
Jack and Djinn
Djinn and Tonic

Jack Wilder Titles:
The Missionary

To be informed of new releases, special offers, and other Jasinda news, sign up for Jasinda's email newsletter at http://eepurl.com/qW87T.

84790327R00290

Made in the USA
Lexington, KY
26 March 2018